State of Love & Trust

Grace Ombry

Whipping

Words and Music by Eddie Vedder, Jeff Ament, Stone Gossard, Michael David McCready and Dave Abbruzzese Copyright (c) 1994 INNOCENT BYSTANDER, SCRIBING C-MENT SONGS, WRITE TREATAGE MUSIC, JUMPIN' CAT MUSIC and PICKLED FISH MUSIC
All Rights for INNOCENT BYSTANDER, SCRIBING C-MENT SONGS, WRITE TREATAGE MUSIC and JUMPIN' CAT MUSIC Administered by UNIVERSAL MUSIC CORP.
All Rights Reserved   Used by Permission
Reprinted by Permission of Hal Leonard LLC

graceombry.com
Ombry, Grace 1964
State of Love & Trust
ISBN-13: 978-0997959703 (softcover edition)
ISBN-13: 978-0997959710 (e-book)

Cover design: Ray York II

Cover image: *Bittersweet Vine*, Mary Jo Hoffman, stillblog.net

theledbetterpress.com

Contents

1

Getting in Tune

Ellie • Okemos, Mich. • Tuesday, May 20, 2006

I pulled the Yield bus into a rest stop somewhere between Grand Rapids and Detroit. Seeing Pearl Jam three times in four days was the kind of thing I lived for, but at two in the morning after the third show, I was cracked.

"C'mon you guys. Break time, then someone else has to take a turn driving this beast." I tossed a pillow at the futon where my boyfriend Reece was kicking back, smearing marshmallow fluff onto an Oreo.

"Yo. Lovebirds. You heard the woman. Let's go." Reece licked his plastic knife and lobbed the pillow at the other futon where Clive, my twin brother, was snuggled down with his new wife, Becca. It bounced off her head. She snickered and flung the pillow back at Reece.

"Enough with your sass," she said.

"Sorry, Ms. Becca. I was aiming for Clive," Reece said. He offered her an Oreo.

"Is there any of my Fiddle Faddle left?"

He shook the empty box. "Oops. It was really good, though."

She took the cookie, bit into it and dusted the crumbs off her yellow T-shirt with a peeling picture of Marc Bolan crouched on a skateboard. I barely knew her, but I trusted Clive's judgment and he was thrilled with her. She was a heating technician with her own business up in Rogers City—sharp, with serious eyes and glossy black hair. But they'd fallen in together fast and gotten married

1

before I'd even had a chance to meet her. There was a lot about Clive that I knew he wouldn't have told her, and it made me nervous for him.

We all got off the bus except for the random fan who'd bummed a ride home with us. He was deep asleep on one of the bench seats, with his long legs slung over the backrest, and his beat-to-crap Doc Martens crossed at the ankles. We'd met in the pit. He'd held my spot on the rail so I could get in the poster line. Before the concert started, we'd gotten so caught up in comparing which shows we'd been to that I never did catch his name. But when he said he'd hitchhiked to Grand Rapids because his tires were too bald to make the trip, I'd offered him a lift back to Detroit.

At the vending machines inside the rest stop, I tried to talk Reece into taking a turn driving.

He dropped some change into the slot and punched the code for a Gatorade. "Sugar, I'm beat. How about I get you a Mountain Dew instead?"

"Blech. Can't you just drive? I have to work in the morning."

"Call in sick."

"Shelby knows we were at a show. I'd never get away with it."

"You back-seat drove me straight up the wall last time."

He was trying my patience even if he did sort of have a point. I had a hard time letting go when Reece drove my refurbished school bus. But I'd put everything into it. Painted it red and white, sewed the ticking stripe curtains myself, installed the futons and bolted the mini fridge to the floor. Clive, who had a natural talent for art and calligraphy, had lettered *Push Me, Pull Me* on the back, and painted a Sacred Heart of Jesus style image that was actually Stone Gossard. It brought on two varieties of commentary in the arena parking lots: *Why not Eddie?* and, *Oh my God, Stone, hell yes.*

"This time, I promise. I won't even look. C'mon, Reece's Pieces," I said.

Clive came up to us and Reece started rubbing his shoulders. My brother groaned. Those futons saved us a fortune in lodging, but we hadn't nicknamed them Satan's beds for nothing. Clive relaxed into Reece's impromptu massage, letting his head hang forward and his wild mop of thick brown curls swing free. He was short but deceptively powerful. I'd watched him smoke Reece at basketball many times.

Reece worked an elbow into Clive's back. "Do me a favor. Take over for Ellie at the wheel, and I'll be your best bud forever."

"Pfft." Clive straightened up and pulled his hair away from his face. "You're going to need to seriously sweeten the pot, my man."

"I'll get you a Cherry Coke."

Clive motioned for more with his hand.

"And Doritos," Reece said.

He kept motioning. "And?"

"What?"

"And?"

Reece dug around in his pockets and passed something small to Clive.

"See?" Clive slipped the contraband into his wallet. "I knew you were holding some flowers out on me. Now, don't forget my Doritos and stuff."

Becca came out of the ladies room and headed in our direction, drying her hands on the thighs of her Levi's. She smoothed down the large bandage across her palm from some kitchen mishap on their recent honeymoon in Canada.

Reece forked over the promised Doritos and pop to Clive. "We good?"

"Stellar. As a matter of fact, at this moment I'm the happiest man alive. I mean, would you look at her?"

"Oh," Reece said. "You know I have."

Back on the bus, I settled onto a futon and tried to concentrate on my latest embroidery project. Clive cranked up a playlist of Pearl Jam covering The Who, and we lurched onto the highway. He sang along with *Getting in Tune* in a baritone that could rival Barry White's. Reece made his way up to the front and joined in at the top of his lungs. What my boyfriend lacked in harmony he made up for in volume.

The singing woke up the random fan. He stretched his slender body from a grab bar and gave me a wide smile. His eyes were round and dark with heavy lids.

3

I waved at him awkwardly with my embroidery hoop. "Hey, by the way, I'm Detroit Ellie."

"Saint," he said.

"Is that like, your real name?"

He plopped back down in his seat and shrugged. "Real as Detroit Ellie, right?"

Fair enough.

"Can I check out your ink?" I asked.

I meant the lettering down the inside of his left forearm, a guitarist's tattoo for sure. I'd noticed it at the show but couldn't tell what it said. Instead, he turned his back and peeled his Mother Love Bone tank shirt upward. The entire first stanza of *Whipping* was inked in a neat typewriter font on his shoulder blade.

Don't need a helmet
Got a hard, hard head
Don't need a raincoat
I'm already wet
Don't need a bandage
There's too much blood
After a while seems
To roll right off ... hmm

That had to have hurt.

"I have seen a lot of Pearl Jam tats over the years, but that one is possibly the baddest yet," I said.

He yanked his shirt down and turned to face me. "My favorite lyric. Do you have any PJ tats?"

I lifted the edge of my batik skirt to show off the Stickman on my ankle. "It's way mainstream compared to yours."

"That's classic. Don't ever apologize for it. I almost got that one too, but ended up spending all my cash on this." He showed me *Tremor Christ* tattooed down the inside of his left forearm in Brad Klausen-style poster lettering. That was the one I'd wanted to get a better look at. It was fantastic, all in golds and rich browns.

"So you must be a *Vitalogy* fan," I said. "It's a great album, but we hold pretty fast to *Yield* around here, obviously."

"Yeah, I figured. I got it for my puppy. That's his name," he said.

"Tremor Christ? It makes him sound tough."

"He's a big boy, but really still a baby. I'm working on teaching him some manners." He reached for my embroidery hoop to see what I was making.

I handed it over, then watched him try to make sense of my highly textured crewel embroidering of a four-leaf clover with jagged edges where the lower leaves were torn away. They lay crumpled at the base of a brown stem. *The Raffertys* curved across the top in elaborate lettering. At the bottom I'd stitched *We're Fuckin' Doomed.*

Saint studied it for a long time before giving it back to me. "What is it?"

"A late wedding gift for my brother, the guy who's driving right now. Clive. And her, too." I tipped my head toward Becca, who was sprawled on the other futon, reading a Superman comic.

"Is that his personal motto?" Saint asked.

"Close. It's our family crest."

"Oh." He shoved a lock of dark hair out of his eyes. It was gelled into something that wasn't quite a pompadour. More like a pompa-oops. "That's pretty grim for a family motto. Is it meant as a joke? Or do you guys actually live by it?"

I thought about it before answering, "Both. It's one thing to accept your reality, and it's another to be able to laugh in its face."

2

Corduroy

Ellie • Detroit, Mich. • Sunday, June 25, 2006

I rang up three soft pretzels with five sides of melted cheese and a mega large Diet Pepsi for a lady who was paying in rolls of nickels. My shift didn't end for another fifteen minutes, but Reece had already parked his Buick Roadmaster in front of Mr. Salty's House of Pretzels. Shelby Williams, my manager, frowned on early departures. She also didn't like employees having visitors.

We'd called that car the Roadbastard since before Reece's dad sold it to him. It was a freaking yacht, a shameless gas hog, a rolling representation of why Detroit was all but out of business. Old Mr. LeFanch still got misty-eyed about that car. Water droplets glimmered on the front bumper—Reece had the car ready for his dad to inspect. I, on the other hand, was hardly ready to choke down my least favorite meal of the month, Sunday dinner at the LeFanch's.

I swiped at the mustard stain on my polyester Mr. Salty's uniform and hoped Reece remembered to throw a clean T-shirt in the car for me. I already had shorts on under my work pants, even though they made my butt look lumpy.

Shelby pulled her nose down in disapproval when Reece walked in. Sometimes I spied her practicing that look while polishing fingerprints off the door after dark.

"Hey there, Ms. Shelby," Reece said. "Your pretzels smell heavenly. I'll take two, with cinnamon."

"They'll ruin your appetite," I said, though he wasn't talking to me.

"That's barely enough to whet it. Shelby, do you ever think about rolling pretzels in caramel and pecans?" He licked his lips.

"It's a franchise." She smoothed her hands over her already perfect magenta hair and adjusted her bright blue visor. "We can only sell what corporate tells us. But boy do I adore pecans. And caramel."

"And toffee," Reece said. "Toffee's pure awesome."

I bugged my eyes at Reece and dragged a finger across my neck. My boss and I had enough issues without Reece flirting with her. She wrapped two cinnamon pretzels in waxed paper and pushed them across the counter to him. "No charge. Save 'em for dessert."

He didn't. He ate them sitting crossways in a booth while I worked to the end of my shift. I didn't take the free pretzel I was entitled to after my four-hour shift because Reece would eat that one too. Then Marjorie LeFanch would pout when her baby boy didn't take seconds and she'd probably blame me for spoiling his din-din.

⚬

Reece's folks lived in an aluminum-sided one-story in Hazel Park, which we called Hazeltucky.

Today their house smelled like green apple ReNuzIt, corned beef and cabbage.

"I made it especially for you," Marjorie LeFanch said. "There's plenty of veggies." After four years, she'd finally quit putting meat on my plate and lecturing me about iron. Tonight she'd serve me limp cabbage with overcooked potatoes in meat juice, with a side dish of boiled celery. Like being a vegetarian made me the rabbit in *Fatal Attraction*. I should have eaten a pretzel.

Reece and his dad sat down to watch the Tigers game. I counted Marjorie's thirty-nine doilies, seven crucifixes, and three parakeets. I started in on the framed photos encrusting the walls. Twenty-two of Reece and his four older sisters who'd fled to New York, Atlanta, Chicago and Seattle. My favorite was blond baby

Reece laughing with one tooth. He was the youngest, the only boy, and their prize. I tried to count the pictures of all of the LeFanch grandkids but lost track around thirty-seven.

A wedding photo of Reece and his ex-wife leered at me from a fussy pie table. What had possessed Marjorie to move it from the guest bedroom? I used to hate the ex because she got their brick ranch in Warren in the divorce, plus a ridiculous settlement that I still didn't understand. She was the reason he'd ended up moving into his last piece of income property in Detroit, at the edge of Corktown where the houses were crammed together so close you could stand between any two and touch them both without stretching.

But I couldn't hold a grudge against someone I hadn't met, and I respected that Reece never trash-talked her. Whatever had happened, they'd moved on. Everyone had moved on except Marjorie, apparently. And the divorce lawyer Reece was still paying off on an installment plan.

All of that, by the way, was why we invited Saint to rent our spare bedroom. We'd run into him again at the Pearl Jam show at The Palace of Auburn Hills, and it all just kind of fell together from there. He had a steady job as a busboy at a fancy restaurant at the Ren Cen and was out a lot of nights playing gigs at the local bars. At least he kept most of his guitar stuff in his room where we didn't have to trip over it. But his dog was no puppy, and that was sort of getting to be an issue.

Reece spotted me looking at his old wedding picture. He got up, walked over to the little table and set the photo face down.

"It doesn't bug me," I said. Partly true. His previous marriage didn't bother me, but the photo's new location did.

Reece leaned over me and whispered, "You are exactly nine-point-two times hotter than she'll ever be." As a junior accountant at Tax Break, Reece could be precise like that.

He grabbed an armload of beers from the kitchen fridge, one for himself, one for me and two for his dad. Marjorie didn't touch anything but mixed drinks with cute names. Already she was sipping a fuzzy navel and baby-talking to her parakeet.

"There's what's wrong with this country," Mr. LeFanch said, pointing one of his beer bottles at the Volvo commercial on TV.

Reece nodded, but I knew it was only because he didn't want to argue. Whatever was wrong with our country, I was pretty sure it wasn't on Volvo. Besides, I liked the idea of a safe car that would last. Lasting safety was something I'd never had. I didn't even own a car, just the Yield bus. It was impractical, but it justified its existence every time we loaded it up and took it to a Pearl Jam show. Otherwise, it quaffed gasoline and was a post-apocalyptic nightmare to park, so I walked, rode my 10-speed, took the SMART bus or got rides from Reece. Earlier today, Saint had given me a lift to work in his rusted purple Geo Tracker with fresh whitewalls that must have been on special at Belle Tire. He'd been pretty excited about them, but Reece had laughed his ass off at how ridiculous they looked on the Tracker.

At the dinner table, Marjorie pestered Reece about going to Mass with her. "It's the family thing to do. Even if you are living in sin."

"Don't push it, Ma. I'm still paying off that last piece of paper."

"Things didn't have to turn out that way. Counseling. If you two had gotten counseling. She was a smart girl from a nice family."

My cheeks burned. I didn't go to Michigan State like Reece and his ex. Or any college. But I wasn't stupid, either. I had my GED. Maybe Clive and I didn't come from the best family. To be honest, we pretty much came from no family at all. But we stuck together and we were good people, nice as anyone Reece had ever divorced, for sure.

Reece squeezed my thigh under the table. That meant a lot.

His mother said, "Prayer. A couples' retreat. You should have tried harder to work it out with her. I still believe that."

I pushed a limp chunk of cabbage around my plate and changed the subject. "Dinner was special. You know how I adore vegetables."

"Especially cabbage," Reece said. "Cabbage rocks, Ma. We'd love it if you'd package up some of the leftovers."

Later, I elbowed him as Marjorie spooned the leftovers into a plastic container for us. I was already planning to forget them on the pie table, right atop the face-down wedding photo.

We backed the Roadbastard onto the street, pretending not to see her rushing after us, Tupperware in hand.

3

Pilate

Ellie • Detroit, Mich. • Friday, June 30, 2006

Saint caught me dangling his codpiece over the kitchen wastebasket. He stomped in and snatched it from my hand. "You wouldn't dare." He half smiled, clutching it to his chest.

"Yeah, actually I would."

"Harsh. You know I need it." His round eyes were all innocence. "You were really gonna toss it?"

"Yup. Don't leave it on my counter again. Man, that's just gross."

"Sorry. I only set it there for a second."

"One second too long, friend."

He was only twenty-one, but c'mon. A codpiece. On my counter. That's just … *ew*. If he was ever going to work out as our roomie, I had to get him trained. Pronto.

He strapped the leather piece over his skinny jeans. It was a weirdly intimate process to watch so I made a point of looking at Reece's collection of Lions, Tigers, and Red Wings refrigerator magnets. Saint buckled on thick leather arm guards and a wide, studded collar then yanked open the door and pounded down the back steps without another word. I didn't get how he could love a dog that he needed to armor up against.

I one-hundred percent hated Tremor Christ already. Sure, the Rottweiler/pit mix was named after a truly great song and I could respect that. But the admiration stopped there. The dog was a hundred and fifty pounds of muscle and teeth, with yellow eyes far too wise for a creature I might need to outsmart. Rescued from a kill shelter after three or four failed re-homing attempts, he was more of a wild beast that could momentarily pretend to be tame than he was a pet.

I peeled carrots at the sink, the window providing a decent view. I shoved it open, letting in the soft summer air and the scent of warm grass. All the commands Saint used were in German. *Sitz, platz, hol, aus, packen, nein, varous.* Everything. He'd told me there were two good reasons he trained Tremor Christ in German: it sounded more forceful than English, and it prevented strangers from commanding the dog.

That didn't seem like the greatest idea to me. I'd flunked German before I dropped out of high school. If I ever had to command Tremor Christ what would I do? I'd probably panic and say *gesundheit. Volkswagen. Tannenbaum. Heil Hitler.*

Face it. If that dog ever got loose, I'd be screwed.

I never went out to my bus after the dog took over the yard. He was always chained, sure, but I didn't trust him. Not after what he did to Judas, the neighbor's yellow tabby. Oh, Reece thought it was real funny about their names. But there had been fur and guts all over the chain link fence, blood spattered on the side of my bus, and Judas's ear stuck to the step on the deck. That rescued monster of Saint's was pure evil.

Saint had apologized to the neighbors and even offered to buy them a kitten, but the whole incident burnished our white trash reputation on our street of tightly packed old houses.

Every time I stood peeling vegetables or washing dishes while Saint worked with Tremor Christ, his thoughtless courage floored me. This might be it, the time the dog didn't obey him. The time an ambulance would come to take Saint away, sirens silenced.

I left cold water gushing from the tap while Saint held his arm high and commanded the dog to *packen.* Tremor Christ jumped and clamped his massive jaw on Saint's leather arm guard. No matter how many times I witnessed this exercise, I'd almost pee my pants.

Reece squeezed my hips from behind, his lips and razor stubble tickling my neck. "What's for dessert, sugar?" It wasn't a question. Dinner wasn't even on the stove yet.

14

Saint threw this week's woobie for Tremor Christ. It was a sock monkey I'd picked up at a rummage sale for him a few days earlier. Already it was torn and filthy, spinning lazy circles through the air. Tremor Christ loped after it over our carpet of dandelions, jumped skyward and snatched it in his teeth. He shook it hard.

"Phooey," Saint commanded the dog. At least, it sounded like *phooey* to me. Tremor Christ released the limp monkey atop Saint's boots.

I'd have to try to remember that command.

"He's such a freak," Reece said.

"What do you mean?"

"Just look at him. Studded collar. A fucking codpiece? Get real."

Reece took my hands out of the sink and kissed them. They were dripping wet and covered in bits of carrot peelings. The orange specks clung to his chin. I let him lead me away from the window, from the kitchen, from Saint.

4

All or None

Clive • Belknap Township, Mich. • Thursday, July 20th, 2006

The happiest man alive. That was me from the snowy day last March when Becca had agreed to marry me, until this very moment in the blazing heat. I should have known something like this would happen. I had my reasons, I swear, that one little word could double me over with the force of a gut punch right there in our backyard garden.

I stumbled backward and stepped on a rotting tomato. Embryonic slime oozed warm between my toes. I scraped my bare foot in the rough crabgrass while she continued kneeling in the dirt. Steady. Stable. Oblivious to the earwig flailing in her water glass. She quit looking at me for a reply and forced her weed digger between twin dandelions.

"Maybe we should have planted popping corn," Becca said, as if she hadn't just detonated a neutron bomb.

I stood there, fists involuntarily clenched, mind scrambling to grasp the implications. Cicadas played an alien battle of the bands in the cedars lining our deep lot. The stench of cow manure wafted from a neighboring pasture. Her beagle, Cubby, continued snoozing peacefully in the thin shade of my weeping willow.

We'd been careful. So damned careful. She was on the patch.

"Please. Don't change the subject," I said. "How did this even happen?"

She tugged off her flowered gardening glove and showed me her palm. The stitches were gone but the fresh scar, where the boning knife had slipped through the avocado and pierced her hand, was still a deep shade of red. "I'm thinking it was those Canadian antibiotics."

The week before the Pearl Jam shows, we'd taken a belated honeymoon at her brother's bed and breakfast in Montréal. That's where the stupid knife mishap occurred. It was completely my fault. I never should have asked her to make guacamole for me.

She shrugged. "I guess they deactivated my birth control."

I was trying to be patient. Trying to understand. Sweat rolled down the backs of my knees. I weighed what to say next to this woman I adored, who'd taken a chance on a broke-ass artist from Detroit when every busybody in Presque Isle County was sure she should have married the Hollywood-handsome foreman from the quarry.

"We talked about this. Remember? You said, 'Maybe in ten years.' And I said that seemed soon but I was open. Was I dreaming, or did we not have basically that exact conversation?"

She pushed her sunglasses on top of her head and squinted up at me. "Yeah, you're right. We did."

I went for it. "So you don't plan to go through with it or anything."

"Seriously? I think, I mean, now that it's happening, why wouldn't we?"

I swallowed. The bitter taste of fear burned in the back of my throat. "Are you ready for this? Because I'm sure as hell not."

She stabbed the earth and worked a furious circle with her weed digger. "It was an accident, but it's something. You know? It's ours." She wrestled a dandelion from the dirt and pointed its wicked white root at me. "You're giving me a knee-jerk reaction. An automatic hell no."

"Someday. Alright? Someday we'll try this. I've already promised you that. But this wasn't part of our plan. A dumb accident that's nobody's fault doesn't mean we have to totally abandon our plan."

The plan was that I'd continue growing my business, Retro Replicas, from my home studio while she gradually expanded the service territory of Crowe & Father Home Heating, the business she'd inherited when her dad died. A surprise baby that would probably arrive in time for our first wedding anniversary did not fit anywhere into that plan as far as I could tell.

Becca took a sip of her water and spotted the drowning earwig. She jumped to her feet and flung the glass across the yard. It smashed against a stump near the fire pit. "Crap. I'll get that. Oh!" She put her hands to the sides of her head, blinked hard and swayed.

I grabbed her by the waist and steadied her. "Hey? Bec? You alright?"

"I'm fine. Jeez. I'm just hot. I stood up too fast." She stumbled toward the hose coiled at the side of our peeling white bungalow. Her sunglasses fell to the grass as she splashed water on her face.

My inadequacy at this husband gig nauseated me. What was I supposed to do, though?

She dried her cheeks with the bottom of her tank top, her bellybutton a tall O centered at her narrow waist. Her shirt fell into place, rumpled and wet. "So, I know it's not perfect timing, I'll give you that. And believe me, I'm as scared about this as you are. But you freaking out on me hardly helps."

Water burbled from the hose. She kicked off her rubber gardening clogs and rinsed her feet. "Fine. I get it. It's a screw-up, and it changes our plans. But we'll get by. I mean, it's just a baby. It will be small. It won't eat all that much."

"Don't call it that. Right now it's a little clump of cells."

"That may be." She dropped the hose. Her onyx eyes narrowed. "But it's my clump."

"Bec, please. Don't do this to us. Not like this. Not right now."

"It happened. It's done."

"These things can be undone, you know."

Ignoring my last remark, she refastened her sweat-damp ponytail into a sloppy bun. Water continued to pour out of the hose. She wouldn't even look at me. Usually, she was so reasonable. But this, this was different. There had to be some way to get her to reconsider. I picked up her sunglasses and handed them back to her, then tried appealing to her practical side.

"We're in a one-bedroom house. Where's it supposed to sleep?"

"Two-bedroom."

Ouch. That other bedroom was my art studio.

"Seriously, Becca. I mean, come on. Are you really going to go there? My replicas are bringing in good money. If this is your new plan, you won't be expanding your business anytime soon. Can you show me your thinking on this?"

She chewed her lip and looked away. This had to be sinking in. Bringing up her business was a good angle.

"Who do you imagine is going to take care of it while you're off fixing boilers?"

"Simple. You're always home. You'll be a stay-at-home dad."

Jesus. I could just see myself painting *Houses of the Holy* with a baby on my hip.

"Try to be realistic. This is my livelihood you're messing with. You're going to leave a baby here and just go off and work. And the kid, it's going to be crawling around the studio knocking over jars of turpentine. Think of someone other than yourself."

"That's exactly what I am doing. You should try it sometime."

I toed the deepening puddle of cold water in the grass and swished my foot around until the last of the tomato goop washed away. Me, a stay-at-home dad. I stepped out of the puddle onto the dry grass and made another pass at reasoning with her. "They're not cute."

"What is that even supposed to mean?"

"Alright, so maybe they're cute."

"That's irrelevant. Cute or not. We're talking about our kid. You're saying you don't want it because it might not be cute? I feel like I don't even know you right now."

That wasn't what I'd meant. I tried again. "Well, obviously it'd be cute. What I'm saying is, so what? That doesn't stop them from crying and barfing and crapping. They're helpless. Needy. Fragile. Their whole lives depend on you. It's exhausting. And if you fail, you can never forgive yourself."

"You talk about having kids like you think you know some-thing. You didn't even have little brothers or sisters. Just you and

20

Ellie. Where do you even … how can you just?" She flapped her hands in frustration.

She was flat out wrong about that, but this was hardly the time to lay it on her about how Ellie and I were, or were not, raised and how many siblings we'd actually had.

The nachos I'd eaten for lunch were rioting in my stomach and about to organize a protest march right out of my throat. I staggered forward and grabbed the garden hose. I needed to be doing anything other than discussing this doomsday scenario with the woman I loved. I did love her, really, despite any apparent evidence to the contrary.

I let the hose water splash against my feet until my bones ached from the cold.

"You're upset," she said. "It's a lot to process, I know. But let me say this. There's a tiny piece of you stuck inside me now. And I'm its mother. I don't think I'd know how to say goodbye to that."

Pressure welled against my esophagus. I made for the sliding doors and staggered through the house and into the bathroom. My knees smacked the floor tiles. I clutched the toilet rim as wave after wave of the nacho brigade stampeded out of me.

ᅇ

By the time I was out of the shower, Becca had split. Still queasy with the news, I drove my ancient Toyota Land Cruiser the six miles to her shop on Third Street, Rogers City's main drag. I'd taken the top off the vehicle, and my wet hair had dried into some kind of dreadlocked nightmare by the time I arrived. Sure enough, there was her work van with *Crowe & Father Home Heating* emblazoned on the side. I'd lettered it for her myself, copying the font from her storefront awning. You get pretty good at lettering when you replicate album covers for a living.

I was in severe need of a smoke, but I'd quit right after I met her. Damn this clean living shit. I tried to wrestle my hair into a ponytail, but it was hopeless. Everything felt hopeless. I had to slow down and think through how to deal with this mess. What kind of guy tells his wife of four months to abort an unplanned pregnancy? That's easy, an asshole. *Next?*

So I was an asshole. That was a starting point. Something we could both agree on. I sat behind the wheel and let the sun pound me, considering what to tell her and what to leave out, while trying to untangle my hair one byzantine knot at a time.

She knew my family consisted of Ellie, period. She deduced correctly that some major tragedy had befallen us, and that I really didn't like talking about it. I told her I'd survived by looking ahead, always ahead. Who could argue with that? She probably thought it had been some one-time, normal-people disaster like a car accident. Ha. I wish.

Now what? Make a maudlin explanation for why I was being an asshole about this pregnancy thing? She only knew some oversim-plified and thoroughly fumigated version of my past. My stupid story hung over me, clouding everything. Couldn't we just skip past the part where I relive my bullshit childhood and my mother and brothers and LuCretia—all the real reasons that Becca's pregnancy terrified me—to the part where she'd understand that no way in hell was I ready for fatherhood? Was it asking too much for her to just take my word for it? I'd never lied to her and I wasn't about to start.

Sorry, I'm just not ready.

Sure Clive, that's cool.

As if.

And then maybe a miracle would happen and the pregnancy would be a false alarm. We'd laugh about it and double up on birth control and wait ten years to have kids. Or fifteen. I'd only be forty by then. Lots of guys put it off that long.

The sun made me sweat. I was pulling my mass of hair up off my neck when Howie Peterson cruised by in his American-cheese colored Dodge Ram with the lift kit. He spotted me and gunned the engine. What a tough guy. That ex-boyfriend of hers was never going to let it go. Yeah, I know Rogers City is small and her shop is on the busiest street, but come on. He drove by all the damned time. Get over her, bro.

I was firm. I would not use my story to talk her out of this, because if there is one thing I didn't need it was pity. I hated pity, hated that look people got like *I never had it as bad as you, thank Jebus.* Better to have her think I'm an asshole than pity me. I didn't need that story. My reasons were legit right now, in the here and now. We were newlyweds. Only twenty-five years old. Fledgling entrepreneurs. Scraping by financially. Our house was tiny. We both had other plans. There would be a time for us to start a family, absolutely, but this wasn't it.

I steeled myself and went in through the side door. She'd propped it open with a pudding stone to let in the Lake Huron breeze, but that breeze was limp today.

Cubby eyed me first and gave me half a tail wag from the spot where he'd splayed himself on the cool cement floor.

The shop was so Becca. The pipe cutter squealed, nearly drowning out Bowie's *Panic in Detroit* blaring out of a dusty boom box. Her old apartment was upstairs, still furnished because we were eventually going to rent it out to bring in some extra cash. The only piece of furniture she'd moved into my house on Rabbits-Honey Road was her bookshelf, loaded with the tomes of her trade: *The Lost Art of Steam Heating; German for Engineers and Technicians; The Pipefitter's Math Guide.* She also had about two-hundred vintage Superman comic books. God yes, I loved this woman.

Her back was still to me. She was chopping lengths of pipe and tossing them into a big box.

The whole verbal apology thing was going to be awkward. I moseyed over to the antique refrigerator nestled between some tool cabinets and extracted a couple of bottles of Corona. My stomach wasn't quite ready for a beer, but my brain sure was. I opened both and brought them over to her.

I held out the cool, refreshing olive branch and said, "I'm still in shock. If I acted like an ass, I'm sorry."

She wiped her hands on her canvas apron and pulled her industrial goggles down around her neck. "Clive. Honestly."

"What?"

"I can't even drink that." She brushed her hand across her lower abdomen.

I stood there clutching both beers like a moron. Obviously, pregnant women shouldn't drink. Or smoke black tar heroin. I knew these things first-hand.

She pushed a stool toward me, an invitation to sit down. "On my way here I was sort of talking this over with Cubby and I realized I really didn't listen when you tried to give me your reasons." She hoisted herself onto the workbench. "This was just an accident, and it's not exactly fair to you."

"Right," was all I could manage in the face of her overwhelming reasonableness, her tolerance for my blatant rejection of our shared crisis, the bald fact that I wasn't good enough for a woman like her. "Right," I said again. I couldn't help myself.

"And if you're absolutely certain you don't want it," Becca continued, "it's not going to be fair to any of us. I'm going to shut up for ten, fifteen, twenty minutes, and open my mind, and listen while you explain why you're so dead-set against this." She pinched her thumb and forefinger together and drew them across her lips.

"Thanks," stuck in my parched throat. A sip of cool beer helped that, but my stomach didn't appreciate it. What was I supposed to say?

Presque Isle County. Belknap Township. A 1940's bungalow on a land contract. Making my paintings, drinking beer and smoking weed by the fire pit in my backyard, not being responsible for anyone else for the first time in my life. It had been a fat slice of heaven on earth. Then my furnace craps out in the dead of winter and this goddess shows up to repair it, and it turns out she's my soul mate. Sure we were raised completely differently, but still we had everything in common. We loved classic rock, Mystery Science Theatre 3000, comic books, Mexican food, bonfires and beer. We were both left-handed, our own bosses, and preferred roasted garlic on our pizza. We'd blended our lives together peacefully and easily, and had yet to be truly angry at each other.

That's the Cliff Notes version of what I was on the verge of completely fucking up no matter what I said.

Becca untied her shop apron and slipped it off. Folded it. Set it on the workbench. Waited.

"Think about the Rafferty family crest," I said. "I mean, our motto is 'We're Fuckin' Doomed,' you know? I can't see bringing a kid into that."

"Oh, come on. You and Ellie made that thing up."

She had me there. The embroidered crest in its Dollar Store frame didn't prove anything even if it did resonate with the truth about my sister and me.

Screw my reasons. Screw my past. When I boiled it down, there was only one factor that meant anything.

"What if I can't go through with this?" I asked. "Is that going to be it for us?"

She twisted her wedding ring around her finger several times, no eye contact. A bead of perspiration collected at her throat and slid beneath the front of her thin tank top. I allowed myself a glimpse at her lower abdomen. Perfectly normal. No one would ever guess my microscopic doom had invaded her.

"I want it," she said. "But not if it costs me you."

I let out a breath I didn't even know I'd been holding. "That was never on the table, Bec. I'm here whether or not you have a baby. I'm not the one with the choice."

"Yeah, you are. I'm not having this child unless you want me to. That wouldn't be fair to anyone. Would you want to be born by mistake? Wanted by one of your parents and resented by the other?"

I couldn't relate to what she was saying. Two parents sounded like a straight up luxury to me no matter how they might have felt.

"I already know what I want," she said. "Now you need to decide."

I hated that she was putting it all on me. I couldn't agree to it, but I also didn't want to be the villain. My only option was to stall. "Can I have some time to think it over? A few days? A week?"

"If that's really what you need, I guess so."

5

Just a Girl

Ellie • Detroit, Mich. • Thursday, July 20, 2006

Invisible. Nosy. That was me, leaning against the bathroom sink and listening to Saint and whoever she was, their private noises coming through the air vent on the shared wall.

A cool shower had brought my body temperature down enough for sleep that sweltering summer night, but I was wide awake. My cotton robe stuck to my damp skin. My hair dripped cold water onto my feet. Eavesdropping wasn't my style, but their sounds riveted me. Alright, so maybe eavesdropping was exactly my style. Whatever. Reece had gone to bed really early and I was super bored.

The paint on my toenails was chipped. Maybe I should have shaved off those fine blonde hairs on my big toes. Shaving my legs defied my animal nature, but I did it because when I skipped it too long, Reece called me his love monkey.

I hadn't even seen this girl but I could guess how she'd look. She'd be another standard-issue Saint groupie. Hair dyed midnight black. Eyes ringed with thick liner. Dark lipstick. Tight black skirt, tortured tank top, high-top Chuck Taylors. Twiggy, with tattoos. Roses, butterflies, moons, stars, or a cross. Every last one of them sported ink on her clavicle, which was highly useful in telling them apart. Butterfly, Moonie, Cross, Rose, Star, and the Other Rose, so far.

Their voices were muffled, Saint and whoever she was. Here's the thing that killed me: sinewy, hard-ass Saint, all ink and piercings and attitude going on for days. Mr. Badass, playing his beat-to-shit Fender Mustang or his vintage Strat in some probably terrible psychedelic rock cover band called Quadraphonic Space Trip. But whenever he had a girl in bed, he'd be giggling his ass off. Like a little kid watching cartoons, right? I'd thought I'd heard him giggling before, but I could never be sure. Tonight, in the bathroom, there was no mistaking it. High-pitched, sweet, delighted giggles coming out of that boy. I grinned.

It was him for sure, not the girl. Her voice was low, husky, working overtime at being so cool and detached. I couldn't tell what she was saying. Everything got quiet.

"Um. Can I use it?"

And there she was in the bathroom doorway. Eyeliner smudged, magenta lipstick worn away. In the bright overhead light, pale roots were visible at her part line. A long white tank top that had to be one of Saint's skimmed her narrow frame. Instead of a rose inked on her clavicle, this one had a tulip. I gave her half a point for originality.

"Yeah. It's all yours." I tightened the belt on my robe and headed down the hall.

We had a rule against Saint's guests spending the night. Ridiculous, right? He thought so. But for $300 a month I didn't want to wake up to strangers in my kitchen. Or share my bathroom in the morning. I didn't care if they stayed over, as long as they were out of the house before my feet hit the bedroom floor. If we let them stay, the next thing you know we'd end up with a roomie by default, eating the organic eggs, sucking up the electricity, blasting craptastic music on the stereo, pissing off the neighbors, leaving G-strings on the bathroom floor.

I was strict about these things. When Clive lived here, it was harder to say no. He belonged here. He was one of us. He and Reece were best friends before Reece and I were even a thing. We'd tried to give him the space he needed, but LuCretia had made that damned near impossible.

Whenever she'd stayed, I'd locked my knapsack in the closet. Nothing was safe with that crazy bitch around. Clive would find her completely smacked out somewhere—shades of our mother—

and drag her home to sleep it off. He never took his eyes off her. Some mornings I'd find her collapsed across our purple paisley U-shaped sectional, arms, legs and auburn curls everywhere. Clive would be on the floor, always the floor, lucky if he even got one throw pillow. I'd rummage through her big leather bag, reclaiming whatever stuff of ours that she hadn't already sold off to fund her damned habits.

When Saint signed on to be our roomie, I laid down the law.

Tulip showered. No giggling, so Saint wasn't in there. She better not have used my shampoo. And no way was I washing any funky biznotch post-sex towels.

After I slipped into polka-dot boxer shorts and my Bonnaroo tank top, I sat on the arm of the sectional and plucked at my ukulele. The living room was strung with tiny Christmas lights that I left up year-round. I loved the dreamy, peaceful atmosphere. My fingers were screwing up a B chord when Saint sauntered in. Cut-off sweat pants. No shirt. His big, dark nipples unnerved me. Secretly, I tried to count his piercings.

He noticed because he was observant like that. "Quit staring."

"Where's Tulip?" I didn't hear the shower anymore. Trying to play music always made me lose track of time.

He shrugged, reached for my ukulele and put his eye to the sound hole. I'd had that ukulele for years but still couldn't play it worth a damn. It was a rich, golden-brown, made from some genuine Hawaiian wood, koa or something. I'd picked it up at a garage sale.

"Reece left you a present in there," he said. He sat not too close on the sectional and stuck his long fingers through the sound hole. "Would you look at that?" He extracted a baggie of weed. "Your man was feeling generous. Share?"

It wasn't a gift. Reece made a habit of storing his "flowers" in my uke, which he saw as more of a wall decoration than an instrument that I might actually want to learn to play.

"Sure," I said. "You're rolling it, though. I'm too hot."

No one rolled a joint slower than Saint. The anticipation killed me. To make the time go faster I went into the kitchen and poured some fresh limeade into two tall glasses filled with ice.

29

I returned, the glasses dripping condensation with my every step. Tulip glared at me from Saint's lap as if I was the interloper. Other than a fresh coat of dark lipstick, she looked the same as she did when she'd entered the bathroom. Even the eyeliner smudge remained on her cheek. Maybe she'd only washed her business.

"Is this your mom?" she asked Saint.

I was only four years older than he was. I set down our lime-ades and snatched the joint from her. She'd left lipstick on it.

I took a long hit anyway.

"Get it right. I'm his granny," I said.

6

Animal

Ellie • Detroit, Mich. • Tuesday, July 25, 2006

I was pretty mad at Saint. Scratch that. I was furious. I'd worked hella late the night before doing inventory at Mr. Salty's. That's right, I'd had to count frozen pretzels, so many that I actually had dreams that everything had to be counted, and everything I counted turned into a pretzel. Reece was at some work dinner thingy that ran late, so Shelby had given me a ride home. I'd crashed on the couch and didn't really pay any attention to who or what Saint brought home from the bar that night.

That morning I'd found lacy black panties under my bed.

No, they weren't mine. I tried not to judge the girls he brought home, but I had a major problem with them using our room. Our bed. Like we needed a case of the crabs. By the looks of some of those chicks, maybe even a case of the lobsters. I had to wash all of our bedding. Pigs. The extra work took up half my morning, and I had a double shift at Mr. Salty's in an hour.

Clive would have never pulled something like that when he lived here. Not in a million billion light years. And anyway, why? Saint had his own damned room for that, even if it did only have a twin-size bed.

I wasn't about to touch those panties. I hauled Saint into our room and pointed at the offending garment.

He grabbed the panties into a wad and crammed them into his pocket. Didn't utter a word. No denial, no explanation, no excuses. No shame either, just a knowing smirk. He stomped out of the room and left the house, taking that beastly dog with him. Like I was the one with a problem.

There are some lines you don't cross with roomies, and he'd taken a flying leap over a big one. Thinking about it while cramming our sheets into the washing machine, my scalp tingled with rage all over again.

ଓ

I was in the basement folding sheets hot out of the dryer, careful not to let them touch the grungy floor. The back door slammed with the familiar rattle of the metal grate that covered its window. Saint pounded fast and heavy down the basement stairs, Tremor Christ clamoring behind him. I jumped onto the dryer. Half of Reece's clean white T-shirts hit the floor.

"Get that beast out of here. Hook him outside," I said.

All of Saint's focus was on the dog. I gasped when I spotted the mess of torn flesh hanging from his left forearm. Blood soaked his T-shirt and jeans. His boots were spattered in red, even his chin was smudged with it. There was blood all over the dog's face. I curled my knees to my chest atop the dryer and stifled a scream. Saint sweet-talked that devil creature with *liebe* and *welpe* until he managed to get him hooked to a short chain attached to an eyebolt in the floor. The whole time, Saint's blood dribbled on the cement.

I slid off the dryer. "What the hell has he done to you? Let me see it."

He turned away from me and took a long look at his arm, maybe for the first time since whatever had happened.

"Damn it. Oh, man. How am I supposed to play tonight?" His knees buckled and he caught himself on the edge of the washer. "It wasn't his fault." He slid down the washer and sank to the floor. "Damn. I might need some help."

I grabbed one of Reece's clean shirts and wrapped it snug around his shredded forearm. Call 911 or drive him to the hospital? Emergency response was slow around our neighborhood, more like a clean-up crew. I found Saint's keys and drove him myself, readjusting the seats and mirrors in his white-walled Tracker while he

32

hunched over his arm in the passenger seat, muttering "Man, oh man," over and over.

വേ

The wait in the hospital emergency room was endless. Saint was ghostly pale and shaking, but he pulled out his cell phone and left a calm, matter-of-fact message. "Hi Ma, it's Tim. Am I still on your insurance? Hey, call me back."

I rubbed his shoulders and told him everything would be fine, although I knew no such thing. The hospital had the air conditioning set to glacial. The T-shirt I'd wrapped around his arm was soaked bright red. Saint's blood had spattered my Mr. Salty's polyester uniform pants. A smudge had dried flaky and brown on the back of my hand.

I called into work to let Shelby know I'd be really late.

She said, "Uh-uh girl, get that rear in gear."

"I can't leave him. He can't even drive. It's really bad."

"Fine, Ellie. That's just grand. Leave me to pull the lunch shift by myself. You know what? Don't come in at all. And don't go pestering me for extra hours later to make up for this."

Saint folded himself protectively over his trashed arm.

"Think about having him put to sleep," I said.

"Shush," he said into his knees. He turned his head and looked up at me, eyes puffy and bloodshot. "He was provoked. Another dog went after him. I was breaking them up."

"It doesn't matter. A dog that'll attack when provoked ..." I didn't need to finish. He knew damned well what I was getting at. I didn't even bother to ask how it went for the other dog. Remembering the bits of Judas kitty stuck to the fence was enough for me.

"I rescued him from a kill shelter. Everyone gave up on him. Who knows what he's been through? He's loyal. And grateful. He's my forever dog. I'm not getting him put down just because he made one little mistake. He was trying to protect me, in his way." He straightened up and peeled back part of the bloody T-shirt. "Man, he really fucked up his name."

Where the *Tremor Christ* tattoo had been there was now a fleshy mess of purple, red, white, and yellow. I gagged involuntarily.

"C'mon. It's not all that bad," he said. "I'm sitting here talking to you. Hey, can you stick around?"

"Sure."

"When it's my turn, come with me, OK?"

They called him back to triage. I told the nurse, "I'm Timmy's aunt," and she let me go in with him. He gave me a sour look for calling him Timmy. I guess only his mom was allowed to call him that.

The doctor said, "Do the world a favor. Have that dog euthanized today."

"I can't," Saint said.

"We're required to report dog attacks to Animal Control," the doctor said. "You can put him down or you can let Animal Control come and take him away. He'll have a more peaceful death at the vet." He plunged a needle into Saint's shoulder. "That should numb it a bit."

Saint refused to look at anyone. He lay flat on his back, staring at the ceiling while the doctor embroidered his arm together. The black lace panties were peeking out of his front pocket. I felt a slug of guilt for shaming him over that, even if he did have it coming. He was young. I remember doing stupid stuff a few years back, before I got involved with Reece. I should have cut Saint some slack. I took his other hand and held it. His skin was soft except for the guitar calluses on his fingertips. His palm was cool and dry. He let me hold his hand for a while before pulling it away and drawing his fist to his chest. He swallowed hard. His nostrils flared as he breathed steady, determined breaths. He was shaking. The doctor kept sewing. Saint bit his lip and winced. The heels of his bloodied Doc Martens worked back and forth on the exam table. His eyes rolled back in his head to the whites. Still, the doctor sewed and sewed. Saint didn't complain. Not even once.

When the doctor had finished, Saint sat up and puked into a pink disposable tray. That made me want to hurl, too. I grabbed a cup of water for him while a nurse wrapped a long cotton bandage around his injury.

They prescribed Vicodin for the pain along with strong antibiotics and put his arm in a sling. The doctor explained aftercare to me like I was Saint's guardian. It was strangely flattering.

ભ

I took him home, then ran out and got his prescriptions filled. I spent all my cash on canned soup, pumpernickel bread, Puddin' Packs and milk for him.

Tremor Christ howled in the basement while I put the groceries away. Saint shivered in a fetal position on the sectional despite the afternoon heat. He was shell-shocked, vacant. Like all that stoicism in the emergency room had scraped him empty.

I hauled the Rafferty family quilt downstairs and tucked it around his shoulders, careful not to let it brush his injured arm. He smelled like roasted cashews, blood, and Betadine. A stray eyelash had fallen onto his cheek, but I let it be. I brought him milk and pudding. Tomorrow, I'd have to work. Maybe one of the funky biznotches would want to play nurse. Tulip or Rose or the other Rose. Or maybe Cross, although she was the least tolerable of the bunch. I wouldn't know how to find them on his phone because I never paid attention to their real names.

"I'll call someone if you want. Maybe your mom?"

"Nah. I'm OK." He started to push himself up. "I just need to go downstairs and feed him."

Oh, dear God. The last thing Saint, woozy on painkillers, needed to do was to face that howling monster.

"You should stay away from him," I said.

"He's chained. I'm offering food. He only bit me because I was pulling him off that other dog."

I failed to find any of this reassuring.

"Maybe I could do it instead," I said.

"Nah, he scares you. You don't have to do that." Saint's eyelids drooped and he covered a yawn. "You've done so much already. Taking me to ER, sitting with me, getting my prescriptions. Pudding, even. You're the best." He sat the rest of the way up, then flopped back against the cushions.

"It's alright," I said. "I can feed him."

"I'll get him in a minute." He leaned back and closed his eyes.

Both my hands shook as I filled Tremor Christ's metal dish from the bin of dog food in the kitchen. A trail of muddy and bloody dog and Doc Marten prints led to the basement door. I peered down the steps to make sure he was still chained. Yep. I crept down the stairs. The blood spattered on the basement floor had dried to black. Tremor Christ's muzzle was crusted with blood, but his tail stub wagged when he saw the dish. I set it on the floor and used a broom to shove it in his direction. While he was distracted by his dinner, I grabbed my clean sheets and dashed to safety.

7

It's OK

Ellie • Detroit, Mich. • Wednesday, July 26, 2006

Reece and I were sitting on stools at the butcher block kitchen island. I was telling him all about yesterday's dog fiasco. Well, everything but the part about the panties in our bedroom. That would have made him flip his wig. Karma, harsh and swift, had already walloped Saint. He didn't need Reece piling on.

"If he's attacking his master, that's completely out of hand," Reece said.

"Another dog went after him. Saint was breaking them up."

Reece shook his head. "What if he attacks you next? Then what's the freak's excuse going to be?" He sprinkled sugar on the butcher block, drew a dividing line in it and licked his finger. "Either that dog goes or they've both got to go. Immediamente."

"I can talk it over with him when he comes downstairs," I said.

Poor Saint. I couldn't get behind forcing him into a decision in the state he was in. And he wasn't a freak. He was just an individual. Reece had never even tried to understand him.

"Nope. I'm telling him right now." Reece marched upstairs and pounded on Saint's bedroom door. I hated how he was making it all confrontational. A finch chirped outside the open kitchen window. I strained to hear what Reece was saying to Saint, but the loudmouth finch drowned out everything. I got up and slammed the window shut.

A few minutes later, Reece returned to the kitchen and stood at the sink, clutching the edge of the countertop and staring outside.

He breathed hard, his neck an angry pink. That was the thing with Reece. It took a lot to make him mad, but boy did he get mad when he got mad. I knew not to press him. I waited. Finally, he turned to face me. He looked at my feet, then upward until our eyes met. "I love you, sugar. I want you to know that. I love you so much. Damn it. If anything bad ever happens to you … if that dog …" Tears welled in his blue eyes. He stumbled over and hugged me. Sniffed. "Don't feed him. Until this is over, don't you go anywhere near him."

I thought he was being a little melodramatic, but who knows? Maybe I just found it hard to believe anyone could care about me that much. At least, anyone besides my brother.

"Wait. So, you mean he's moving out?"

"Yep. The freak refuses to get rid of the dog, so that's his only option now."

I was surprised how disappointed I felt. It wasn't about the rent money, although we sure could use it. We weren't exactly close. But Saint had made things interesting. I missed him already. His floppy hair. His tattoos. His sweet smile. Maybe even his groupies.

Nah.

CR

The following week, Reece spoiled me with painted daisies and snapdragons from the Eastern Market, Mexican take-out from El Comal, homemade chocolate chip cookies, rhubarb-raspberry cobbler, and peanut butter bars. I gained two pounds.

Saint ghosted around the house, an occasional noise or shadow, but mostly he stayed in his room. No girls came over. He took care of the dog's basic needs but there were no training sessions, not with the load of painkillers they had him on, and his arm heavily bandaged and in a sling. He couldn't work at the restaurant or practice with Quadraphonic Space Trip. Rain soaked the sock monkey woobie. Tremor Christ slept under the Yield bus, dejected. Maybe even sorry. I wanted to know when Saint was moving out, but I didn't ask him. There was no way he'd choose this roof over his head when it was Tremor Christ that he loved.

CR

Saint's plastic laundry hamper thumped as he dragged it one-handed down the steps.

"Let me do that for you." I sprinted up the stairs and took it.

"That's silly."

"For real. I've got loads going anyway."

This wasn't exactly true. My laundry was done. I wanted to do something for him because I felt awful about his arm and even worse that we were kicking him out. He was badly hurt, but instead of being supportive the way friends should be, we were making him choose between moving out and getting rid of his dog.

His bloody clothes were stuck to the bottom of his hamper. I poured hydrogen peroxide over the stains and let it foam into a brownie-pink goo. Some quarters tumbled out of his jeans and rolled across the floor. I checked all of his pockets for whatever else shouldn't get laundered. Papers from the emergency room, a pink Bic lighter, two Trojan Magnums, four one-dollar bills and a Canadian loonie. Dunlop guitar picks. I dumped everything on top of the dryer.

The front pocket of the bloodied jeans still held the wadded black panties. I extracted them and wrinkled my nose. Trash can? They weren't mine to throw away. I tossed them in with his darks.

Who'd he screw in my bed? Tulip came to mind first, but those panties were bigger than her narrow rear. Probably one of the Roses, or maybe Cross. Yeah, I'd say they were Cross's style. But I didn't want it to be her. She always gave me the stink eye. I don't know what I ever did to deserve that.

When the laundry was done I folded his things into a neat stack and piled the sundry items on top. I tucked the panties between two pairs of jeans. I didn't want to make it an issue. If I was honest with myself, his injury was at least partly my fault. I'd been furious with him the morning it happened, maybe even angrier than I'd been admitting to myself. My angry energy drove him out of the house. If I hadn't been so mad, he wouldn't have rushed to take Tremor Christ for a walk in the first place. Maybe my negative energy had followed him like a cloud, a fog that stopped him from seeing the other dog coming in time to get Tremor Christ under control.

I'd had every right to be angry, sure. But that didn't change the consequences for Saint.

I hugged his clean laundry to my chest and concentrated on sending him pure and positive vibes. I carried it all to his room and set the pile on his unmade bed.

His voice was coming from the bathroom. "Man. Aw, damn. Man. Goddamn."

I tapped on the door. "Everything alright?"

"Ellie? Hey, can you help? Come in here."

Saint opened the door. He was shirtless and holding his injured arm by the elbow. The bandage was partially unwound. One end lay crusted and brown in the sink, the other end was still wrapped around his wrist. His arm was lumpy and swollen. Black stitches ran at crazy angles over what was left of his *Tremor Christ* tattoo. I blinked stupidly at the excruciating mess.

"It's stuck," he said. "I can't pull it off. I'm supposed to change the bandages today."

His hair obscured his face and his giant nipples stared at me. I didn't quite know where to put my eyes. Every time I looked at his arm, a stabbing pain ran from my solar plexus to my groin.

I did the only thing there was to do. I helped him. Gently, I lifted the bloody bandage and tried to detach it. Saint squeezed my shoulder. It hurt, but that was good because it let me gauge his pain.

He sucked air past his teeth. "Stop. Stop." He hadn't even said that when he was getting the stitches.

"Wait a sec."

I rummaged under the sink until I found an empty spray bottle. I filled it with warm water and squirted the stuck part of the bandage. It loosened a little. Saint was tense as hell, his fingers digging into my shoulder, his eyes watering. Taking my time, my stomach in a hard knot, I gently worked at the bandage until it came loose.

"There. It's done." I tossed the damp end into the sink.

He collapsed against me—in relief or exhaustion, I didn't know. He was skinny, but felt heavy as bridge cables. My head swam. I must have been holding my breath almost the whole time I was unwrapping his dressing. He pulled away and asked me to help him put the fresh bandage on.

The new bandage box sat atop Reece's pill organizer. He took so many health supplements, I didn't bother trying to keep track. He spent a fortune on those. Sometimes we argued over it. I was an agnostic in regard to vitamins. Reece was a true believer.

Wrapping Saint's arm was much easier than unwrapping it, but the ordeal was getting to him. He was shaky and pale. I thought he might faint. I closed the toilet lid and sat him down, then knelt to finish securing the clean dressing.

I gave him his painkiller and a Dixie cup of water. After he swallowed, I told him to put his head between his knees. He leaned far forward. I reread the stanza of *Whipping* tattooed on his back even though I'd known it by heart for years. I perched on the edge of the bathtub across from him. Our knees almost touched. He sat up straight and looked into my face, the color slowly returning to his cheeks. His dark eyes were sad.

"Sorry, but I haven't found a new place yet," he said.

"Yeah, hardly anyone allows pets anymore."

"That's not really it. I don't actually want to move. I love Cork-town. This house is cool. You're cool. But that's my dog. I can't just have him destroyed."

"Couldn't someone take him for you?"

He looked at me like I was speaking Swahili.

"What about your guys in Quadraphonic Space Trip? Someone in your band should make a spot for you. You're like, lead guitar and vocals, right?"

"You don't know how crazy they live. They've got an entire Nissan GT-R torn up in their apartment. It's practically an auto body shop up in there. Anyway, the bassist has terrible dog allergies."

I understood. I too was allergic to terrible dogs.

"Maybe you could stay with, I don't know, one of those chicks you date."

41

"Date?" He snickered. "What is a date? I don't go out on dates. Like, I guess my ma goes on dates. My granny probably went on dates to like, a hoedown or something. Chicks I date. That's a scream."

"Well, you know what I mean. Girls you hook up with or whatever. Rose or Tulip or one of them."

"Uh, you mean Lizzie or Nicki? No thanks. That takes shit to a level I don't even want to think about."

"Have you ever lived with anybody?"

"My ma."

"Just your mom?"

"Just my ma. For my nineteenth birthday, she gave me this huge duffel bag and enough for a deposit on an apartment. Said, 'I love ya, Timmy but it's time you were on your own.' She moved into a smaller house in Mount Clemens with my little sister. There's no room for me there and anyway, I can't move back in with her. It's a point of pride."

This wasn't going anywhere, so I decided it was time to throw in a Pearl Jam pop quiz.

"So, let's say you absolutely had to give your dog to a member of Pearl Jam, which one would it be?"

"Easy. Matt-Cam. He'd throw sticks for him." He swept my hair away from my face. "You're the best, girlfriend. I think I'm gonna miss you most of all."

Before I could process that, he'd left the bathroom. I ran my big toe across a scar on the linoleum floor and thought about what a funny word *girlfriend* was.

8

State of Love & Trust

Ellie • Detroit, Mich. • Friday, July 28, 2006

Reece brought me coffee in bed Friday morning. I sat propped against my pillows and waited for it to cool. He chugged his down piping hot with a handful of vitamins and supplements, then got busy ironing his dress shirt. Six-thirty in the morning and already it was too steamy for ironing. Reece's forehead was shiny with sweat despite the fact that he was freshly showered.

"We're probably going to be working late again tonight," he said. "Don't wait dinner for me."

This was getting to be a regular thing, but I didn't dare complain since Shelby was hogging half my shifts at Mr. Salty's. With Saint moving out soon, our budget was going to be super tight. Reece working overtime was crucial, even if it was a drag.

"That's fine. I'll just eat with Saint."

"Don't encourage him, sugar. He needs to get his ass out of here. You're too nice to him."

"I'm not any nicer to him than he is to me."

He set the iron down and looked at me. "Do you even see how that sounds?"

I didn't. I took a sip of coffee. Reece had made it too sweet. Some dribbled on my yellow quilt and I tried to dab it up with the edge of my T-shirt, but it had already soaked in. I loved that quilt. I'd picked it up for two bucks at a rummage sale when I was ten, and Clive and I decided to treat it like our own family heirloom. When he moved up north, we'd agreed to take turns having custody of it, but so far he'd forgotten to ask for it—and I wasn't about to remind him.

"I'm working long hours and you and Saint are home being all nice to each other, meanwhile that stupid dog is tearing up the backyard, barking at the neighbors, gnawing on the bus tires …"

"He chewed my bus tires?"

"No, but I got your attention. He needs to go. Saint needs to go. I don't know why you're letting him drag this out." He ironed the collar of his shirt like he was smashing a bug.

"But you own the house. You're the one who said he has to move out. Why is it up to me to get rid of him all of a sudden? I don't have any authority here. I'm just an underemployed high school dropout. Why are you putting it on me?"

He shrugged into his shirt and started buttoning. "You're here all day. You can talk to him anytime. He avoids me completely. As soon as I come home, the freak goes in his room and slams the door."

God, I hate-hate-hated when Reece called Saint a freak.

"Well, maybe if you were nicer to him."

"That's the whole problem. You're too nice to him. Like I said. He doesn't want to leave because why would he? He's got pretty Ellie at his beck and call all day. 'Oh Ellie, help me with my Band-Aid. Oh Ellie, feed my dog and make my dinner. Oh Ellie, fold my laundry. Oh Ellie, it's too hot in here. Fan my smelly feet.'"

I didn't like this conversation at all. Reece was being completely unfair. Naturally, Saint would be home all day since he couldn't bus tables with one arm. How was he supposed to make his dinner or fold his laundry single-handed? I was just doing what any decent human being would do. And Reece was acting like that was devious or flirting or something. Besides, whose beck and call was I at when he was the one who'd just left his wet towel on the floor?

"I have talked to him about it," I said, stuffing my aggravation. "He's looking for a place right now. He just hasn't found anything yet. He totally respects that you want him to move out."

Reece adjusted his salmon-colored tie in the mirror. "We want him to move out. *We*. You're making it sound like I'm the bad guy."

When he left for work I stayed in bed, still holding my cup of tepid, hyper-sweetened coffee. A ladybug crawled up the painted white bedpost. I imagined what the world looked like from her point of view. Had she heard us arguing? Who did she side with? Had she seen Saint going at it in our bed with one of his groupies? All of his tattoos revealed. Those enormous brown nipples. Giggling. My imagination was vivid. I felt dirty reveling in just how wrong it all was. I was supposed to be mad at him for using our bed, but now I wanted to thank him for giving me this cheap thrill on a lousy, hot Friday morning.

I slid out of bed and picked Reece's damp towel up off the floor. It was my Pearl Jam beach towel. It had a classic Klausen design in orange and gold with a silhouetted surfboarder. Gorgeous. I'd bought it off eBay. Oh, did Reece have himself one fat Guernsey cow that day. That's why I still referred to it as *the crying towel*. I mean, come on. What could I have possibly done with seventy-eight dollars that would have been cooler than this towel? I threw it in the hamper.

☙

Saint and I hung out at home all day. With neither one of us working and the summer heat unbearable, we took slacking off to unprecedented levels. He put Tremor Christ in the basement with a bowl of ice water and some chew toys while I covered the windows with tapestries to keep the sun out. We set up three box fans to get the air moving.

We started in the morning listening to my vinyl collection and eating Saint's favorite: burnt pumpernickel toast slathered in butter. He showed me the chords for *State of Love and Trust* on my uke, and I knew I could play it since he was doing it single-handed on his vintage Strat even though his wounded arm was still in a sling.

"Do you think if the Beatles had stayed together longer, they'd have eventually written *All Those Yesterdays*?" he asked.

I loved that his question pertained to *Yield*.

"No. Not unless Lennon and McCartney also read *Ishmael*. And probably not even then." *Ishmael* was a Socratic dialogue posing as a

45

novel, where the teacher was a gorilla. *Yield* was loosely based on the ideas in that book.

"It's totally Beatles-esque. So is *Parachutes*," he said.

"I don't know. I'm tired of having to give The Beatles credit for everything."

He started plucking *I've Got a Feeling* on his strat, definitely my favorite Pearl Jam cover of a Beatles tune. He sure knew how to make a point.

ରୁ

In the afternoon we shifted to the TV, watching Judge Judy, Maury Povich and our favorite, Jerry Springer, while eating through a mountain of nachos and drinking pitchers of sweet tea. Saint was experimenting with cutting back on painkillers and boy, his appetite was something else.

Filling the day with loud music and television circumvented any awkward discussions about when he was moving out. I'd decided not to bring it up. Reece was the one who wanted to push Saint out. I wasn't going to do his dirty work.

Jerry Springer had just come back from commercial break with paternity results in his hand when someone pounded on our front door.

"Don't answer it," Saint said.

They pounded again. I knew that kind of pounding. That was how police knocked. That was how truancy officers knocked. That was how CPS knocked. Shoot. It had always been Clive who'd answered the door when the authorities showed up. Even when we were five or six years old he could convince them to go away with that wide, dimply, *really everything's great here* smile.

More pounding. Not answering didn't feel like an option. God, if only I could channel my brother's gift for passing his contempt for authority off as compliance. I stood and faced the door.

"Just leave it. They'll go away," Saint said.

He obviously hadn't spent his childhood ducking CPS. These authority folks don't go away until you've dealt with them. It's their job to give you shit, so you open the door and take as much shit as you have to until they can leave satisfied that they've done their duty.

"Animal Control!" announced a male voice on the other side of the door. This was punctuated by more banging.

Tremor Christ barked.

"Ah, shit." Saint cranked up the TV volume as Jerry Springer tried to mediate a shouting match between a sumo wrestler, his wife, and his girlfriend/cousin. "OK, answer it. But give me a few seconds. You stall 'em. I'll get down there and keep him hushed up."

I called "Just a minute" toward the door, and let the TV blare until the barking subsided. The only way to get through this was to put on my best Clive imitation. I fluffed my hair, cracked my knuckles and sauntered into the front vestibule. I flung the door open and grinned. "Afternoon. How can I help you?"

The Animal Control officer wasn't much older than I was, if at all. The soul patch on his chin was bleached to match his hair. His truck was double parked, blocking the narrow path down our street.

"Animal Control." He showed me the ID tag hanging on a lanyard around his thick neck. He was sweating and slightly sunburned. "I'm looking for a Timothy C. Wozniak. Do you know him?"

"Yeah, I do."

"Is he here?"

"Sorry, no. He used to live here but he moved out a while ago."

"Are you a girlfriend?"

"Ha. No." I leaned on the doorframe, all casual. "He was our boarder. My boyfriend, Maurice LeFanch, owns this house. Tim moved out a few weeks ago." It felt really weird to call him Tim, knowing how much Saint hated his given name.

"Is there a dog on the premises?"

I had to think fast. If he'd checked around back he'd have already seen evidence of a dog. The tie out, probably some poop, a few battered toys. If he came inside he might notice the dog food bin in the kitchen, the leash looped over the basement doorknob, and maybe random muddy paw prints or fur.

"There's not at the moment, but I dog sit my mother's black lab when she has to work overnights. She's a nurse in the ICU up at Henry Ford Hospital."

Oh, the lies.

"Mind if I come in and look around?"

Didn't he need a warrant or something? I weighed telling him to come back with some kind of court order, then asked myself what Clive would do.

"Sure. That's fine. The house is a little messy. Who wants to do housework in this heat, right?" I opened the door wide and moved aside to let him through the vestibule. "Can I fix you a glass of sweet tea?"

"No thank you. Actually, could I get some ice water?"

"With lemon?"

"Sounds real nice."

We went into the kitchen. I sprang into action and put a drink together for him with a purple straw and everything. "Can I ask what's up with Sai—er, Tim Wozniak?" I handed him the glass of ice water.

"Thanks. He's been reported as harboring a dangerous animal. Do you know anything about that?"

I did my damndest to look surprised. "That doesn't sound like Tim at all. He didn't have any animals when he lived here. What kind of dangerous animal was it? Like, a wombat or something?"

The Animal Control officer nearly spit out his water laughing. "Nothing so exotic. Just your run of the mill vicious Rottweiler mix. Tim turned up at the hospital with some pretty severe wounds and the ER surgeon reported him to us. This was the address on his medical forms."

"He probably just wrote down our address out of habit. If he was hurt, I'll bet he wasn't thinking straight. Anyway, if he got a mean dog and was attacked by it, it had to have happened sometime after he moved out of here. Taking care of Fluffball—that's my mom's dog—as often as I do, we never allow our boarders to have pets. Don't want her to get fleas and stuff."

Just as I was saying that, Reece came in through the back door. He must have parked in the alley behind our house, what with the Animal Control truck blocking our street.

"Don't want who to get fleas? Who's this?"

"Hi, baby. This is Animal Control. We don't have what they're looking for so we were just standing around chatting about my mom's dog. Fluffball."

"Your mom? Fluffball?" Reece looked genuinely perplexed. I didn't bring my mother up with him much because it was just too depressing. When I needed to vent about that garbage, Clive was my go-to. But Reece knew my mother was long gone. It wouldn't take much for him to catch on to why I was nattering about my non-existent mother and her non-existent dog to an Animal Control officer in our kitchen

"Yeah, Fluffball." I pointed at Tremor Christ's leash on the doorknob. "Probably won't have her again for a few more days."

The Animal Control officer set his glass on the kitchen island. "I'm sorry to have troubled you folks, and I appreciate your friendly cooperation. That's rare in this job." He handed me a business card. "If you see Mr. Wozniak, tell him we're looking for him. Please. It's a matter of public safety. The next person that dog attacks might not be his owner." With that, he shook Reece's hand and headed for the front door. I followed him, said another friendly goodbye and locked up behind him.

Reece was tearing off his necktie and rolling up his sleeves. "That's exactly what I thought this was. Animal Control coming for that freak and his demon dog. And you covering for him, and trying to drag me into covering for him."

Guilty as charged. What could I say? I shrugged.

"Fine. Where is that worthless skid mark?"

I truly did not mean to glance at the basement door.

Reece marched over and yanked it open. "Wozniak! Get your ass up here!"

Saint emerged out of the dark stairwell and blinked in the bright afternoon sunlight streaming through the kitchen windows. "What?"

"I've had it with you. You're making Ellie lie for you. Your dog could kill anyone, anytime. We gave you a choice to get rid of it or move out, and you haven't done either."

Saint leveled a cold, hard glare at Reece.

"We can start legal eviction proceedings if that's how you want to play it," Reece said.

I touched Reece's arm. "But he's still in the process of healing. He can't work yet. He doesn't have any place to go. He's tried to find something but there isn't anything right now."

Reece ignored my comments and folded his arms across his chest. "Get your shit and get your dog and get your skinny ass out of my house. Comprende?"

Saint kept glaring—as if that conversation where they'd settled everything right after the dog attack hadn't even happened. He refused to look at me, which felt all wrong since I was defending him.

"You guys, don't fight. C'mon, just cool it," I said.

Saint looked at me and shook his head, then left by the back door without taking his stuff or his dog. I felt like I'd disappointed him, maybe even more than I'd disappointed Reece. But why? What did I do wrong?

"You're too soft, Ellie. Too nice. You could get in serious trouble lying to Animal Control like that. You could get us both in trouble. For all I know, we already are in trouble. I know you're trying to do what you think people want, but you've got to think this shit through all the way to the back."

"He said he's moving out. I'm trying to give him the benefit of the doubt," I said.

"That freak doesn't keep his word. He's such a liar. And he's so secretive."

I couldn't think of a single instance of Saint lying to me or not keeping his word. If he said he would pick me up at work, he was there and on time. He never made excuses about the rent. I didn't even see him lying to those girls he brought home. It was like they knew he was seeing multiple girls and they didn't care as long as he'd be exclusively theirs for the night.

"Cut him some slack. He's got no place to go and that dog is his baby. And I don't think he's a liar at all."

"You're too innocent. Every scam he's running goes right over your head. Don't get me wrong—I love your innocence. But in this case, it's a real problem. You need to open your eyes and see that freak for who he really is."

9

Hail, Hail

Clive • Belknap, Mich. • Friday, July 28, 2006

Becca and I were on day eight of *Geez Clive, can't you make a decision?* I'd spent the day painting a three-by-three replica of *Bat Out of Hell.* With each stroke of my brush, I'd rehearsed breaking it to her: *No baby. I'm sorry. I just can't. Maybe someday, but not now.*

Right before she was due home, my resolve turned to chicken shit. That's how I'd ended up at the Buckshot Tavern.

The place was nearly empty, just the way I liked it. I ordered a Natty and grabbed a table near the back, far from the jukebox churning out stale pop country. I felt out of place here, but not as much as I felt out of place in my own home.

I'd been so ready to tell her. But then as I was cleaning up my studio I swirled a paintbrush in a jar of turpentine. The liquid turned fire engine red, and I swear I saw my future in it. The moment I told her not to have it, our entire relationship would change. Yet things would never be the same if she went ahead. When I married Rebecca Crowe I'd never been happier. All I wanted was to go back in time to how it was when we were just us— two kindred lovers in a rural bungalow. No impending kid or looming abortion.

We had something beautiful and whole and perfect. I was about to put a big crack in it and hope that it would still hold water.

I took a slug of my Natty. My eyes were adjusting to the Buckshot's dim interior, but my nose wasn't getting over the mélange of fried onions, stale cigarette smoke, and beer-soured carpet. That this place was preferable to home right now spoke volumes about my predicament.

The door swung open and a handful of guys in dusty Calcite Quarry work uniforms tromped in. Shit. There was Howie Peterson. He headed straight for me and clapped me on the back.

"If it ain't Becca's ex-pet midget."

Her *what?* This was how every conversation with Howie Peterson went. I barely understood what came out of his mouth, and there wasn't even the fun of wondering what she ever could have possibly seen in him because that was blindingly obvious. He was six-foot-four with a chest like a packing crate. He had short, blond curls and the kind of wide blue eyes and friendly smile that made you want to like the guy despite yourself. He moved with the easy grace of a hockey star, which locally, he was. His emotional fault line for Becca ran as deep as his intellect ran shallow.

She'd told me, "I was always forgiving him for being mean because he could be so dumb it was like he didn't even know he was being mean. If you knew him, you'd understand."

I didn't have any desire to know him and anyway, I already understood.

"I see little Petey Townshend's crying in his beer now that Crowe's run off and married."

Seriously. It was like the guy lived in his own tiny universe of misbegotten notions. He'd once snickered at Becca for saying spiders had eight legs because in The World According to Howie, spiders were insects and everybody knows they have six. The Pete Townsend thing had been an inside joke between me and Becca, yet he was still convinced that was my name. Howie had no clue who Pete Townshend was. Of course not. Why would he? Cultural literacy was for short men like me who had to actually make conversation to get by socially. All that guys like Howie needed to pay attention to was ball scores.

He clapped my back again, hard enough to make my Natty splash onto the table.

"The chick smoked us both, dude. We never saw it coming."

I tried to sop up the beer with a handful of cheap napkins. "What are you even talking about?"

"Oh, you really are out of the loop." The corners of his mouth turned down. "It happened, I dunno, maybe in March?" He flipped a chair around and straddled it. "Crowe up and married some Cliff Rastafarian or something. Didn't you know?" He pulled out his billfold and fished a torn newspaper clipping from behind Becca's high school graduation photo.

I scrutinized the scrap of newspaper. We hadn't bothered with a wedding announcement, but our names were listed with a half-dozen others in a tiny font under Marriage Licenses. It had never occurred to me that her ex-boyfriend didn't already know we were married. In Presque Isle County it seemed like everybody knew everybody else's business, especially Becca's.

"See right there? Rebecca Jane Crowe and Clive Ellis Rafferty," he said.

That explained it. He knew she'd gotten married, he just didn't know she'd married me. But he'd spotted me sitting in the Land Cruiser outside of her shop last week. What did he think I was doing there if he believed she was married to some Rastafarian stranger? Just stalking her around Rogers City, like he did? It was ludicrous.

I said, "Nothing gets by you, brother."

"Hell kind of name is Clive? Sounds kinda black, don't it? I didn't think we had any coloreds around here."

It was news to me that my name was reserved for "coloreds." I decided to play into his racist assumptions.

"Maybe he was named after one of his mother's dealers."

This was actually a theory I had. Look, I can't pay you today but I named this here kid I just squirted out after you. That's gotta be worth a hit, right? Give me a few more and I'll name the girl after you too.

"I'd like to pound this sneaky asshole, but hell if I know who he is," Howie said. "And I know every single person in Presque Isle County, plus their grandma. You sure you don't know who he is? I mean, she dumped you for this rat, didn't she?"

"What? No."

This had gone far enough.

"Oh. Oh! Don't even try to tell me you dumped her, pet midget. She's way too good for you and your hippie-ass hairdo."

"Um, actually—"

"You didn't even know she got hitched? Geez, seriously. I thought you two were getting pretty thick for a few months there."

"Yeah, I can be damned thick," I muttered. I downed some more beer and motioned the waitress over. She waved me off and kept talking to the bartender.

"I never figured on Crowe sticking with a runt like you," he said. Words like *runt* and *midget* never fazed me. I'd been called that and worse my whole life. I wasn't tall but damn it, I was tall enough.

He folded the newspaper clipping and tucked it gently into his wallet. "This Rafferty prick stole our bird. We gotta fry this sneaky fuck. You in, Townshend?"

Our bird. I briefly considered the escapades that might follow an offer to help kick my own ass with Howie Peterson. This could be a hoot. But no. I'd let this go on too long already.

"No way," I said. "I love her. And I want her to have whatever makes her happy."

"You don't love that girl. Man, I smashed shit up when I found out. You're sitting here, all 'Hey man, whatever makes her happy, man.' That ain't love. That's being a pussy. A hippie-haired, light-beer-drinking pussy."

The waitress deigned to come over. I ordered another Natty. Howie asked for Budweiser and onion rings and told her to put everything on his tab.

He pinched my Natty can and held it at arm's length. "The hell you drinkin'? Natural Light? Lemme piss in your can—it'll make a better brew. Budweiser, now there's a man's beer."

I snatched back my Natty. I didn't appreciate him taking pot shots at it.

"Guess we're two peas in the same damned boat now that Crowe's married," he said. "Up shit crick with no visible means of paddlefication."

Howie and his mangled clichés. Becca sometimes imitated them and laughed, little pink splotches blossoming on her cheeks. Her laugh. God, how I loved her laugh.

"What the hell you smiling about?"

"Nothing. Looking forward to some onion rings, that's all," I said.

"Get your own damned basket. This ain't a date, princess. Shit, buy the midget a beer, he thinks he's at the goddamn prom."

I called to the waitress from across the bar, "Make it two baskets of rings and a corsage for my lady-friend here."

Howie's group of quarry coworkers looked up from their billiards game and laughed.

"We don't have corsages," the waitress hollered back, "but on Tuesdays we sell carnations. Buck-fifty."

"We'll be in to buy some for Rafferty's grave." Howie guffawed at his own brilliance.

I put my hands up. "I'm Rafferty. She let you think my name was Pete Townsend because, well, damn it, it was kind of funny. But I'm actually Clive Rafferty. I married her. March twenty-fourth."

"Ha. Good one, Townshend. You're not even black."

Christ almighty. It was like trying to level with a manatee. I flipped my wallet open to show him my driver's license.

He peered at it, then shook his head. "No way. Stolen wallet. Crowe wouldn't lie to me."

"Check the photo."

He grunted. "Could be anybody. How'd you get his wallet? Let me see this dickweed." He squinted at my license and read it aloud. "Eyes, blue. Height, five-oh-seven ..." His mouth twitched as reality sunk into his thick skull.

I rocked backward on the vinyl bar chair, balancing on my toes. "Don't bust an artery, friend. It's not like it's personal."

"Yeah, well, I got there first." He leaned closer. "So, you like my sloppy seconds when she makes you eat Crowe?"

I let the chair drop onto four legs and slammed my beer can on the table. Foam seethed over the lip.

"If you're so sure you love her, try to show some goddamned respect for her choices."

Yes, I heard the hypocrisy in my own words.

The waitress delivered the onion rings and Budweiser. I stuffed a twenty into her hand to prevent anything from going on Howie's tab. I didn't ever want it said that I'd kicked the ass of a man who'd bought me a beer, if this shit came down to that. And it looked like it might.

He crammed an onion ring into his mouth and sucked cool air around it. "Yeah, I see how it is. You're at the bar, she's home alone. It's drying up now that you're married."

"She can't get enough of me."

"Bullshit." Onion ring crumbs spewed across the table.

"It's true. She's pregnant. All she talks about is how she can't wait to have my baby. She loves being pregnant. She's never been happier."

"No shit?"

"Oh, you should see her. She glows like the Madonna."

His ruddy cheeks faded and his Adam's apple bobbed. For a second, I thought he might burst into tears.

He slapped his palms onto the table. "Here's the deal, Townshend. Rafferty. Whatever the fuck your name is. If I find out you're not taking care of her, I'll string you up by the acorns. Count on it." He stood up, knocking his chair over.

"Cool. I'll pass your congratulations along to our bird."

10

Yellow Ledbetter

Ellie • Detroit, Mich. • Friday, July 28, 2006

I was flat on my back in bed. I had pretended to agree with Reece so he'd drop the subject of kicking Saint out, and leave me alone. He was snoring softly beside me.

I heard Saint come home, tend to his dog, tiptoe upstairs, shower, then go into his room and shut the door tight. The tension between them was like an entity in the house. Reece was righteously angry. Saint was facing the loss of his place to live, his dog, or both. I cared about each of them but was powerless to help them reconcile.

The window fan hummed but failed to cut through the sweltering heat. All I wanted was for Reece and Saint to get along, for Saint to stay and Reece to be happy again. Tremor Christ worried me, sure, but his fate wasn't up to me. I needed to yield to whatever Saint decided about his dog. Or whatever Reece decided about Saint. After all, it was Reece's house and Saint's dog. I was just along for the ride, but tonight the ride was making me sick. My temples throbbed. Heat lightning flashed. The barometric pressure was oppressive.

I crept down to the bathroom and got a bottle of ibuprofen out of the medicine drawer. I set it on the counter and picked up Saint's Vicodin. I read the prescription label. Maybe I could pop one to knock out my headache, take the edge off my anxiety and get some sleep. I decided against it, number one because it was Saint's. My tension headache couldn't compare to what he was going through with his arm. Number two, because it would be stealing—something I'd been accused of too many times and had prided myself on the fact that those allegations were always false— even the time it had landed me in a girls' correctional facility. Number three, and the biggest reason of all, was that it's addictive and one thing I'd never allow myself to become was an addict like my mother. Or Clive's nightmare ex, Lu-Creep-Show.

Saint clucked his tongue at me. He'd been standing in the dark hallway, watching me for I don't know how long. He was wearing baggy basketball shorts and nothing else. It was a major effort to ignore his giant brown nipples.

"I wasn't," I whispered, setting the bottle down. "It's just … my brain really hurts."

He shrugged. "Go ahead, try it. I'm done with them anyway."

I didn't. I washed down three ibuprofen tablets with a handful of water, careful not to dribble on my Pearl Jam *Yield* T-shirt that was softer than kittens and fell halfway to my knees. On the back I had scrawled *I've Come in Peace* with a white fabric pen. That was all I wanted at the moment. Just peace.

Saint pinched his thumb and forefinger together and brought them to his lips in the universal gesture for *burn one?* I raised my eyebrows. He jerked his head almost imperceptibly toward the stairs. I smiled and followed him down to the kitchen, grabbing my uke off the coffee table on the way.

I flipped the kitchen light on and Tremor Christ barked from the backyard. Saint yanked open the casement window over the sink. The humid night air was tinged with the charcoal smoke of our neighbor's patio grill.

"See that? All you did was turn on the light," Saint said. "He's a great watchdog."

"That's one way to put it."

"I think it's about to rain. I should bring the dog in."

"First, check this out." I handed him my uke. Boy, was he in for a treat. Reece had scored some Thai stick from a Tax Break client who was short on cash. I'd watched him stuff the baggie into the sound hole for safe keeping.

Saint extracted it, gave the bag a long sniff and grinned. "You gotta be kidding me, girlfriend. That's some old school primo shit right there. Where'd you even get this?"

"It's Reece's."

"Ha. Then I'm gonna smoke all of it."

"Long as you're doing the honors."

"Oh yeah, sure."

I grabbed my cheap Mp3 player and started a playlist consisting entirely of bootleg versions of Yellow Ledbetter, and dropped it into a clean mug to amplify the sound. He took a pack of rolling papers out of a box of wooden matches on the stove and began rolling in that meticulous way of his. The process took him even longer with the limitations of his injured arm, but the fine finger work was probably good physical therapy.

I hoisted myself onto the island and sliced a Mineola orange, juicy and fragrant. Saint might have been the world's slowest joint roller, but I was a big fan of anticipation.

We smoked the entire joint in silence, trading it back and forth, our fingers touching, the tensions easing. We ate sweet slices of orange in between tokes.

Thai stick dimmed the corners of my mind and tossed a tattered gray veil over everything. My headache and anxiety linked arms and ran away together. The entire world became the kitchen, the sticky orange juice on my fingers, and Saint's long forelock falling across his dark eyes. He peeled the rind off another orange slice and sucked on it. Softly, I drummed my heels against the island cupboard and felt my brain somersaulting like a child in a rolling meadow filled with daisies.

Saint pushed the cutting board aside and hopped onto the counter next to me. Close. He leaned forward. There was his *Whipping* tattoo. With my fingertip, I traced the words on his shoulder blade. Now that I knew him better, I understood just how perfectly that first stanza fit Saint Wozniak.

I stopped tracing and held onto the edge of the island. The tip of Saint's pinky brushed mine. It was a switch flipping on and electrifying every cell of my being. Was it intentional? Accidental? I stared at our hands, side by side on the edge of the butcher block, and tried to decipher the indecipherable.

He lifted his pinky and hooked it over mine. A thrill coursed through me. *Intentional.* Holy wow!

What, exactly, was he doing? What was I doing? I marveled at this tiny, perfect moment in my messy, unpredictable life. I could have moved my hand away. Slid off the island. Stuffed the last segment of orange into my mouth. Started talking about Stone Gossard or Maury Povich.

Here is what I did: *nothing.*

He laced his fingers with mine. My heart raced and my ears burned. Holding hands hadn't created this much sexual tension for me since eighth grade. I rubbed my bare feet together, my soles sweating.

Saint said nothing. I said nothing.

He released my hand and touched my knee, then caressed it. I was transfixed by disbelief, curiosity, and unexpected desire. I kept forgetting to breathe. His tawny coloring contrasted with my plain, pale skin. Mesmerized, I let his hand wander ever higher.

Reece was upstairs. Right upstairs.

I was afraid Saint wouldn't stop and afraid that he would. He moved his mouth near my ear, sweet oranges and Thai stick on his breath. "Detroit Ellie … is this OK? Want me to stop?"

In answer, I turned my face and let my lips find his. Damn, this boy could kiss.

"You're baked, though," he said.

"*You're* baked."

I moved my knees apart, inviting him to not stop. And he didn't. We were mostly silent from that point on. I let it wash away the bright kitchen lights, the cool, hard surfaces, Reece snoozing upstairs, Tremor Christ out there in the dark crouching under the bus. At some point, I whispered, "Your boo boo," when his wounded arm was cradled between us. He said "Shh," into my hair. That was the full extent of our verbal exchange.

The universe flowed between us. This was pure connection. No expectations. No agenda. All natural, like wildflowers and honey bees and summer breezes. Saint. Me. The thunderstorm that always comes due on the hottest night of the year blew in hard and fast. I smelled the coming downpour even before the rain splattered the window screens. Lightning flashed, thunder growled, the power blinked out then surged on again. Tremor Christ howled in the yard. Saint was all over me like a bare-ass suntan.

I was a mammal, born to do exactly this.

When it was over, I stood barefoot on the kitchen floor, knees trembling, whisker burns high on my thighs. I had no words. I squeezed his hand, ending things where they'd begun.

My panties and shirt were wadded on top of the fridge. I had no idea how they'd gotten there. Saint shook them out and handed them back to me. I pulled them on while he tore the rind off the very last orange slice.

"It's pouring. I gotta let the dog in." He put the orange segment in my hand and kissed my forehead.

"Before you go, I have one question," I said.

"OK. Shoot."

"Was covering *Last Kiss* forgivable?"

"Ooh. I'm gonna have to think that one over and get back to you. Hey, sweet dreams, Detroit Ellie."

Savoring the juicy citrus, I tiptoed upstairs and slid into the cotton sheets next to Reece. I felt delicious and wretched all at once, still quivering with the thrill and barely believing what had transpired.

Two facts occurred to me in this order: Saint had not giggled even once. I'd forgotten my diaphragm entirely.

11

Smile

Reece and I were curled at opposite ends of the sectional, late morning light slanting through dusty windows, the air damp and cooler thanks to last night's storm. I struggled with my latest embroidery project, too distracted by every delectable detail of Saint last night to properly separate the threads of golden floss.

I was an emotional bundle, yet numb to everything around me. Saint had left early, before I was even up, for his first shift at the Ren Cen since his injury. After everything that happened, I'd laid awake forever, then finally conked out at sunrise and slept way in. I still wore the same Pearl Jam T-shirt. *I came in peace.* I sniffed the sleeve and caught the faint scent of roasted cashews. Luxurious. Decadent. I could get lost in his natural fragrance.

Reece pushed his toe into my bare thigh. "Where are you, sugar? Did you even hear me?"

Had he been talking? God, I needed to get a grip. I set the embroidery hoop on my lap. "Sorry, what?"

"Wozniak was actually pretty cool with me this morning. Something I said yesterday must have sunk in with him."

"Huh. Go figure." Something sunk in alright, but it wasn't anything Reece had said.

What if I was pregnant? This enormous possibility paralyzed me right there on the sectional while Reece, who'd given up trying to make conversation, sat next to me and chuckled at the comic section of *The Freep*.

What had I done? How could I atone? I decided then and there to commit the rest of my Saturday to actively listening to Reece and doing whatever I could to make him happy. We'd been together forever. We belonged together. I was going to yield to Reece completely.

One night with Saint wouldn't change anything.

CR

That afternoon Reece and I hit some used record stores looking for album cover samples for Clive. That's the kind of person Reece was. I'd said we could do anything he wanted that day, and here we were shopping for records for my brother. Reece had always had a knack for choosing spec pieces that would bring Clive the best commissions. An album a Baby Boomer had obsessed over during his formative years was pure Retro Replicas gold.

I wasn't finding anything good. The Captain & Tennille sure sold a lot of records. So did Andy Gibb. And what was up with Nazareth? My life made about as much sense as any of that right about now.

I'd never, ever forgotten my diaphragm with Reece. I choked on that irony. Reece never made me forget it, but Saint sure had. I shoved the thoughts of him away and handed Reece *Journey's Greatest Hits*.

He motioned like he was going to fling it. "C'mon. *Escape*? Maybe. *Infinity*, absolutely." He tucked the offending album into a crate. "No greatest hits albums. Greatest hits are for casual fans, and casual fans don't buy album art."

"They might."

"Said the girl who doesn't even own a copy of *Rearviewmirror*."

He had me there. I was a Pearl Jam purist, but I didn't own their greatest hits album or *Riot Act*. I did have two copies of *Yield* on vinyl, though, and several on CD. If I ever saw one in a used CD bin I snapped it up to give to the needy—meaning anyone who didn't already have that album in their life.

If I was pregnant, I'd have to learn to survive without Reece. On my Mr. Salty's wages, I could afford a sturdy appliance box on

Nine Mile—maybe. I counted on him for so much. At thirty, he was older and better educated. He had the full-time job, the house, the reliable car. But it was more than that. I loved him, and I knew he loved me. These facts came rushing at me with an enormous side helping of guilt and shame.

Reece had already scored a copy of *Licensed to Ill*, and now he was waving *Welcome to My Nightmare* at me, beaming. He didn't need to elaborate. That one was right up there with *Kiss Alive* and *Montrose*. I knew my classic rock, even the stuff that was long before my time. Clive and Reece had taught me well.

Reece started singing *Only Women Bleed* with the "Oohs" and everything, keeping a completely straight face while I tried not to pee my pants laughing. I'd been insane to betray him. Saint had uncovered a side of me I didn't even know existed. Had he always seen it there? Did Reece see it? How had I not known about it before all of this?

ભ

We stood in line outside of a theatre on Woodward that night, waiting to see some band I'd never heard of that Reece was excited about. This was all part of yielding to him, and I was feeling pretty good about it. Anyway, I was mostly just grateful that he wasn't dragging me to this year's Van's Warped Tour at Comerica Park. He went to talk to some people he knew, and when he came back he handed me a couple of magic mushrooms.

"Just sharin' the love."

Reece was crazy about 'shrooms. Personally, I hated the little shit bombs. Last time I ate one I'd ended up in a heated argument about Anthony Kiedis. With a doorknob. I'd planned to never eat another one as long as I lived.

I sniffed it and wrinkled my nose. It smelled like a sun-dried cow patty. Worse, even one little 'shroom could be enough to make me slip up and blab about last night. There was maybe a two-percent chance I was pregnant. Given even that tiny possibility, I had enough to worry about with the damned Thai stick. There was yielding to Reece, then there was colossal stupidity.

"I'll take them later," I said.

"You're not going to, are you?"

I shrugged. "Somebody's gotta drive the Roadbastard home, remember."

"Good point."

He put his hand out and I gave them back to him. I swore to myself I'd yield to absolutely anything else he asked of me for the rest of the night.

෨

After the show, we were starving. I drove us to this hole-in-the-wall Middle Eastern place in Midtown where we could get falafel. The lights were bright, the furniture cheap, and a sitar was playing *Love Hangover*. That was about the last thing I needed to hear. But the aromas in the place were straight from the kitchen of the gods. Roasted garlic, smoked eggplant, Kalamata olives, warm pita bread. My stomach rumbled loud enough that the woman in line ahead of us turned and gave me a shy smile. She wore a candy pink sari with shimmering gold embroidery. Her baby, fastened to her body by a swath of matching fabric, peered at us with onyx eyes. She had two bottom teeth like tiny pearls. Her thick hair sprouted from a plastic barrette. Reece made funny faces at her and played a silent game of peek-a-boo until she squawked with joy.

I thought I was going to melt, and Reece already had. As we ate our warm falafel and hummus, he continued flirting with the smiling baby. The magic mushrooms had him flying. Cucumber yogurt sauce dripped down his chin. I was dabbing his face with my napkin when he said, "Just think. Between you and me we have everything we need to create one of those."

"Whoa. Oh wow. That's actually true."

"Wouldn't it be neat? I mean, we could do that. Me, you and a bed is all it would take to create a whole new human being."

"The bed is optional."

I couldn't believe I blurted that.

"I'm digging your thinking. So you want to?"

I nodded, not sure whether I was yielding to sex or to actually attempting to make a baby. I figured he'd come down off those mushrooms by the time we got home, return to his senses, and then he'd be all about my diaphragm.

It didn't happen that way. Oh, he came down alright. He was his normal, clear-eyed self by the time we crawled into bed that night. But he was still in love with the idea that we could make a whole human being from nothing but our own cells.

In the end, I made my apologies to Reece with my whole body, and without my diaphragm.

12

Gimme Some Truth

Ellie • Detroit, Mich. • Monday, Aug. 7, 2006

S helby finally scheduled me for some hours at Mr. Salty's. After my shift, I caught the SMART bus in the warm summer drizzle. The vibrations of the bus, the frequent stops and starts, the hydraulic shushing of the door, the scents of exhaust fumes and fruity bubblegum were almost soothing. The people boarding and departing look damp, overworked, weary. As big as my problems were, I was still better off than most of them.

Ten days had passed since my indiscretion with Saint and my flawed attempt to set things right with Reece. He'd been asking me if I wanted to keep trying, and I told him that if it was meant to be, it would happen.

I'd been checking myself daily for any pregnancy symptoms— breast tenderness, nausea, changes in appetite, fatigue. But other than nagging guilt, I felt no different. Waiting to get my period was an option, but the suspense pushed me to drop fourteen dollars at Rite Aid for an early pregnancy test. I'd removed the instructions from the box and read and reread them every time I was alone. August twelfth was the earliest I could test and not risk a false negative.

Raindrops splattered the bus window. It's not like I wanted to go back to the health clinic in my Mr. Salty's getup, but taking the bus straight from work was the only way to get there without raising eyebrows. I had a lot more to rule out than pregnancy.

Having unprotected sex with two different people within twenty-four hours was possibly my stupidest behavior to date. Who knew what Saint might have picked up from one of those chicks he brought home from his gigs? Genital warts. Herpes. Hep C. AIDS. Pregnancy began to seem like a comparatively minor concern that might even end with something cute.

A week earlier the free clinic had tested me for every STD known to man and beast, then lectured me about bloodborne pathogens, condoms, and responsibility. They offered me a pregnancy test but I said I already had one. Today I was going back for my STD results, with all my fingers crossed that they'd be negative.

The prison-orange plastic chairs in the windowless waiting room made my butt numb. I wondered if I looked as desperate as everyone else there, with my frizzy hair shoved back in a Mr. Salty's visor. The damp polyester uniform made me itch. Jerry Springer was on the waiting room television attached to the wall. I couldn't look away. If I was pregnant now, I'd be exactly like those losers. *Paternity test! Up next, Jerry has the results. Does Tiffany's baby, little Fresno, belong to her cousin Jim-Leroy, or her half-brother, Jim-Bob? Find out after the break.*

If I was pregnant, the only things separating me from Tiffany was I didn't share any grandparents with the putative fathers. Other than that, me and Tiffany could be soul sisters.

They called me to the counseling area just as the wrong Jim won the paternity lottery. Or maybe lost. The guys swung at each other. Springer ran for cover. Tiffany waddled over and decked the father. The baby, forgotten in his car seat, sucked his fist. He was going to need it.

My results were good news/bad news. The good news was I was negative for almost every STD. The bad news was I had Chlamydia. Tiffany from Jerry Springer didn't even have that, I'd bet.

"Next time, use a condom." The nurse handed me a prescription for Zithromax. "Fortunately for you, this one's curable."

I wondered if that was how I should break it to Saint. *Don't sweat it, kiddo. This one's totally curable with a course of strong antibiotics.* And Reece. Holy crap. I'd have to tell Reece. I was lower than the dirt stains on the clinic's carpet.

The nurse cheerfully added, "Be sure to inform all of your partners, and have every single one of them tested."

All of my partners. Not my partner, or even *both* of my partners, but *all* of them. Like there were dozens. I flashed her my best *Jerry Springer Show* smile. Why not? She'd earned it.

ɕ

The hardest talk I'd ever had to have with anyone had taken place two years earlier, with Clive. Somebody had to tell him he was enabling LuCretia. And who cared about Clive more than I did? I think in a way he knew he was becoming part of LuCretia's problem, or at least not solving it, but he was too caught up, too in love, too desperate in his attempts to save her to realize those things. He'd needed to hear it from someone who understood him and didn't doubt his intentions, which with Clive were always golden. I was proud of how I'd handled that with him. I hadn't called her Lu-Creep-Show even once. And now he was married to someone else and happy, as far as I could tell.

The conversations I needed to have with Reece and Saint would be much harder. Every time I rehearsed what I needed to say, my stomach knotted like a macramé owl. Reece was out for euchre night with his work buddies, so I was temporarily off the hook there. But when a girl I'd never seen before trailed Saint home, I had no choice but to warn him before it was too late.

They were playing *Guitar Hero* in the living room. The game's CGI crowd booed Saint off stage before the end of *Thunder Kiss '65*. I could play that one with my toes, in my sleep. Poor Saint. That plastic game-controller guitar always had confounded him. With his arm all messed up, it was even worse. He sank into the sectional and nursed a twenty-ounce Budweiser. I was on the opposite end, embroidering away my various frustrations on a pair of cutoffs.

This new girl had a yellow rosebud tattooed on her clavicle. She wore daisy dukes, thigh-high baseball socks, and high-tops. Her hair was divided into two short ponytails, like puppy dog ears. She was kicking some serious *Guitar Hero* ass. She charged through

Cowboys from Hell, making eyes at Saint while he sulked over his beer. She flipped the fake guitar behind her head, turned away from the TV to face me and without missing a single note said, "Wanna play?" She was cute, a scrawny, Harajuku Goth version of Mike McCready. I liked her instantly. For sure she didn't deserve Chlamydia.

"You know, I would. But I need to talk to Saint for a minute. If that's alright with you."

Saint didn't wait for her permission. Before she'd even uttered, "Sure. Whatevs," he was in the kitchen waiting for me.

He swung the door closed. "You OK? Whatcha need?"

I'd avoided being alone with him since our night together, and now I remembered why. He smelled delicious. I braced myself against my stupid desires that had caused so much trouble already.

There was no elegant way to put it, so I went with the facts. "I, um, I guess I have Chlamydia?"

"What's that?"

"Um, an STD. One I didn't have before we, before…"

His eyes got round. "Well, you didn't get it here."

"Yeah, actually, I did. I had to have."

He shook his head.

I knew he gave it to me, but spreading blame around wasn't my purpose. "Regardless. You sleep with Rosebud, you'll give it to Rosebud."

"Who?"

"That girl. The one playing *Crossroads* out there in the living room."

"Her name's Lizzie."

"Right, well whatever. Whether I got it from you or not, you've been exposed. Get yourself tested before you do it with anybody."

"You're being possessive. You don't want me hooking up with anyone but you."

I opened and closed my mouth like a beached trout. I hadn't even thought about whether I wanted him to sleep with anyone else, but nothing could be further from the point.

"I'm in a relationship," I said. "You can sleep with whoever. But I'm trying to warn you, you've been exposed. Don't be the Johnny Appleseed of Chlamydia."

"I always wear a raincoat." He said this with a straight face, even though his *Whipping* tattoo literally said he didn't need a raincoat. Maybe Reece was right and Saint was a total liar.

"You do not."

"Yes I do. Always. I mean, always, always."

"You didn't with me."

He slumped onto a stool and hung his head. His hair flopped forward.

"You didn't," I said. "Why didn't you?"

He grabbed my wrist. A jolt of electricity. For Saint Wozniak, I had no ground.

His eyes were intense. "I'm not sure. That moment. With you. Man. It was the most natural thing I've ever experienced. Animal. Like, pure instinct. You were the aurora borealis."

My knees threatened to collapse.

"Girlfriend, I can't shake that night out of my head. This situation's messed up. I'm trying. I brought that girl here because I'm really trying. I know, I know. I gotta move on. I get it. I'm sorry."

Why was he apologizing when I was the one who'd wronged everyone? All I wanted was to keep that wrong from spreading to Rosebud/Lizzie and the rest of greater Detroit. I touched his cheek. He pressed it against my palm and closed his eyes. He let go of my wrist and put his good arm around my waist, drawing me in close, closer until his head was against my chest.

Good lord, we could not be doing this. What the hell was wrong with me? I pulled away. "Promise me you'll at least wear a condom for her tonight. And get tested tomorrow."

"No. I'm sending her home."

"You don't have to, but it's probably a good idea. Better to get tested and treated than chance anything."

He winced. "Yeah. I'll do that. So, Reece won't be back until real late, right?"

"He'll be home any minute."

"Nah, he won't. Let's hang out."

Had I not just told him I had Chlamydia? Besides, what happened between us was a one-time thing. A titanic Thai stick mishap. Phenomenally stupid. If he thought tonight was going to be a repeat performance, he was dead wrong.

"I'll be good, I swear," he said.

Lizzie went home. Saint and I made popcorn and watched *The Big Lebowski*. We sat facing each other on the sectional, the soles of our feet touching through the entire movie. That's as far as I let it go, but even that was too far, I know.

13

Funky Crime

Ellie • Detroit, Mich. • Saturday, Aug. 12, 2006

The urge to pee woke me at dawn. I reached under my pillow for the pregnancy test. It was there in all its idiot-proof glory. When I sat up, Reece did too. His hair was mashed to the side of his head. I did not need him awake for this.

"I've been thinking," he said.

I wanted to know what he'd been thinking. I slid the pregnancy test box under the sheet before he could notice it.

"If it turns out you're pregnant, do you want to get married?" he asked.

If. Do I want to? Was that a proposal?

"Do you think it's necessary?" I asked.

"I don't know. There's insurance to consider." Ladies and gentlemen: my boyfriend, the bean counter.

"A. I'm not pregnant—"

"—You sure? You got your period?"

"Not yet, but I'm probably not. B. If we get married it should be because we want to commit the rest of our lives to each other. Not because of a pregnancy. Or some insurance hoo-ha."

"I was just offering, in case, you know."

"Well, thanks for that."

He was trying to do the right thing, in his way. There are worse things your boyfriend can do than offer to marry you *if* you're pregnant. Still. If he'd asked me to marry him a month earlier, with a ring and maybe flowers, I'd have said yes. No *ifs* about it.

"I'm kind of horny," he said. "You want to frog around?"

"I gotta pee. My neck hurts." That was no lie. Stress always made my neck stiff. Lately, I was Quasimodo with Chlamydia.

"You won't mind if I take care of a little business, then?" He pushed his covers down to reveal a bouncing, fat erection.

"Have at it." I couldn't hang around for the festivities. While he distracted himself I smuggled the pregnancy test into the bathroom and locked the door.

I took the test and laid it on a pile of Kleenex on the back of the toilet, then got busy washing my face and brushing my teeth to kill time. The instructions had said that if I tested too early, the lines might be faint and I'd need to retest in a few days. If that happened, maybe I could will it to be negative a few days from now. Toothbrush still in my mouth, I checked the test.

Two strong blue lines had already formed a cross. There was nothing faint about them. This meant *positive* according to the fool-proof, clear-and-easy, no-confusion instructions I'd memorized. I spat my toothpaste into the sink.

A cross. My cross.

Pregnant. Goddamnsonofabitch. I couldn't get away with cheating even one time. With unprotected sex two times. First Chlamydia and now I was pregnant, and I didn't even know who the father was. Someone call Jerry Springer STAT.

ଓ

Monday, I called the health clinic and told them I was pregnant after all. The nurse said the Zithromax wouldn't hurt the fetus, but if Chlamydia was present at birth there was a risk of severe complications for the baby, including blindness, pneumonia, and death. Again she reminded me to tell all of my partners. *Great news, guys. If we don't get this shit cleared up we're going to have a blind, dead baby with pneumonia.*

She also wrote me a prescription for prenatal vitamins. I knew I'd take them even though I didn't believe in supplements. Even though I wasn't completely sure I should have this baby at all. I've always been pro-choice, but as messed up as this whole thing was I just couldn't see getting an abortion. This was my turn to be a better mother than Honey Jane. Clive, David, Donald and I had a train wreck of a mother. David and Donald were dead before they were dry through the night. I knew I could do so much better.

Riding my old ten-speed to the clinic, I imagined this baby of mine. She or he didn't yet have limbs or eyes and was the size of a pencil dot. This little dot had nothing to claim but potential. This small life was my fault, my responsibility, and with any luck, my joy. Some people believe a baby chooses its mother. If that was true, I'd be giving birth to either the dumbest or the most compassionate human ever.

No way did I choose my mother. If I could have picked one, she'd have been this one foster mother we'd had before the fire and everything. She'd had all four of us together. A big Italian Catholic woman with a big Italian Catholic family. She had crazy brown curls, happy eyes and the warmest hugs. She laughed a lot and so did her kids, and there was tons of food all the time. Her daughter Janice was the closest thing I'd ever had to a sister. I wondered whatever had happened to Janice Marconi. She was maybe a year older than me.

Clive and I had rated our foster care homes on a five-star system, like they do for hotels. The Marconis had set the standard for five stars. We shouldn't have lost touch with them, but I'd heard somewhere along the way that Mrs. Marconi was super broken up and had quit fostering when our brothers died.

God, I needed Clive. He probably wouldn't understand my predicament, but he'd care. Reece was going to have a moose about the Chlamydia thing. Maybe Clive could help me break it to him.

But wait, that was dumb. I had a better idea.

There was a way around this without telling Reece I'd cheated, or was diseased, or that he needed testing. It would require a lot of riding my bike all over, but I was pretty sure it'd work. Besides, it was a warm, cloudy, windless day, perfect for my tasks.

I got myself back to the clinic and locked my bike to a No Parking sign. I took a walk-in number and waited alongside the desperate people. I was one of them now. When I had my turn with the nurse, I told her my purse had been stolen with the rest of my Zithromax pills and I needed the prescription again. She looked at me like I was a lying turd bag, like I was trying to score narcotics, like the hardest part of her job was faking not being judgmental and I was making that damned near impossible for her.

"You can't get a prescription for your partner, missy. That's dangerous. He needs to be seen by a medical professional and tested for everything. They all do."

No doubt everyone heard her over the beige partitions.

"Honestly, my purse was stolen. I swear. Anyway, he already got tested. You can even check your patient list. Timothy C. Wozniak. I'm sure he's been by." In reality, I had no idea whether Saint had followed through after our conversation, but assuming he had half a brain, he would have.

I swore right and left that the prescription was for me, and explained that it was super important because if I didn't get the infection cleared there could be severe consequences for my baby. I didn't shut up until a new Zithromax prescription was in my hand.

Babies. Yep, they trump everything. I'd have to keep that in mind.

I had the prescriptions filled before riding to Reece's personal mecca, Supplement City. I bought an empty plastic vial.

After dinner, I told Reece I'd heard about this ancient herbal supplement that hadn't even been FDA approved yet, and I'd checked Supplement City for him while I was out and about, and sure enough they'd sold me a sample under the counter.

"They're supposed to improve your stamina. Not that it needs improving, if you know what I mean. Ha ha. But it might be fun."

"You? In Supplement City? You really do love me."

I took the store bag out of my knapsack. I'd spent about an hour locked in the bathroom, filing the markings off the pink Zithromax pills with an emery board and dropping them into the vial.

"The guy said you take it three times a day for ten days, and they'll increase your time by like, up to twenty percent."

"Coolness. Let's try 'em out tonight."

"Oh, no no no. That's not how it works. He said no sex during the ten days. You can't even spank your monkey. You have to let it build up in your system."

It was that easy to get the antibiotic into Reece's pill sorter. When the hell did I get so good at lying? Maybe it's a symptom of Chlamydia.

14

Anything In Between

Clive • I-75 Southbound, Mich. • Saturday, Aug. 26, 2006

I didn't tell Becca about my run-in with Howie at the Buckshot Tavern until we were headed to the D to spend the weekend at Ellie and Reece's. She laughed at a few of the details, but when I was finished she said, "As long as you didn't tell him I'm pregnant."

Well shit, I didn't think I was going to have to lie to her.

"How did he not realize you'd married me? I mean, how does he imagine that after we'd been an item for months that you'd up and marry some random black guy? Just because my name is Clive. All this time, he really thought my name was Pete Townshend. Pete Townshend! I can't possibly be a Clive just because I'm white. That's moronically idiotic. And more than a little racist."

I cracked the window. The late summer sunshine was beautiful. A cigarette would have been perfection at this moment.

"Racist? I don't follow," she said.

I decided to let it go. He was a jerk. He'd made an ass of himself. I didn't need to convince her that he was a racist, too.

She turned the stereo volume up for T. Rex, *20th Century Boy*. I always had her DJ on long drives. It made her happy, and I needed her as happy as possible. I'd be breaking it to her this weekend that I wanted her to end the pregnancy. Telling her was going to suck, but I was trying to set the scene for a soft landing. Ellie would help her understand where I was coming from, and Reece was a genius when it came to diffusing emotional situations. I probably should have called them beforehand and given them a heads up, but I could work it out when we got there.

"I hope you didn't tell Howie I'm pregnant."

"Why would I? It's none of his business." I downshifted and stamped on the gas to blow by a trio of semis, and didn't bother slowing back down to the speed limit. If she got on me about my driving it'd derail the topic of her pregnancy.

"If you're not going to let me keep it, I really don't want anyone knowing. Especially not Howie Peterson."

I changed lanes without signaling.

"And since we're on the subject," she said.

Ugh. Not yet.

"You were going to take a few days to decide. It's been a month now. I've been more than patient."

A state police patrol car was idling in the median up ahead. I gunned the engine and pushed the Land Cruiser up over eighty-five. Getting pulled over would be the fastest way to derail this conversation. I desperately needed this to wait until we were at Ellie's.

"Five weeks, Clive. And I still don't know if I'm having a baby or an abortion. It's not fair." She pressed the soles of her Teva sandals against the dashboard and crossed her arms.

She was right. It wasn't fair. But I only needed her to wait a few more hours, a day at most. I checked the rearview mirror. Nothing. Damned state bull ignoring me the one time I needed them riding my ass.

"I'm dead sick of hanging in limbo. Rogers City is a very small town, everybody knows me and I've got my reputation to consider. Pretty soon this pregnancy is going to be obvious," she said.

Except for the more generous curve of her breasts, she looked no different than before this disaster struck. Smooth skin, a sweet figure, silky chestnut hair swept into a ponytail. I loved her so much that it hurt to look at her. It hurt me to hurt her. I wished I could get on board with this baby thing, but every time I tried to I was hit with waves of panic and despair. She was from a stable family, and the youngest. She had no idea of the realities of parenthood.

84

"Honey, I know. I know. You've been beyond patient. But right now I really need to pay attention to the road."

"You blew past the state bull doing eighty-eight in a seventy and changed lanes without signaling. I doubt you could do much worse."

Damn it. She was everything to me. And she was right. Making her wait as long as I already had was unfair. I needed to man up. Quit stalling. Tell her. Tell her. Tell her to abort. It was mine too; it wasn't like I had no say. Hell, she'd given me a say. This whole mess was about my say.

I'd tell her, we'd probably argue, maybe we'd pull over and cry about it. Then we'd find a way to make up and get on with our lives. It was weak of me to use Ellie like a crutch. This was my shit and I needed to deal with it.

"If you're going to make me end this, tell me right now. I'm not going to be one of these people who wait until the second or third trimester." Becca pulled off her sandals, drew her legs into the lotus position and arched her back. "The longer you take, the more attached to her I'm getting."

"I'm not going to 'make' you do anything. It's your body. And why refer to it as 'her'? That's not going to make it any easier in the end."

"So, there is going to be an end?"

Well, it was out there now. Might as well run with it.

"You wanted my decision."

My words hung in the air between us, foul as a taco fart. She stared straight ahead, expression inscrutable behind her sunglasses. Her posture was rigid. She dug her fingers into her kneecaps. *Gone.* Just like that. For Christ's sake, she had to have known it was going this way. Why else would I have delayed? Hadn't she heard that yes comes quickly and no never comes?

I put my hand on her shoulder. "I'm sorry. Really, I am. I just didn't know how to tell you."

She brushed my hand away, tipped her head back against the seat and blew out a long stream of air as if she'd been holding her breath for five weeks. I know I had been. But maybe she'd get used to the idea. Maybe she'd forgive me.

85

Maybe I was screwed.

"You didn't even want to leave your dog at the kennel. How are you going to leave a baby all day, every day?" I asked.

"Cubby would have been fine coming with us. In case you haven't noticed, Ellie exaggerates. If that roomie's dog was as terrible as she says, he'd have killed someone by now."

"He attacked that guy. Saint Whatever-iak."

She shrugged. "He doesn't know how to handle him, then. I would. God, it's like you're afraid of everything. Afraid of a dog. Afraid of a baby."

There was no defending myself. I turned the music up and let the discussion drop.

We were well past Flint before she spoke again. "Last night I dreamed about her. She was a young woman, and she was walking away from me. I knew her scent. I could feel her presence. But I couldn't see her face."

"Then you can't know for sure it was her." I heard myself say *her* and felt tricked.

"It was in the way she walked, too. She was ours, Clive. Ours. She walked exactly like you."

"What's that supposed to mean? Now I walk funny?"

"You walk..." she paused in search of words. "You walk as if tragedy is right at your heels. Like you can outrun it as long as you refused to look back. And that's exactly how she walked in my dream."

I don't know how I walk, but that was exactly how I lived my life. She *was* mine, whoever she was. Goosebumps smacked my right side from my thigh to my cheek. She was really mine. I wished that was enough information for a change of heart, but no. It only made me want a cigarette.

15

Last Kiss

Ellie • Detroit, Mich. • Saturday, Aug. 26, 2006

I smashed overripe bananas with a fork while Reece measured the dry ingredients for the sourdough banana bread he'd insisted on baking for Clive and Becca. I had about a zillion other things to take care of before they arrived, but Reece had asked for my help. He was dancing around the kitchen and singing along with The Darkness, *I Believe in a Thing Called Love*. Goofball. This seemed like as good a time as any to tell him the secret I'd been carrying around for the better part of two weeks. Before saying anything, I'd had to wait until I'd gotten used to the idea enough that I could say it aloud without crying.

Some people make a big, cutesy deal about these announcements, but all I did was peel another black banana and say, "By the way, it was positive."

Reece spilled flour on the counter and down the front of the striped, faded polo shirt he wore every Saturday. He picked me up and set me down. "I can't believe it. I'm going to be a daddy." Happy tears sparkled in his eyes.

I appreciated Reece's joy but felt hardly any for myself. I'd put us on this train and I wasn't convinced it was on the right track.

"So, wow. What do we do now?" he asked.

"I'm not due until April nineteenth. I think that gives us time to finish making banana bread."

He chattered the entire time we blended the ingredients, telling me his favorite childhood story was *In the Night Kitchen*, and going

87

on about the games and cartoons he'd loved best. I indulged him in thinking this pregnancy was all about him, while mentally tabulating the five-hundred errands I still had to run to get ready for Clive and his wife.

"Shouldn't we get married?" Reece asked. He wasn't a practicing Catholic, but his upbringing in the church explained his notion that marriage was the answer to pregnancy. I'd never seen what one had to do with the other.

"I don't know. Do I have to become a Catholic?" Maybe this wasn't a romantic response, but c'mon. Couldn't he ask me to marry him in some way that involved, I don't know, romance? Flowers? Dinner? Maybe even a modest piece of jewelry?

"I haven't been to church lately, but Catholicism sure has a lot of beautiful traditions," he said. "You should think it over."

Yeah, right. Traditions like codified misogyny, child molestation, and the impoverished tithing to support the world's wealthiest organization. *Beautiful.* I stirred chopped walnuts into the batter. Reece dumped in an entire bag of chocolate chips.

"Whoa there, sugartooth. Slow down."

"But you love chocolate chips." He popped one into my mouth. "And you're eating for two now."

I chewed it and swallowed. "Yeah, and one of us is about the size of a chocolate chip."

"Who is?" Saint stood in the doorway, that ridiculous codpiece strapped over his jeans. He wrapped a clean dish towel around his bandaged arm and held the leather forearm guard out for me to buckle into place.

I couldn't remember the last time Tremor Christ had had a training session. I didn't trust him not to finish Saint off. I dropped my spoon into the batter and helped him buckle his protective gear. The slippery metal tine refused to go through the little hole in the leather strap.

"Who's the size of a chocolate chip?" he asked.

"Our baby," Reece said, like he'd just won the Michigan Lotto.

Saint lurched backward, sending the greased bread pan clattering to the floor. The silence that followed made me want to cover my ears. He stared at the pan, his breaths short and panicky, then grabbed it and slammed it onto the counter.

I started fumbling with the buckle on his arm guard again. Now he was shaking.

"It's fine. Really, it's alright." I didn't mean the pan.

He jerked away from me as soon as I got the buckle fastened.

"Aren't you happy for us?" Reece was all smiles. I hadn't seen him that sunny since last time the Spartans beat the Wolverines.

"Thrilled," Saint muttered. He opened the back door, then turned around and stared straight into my eyes. "And by the way, no, *Last Kiss* is not at all forgivable." He stomped outside and began commanding Tremor Christ to *sitz* and *gib* in the relentless sunshine.

Reece poured the batter into the pan. "And that's why, thanks to Saint, we have banana bread every morning."

 C3

Saint took me to run my shopping errands while Reece waited for the banana bread to bake. Obviously, we had a few details to hash out. We were in his Tracker in the parking lot of a Midtown grocery store. There was a case of Natural Light on the floor at my feet, a bag of fancy cheeses that Reece had asked me to buy, and a sack of Granny Smith apples. I still needed to change the sheets on the trundle bed in the loft for Clive and Becca, since Saint had Clive's old room now. So much to do, and now I had to deal with this.

Things had been a lot simpler when Clive lived with us.

"Did you get tested?" I asked.

"Yup. I'm clean."

I slid down in the seat and pushed on the case of beer with my flip-flops. There was no way that I didn't get that STD from him.

"How is that possible?"

"I told you from the start it wasn't me." He looked straight ahead, his voice low, conspiratorial. "But did you ever consider it might have been Reece?"

Was he that desperate to pin this STD on Reece? Reece was the victim. Our victim. And now Saint wanted to blame him for the consequences of our misdeeds. Consequences, part of which Reece was excited to be taking on a lifetime of responsibility for. I could hardly keep up with how wrong all of this was. I needed to escape all of this bull crap, but I had one final errand. I asked Saint to drive me to Brush Park.

"What? Why do you want to go there? Did you forget to pick up an abandoned house?"

I gave him my sternest *don't ask* look and he shut up and drove me there.

Brush Park's empty Victorian houses sagged pathetically; turrets leaning at odd angles, complex gables reduced to charred timbers, Juliet balconies collapsing, and arched doorways boarded with graffiti-covered plywood. I directed him to an empty lot between two sorry old brick mansions. There, in abundance, was exactly what I'd come for. Queen Anne's lace, black-eyed Susans, snapdragons, bittersweet berries, chicory, and clover. I hopped out of the Tracker and gathered an unruly bouquet. Sunshine baked the top of my head. Dragonflies and bumblebees buzzed around me. Weeds scratched my bare legs. I didn't care. I shook the bugs off of the flowers and climbed into the Tracker, then laid the bouquet across my lap and breathed in its sweet aromas.

"What's that all about?" Saint asked.

I didn't bother trying to explain. These flowers were for me, for Clive, for the little brothers we'd lost. Most of all, they were for my baby. They represented glimmers of peace and hope in my wretched world. Clive would know exactly where they were from.

"They're actually kind of pretty. I mean, for weeds," he said.

"I'd call them volunteers."

I pulled a spray of bittersweet out of the bunch and handed it to him. He tucked it behind his ear, the deep pink and orange berries bright against his dark hair. They softened his edges.

"I need the truth, so I gotta ask," he said. "Any possibility it's mine?"

"We did it one time. It's not yours. I wouldn't do that to you, you know?"

90

"I think maybe it could be mine. There's this vibe."

"The only vibe I'm getting is that you're being a tad dramatic. Up until a few hours ago, you didn't even know."

"Maybe I did, though. I think. I wondered. Especially after you brought up me not wearing a raincoat. I'm always more careful than that. But if it's mine, well, I'm sorry."

Who was this Saint who apologized? What happened to the old, indifferent, hard-ass Saint? And no, I didn't need his apology. Any blame was far more mine than his.

He pushed his hand through his forelock. It had grown too long to hold a style, yet somehow this was an improvement. "Look. If it's mine you can tell me, I'm not going to freak out or anything."

What could I say? There's a fifty-percent chance it's yours but I'm running with the theory it's Reece's because he'll be a better father and conveniently, I'm already in a relationship with him. I knew how bad that sounded. No way was I saying it aloud. Besides, there was no earthly way for me to know which one fathered my baby at this point. I told myself it wasn't that big of a deal. Nobody knew who my father was. There weren't even any candidates to narrow it down. And I'd turned out fine, considering. Paternity couldn't be all that important. Wasn't it about males wanting to take credit for things that had very little to do with them? A woman always knew which kids were hers. A man had to take her word for it, even if they were married.

"I'll tell you exactly whose it is," I said. "It's mine."

"Great. You're going to do whatever you damned well please about it, and I get no say."

"It's probably not even yours."

"Whoa, whoa. Wait a sec. A minute ago you were certain it was Reece's. Now it's just probably not mine? Probably? Girlfriend, this situation is every kind of fucked up."

Welcome to my world, Saint Wozniak. We've got fucked up in a rainbow of flavors. Take your pick. Tears were coming on. I fought them with everything I had.

He brushed my cheek with his callused fingertip. "Aw, Detroit Ellie. C'mon. Don't cry."

He scooted over and sat on the edge of my seat, practically on my lap, and gently moved my bouquet to the dashboard. I melted against him. How could he feel this natural, smell this edible, yet be entirely wrong for me?

"All I want out of this is what's right for you. I wanna do what's right. Help me," he said.

I squeezed him and swore to myself it was the last time ever. Because I knew it had to be.

"You're a good girl. An angel. I respect you."

This was the craziest, stupidest thing he'd ever said. I'd been awful and wretched and evil and lying. I was way less forgivable than *Last Kiss*. Reece deserved better. My baby deserved better. Saint did, too. He should have run away from me, screaming, with a bag over his head. But no. He cried into my hair. He kissed my ear. He whispered that it was going to be OK. Then he moved back into the driver's seat and wiped his wet eyes with his fist.

The bittersweet he'd tucked behind his ear now lay crushed on my lap. I inserted it into the bouquet. It had earned its place among my collection of beautiful weeds.

16

Leash

Clive • Detroit, Mich. • Saturday, Aug. 26, 2006

I squeaked into a tight parking spot for the Land Cruiser across the street from Reece and Ellie's house. We sat there, unready to go inside. The tick of the engine cooling underscored the stubborn silence between Becca and me.

Their tired two-and-a-half-story stood on the hairy edge of Corktown, on a block where the houses were packed together so tight that no one could have a driveway. This had been my first real home. Real, because CPS couldn't remove me. The state couldn't decide to place me with strangers. I'd rented it cheap from Reece, who I'd known since the period when we'd both worked at Rite Aid while I was in high school and he was in college. He'd earned a degree, had a real job, had married his college sweetheart, had a tidy brick house in a decent neighborhood in Warren, and a few low-rent income properties scattered around Detroit. I'd really looked up to him. When he got divorced and lost nearly everything, he'd moved into his last remaining rental, where I already lived.

Nowhere else embraced life's decrepitude and hope like Detroit. If it hadn't been for the mess with LuCretia, I'd still be living here. I wouldn't have moved up north or bought my country bungalow in Belknap Township, or met Becca. Even with this rough patch Becca and I were facing, I still felt like maybe I should send LuCretia a thank you card for never getting sober.

Metal grates secured the cheap replacement windows, the steel front security door was scarred, the asphalt shingle siding had fallen away in more than a few spots, and a rusted chain link fence surrounded the patchy scrap of front lawn. Cornflower sprouted through the cracks in the short walkway to the front stoop.

Home. It was beautiful, especially today.

"Before we go inside, clue me in on how to fake newlywed bliss," Becca said.

"Don't pretend anything for my sake."

"Maybe everything isn't just for your sake. Did you ever consider that?"

"Right. If you want to fake bliss, you can start by laying off me," I said.

"I see. That's your answer for everything. Cut you some slack, and if that doesn't work, cut you some more slack. And if that doesn't work, then just pretend to cut you the slack."

"Look, if you want to have this baby so bad, just have it. I never said you couldn't. The problem is you want it both ways. You want to have it and you want me to be happy about it. I never said I'd leave you over this. And I won't. So have it. Have it. I guess I'll just suck it up and deal like I always have."

"My God. When have I ever asked you to suck it up and deal?"

She was right. She'd never said anything like that to me. A lot of people had, but not Becca. I started to apologize but she was already out of the Land Cruiser, hauling her duffle bag to their front door.

ଓ

Inside, their house was a lot like a Hard Rock Café except all of the music memorabilia was for Pearl Jam. That was Ellie. Reece was more pragmatist partier than fan. He'd missed half of the Grand Rapids show because he was "out in the parking lot, being awesome," whatever that meant. Ellie compensated for Reece's lack of Pearl Jam fidelity by plastering their walls with every Klausen and Ames Bros. poster she could afford with her Mr. Salty's paycheck. I'd helped her frame some of the early ones, but now she was taping them to the walls, willy-nilly.

There was nothing remotely normal about her décor. I wouldn't have given much thought, but this was only the second time Becca was seeing how my sister lived—and how I used to live. I was acutely aware of the colorful tapestries covering the windows, the random Yield signs, her not-so-subtle shrine to Stone Gossard on a side table, and the framed album covers on the wall alongside the stairs. She took Pearl Jam as seriously as other people take religion. If Pearl Jam was a belief system, Ellie was its high priestess.

In the middle of the square coffee table that filled the center of their ungodly purple sectional, there sat a basket of green apples and a mason jar teaming with wildflowers. Those made my heart hurt. I knew where Ellie had picked them. I knew they were for me. For us. For our brothers. The thought of her there, gathering those flowers because she knew I was coming ... oh, Ellie. I had the best sister in the world. Of all the things I missed about life in Detroit—concerts, festivals, the Eastern Market, Greektown, Corktown, Midtown, great restaurants, old friends—my sister and our sacred spot in Brush Park were what I missed most of all.

I was wrung out. I hugged Reece and Ellie then asked if I could go check for a lighter I'd left on the Yield bus. I needed a few minutes alone to try to screw my head on straight.

ॐ

The backyard looked rattier than ever. The deck was severely in need of a fresh coat of stain. Ellie's bus took up half of the narrow lot. I remembered dismantling part of the cyclone fence along the alley to get it parked there. The lawn was patchy, yellow and strewn with mutilated dog toys. I pushed open the bus's folding door and got on board. This had always been a happy refuge, either on the way to see Pearl Jam, tailgating in an arena parking lot, or heading home. Today it seemed sun faded and weary. I slid behind the wheel and laid my head on it. There was my red Zippo lighter on the floor near the shifter. I didn't bother to pick it up. Everything felt impossibly difficult.

My decision was out there and now we just had to deal with it, heal, move on. Rock bottom had been on the drive down, arguing.

We were past the worst of it. Now all we had to do was renegotiate our relationship. From here it was all ups. It had to be.

Well, there was still the actual abortion to get through. That wouldn't be pretty.

Nein! Aus! Aus! Nein! Phooey!

I sat at attention.

Aus! Braver Hund! A tall, skinny guy with a leather guard on his arm was trying to command the ugliest Rottweiler mix I'd ever seen. He hurled a stick. *Varous! Hol! Aus! Aus! Aus!*

Jesus. That dog obviously did not care to *aus* and he sure didn't look like you could make him.

Nein! Phooey! The guy dragged the dog over to a tie out and chained him. He spotted me and headed toward the bus. Great. I'd come out here to be alone, so why not spend that time making shallow conversation with Ellie and Reece's housemate who I didn't even know?

He came through the door and stood on the first step. "He's secured. You'll be fine as long as you don't mess with him. Just be sure to head straight back to the house when you're ready to go in." He was wearing a faded Green River tank shirt and a wide leather collar. Bandages peeked out of either end of his arm guard. For fuck's sake, the guy had an actual codpiece strapped over his jeans. I stifled a laugh.

"By the way, I'm Saint."

"Sure. We met on the bus home from Pearl Jam in G.R."

"Right. Right. You're her brother, Clovis."

"Clive."

"That's right. Sorry. I remember your hair."

Yes, my hair. Of course. It's so memorable.

"Hey, can we talk for a second?"

Stellar. I scratched my forehead. "I guess."

He stood mutely. The awkwardness grew heavier with each second that passed in silence. I prompted him with, "Yeah?"

"OK, well, see I'm a little concerned about your sister. I mean, I'm genuinely worried about her."

He had my full attention.

"It's Reece. I don't know how well you know him, but, I dunno. Do you think he's cool, or do you think he like, runs around on her and stuff? I mean, he acts nice sometimes, but the brother has a temper and he's gone, like late. A lot. What do you think?"

"Reece?" I laughed, hard. "You're worried about her and Reece? That guy has been my best friend since high school. Christ, I'm the one who introduced those two. I lived with him before she even did." I put my foot on the pole between us and leaned back. "So, yeah. I'm not the least bit worried about either of them."

He shifted from foot to foot in scuffed Doc Martens and scratched at the part of the cotton bandage covering his elbow. "Sorry but, I just get the feeling he's screwing off. He's always working late." He made finger quotes around the word *working*. "You know, she could get a disease or something."

"He's working to support her. I doubt he's giving her diseases, but I'm pretty sure that's none of your business, regardless. You've known her for what, three months? What's your stake here?"

"Nothing." He pushed his hair out of his eyes and I knew he wasn't leveling with me. "She's my friend. She deserves to be treated well. That's all."

There was something about the way he was talking that made me think he was lying, or hiding something, or shining me on.

"I heard your dog did that to your arm," I said.

"Yeah. It's OK. He was provoked."

"Hmm. Right. The truth is I'm a lot more worried about what your dog might do to Ellie than I am about Reece"—I mocked his finger quotes—"working late."

He reached down and scooped my lighter off the floor. "Nice? Yours?"

I put my hand out and he dropped the lighter into it. He hopped off the bus and disappeared through the back door.

I'd heard Reece was hot to get rid of that roomie, and now I understood why. What a complete weirdo.

 C3

Ellie was slicing banana bread at the kitchen island, looking all pink and happy with her honey-blond hair tied back in a peach bandana. Becca and Reece were sitting on stools around the island, Reece nursing a bottle of hard cider and Becca absently stirring her iced tea with a straw. She was doing a pretty good job of acting like things were normal, considering. I wasn't sure if that was a good thing, or if I was road kill.

I nudged my sister.

She took one look at me and pushed the cutting board in Reece's direction. I headed toward the front vestibule—always our go-to spot for private conversations—and she followed, softly closing the door behind us. "What? What's wrong? You look like hell."

"That roomie of yours. Saint? He's nuts."

"What happened?"

I told her what he'd said about Reece. "It doesn't make any sense. What's that moron's problem?"

She shoved her hands into the pockets of her wildly embroidered cutoffs. "He's been out of sorts lately. He's on Vicodin for that arm injury. I think it's making him paranoid."

"Oh, fucking brilliant. He's a narcotics addict?"

"No. No. I didn't mean it like that. It's just the injury. He doesn't actually take that much. I'm not sure if he's even taking it anymore."

"Well, that explains absolutely jack. Why is he trashing Reece to me? Why is he all wrapped around the axle about you?"

She shrugged. "I don't know. He's super nice when you get to know him, but he's really stressed out right now. There's that injury, and he only just got back to work, and Reece is pressuring him to move out and he can't find a place."

"You mean with that Nazi-ass dog of his, landlords aren't lining up to offer him free apartments? Shocker."

"I'm trying to cut him some slack. Reece has really been harshing on him."

I shook my head. I couldn't believe how naïve she was being. Did she not see the teeth on that dog? She was glossing over everything. I tried again. "Why is he so concerned about you? Are things still cool with you and Reece?"

"Totally coolio. It's just that Reece has Saint in a bind. He's kind of gridlocked."

Gridlocked. Right. More like obsessed. Her muddled explanations didn't clear up anything. But if she didn't think Saint was any threat, maybe I was off base. I reached for the doorknob. "Hey, one other little thing. I might need some help with Becca this weekend. Because I uh, well, she uh…"

Ellie squealed and giggled. She pointed to the inside door. I turned to see Reece's face distorted against the glass, his nostrils making steam clouds.

"Still don't have him trained, eh?"

"It's a lost cause."

∞

Becca looked stoic sitting cross-legged on the sectional. I sat opposite her. Reece plopped down next to me and pulled Ellie onto his knee. She unleashed her dimpliest grin. "Cliver," she said. "Cliver, Cliver, Cliver. All married now. And super happy, right?"

Yeah, I'd been trying to bring that up in the vestibule. Now sure wasn't the time. "I love it," I said. "Happiest man alive, remember?"

Becca turned away from us and looked at the hodgepodge of posters taped to the wall behind her.

"You have a taste for Klausen, Becca?" Reece asked.

She jerked her head around. "No pickles for me, thanks."

Great. Now she probably thought I'd told Reece she was pregnant.

Ellie guffawed. "Clausen pickles? I want one!"

"Posters," Reece said to Becca. "I meant the posters. Klausen is the artist. Ellie, calm down. She didn't know."

"So. It was still funny," Ellie said.

Saint clomped down the stairs and stood at the open end of the sectional. He turned to Becca and stared, ignoring the rest of us.

Her shoulders lifted slightly, an unconscious gesture she made when she felt threatened.

"Is there something you need?" she asked.

Man, I'd pounce on that crazy fuck if he said even one thing out of line to her.

Saint cleared his throat. "I need to warn you. Tremor Christ? He's not real good with strangers yet. Just keep your distance. For your own safety, you know? I have a gig tonight. I won't be around to monitor people with him." He spun on the heel of his boot and headed out the door.

"Tremor Christ?" Becca asked.

"A demon he's mistaken for a dog," Reece said. "Did you see his arm? The dog did that. And he refuses to have him put down. We've got Animal Control breathing down our necks. It's insanity."

Becca was crazy about dogs, but how had Saint picked up on that? He was obsessed with my sister, and now he was reading my wife's mind. Creep.

"Well, enough with that scrawny Martian," Reece said. "In other news, Jet are a better band than Pearl Jam."

"Don't even start," Ellie said. "Anyway, it's *is* not *are.*

From seemingly out of nowhere, Reece tossed a joint into the air, caught it between his lips and sparked it up. "Flowers?" He passed it to me.

I took a hit. Becca would hate it, but this was a longstanding tradition between the three of us. Anyway, I needed to cut some tension. She hadn't looked at me once since we'd arrived, and she was free to continue not looking at me while I burned one with my twin sister and my best friend. I passed it to Ellie. She stretched her arm toward Becca, who pursed her lips and shook her head. Ellie gave it back to Reece. I'd never known my sister to pass up marijuana, especially not the shit Reece scored, which was always magical. Ellie wasn't a heavy pot smoker, but if you were offering, she was having.

I had to ask, "What's this? The queen of green, not partaking?"

Ellie and Reece exchanged mischievous looks.

"Let me tell," Reece said.

"He's my brother. I get to be the one." Ellie pushed my hair back and cupped her hands over my ear. Her warm breath tickled. "Looks like you're going to be an uncle." She leaned back and waited for my reaction. I'm sure it was all wrong. Flabbergasted isn't an emotion I've ever been good at disguising.

"That's wonderful news." I squeezed her. She was soft, warm, and smelled of vanilla. "You'll be a fantastic mom, Elsworth." That part, I meant with all my heart.

But Jesus fuck us all. Why today? Of all days?

Becca couldn't have looked more betrayed if I'd shoved her off the Blue Water Bridge. But what was I supposed to do, not congratulate my sister on her pregnancy?

"Hey, nice going, man." I whacked Reece's shoulder and gave him a hug. "I'm happy for you, brother. And we should not be smoking any shit around her. Come on. Use your noodle."

"Oh, yeah. Didn't even think of that." Reece tapped the joint into the ashtray and left it there.

"I'm so glad Clive realizes it's bad to expose a developing fetus to pot smoke," Becca said in a schoolmarm tone, still not looking at me. "What a totally cool surprise, you guys. I mean, how exciting for you both."

"Pearl Jemima," Ellie said. "That's what we'll name her if it's a girl."

That poor kid. I'd have to convince her to rethink that. If our mother had named us for what she'd like best, we'd have been called Crack and Smack.

"Oh, girl or boy, if it were me I'd go with Ziggy Stardust," Becca said.

That was a dig at me. I'd painted the jacket of that Bowie album for her before we were even really together. She'd left a wrench behind that time she fixed my furnace, and when she'd stopped by to pick it up a few days later, we got to talking and I'd ended up showing her my studio and my album cover replicas. She'd mentioned that she loved Ziggy Stardust. I'd later painted one for her, with her own face in place of David Bowie's. We'd started going out after that. I may be short, but my long game is killer.

Becca would never name a kid anything weird. She believed a child should be given a name, not an affliction. Our kids, if we ever had any, would be named like they were in the line of succession to the British throne.

"The baby is due on April nineteenth," Ellie said.

I knew Becca's due date because I'd seen it circled in pencil on the wall calendar in her shop. March twenty-sixth, two days after our first anniversary. This entire scene had to be killing her. I tried to give her a sympathetic look; she returned it with a death glare. She took a green apple from the basket on the coffee table and polished it with the tail of her sleeveless blouse.

"Our kid will need cousins." Reece jabbed me. "I think you and Ms. Becca better get busy."

I tried to shoot him a *not now* look but he was even more oblivious than usual today.

"Nah," I said, "We're not into that. Not for another ten years or something. She's got her business to run. It'll wait."

Becca whipped that apple at me. It slammed against my chest and bounced to the floor. That stung, to say nothing of what it did to my feelings.

"I'd love to have your child," she said. "It's all I think about."

Reece reared back. "Dang. Need to borrow a bed?"

She batted her lashes, something I'd never seen her do. "We'll make a little Rafferty of our own. I'm sure Clive would be almost as good a father as Cubby."

"Cubby?" Ellie asked.

I wasn't about to explain that my wife had just said I'd make a worse father than her dog, an escape artist beagle who been accused of spawning many random litters before she'd rescued him and gotten him snipped.

"Someday we'll be ready for that. Not yet, but someday. Bec, I mean it." I picked up the bruised apple and set it back in the basket.

"So, you two were actually trying for this?" I asked Reece.

"Trying was the best part, brother."

"How'd you reach such a mature decision?" Becca asked. "Some people crap their panties at the mere suggestion of parenthood."

She was angry, sure. And hurt. She had every reason to be furious with me. Ellie's announcement had cranked the burners up under the toxic stew pot we were already in. But I wouldn't stoop to arguing in front of Ellie and Reece. I'd just have to absorb her anger somehow.

She reached for another apple. My chest still ached where she'd beaned me with the last one.

"It was easy," Reece said. "We did some 'shrooms at a concert. After, we had this revelation that we had everything we needed to make a whole human being right there between us. That seemed so cool, we had to go for it. Almost like an experiment."

"If they'd assigned that for science lab, I might have finished high school," Ellie said.

Becca pitched another apple at me. This time I was ready. I snatched it from the air with one hand and took a big bite.

17

Tremor Christ

Clive • Detroit, Mich. • Sunday, Aug. 27, 2006

Under a thin slice of moon, Becca was sprawled sound asleep on the back deck in a flannel nightshirt. Her head lolled against the railing, throat exposed, lips parted. Loose ribbons of dark hair obscured the rest of her face. On her lap rested Tremor Christ's enormous head. Heart in my throat, I pressed my forehead against the grated window in the back door.

Why Becca? Why? Why? Why?

She'd always trusted dogs more than people, always gave them a chance. She'd given me a chance, hadn't she? Tonight, Tremor Christ must have looked like the safer bet.

"Thought I heard you come down," Ellie said from somewhere in the dark. "It's two in the morning. Have you seen Reece?"

"No."

"What are you doing?"

"Leave the light off. Check this out. I'm worried, El."

She peered through the grate. Her mouth dropped into an O. "He's off the chain? She's screwed."

"How bad is he, really?"

"Motörhead bad. Think, love child of Lemmy Kilmister and Ann Coulter." She turned away. "I can't even look anymore."

I couldn't stop looking.

"Well Cliver, if you want out, this will be a darn site cheaper than divorce."

"Christ. How can you say that to me? I'm scared shitless."

"Something is seriously wrong between you two. I can feel it."

"We're great. Never better." That didn't come out nearly as convincing as I'd hoped.

She laid her hand on my forearm, warm and reassuring. "Out with it. You can tell me. We've been to hell and back so many times we've got frequent flyer miles. Something's gone really wrong with you two. I've felt that all day. Did you bump into LuCretia or something?"

"What? No. Don't even say that name. God, I'm not that stupid."

"Well, 'scuse me. I figured if Lu-Creep-Show's sucking you into her druggy drama, that'd explain Becca chucking apples at you. And napping with Devil Dog."

"Look, she has her reasons. But LuCretia isn't one of them. Now, tell me how to get her into the house without pissing off that, that monster."

"Alright, alright, here's what I know. You wake him up, it's over. But if she wakes him, I don't know. Maybe she'll get lucky. She did once, obviously. I can't believe she unchained him. She's brave. And when I say brave, I mean really goddamned stupid." She clutched my wrist. "Now tell me what's going on with you two already."

"So, as it happens, she's pregnant."

"You did not just say that!" She pressed her face and hands against the window. "We've got to get her out of there. That's your baby, right under Tremor Christ's head."

"No."

"Holy hell. It's not even your kid? What is this, Lu-Creep-Show part two?"

Ellie had never believed the baby my ex had miscarried was actually mine. The truth was, I didn't know and never would. It didn't bother me, but it bugged the shit out of Ellie.

"Whoa. El. Settle down. You don't get it. It is mine. Absolutely. But it's a mistake. There's not going to be a baby."

"She doesn't want it? Is that what you meant when you said she's all about work? Can't she slow down?"

"Oh my God, don't blame her. This is my fault, all of it. It was an accident. She wants to keep it. I'm the one who doesn't."

"Why'd you marry her if you don't even love her enough to have a baby?"

"It's not like that. It's all the other stuff. Like the fire."

She shook her head. "That fire is not stopping me and you do not have my permission to let it stop you. Remember what we did? We survived. And we're going to keep on surviving. Come on, Cliver. Live! Live 'til it fucking hurts."

"But last time …"

"This is totally different. LuCretia was an addict. That baby wasn't even yours, probably. Of course she miscarried. Of course she went right back to using because A. She's an addict and B. She's an addict and C. That's what addicts motherfucking do, dummy. Rebecca is not an addict. She's a pipefitter."

"Your announcement today—we didn't see that coming. I had finally given her my decision to end it on the way down here."

"Finally? What the—how far along is she?"

"Maybe a month ahead of you." Jesus. That did sound long when I said it aloud.

She shoved me. "You asshole. You goddamned little twerp. What the hell is wrong with you?"

"Don't hate me. She hates me now." I choked on the words. "If you hate me, I've got fuck-all."

She backed away in the dim kitchen, features crumpling. Ellie, the one person who'd always understood me. My shame inflated under the glare of her judgment.

"If I was her I'd have drop-kicked your sorry ass all the way to next Tuesday," she said. "The chick has restraint. Too bad that dog will be picking her out of his teeth before I can tell her what I think."

I looked through the window. Becca still slept, her skin milky under the sodium light, arms open like a sacrifice.

"We've got to get her inside. Please. Just help me do this. You can concentrate on hating me later."

Ellie's expression softened. "I see what you're doing. You're blaming yourself for our brothers, for everything. You can't punish our mother, so you take on the guilt and punish yourself instead."

"Is that wrong?"

"Look at her, Cliver. Who are you punishing now?"

I turned to the window. Becca startled awake and the dog did too. His muzzle was inches from her face. The stub of his tail jutted back and the fur on his spine stood straight up. I swear my heart stopped. Ellie skittered behind me and pressed her face between my shoulder blades.

Becca dropped her head to her knees and exposed her wrists to the dog in a believable show of deference. He sniffed her hand. His fur Mohawk settled and he headed down the deck steps. He was all business, surveying the perimeter of the yard, sniffing the bus's tires, stopping every few yards to mark his territory.

Becca stood up, but instead of heading inside she went down the steps. I cracked the door open and tried to get her attention without the dog noticing, whispering her name into the cool night air. She scooped up the dog's chain, sank to her knees and made kissy noises.

I leaned out the door and whispered, "Becca, hurry. Get in here."

Ellie grabbed my arm. "Don't go."

The backyard sodium light buzzed. I opened the door wider, hoping Becca would see me there and get a clue. Ellie let go of me and ducked over to the far side of the kitchen island.

Becca coaxed Tremor Christ over to her. He sat down. She was going to tether him. It was going to work out. But I was ready to jump in between her and that dog if she needed me to.

"Close the door," Ellie whispered.

I shook my head.

Becca stroked the dog's ear. The chain was still in her hand, still not fastened to his collar.

The kitchen light came on and just about blinded me. Ellie said "No!" at the same time Reece yelled "Gene Simmons rules!"

"Turn it off!" Ellie said.

"You guys playing hide and seek in here or what? How come you get to have all the fun? Can't I play?"

"Oh my God would you shut up? Becca's out there. With Tremor Christ," Ellie said.

"No shit?"

I turned around to tell Reece to cram it.

Ellie was scrambling up onto the island. "Clive! Oh shit!

I spun toward the door and Tremor Christ slammed into me like a runaway truck. My head smacked the edge of the island. He flattened me against the floor. I couldn't breathe. I pushed against the crushing mass of muscle and fur. He was barking and growling, his breath like steamed carnage in my face. Ellie was shrieking hysterically.

"Reece. Get Ellie out of here." It was Becca, next to me on all fours.

My sister's shrieks dissolved to whimpers as Reece dragged her away to safety.

☍

Becca was right there, her shoulder pressed against mine on the kitchen floor, her lips to my ear. "Close your eyes. Do not look at him."

The dog weighed a metric fuck-ton. Getting words out was a struggle. "Go with Ellie. Just go."

She didn't budge. "Shh. Be still. Don't make a sound. Close your eyes."

I squeezed them shut.

"Not like that. I mean relax. Play dead."

Relax? As if.

"Quit pushing him. Seriously. Give in. Let go."

Impossible. I had two priorities: get Becca the hell out of there, and survive.

She put her hand below my jaw, blocking my jugular from Tremor Christ's teeth. That dog could snap her hand off in one bite, but that she'd offer it as an appetizer meant more than everything.

"Do as I say," she whispered. "We might get you out of this."

"Please go. I've got this." My plan was evolving rapidly. If I let the dog kill me, she'd have time to get to safety. It'd work if she'd just get her ass out of here. Sure, it would probably hurt for a few minutes, but then it'd be over and she could go on with her life. Baby and all.

"Shh. Not one sound."

Her thumb pulsing against my jaw offered the tiniest comfort. Her short breaths were warm on my cheek. I felt the rapid thump of her heart as she pressed against me on the hard floor. Maybe this wasn't a completely terrible way to die.

"Come on now. Release him slowly, pretend you're dying," she said. "Sneak your arms down, close to your ribs. Protect your organs."

This was it. It was time. I stopped pushing him away. It was as easy as falling off a building. His growls deepened.

"Good, good. Now play dead like your life depends on it. Relax every fiber of your being. You've got to trust me here. There's no other way."

Hot saliva dripped across my nose. I remembered something crucial. I'd tell her. Maybe these would be my last words to the woman I loved. "Speak German."

The dog's guttural snarl covered me with chills. That was it. My one chance, and I hadn't given her enough detail to make any sense of it. She probably thought I wanted her to tell me *auf wiedersehen*. I was good as dead anyway, but if she understood what I meant it might help her save herself.

"German. He understands commands in—"

"Shh. Breathe, love. Breathe."

I let my nostrils fill with the hot stink of canine rage. She continued channeling all the love in the universe through the pad of her thumb. I focused on that, and that alone.

"I'm sorry I let him loose. God, I do love you," she said.

I swallowed, knowing she'd feel it, hoping she'd understand. And maybe someday forgive me. My heart pounded so hard I thought it would split.

Becca lifted her hand from my jaw. I opened my eyes enough to see the beast's expression change as she proffered her wrist. The dog took the bait. Her body stiffened as her hand disappeared into the sinister maw. She melted, submitting herself to the dog in exactly the way she'd been trying to convince me to do.

She rolled onto her back. "Komm."

The dog shifted his weight off me. It was no relief. He was on top of her now.

"Clive, play dead," she said through clenched teeth.

I half-closed my eyes and tried to lie still. Doing nothing felt like a felony.

"Gib?" she said.

Nothing happened.

"Gib. Gib."

Nope.

I whispered, "Try *aus*."

"Aus!" she said.

Tremor Christ unclenched his jaw and let her remove her hand. The bite marks were an angry purple.

"Braver Hund!"

His tail stub wiggled. She stroked his ear, her brow furrowed and her lower lip caught in her teeth. The dog moved off her, sat on his haunches and looked around the kitchen like he'd just awoken from a strange dream.

"Don't move. I'll get him hooked up outside," Becca said. "I'll need you to shut the door. Lights out. Stay away from the windows. Don't open up until I knock. And for God's sake, keep Reece and his big mouth out of here."

She'd lost her fucking mind.

"Komm." She scooted to the food pail next to the door and tossed a piece to the dog. He swallowed it whole. She rolled pieces closer and closer to the doorway, at last pitching one outside. "Voraus."

The dog bounded after the morsel. I prayed she'd slam the door and be done with it. But she followed him out into the night. This was crazy. Stupid. I should have put my foot down. I should have let him kill me. I had to fight every instinct I had just to give way to her judgment and follow her instructions.

My hands were trembling but I managed to turn off the kitchen light. I crawled to the back door and closed it softly, only because I'd promised her I would. I crouched with my hand on the knob, my ear pressed against the door.

∞

The doorknob grew hot from my hand as I waited. My calves went numb. My head throbbed. I thought of all the times I'd been sick at the thought of the pregnancy, the baby, the responsibility, the risk of everything going wrong. Losing a child is different from any other kind of loss, and I'd already lost two. Yes, they were my brothers but our mother had left it to me to raise them. LuCretia's disastrous miscarriage was just the poisoned cherry on top. But what all of my fear and misery had made me miss in this new equation was Becca herself.

She didn't have to save my life to prove her worth. With her, my tattered past didn't matter. She saw me as a gifted painter, an entrepreneur, an individual. I downplayed my upbringing because I didn't want it to color her image of me. Sure, she knew I was an orphan who grew up in the system—I couldn't exactly fake a bigger family than what I had with Ellie. But burden her with the details? Hell no. If it were up to me I'd have my childhood memories removed like a gangrenous foot.

Small wonder she couldn't understand the reactions I had to her pregnancy. I'd never given her enough information to make sense of it.

On our first date, we'd gone to the beach at Forty Mile Point Lighthouse. There was still snow on the ground. Some little kid pelted her with snowballs. I wanted to ship him off on an ice floe. But Becca didn't get mad, she got curious. She offered him some of our hot chocolate, and pretty soon he was following us across the frozen sand, talking about missing his mommy. He thought she'd forgotten all about him. I don't even want to get into how spookily me-at-age-six that kid was. I was checking myself, wondering if he was a little time traveler version of me, bad haircut, floods and all. I'd half expected to stumble across a converted DeLorean on the beach that day.

I hadn't been charmed by this. I'd felt completely exposed.

She'd given the boy a pudding stone—we'd collected a few pretty ones while walking in the sand. It was pinkish beige with deep red flecks of aggregate.

"See the little pieces of rock stuck in the stone? Little pieces of you are stuck inside your mommy's heart, just like that. She can never forget you. It's impossible," she'd said to the boy.

I'd envied Becca's blind faith in motherhood. The things Becca said to that boy were what I'd needed to hear my entire life, even if they were the sum of privilege and naivety. I wanted to be stuck in her heart and never forgotten.

I pressed my ear to the door but heard nothing over the thrum of my own pulse.

A little piece of me was literally stuck inside of Becca. She'd told me that. And she welcomed it. Why hadn't I?

It didn't matter. I was done making her suffer for my tragedies. I was going to do what Ellie said. I was going to live until it hurt.

The doorknob turned against my sweaty palm. I jumped up, yanked the door open and pulled her inside. I squeezed her to me. Relief tore out of me in choking sobs. She put her fingers in my hair and found a tender spot and broken skin that I hadn't even known was there.

She flipped the light switch. "You hit your head when you went down. Let's get you some ice."

"No. I don't care. Stay here." I wiped my eyes with the sleeve of my T-shirt. "Bec. God. I'm so fucking sorry."

"You're—no, Clive. This whole mess was my fault. I had him by the collar. But the light, the noise. I mean, Gene Simmons? Honestly, what was Reece thinking?" She opened her palm and showed me a fresh, red welt running across her fingers. "I really tried to hold him but he's too strong. He dragged me. His collar did that."

I cradled her hand in mine and looked her over. Her forearms and elbows were scraped raw. Her flannel nightshirt was muddy.

Dirt smudged her pale cheeks. She'd never looked more beautiful. I pulled a dry leaf out of her tangled hair and kissed her forehead.

"You should've let that damned dog have me. You're pregnant." I put my hands on her abdomen. "And if it's still up to me, you're going to stay that way."

"Yes," she said. "Yes, I am."

18

Whipping

Ellie • Detroit, Mich. • Monday, Aug. 28, 2006

Rosebud/Lizzie was doing Guitar Hero battle in my living room again, her cute little ponytails bouncing everywhere. This time instead of Saint, her opponent was a new girl with a nose ring thick enough to be right at home on a Heifer. That was the only interesting thing about her. Otherwise, she was a standard issue Saint groupie right down to the heavy black eyeliner and cheap body splash. Tonight these two had trailed him home from band practice. He'd walked in well ahead of the girls and gone straight out back to deal with Tremor Christ. He'd been out there for half an hour. It was easy to spot when Saint was in no mood for company.

I was up after midnight, feeling queasy while scrubbing the pots and pans left over from having company all weekend. Once we'd gotten over the shock of the dog attack, we'd spent the rest of our time together giddy about our pregnancies. I was super proud of Clive for changing his mind. Reece had gone overboard with cooking, probably trying to get back on Becca's good side after his big stupid mouth had caused so much trouble. When Clive and Becca had started to clean, Reece shooed them out of the kitchen swearing he'd take care of everything later. Now they'd gone home, Reece was in bed, and I was up after midnight playing scullery maid.

Saint banged through the backdoor and faced me for the first time since our painful conversation in Brush Park. He knew Tremor Christ had attacked Clive; Reece and I had both desperately messaged him from the front stoop while arguing over what to do next.

"You're lucky Reece is asleep," I said. "He wants you gone, and that dog. And after what happened to my brother and his pregnant wife, I'm sorry, but I have to agree about Tremor Christ. You at least need to turn him over to someone who can manage him." That was as close as I could let myself get to begging him to stay. I never wanted him out, but his dog was a nightmare.

"Excuse me, but I handle him just fine. Sure, he might be getting a little rowdy because I couldn't work with him while I was recovering, but—"

"Recovering from him attacking you. The ER surgeon even said you should put him down."

"No. Hell no. I rescued him. He's my forever dog. You were sitting right there when I told your sister-in-law he wasn't friendly and to leave him alone. I made a point of warning her."

"Why her?"

"I know a dog person when I see one. Then she runs off and unchains him anyway. What is she, special or something?"

I turned back to my soapy dishwater, letting his last comment slide. He was on the defensive. He knew that the attack would be the catalyst forcing him to get rid of the dog or move out. Plus, I think he was shaken by the slight possibility that my baby was his. I bitch slapped that thought out of my head. No way was this baby Saint's. I was in a long-term relationship with Reece. My baby was Reece's. Life would go on normally as long as I managed to keep stepping over this dangerous soft spot I had for Saint.

We stopped arguing, but instead of going into the living room where his guests were hooting and hollering their way through *Cochise,* he stayed in the kitchen. I silently handed him a hot, wet rag and he started wiping off the countertops and stove. That was one upside of living with a busboy.

"October thirteenth, will you come with me for dinner at my ma's?" he asked, completely out of left field. We'd just been fighting about his dog, and now he wanted me to meet his family. This boy.

"Nah, I don't think that's a good idea."

"Oh, come on. For my birthday. I'm supposed to bring a friend. It's this tradition we have."

I was normally a huge fan of traditions, but I didn't have a lot of use for mothers or birthdays. Reece's mom always made him a birthday dinner, but going to that I felt like an extra, an interloper.

"Your mom wants you to bring someone she doesn't even know?"

"It's important to her. And to me, maybe."

Fantastic. Would motherhood turn me into a head case, too? Maybe rationality got expelled right along with the placenta. He moved to the sink and stood elbow to elbow with me as he rinsed his rag. I concentrated fiercely on scrubbing popcorn ball goo out of a pan.

"It's this tradition, see? We always have one extra person at the table for my birthday. I'm asking you early 'cause it matters. I want you to say yes."

"But why?"

He started wiping popcorn crumbs from the island. "I was conceived as a twin. Fraternal."

I'd never known this about Saint. "Hey, me too. Me and Clive."

"I know. Except my twin didn't make it. Something went wrong. He died, but they couldn't remove him because I had to finish baking in there."

"Ugh. Your poor mother."

"Yep. She picked out a layette for me and a grave marker for him. When my lungs were ready they did a Cesarean. They took me out and handed me to her, then they took out what was left of Brody. That's what she named him. I guess he was in a pretty bad way by then. Like, deteriorated."

Picturing that grisly scene made me hurl into the kitchen sink. Saint was right behind me, holding my hair out of the way. He rinsed the mess down the garbage disposal with the sprayer and patted my back. "I didn't mean to sick you out. I'm sorry."

I sucked water from the tap and rinsed my mouth. He handed me a fresh dishtowel and I dried my face and plunked down on a stool, dizzy.

He found a box of saltines and tore open a fresh package for me. The bland crackers helped. I chewed them and thought about how it must suck to be Saint, to have a birth story that's a gross-out and a tragedy. I didn't know my own birth story, and now I didn't even want to. He apologized again and split a warm can of Vernors into two mugs. He gave me one and sat next to me.

"So that's why we have this tradition. My ma has me bring a friend, and then we all celebrate because that makes the right number of people. But it has to be my friend, you know? Someone I choose. Special. Not just some random person."

"So basically I'd be a birthday stand-in for a deteriorated baby?"

On a cosmic level maybe it would balance out some of the crap I'd been pulling lately. Saint was selecting me for this honor when any of his groupies would have jumped at the chance. It was sort of touching. Anyway, I was curious to meet his mom in case she was this baby's grandmother. I bitch slapped that thought out of my head.

It struck me how harshly I'd judged LuCretia, suspecting that the baby she'd lost was never Clive's to begin with. I was really not one bit better in that regard. I'd tried to tell myself this was different, but I could see now that it wasn't.

"Am I supposed to bring a present?" I asked.

"Your presence will be present enough for me."

That was a relief. I had no idea what would be an appropriate gift for a roommate I'd had sex with once, who my boyfriend was trying to kick out, whose baby I might be carrying, whose friendship meant so much to me, and whose dog had terrorized my brother. Even Dr. Phil probably couldn't figure out that one.

Still, it seemed like I should probably bring him something.

19

Long Road

Clive • Belknap Township, Mich. • Friday, Oct. 13, 2006

Becca leaned in the doorway of my former art studio. I'd spent three days clearing it out, painting the bead-and-cove walls a mossy shade, and putting up Winnie the Pooh wallpaper borders.

She offered me a Lemonhead, all smiles. "This is adorable. Winnie is a great choice. I hate when kids are stuffed into pink or blue boxes. I'm so glad I told you to surprise me. I love it when you're decisive."

She faced plenty of sexism day to day as a heating and cooling technician. Her parents had assumed she'd be a teacher like her mother, while her older brother would follow their father into the heating business. Instead, Marshall had moved to Montréal and opened a bed and breakfast with his boyfriend. Becca began apprenticing with her father at age fifteen.

"It makes the whole baby thing seem so much more real. I'm getting pretty stoked," I said.

Becca bent and unlaced her heavy work boots. Her burgeoning belly had outgrown her *Rebecca* work shirts and she'd switched to her father's old ones, labeled *Walter*. She kicked off her boots and pulled the ponytail holder out of her hair, letting it spill over her shoulders. She was one cute Walter.

"Tomorrow I can set up the furniture," I said.

We'd ordered all the usual stuff, which was unassembled in boxes piled high in the living room. I'd moved my art equipment and supplies to a cramped, windowless room in the basement. If I installed some decent lighting it might do until we could afford a bigger place. I thought we should be more aggressive about getting the apartment above her studio rented out for the extra income, but she kept saying she wanted to paint it and make some repairs first. Now, that place would have made one sweet studio, with gallery space too. But she'd always been a little funny about her apartment. I knew better than to ask her for it.

"What's up? How'd your day go?" I asked.

"It was productive. I corrected a screwed up Hartford loop on a church boiler. It floors me when something that fundamental gets installed wrong. I mean, come on people, are we professionals or not?" She shook a few Lemonheads into my palm. "Also, my OB called. Looks like I get to have a level-two ultrasound. It should be pretty neat. He said we'll get an excellent view of the baby and most likely find out the sex."

"Cool. Can I come?" I popped the sour candy into my mouth.

"You better."

"Wait. Didn't you just have an ultrasound a couple of weeks ago?"

I hadn't tagged along for that. I'd been too caught up with working on a four-piece series for *Joe's Garage*. When it comes to perfecting Frank Zappa's nose, you can't just drop everything for a prenatal appointment. Anyway, Becca didn't need me holding her hand through all of that.

"This one's different. More detailed. Traverse City, Tuesday the thirty-first. Halloween. It'll be fun. We'll make a day of it."

Traverse City was three hours away. It seemed like they'd only send her that far away for an ultrasound if they suspected something wasn't right. But her pregnancy was going so well. She looked great. This wasn't adding up.

"What's up with Traverse? That's kind of a long haul."

She shrugged. "It's the closest one our insurance covers."

"Becca, honey, I don't think so. What's wrong with the last place you went? They had ultrasound machines."

"Oh. Well, it's not about the equipment. They asked me to see a specialist."

When you've got Rafferty luck, this is not the kind of thing you can shrug off.

"Tell me they don't think something's wrong," I said, as gently as I could.

"No. Not exactly." She ate another Lemonhead and inserted the box with its grinning lemon face into her shirt pocket. "It's just, well, my triple-screen came back a little wonky."

My breath escaped me in one big whoosh.

"Don't get weird about it," she said. "It's not as bad as it sounds. The nurse told me this happens all the time—I guess because it's only a screening test. They get loads of false-positives. Nine times out of ten, there's not even a problem."

Odds like that were custom made for Rafferty doom.

"Define *a problem*."

"I don't know. Spina bifida? Down syndrome? They say I'm measuring a little on the small side. They've probably just got my conception date wrong or something. They said that could give you a false result on the screening test too, so that might be all it is. I mean, I was on the patch and antibiotics. No telling when I really ovulated."

I failed to find any of those explanations even remotely reassuring.

"You don't sound worried," I said. "But are you?"

She held her thumb and index finger apart to indicate pea-sized concern. "Really, it's no big deal. They said they refer people for these all the time. I'm excited to find out the sex. If it's a girl, I'm thinking I like the name Louise."

"Louise. That's kind of nice in an old-fashioned way. What about a middle name?"

"If you go along with me on Louise, I'll let you pick out her middle name."

This baby was a Rafferty. I thought of our Rafferty family crest, and how a child of ours might fit in as one of us, hopefully minus the doom. The best choice for a middle name was suddenly obvious. "How about Clover? For good luck."

"Cute." She kissed my cheek. "I like it. But this baby doesn't need extra luck. I'm sure she, or he, is just fine."

Something made me mistrust breezy reassurances like that. Maybe it was the memory of Honey Jane stumbling out the door of our Brush Park tenement for the last time. *Don't look so worried, goofus. I'm just going for ciggies. Watch your brothers and I'll bring you a Coke.* Maybe it was LuCretia promising the pregnancy would keep her sober. *I've totally got this, Rafferty. Calm down.*

And now Becca's screening test results were a little wonky, and I was supposed to relax about this ultrasound because we were just going to find out the sex.

Don't get weird about it.

20

Across the Universe

Ellie • Mount Clemens, Mich. • Friday, Oct. 13, 2006

At first I was pretty proud of the scarf I'd embroidered for Saint's birthday gift. The cheerful sprays of mango and pink bittersweet berries danced across the deep brown, buttery soft fabric I'd found at the thrift shop. It was possibly my best work yet. I'd even included a tiny red and white yield symbol, my embroidery signature. But when I'd shown the scarf to Reece he'd laughed and said I should give it to Becca for Christmas. Then he said it was too girly for her and I should just keep it for myself. I guess he had a point that the bittersweet could be mistaken for flowers.

He told me I ought to embroider a throw pillow for Saint with a picture of a U-haul truck and *Move the Fuck Out*. He was always talking about evicting him, but he didn't do anything. I half suspected he enjoyed complaining about Saint too much to actually get rid of him.

I wrapped the scarf in tissue and tucked it into a used gift bag. It was time to go, and I still had no idea what I was supposed to write inside of the birthday card. There were roughly seven-hundred things I wanted to say to Saint and zero that I had the guts to commit to ink. He was already warming up his white-walled Tracker across the street. I scrounged for a pen and scribbled *It's a messed up world, but I'm glad you're in it*, tucked the card into the gift bag and dashed out the front door.

On our way to his mom's, Saint noticed the gift bag and smiled, but didn't say a word. Good. We didn't need one of those awkward *you shouldn't have* conversations. When it came to Saint, there were any number of things that I shouldn't have.

His mom's house in Mount Clemens was a two-bedroom cottage with plastered archways and lots of windows. Saint was too tall for it, too dark and angular for all the pastels and shabby chic furniture. It smelled like garlic bread and eggplant parmesan. The table was set with vintage Fiesta ware, tapered candles and cloth napkins. A brilliant salad with crumbled cheese and golden croutons sat at the center. Too bad I couldn't eat more than a quarter cup of food at one sitting with the baby hogging all the room in my belly, because this dinner was shaping up to be incredible.

Saint's mom, Patricia, called him Tim and Baby and frowned at his latest piercings. She fussed over his bandaged arm and insisted he update her on his physical therapy, which I hadn't even known about. She was dark and pretty, with the same round, heavily lidded eyes as Saint—except hers had laugh lines. I liked her instantly.

His teenaged sister came in wearing a Red Wings sweatshirt with *Maddie* emblazoned across the back. She high-fived Saint, gave me a shy finger wave and slid onto the piano bench. She played the theme from *The Legend of Zelda* flawlessly, then segued into the staccato *Super Mario Brothers* theme. She started to play the Beatles' *Birthday*, but Saint groaned and she switched to *Across the Universe*.

I liked it here. I liked when Saint sat next to me on the loveseat with its ruffled muslin covering. Not close, but not far. He stretched his arm across the back like we were old friends. No one mentioned Brody, which was a relief.

Patricia poured two glasses of pinot noir, handed one to Saint and offered me the other. I said, "No thank you," at the same moment Saint said, "She can't, Ma. Ellie's expecting."

His mother's face changed. For a split second, it was blank. Like this information was something she'd known, but had forgotten. "Well, in that case, I wish you a very boring pregnancy and a take-home baby."

I had no idea what that meant. A take-home baby? Was there any other kind?

"The eggplant!" She handed Saint the other glass of wine and sprinted into the kitchen.

"Geez, what have you told her about me?" I asked.

"Nothin'." He followed her into the kitchen carrying both glasses. They spoke too softly for me to hear. Lord knows I was straining.

"You don't seem like his usual type," Maddie said, twisting around on the piano bench. "He usually hangs around with girls who are, I don't know, kind of grumpy."

"We're not ... he just shares our house. I live there with my boyfriend. Saint's our housemate. Like, a boarder. Or a roommate. He pays us rent."

"Boarder. Right."

"Really. You should come over and visit sometime."

Nothing too uncomfortable came up at dinner. That was a small miracle because with Saint, even pets weren't a safe topic. We talked about Kwame Kilpatrick, hockey, my thrill-a-minute job at Mr. Salty's, and Beaver Island. I thought I was stuffed until Patricia brought a pineapple upside-down cake to the table. Irresistible. Somehow I found room for two pieces.

She carried a few presents in. I jumped up and snatched the gift bag which I'd left next to the loveseat and nearly forgotten.

He opened a present from his mom first, a new pair of black leather Doc Martens that went right up to his knees. He tried them on, strutted around the dining room and declared that they'd be a perfect fit as soon as he got them broken in. His next present from her was an Orange amp. "No way," he said. "This is too much. You're too much, Ma."

His sister gave him a gift certificate to Detroit Ink, a tattoo and piercing shop. Perfect. I wished I'd thought of that.

"This is the bomb," he said.

My gift seemed less than inadequate. Thrift shop fabric, a dead-simple hem job, wool embroidery thread, and a few pleasant autumn afternoons of freehand stitchery while watching episodes of *A Baby Story* on TLC. It was like a used Kleenex, complete with tears spilled over all those happy births, and admittedly more than one dog food commercial. And to Reece it had looked effeminate. The rumpled green gift bag was on its third or fourth tour of duty. It wasn't nearly enough for Saint, he was probably going to hate it, and they were all waiting for me to fork over that sad little bag on my lap.

I pushed it across the table to him.

He opened the card first, read it and laughed. "Too true, Detroit Ellie. And same here."

"Let me see it," Maddie said.

Saint shook his head and stuffed the card into his back pocket. He pulled the crinkly tissue out of the bag, unwrapped the scarf and spread the brown fabric across his hands revealing the embroidery. He stood and draped the scarf around his neck, then traced the sprays of bittersweet berries with a fingertip.

"That is just stunning," Patricia said.

"Can I have it?" Maddie asked.

"You can't even borrow it," he said.

"The needlework is gorgeous," Patricia said. "My mother used to do crewel embroidery. I didn't think anyone had the patience for it anymore. You made this yourself?"

I rubbed my sweating palms on my leggings and nodded.

"Freehand?" she asked.

Saint answered for me. "Always, Ma. Ellie's a free spirit, unconfined by patterns."

"Sweetie, you're incredibly talented," Patricia said.

Saint kissed the top of my head. "I love it. Absolutely love it." His words flooded me with warmth.

In the car on the way home, he said it again. The scarf was double wrapped around his neck, setting off his jaw, making him look regal. The embroidery was displayed across the right half of his chest. He seriously rocked that scarf. The pride I'd felt before showing it to Reece returned and quadrupled.

ɶ

Saint wore the scarf every day. He wore it to gigs and around the house, to the bar, band practice, the record store. Maybe to bed. It became his signature piece.

"Nice flowers," Reece said when we passed him on the front steps while we were bringing some groceries in.

Saint stroked the scarf. "Indeed."

Reece blinked at the comment and laughed a little too loud. "Why does he have to always wear that thing?"

"I think it's sweet."

"Pfft. He looks like a puss. The only thing crazier than you stitching posies for that freak is him trying to turn it into a fashion statement."

"They're berries. Do you want me to embroider a special scarf for you too, Reece's Pieces?"

"That's not really my bag."

I wished I knew what Reece's bag was.

21

Nothing as it Seems

Clive • Traverse City, Mich. • Tuesday, Oct. 31, 2006

Are we hoping for a ballerina or a ballplayer?" The ultrasound technician asked us.

"Oh wow. I didn't know you could determine the vocation by ultrasound," Becca said. "Neato. I've been hoping for concert pianist or possibly a clinical social worker. Definitely no politicians though. If it's a politician, please don't tell us."

God, how I loved this woman.

The tech asked me to turn off the lights. She worked the transducer over the glossy gel she'd smeared on Becca's belly, sing-songing each body part she spotted. Her scrubs were printed with Jack-o-lanterns and black cats.

The undulating images on the monitor were like watching someone else's head rush. The electric glow of the screen illuminated Becca's wide-eyed fascination.

"Oop, oop, look at that. I see a vagina. You're having a little girl."

"Aw." Becca smiled at me.

"No daughter of mine is having a vagina," I said, deadpan.

Becca snickered.

The tech gave me a dirty look and went back to her sing-song narrative. "I see a foot. There's an arm. And that's the … hmm." She fell silent, continuing to move the transducer. She clicked measurements on the screen and typed notes on the keyboard, frowning.

I wished she'd start nattering again.

"We're probably naming her Louise Clover," Becca said.

The tech grunted.

Becca stayed fixated on the images. "Is that her skull?"

The tech shook her head, never taking her eyes off the screen. Becca grabbed my hand and squeezed.

"Baby's not letting me see the kidneys." The tech set the transducer aside. "It might help if you took a short walk around the hallways. The baby needs a little encouragement to change positions. You can use the restroom, just don't completely empty your bladder if you do. I'm going to get the doctor and see if he has better luck getting a look."

Becca wiped the jelly from her abdomen, yanked up her maternity jeans, adjusted her oversized flannel shirt and stepped into her open work boots. We shuffled aimlessly down the carpeted hallways until she found a bathroom.

I hung around waiting for her, thinking you don't have to be perfect, baby. None of us are. Just try to be alright.

We found a window overlooking the parking lot. The sun had already set. Snow swirled in meaningless patterns beneath the lampposts. My Land Cruiser was one of only four cars left, and the oldest model by a couple of decades.

"Do you think something's up?" Becca asked.

"No. I'm sure it's fine. She probably just doesn't know what she's doing."

"I think she hated the baby's name. Did you see how she reacted when I said we were naming her Louise Clover? She practically oinked."

"Maybe that's her pet pig's name."

We both chuckled over that.

When we got back to the ultrasound lab, the tech stopped me at the door. "Doctor requests you wait in the lounge, Mr. Rafferty."

"Sure. But why?"

"He needs to take a peek trans-vaginally. Some husbands are uncomfortable with Doctor doing a trans-vag on their wives."

"Clive's fine," Becca said. "I want him with me."

"Sorry. That's our policy." She handed Becca a cotton exam gown. "You can leave your bra on. Everything else comes off. Doctor will knock." She closed the door and escorted me to a small waiting room down the hall. A baldheaded doctor hustled past us toward the ultrasound lab.

There were only six chairs in that room. Two were occupied by a couple. The woman was pregnant and reading a *Family Circle*. The guy sat with his ankle over his knee. His foot jiggled to the beat of the Muzak, which was playing *Dancing in the Moonlight*. I sat on the edge of a chair across from them. The walls were covered with Anne Geddes prints of babies sitting in wash buckets, in pumpkins, in flower pots, in watermelons. That looked about as uncomfortable as I felt.

"First-timer?" the guy asked me.

"Yep."

"Relax. We're on our fifth. Trust me, there's nothing to worry about."

"It better be a girl this time," the woman said. "You got your ball team, now it's my turn. A princess to take shopping with me."

Our baby was a girl. That was all we knew about her. If our Louise was anything like her mother, she'd prefer dogs and baseball to shopping. If she was anything like her Aunt Ellie, she'd prefer Pearl Jam to absolutely anything else. I couldn't sit still. I got up and leaned on the door jamb, facing the hallway. The ultrasound lab door was shut tight. I didn't take my eyes off of it. After several minutes, the door opened and the tech stepped out. Her back was to me and her arms were folded across her chest. Another doctor strode toward her and she waved him in.

The door clicked shut behind them.

ଔ

"Relax already. Sit down. Geez dude, you're making me nervous," the five-time father said.

I slipped into the hall and moved across from the ultrasound lab door. Why would they call another doctor in there? What could be wrong with our baby girl? A birth defect? Clubbed feet? A hole in the heart? *Please let it be something fixable.*

I aged ten years waiting for that door to open. When it did, the two doctors emerged, shut the door again and rush down the hall together. I quietly followed them. The bald one held a long streamer of ultrasound images. They rounded a corner and ducked into an office. The door was left open, and their backs were to me. I hovered near the corner, trying to catch what they were saying.

"Look at this," the bald one said, "Bilateral renal agenesis, definitely. Cardiac anomaly, probably Tetralogy of Fallot? And profound midline craniofacial malformations."

An alien tongue, each exotic term more terrifying than the last. This was the most frightening Halloween of my life, hands down.

The second doctor let out a low whistle and took the streamer of images. "Plus, you're looking at omphalocele. Possibly ectopia cordis."

It was a litany of doom.

"With this constellation of anomalies, I'm thinking Pentalogy of Cantrell," he said.

"Mmm, I'd say this is Patau's," the bald one said.

"This is classic Cantrell, I'm telling you."

"Patau's. With midline craniofacial defects like this, the karyotype will come back with T-13."

"Here we go again, Neil. You're on. Chop House this time?"

"Steaks are on you if I'm right. I can taste that porterhouse already."

They shook hands.

The floor dropped away from me like an elevator speeding for hell. Red ringed my vision and my heart pounded in my ears. I cut for the ultrasound lab and pushed through the door. The tech jumped. Her clipboard clattered to the floor. She scurried out of the room.

Fluorescent lights glared off the cold white tile and brushed stainless steel. Becca sat shrunken in her exam gown, legs hanging over the side of the padded table. Her boots were toppled beneath her feet, their leather tongues lolling. I held her. Her skin was covered in goosebumps and her whole body trembled.

"What'd they say?" I asked.

She shook her head. She was crying. "They wouldn't even let me see the screen. I don't know those terms they were using. I asked them what pentalogy meant and they clammed up. Something's wrong, Clive. Really wrong."

"Shh. Bec, you're freezing. Let's get you dressed." I gathered her clothing from the chair, catching her flowered panties before they could hit the floor.

"I wish you'd been in here," she said. "The amnio was creepy. I was terrified they'd poke the baby. The needle is like six inches long. They said we won't know anything until the results come back. That's two weeks away. How are we supposed to get through two whole weeks?"

I didn't know. I really didn't know.

೧

Becca sat stunned and shivering in my old wool peacoat, which she'd adopted around the same time she'd started wearing her dad's shirts. I swung myself around to her side of the pizza joint booth and put my arm around her. I'd have said something, but there was nothing to say that wasn't a false hope or a flat out lie. *It'll be fine. I'm sure it's nothing. Those tests are wrong half the time. It's amazing what they can do with surgery nowadays. If we pray hard enough, God will listen. There might be a miracle. God never gives you more than you can handle. Everything happens for a reason. What doesn't kill us makes us stronger.* If tragedy had taught me a single thing, it was that platitudes existed only for the morons who spouted them.

I squeezed her shoulder. Kissed her hair. "No matter what happens, no matter how screwed up things might get, remember, I'm right here with you. One-hundred percent of the way."

She leaned into me.

The waiter came around for the second time, but neither of us had much appetite and we still hadn't decided what to order. Maybe stopping at a pizza joint hadn't been my best idea, but it was a long drive back home and we were still reeling from the ultrasound. I waved him off and tried to get serious about the menu.

The list of toppings refused to make sense. *Black olives, feta, fetus, pineapple, bilateral, renal, hot peppers, Genoa, agenesis. Bilateral renal agenesis.* That damned phrase was lodged in my brain. It stood out from the rest of the medical Greek because of what the doctor had said right

after it. *Definitely.* I worked the phrase over, trying to parse it out, but the meaning of *renal* eluded me.

"Before she sent us out for a walk, what did the tech say the baby wasn't letting her see?" I asked.

Becca stared at the bubbles in her sparkling water. "Kidneys. Why?"

I pretended to study the menu. *Pepperoni, red pepper, renal, garlic, basil, bilateral, renal.* Renal meant *kidney.* Bilateral meant *both. Agenesis* did not refer to the progressive rock band from the Seventies. I twisted a paper napkin until it was slim as a straw. Wound it around my finger. Unwound it. *Agenesis. Genesis. Beginning.* The prefix *A* meant *not.*

And there it was: both kidneys, not beginning, definitely. A moan escaped me.

"What, Clive? What is it?"

I dropped the strangled napkin and tried to act casual. "I don't know. Nothing. Hey, let's get the deep dish. You want roasted garlic on it?"

She always went for roasted garlic.

"I don't care," she said. "I'm not even hungry anymore."

And what was that other phrase? Prosciutto. Portobello. Profound midline craniofacial malformations.

Well, fuck.

22

Rival

Ellie • Detroit, Mich. • Monday, Nov. 13, 2006

We were in the kitchen when Saint handed me a bank envelope stuffed with $900. "I sold my Strat. Three months' rent."

"But you love that guitar."

"Somebody made me an offer I couldn't refuse."

"You could use this to move out, though."

"If I actually wanted to do that, don't you think I'd be gone by now? This'll help you cover the midwife. She can't be cheap."

"Before I accept it, you have to answer one important question. Are you Team Beth or Team Jill?"

"Ugh, really? Vedder's girlfriends? This is some kind of low for you, Detroit Ellie."

"C'mon, the model or the punk rocker?" I figured he'd be Team Beth all the way.

"I'm gonna have to go with Team Who Gives a Fuck on this one, sorry."

I guess he had a point. I tucked the fat bank envelope into my knapsack. Honestly, I shouldn't have. Reece was still grumbling about starting eviction proceedings. But refusing Saint's rent money would be the same as me kicking him out, and that dirty job was on Reece. I was still holding out hope that we could all hold hands and sing *Kumbaya* around a burning tire.

Saint had been putting in a lot of time training Tremor Christ. Every morning he got up early and took him for a long run. He'd installed a big dog crate in the basement to keep him secure, and used positive reinforcement to teach the dog to love it. All Saint had to say was *kiste* and Tremor Christ would zip right in there, and not even complain when the door was double latched. I'd taken Saint's suggestion to toss a treat through the bars of the crate when I went to the basement to do laundry, so Tremor Christ would learn to associate me with Snausages. These days, Tremor Christ actually wagged his tail when he saw me. I was about fifteen percent less scared of him than I used to be.

I inventoried the things I'd miss when Saint did finally move out:

—The smell of his burnt pumpernickel toast, which he always drenched in butter.

—His ever-changing parade of groupies and their ongoing *Guitar Hero* tournaments. It was entertainment, at least.

—His alarm blasting *Pilate* every morning to wake him up for Tremor Christ's run.

— Our philosophical Pearl Jam pop quizzes.

Saint brought Tremor Christ out of the basement and headed for the door in his training gear. He had the leash in one hand and a naked baby doll tucked under his arm.

"Whoa. What's up with that woobie?" I asked.

"Gummipuppe."

"Goomy poopy yourself," I said.

He grinned at me and banged out the back door, the brown scarf wrapped around his neck. The flat November sky spat snow flurries and a stiff wind blew his hair around. It was long enough to graze his shoulders now. I couldn't hear his training commands through the storm windows, but he held the doll high while the dog jumped at it. He set the doll and a tennis ball on the dirt, and Tremor Christ snatched the doll in his teeth and shook it violently. Saint scolded him. As awful as it looked, I understood what he was trying to accomplish.

It was mesmerizing, but I needed to get ready for work. Reece would be stopping by on his lunch hour to give me a lift to Mr. Salty's. My rapidly expanding waistline made the polyester uniform pants creep into my crevices. I constantly had to pull them lower. I decided to put them on last just to minimize the chore of yanking them out of my beleaguered crotch.

I heard the familiar honk of the Roadbastard and looked out the window. Reece had double parked and was already heading inside. The front door opened and he called up the stairs for me.

"Be there in a sec." I started to rush. That was a tactical error. I got stuck with the pullover shirt on halfway, my arms straight in the air. I wiggled, bent forward and released all of my breath. Nothing. My arms had grown too chubby, my boobs too big. The unyielding polyester shirt didn't fit me anymore and I now couldn't get it on or off. The fabric pressing against my nose was faintly sour because I hadn't gotten my laundry into the dryer soon enough. I was stuck, encased in that infernal shirt, nothing on my lower half but shamrock bikini underpants and fuzzy knee socks—one striped, the other argyle.

What lay ahead was the utter humiliation of yelling for help, of Reece chuckling at me jammed in my polyester prison like Our Lady of Perpetual Doom. He'd have to cut me out of this mess with scissors. And then what would I wear to work? Shelby Williams was going to have a kitten.

"Reece? Hey, Reece?" I called. I could barely get enough air to be heard. "Reece? Honey? Come here!"

I heard his voice coming from downstairs, but he wasn't answering me. Reece's voice, then Saint's voice. Louder, louder, escalating to angry shouts. The heck? Then the commotion started. Swearing. Scuffling. A thump. *Oh, crap.* They were fighting.

Reece yelled something I couldn't understand. Glass shattered and Saint yelled back.

Saint stomped up the stairs and slammed his bedroom door.

"Reece?" I called. "Reece, everything alright?"

Nothing.

Desperate, I fought with that damned shirt, wiggling side to side, panting and sweating. I couldn't get myself into it. I worked my torso in the opposite direction. I don't know how I did it, but finally I forced my way into the stupid shirt. It was cutting into my armpits and bunched over my belly, but it was on.

Saint banged around in his room, slamming drawers and shoving furniture across the pine floor. Reece laid on the Roadbastard's horn.

I tugged the dreaded work pants over my rapidly thickening thighs and didn't bother with the zipper and snap. They wouldn't have cooperated anyway. Besides, my shirt covered that part. I corralled my hair into a half-assed bun and put my visor on. I crammed my swollen feet into my work shoes and stuck my head out of the bedroom door. Saint was on his way down the stairs, dragging a big duffle bag, a guitar case, and an amp.

He banged his way out of the front door. The bandage had fallen off his arm and draped across several steps. He hadn't even noticed.

They'd knocked over the little table with my framed Polaroids of Stone Gossard and my signed Green River handbill. The tiny China bowl of Stone's guitar picks lay shattered on the floor. Was nothing sacred in this house?

Reece blasted his car horn another four times. I didn't even have a chance to set the table upright. I picked up a cracked picture of Stone and apologized to it before running outside.

ᛜ

Saint was throwing all of his stuff into the Tracker, which was parked a few doors down. The scarf obscured most of his face.

I slid into Reece's car, careful not to let the high winds slam the door on my leg.

"About time," Reece said. His ears and cheeks were beet red.

I readjusted the seatbelt around my waist. "What just happened?"

"The short version is that scrawny Martian is finally getting off our planet."

"I heard fighting. Are you hurt?"

"Alls I said to him is a doll wasn't exactly a smart choice for a chew toy. He goes, 'What do you know about anything?' I go, 'I have half a brain.' I mean, for Christ's sake, he's teaching that dog to go after a doll when we're about to bring a baby home?"

138

"I don't think he was—"

"Oh, that's what he tried to tell me. 'You think I'm training him to kill babies?' he says. I go, 'Sounds about right.' And he goes, 'You're really smug for a moron, LeFanch. You think you know somethin' about me. About my dog. You don't know shit.' He wanted it to be a fight."

"Who shoved who first?" I asked.

"I don't even know."

"But you're alright?"

"Yeah, I'm fine. I can take that pussy any day."

The streets of Midtown were empty but for the trash blowing around. It was that first November day where you know winter is inevitable and it won't be warm again for another six months. By the time it was nice out, I'd have a baby. My coat didn't fit anymore and I was shivering in Reece's zip-up Pistons hoodie. I turned the heater up to Nuclear Blast.

"He was using a doll to teach the dog to be gentle with a baby," I said.

"No. That dog had the doll in its teeth, El. In its teeth."

"And was Saint rewarding him for that, or was he telling him to drop it?"

"Who even knows? He was talking German, the little fucking Nazi."

"I know you two aren't getting along like a house on fire, but come on. This is Saint we're talking about."

"You've always given him way too much credit."

Credit. That reminded me. There was a fat envelope of cash in the knapsack on my lap. "He paid us three months' rent today. Ahead. I have to give it back."

"What'd he give that to you for anyhow? He was supposed to move out. What an idiot. Keep it."

"You did not just say that." I turned sideways on the cold leather seat and stared. When was it that Reece, my Reece, had turned into a giant cockroach? "I know you're really mad right now, but this isn't like you."

139

"He pushed me. His dog attacked your brother. Think of it as compensation for emotional distress. Or, you know, an asshole tax. Do you have it on you?"

"No. I left it at home." I lied because I didn't want to hand it over to him. I didn't care what he thought, I was giving it back the minute I figured out where Saint had landed. If that didn't happen, I'd find a way to take it to Saint's mother.

We didn't talk anymore the rest of the way to Mr. Salty's. When he dropped me off, I said, "My shift ends at nine. Can you pick me up?"

"Yeah, I guess. I have a client dinner but I can probably cut out of there by then."

"Great. Thanks." I pushed open the car door.

"Don't I get a hug?"

I gave him a quick one.

"Your shirt smells funny," he said.

☙

I swear Shelby Williams was on the rag twenty-eight days a month. When I told her I was going to need a bigger Mr. Salty's uniform, she bugged her eyes at my swollen uterus and said, "I hope you know whose it is."

"Like Reece didn't just drop me off here?"

"Yuh-huh. I've seen that tall boy picking you up, the way you smile for him."

Saint. No doubt he'd given me my last ride home from Mr. Salty's.

"It's Jerry Springer's," I said. "It was the only way he'd let me on his show."

"Watch it, girl."

Business was slow at the pretzel shop, which was typical for a cold, gray, windy Monday. Shelby assigned me the revolting task of cleaning under the pop machine. It cranked up the volume on the background hum of my constant nausea. I'd forgotten to eat, and that always made my stomach worse. Not to mention, the contortions necessary to clean under the machine were next to impossible in the tight confines of my work uniform. Gooey black resin gummed my knees and elbows. The kneeling, squatting, bending, and reaching made me sweaty and dizzy on top of being sick to my stomach. My hair was escaping its bun and turning into a complete frizz fest.

I took a little extra time in the bathroom trying to set myself right. When I came out, Shelby said, "Take that mess home."

"My shift goes for another four hours."

"We're dead. Corporate wants us to operate on the least amount of crew to serve customers. We've hardly had any today."

"Can I take a pretzel?"

"No. You didn't put in the minimum for pretzel privilege today."

"Well, I would have if you weren't sending me home early. Come on, Shelby. I'm hungry."

"Just go on home and make yourself a sandwich. It's healthier for the baby."

I told myself I was sick of pretzels anyway. Pretzels with cheese. Pretzels with mustard. Pretzels with cinnamon and sugar. I was sick of the very word *pretzel*, of their cutesy shape and sun-tanned crusts and precious salt freckles. But I was starving. The pretzel display rotated and buzzed. My stomach growled. I could have bought the entire store out of pretzels with the cash in my knapsack, but I wouldn't spend Saint's money on even one. He was going to need every penny now that Reece had left him with no place to live.

I zipped into the Pistons hoodie and slung my knapsack over my shoulder. I loved that bag. I'd sewed it myself, and embroidered it with peace signs and daisies. It was the one thing this pregnancy couldn't make me outgrow.

Already it was growing dim outside. Reece wouldn't be done with his client dinner for hours. Saint was gone. Oh crap, he was really, really gone. It wasn't the worst day of my life, but it was making a serious attempt to get in the running.

Day, get behind the day our building burned and my baby brothers died. Get behind the day our mom went to prison. Get behind the day Clive and I were placed in separate foster care homes. Get behind the day I got locked in a girls' detention center.

Day, maybe you suck balls but I've had a lot worse.

Waiting for the SMART bus in the bitter wind, I considered how little I'd done with my life compared to Shelby. She attended Wayne State full-time yet never missed a shift at work. In a year and a half, she'd have her teaching certificate. She drove a new Honda Fit. I was three years older with a GED. My best career hope at the moment was a maternity uniform so I could hang onto my minimum wage position sprinkling salt on soft pretzels in a half-empty strip mall.

The SMART bus pulled up. I climbed on board and found a seat.

Shelby thought I was stupid to live in Detroit without a car. I didn't have the heart to trade the Yield bus for a regular vehicle. I hoped someday we'd take it out on tour again. With my pregnancy that wasn't looking super likely, but to me hope and music are as important as fresh water and clean air. I closed my eyes and remembered my last Pearl Jam show. Auburn Hills. The pit. Our new friend Saint waving Reece and me over to his spot on Stone's side of the stage. Singing along with *State of Love and Trust*. The houselights going up for Yellow Ledbetter.

The better things are, the worse you feel when they end.

Halfway to my transfer, the bus driver pulled over in a plume of smoking oil. He radioed his dispatcher, then announced that another bus would come for us in about forty minutes. I really needed to pee. I couldn't wait that long to get home.

I slid off of the hard plastic seat and jumped onto the curb. A stiff wind knifed through the Pistons hoodie. It was a long walk and really not the safest area, but I grew up in Detroit. I knew how to do this.

I walked fast with my knapsack crammed tight under my arm. I should have worn it inside the hoodie, but I hadn't planned on walking. I kept my head high, my shoulders relaxed. Ignoring the uniform pants giving me camel toe, I walked like my destination was less than a block away. I pretended not to see the group of hard-ass looking kids sitting on the hood of an old Monte Carlo. A girl of about twelve bopped by and I didn't make eye contact with her either. All I knew was, I was getting my pregnant butt home.

I knew exactly who I was scared of—desperate people. That's who you have to look out for in a situation like this. The druggies. The panhandlers who won't take no for an answer. The perpetually angry and entitled. The roving gang of middle schoolers on a dare.

I'd been mugged before, but never in Detroit. It had happened in Camden, New Jersey in 2002. I'd thought nothing could ruin my night after a Pearl Jam show that opened with *Of the Girl*—Cliver's all-time favorite—and ended with *Baba O'Reilly*. I don't know how Clive and I got separated on the way back to the Yield bus, but this gargantuan chick with dead eyes came at me with a flaming propane torch. I threw my bag at her feet and made a run for it. There wasn't one thing in that bag I'd burn for, not even Matt-Cam's drumstick.

When Clive found me he'd wanted to hunt her down and cram that torch straight up her ass. I said no, we should yield to it. All I'd had in that bag was an embroidery project, some homemade granola, the drumstick I'd caught that night, and a stick of deodorant. I was pretty sure she needed it a lot worse than I did.

That bag didn't have anything like Saint's rent money in it. I could have stuffed the cash into my bra, but it was already overcrowded with my pregnancy boobs.

I dug out my cell phone and speed dialed Reece. I needed him to at least know where I was, and it wouldn't hurt for me to look like I was in communication with someone. He didn't answer. I left a message and stuffed the phone into my pocket.

Midtown. I still had quite a ways to go. My shoes were too tight and my little toe was getting a blister. I had a side stitch. Big deal. This day needed to throw a lot worse at me if it wanted to stay in the running for my worst day ever.

Everybody thinks Detroit is so bad, but as long as you know where you're going and what areas to avoid, it's not all that dangerous. A Tracker the same color as Saint's whizzed by, but it didn't have whitewalls. I already missed him and maybe even that crazy mutt of his. If I was walking Tremor Christ, no one would mess with me. Who was I kidding? I'd never had the guts to walk that beast.

I took a shortcut through Charlotte Park, which was not much more than a patch of dead grass, some bare trees and a basketball court. A few scruffy toddlers scrambled around while their moms huddled under a tree, smoking and gossiping. They didn't look more than fifteen or sixteen, but I bet they knew who their kids' fathers were.

About a block and a half past the park, it happened. His smell hit me first. Sour rags. B.O. Vodka. Rage. My scalp tingled. I didn't even turn around. I broke into a run, side stitch, toe blister and all.

He snatched the sleeve of my hoodie. I yanked my arm but he had me. He was a thick, scowling boy. He couldn't have been over 14.

I tried to pull myself free.

"The bag, you stupid cunt. Gimme the bag."

23

Can't Keep

Clive • Traverse City, Mich. • Monday, Nov. 13, 2006

The genetic counselor was a birdlike woman with a pixie haircut and fingernails bitten to the quick. Her office was cramped and hot. On the windowsill were framed photos of simpering, bucktoothed children: a boy and two girls.

She pushed a piece of paper across her desk toward us. "Let's start with your baby's karyotype."

I took the paper and held it so Becca could see, too. It was covered in pairs of squiggles organized in rows over tidy numerals.

The counselor said, "You'll notice there are three chromosomes above the number thirteen instead of the normal two. Your baby has Trisomy 13, or Patau's syndrome."

I wondered if the bald doctor had enjoyed his free steak.

"So, it's like Down syndrome?" Becca asked.

"Only in that it's a trisomy which causes abnormalities. Down syndrome is a trisomy of the twenty-first chromosome and expresses itself quite differently. But let's stick to discussing the issues specific to your baby. This isn't easy to tell you, but the prognosis is extremely poor. She has a constellation of physical anomalies, not the least of which is a severe heart defect called Tetralogy of Fallot."

"My poor little girl," Becca said.

"Her heart is not in the normal location. It's pushed outside the chest wall. That condition is called ectopia cordis."

Becca snatched a pen from the desk, took the paper from me and jotted the term in the margin. "They can do surgery, though. I'm sure. I mean, can't they fix almost anything nowadays?"

The counselor smiled patiently. "Unfortunately, there are additional problems that put cardiac surgery out of the question, including an omphalocele. Some organs, normally positioned in the abdominal cavity, are contained in a sac floating outside of her body."

Becca dropped the pen and it rolled under her chair.

"What about the bilateral ... the bilateral ..." I reached for the pen and handed it to Becca. That damned term had hounded me for days and now I couldn't access it. "The kidneys?"

The counselor nodded. "Bilateral renal agenesis. The kidneys did not develop."

"Couldn't they do, I don't know, dialysis or a transplant or something?" I asked.

At home, we'd frantically Googled whatever medical terms we could remember from the Traverse City appointment. But since they hadn't told us what problems our baby actually had, it was hard to know which defects, treatments, surgeries, or outcomes might apply. It had all been terrifying to contemplate. We'd agreed to quit torturing ourselves, wait for this follow up appointment with the genetics counselor and hope for the best. I believed we were prepared for the worst, but now it seemed like we'd been expecting a 20-car pileup and were getting a nuclear holocaust instead.

Becca was scribbling furiously at the bottom of the page: *Louise. Louise. Louise.*

"Sadly, infants with this trisomy are not candidates for organ transplants. The survival rate is poor, typically a matter of days or weeks, even for those who don't need organs." The counselor cleared her throat. "To be honest, given your baby's condition, your wife would be lucky if she made it full term."

"Please, I'm right here. Don't talk like I'm not in the room," Becca said.

"Rebecca, you're already developing a marked reduction in amniotic fluid," the counselor said. "That's from the non-development of the kidneys. It will become more severe as the baby grows, seriously compromising your health as well."

"How is it possible for someone so tiny to have this many things wrong?" Becca's voice cracked. "I can hardly keep track of it all."

The counselor handed her a box of tissues. "I'm sorry, but that's not everything."

Becca folded her body forward and hugged her knees. "No more. Please. No more."

"We've heard enough for now," I said. I stroked Becca's hair. Tears splotched the toes of her work boots. I knew what was coming next. Midline craniofacial deformities. Becca did not need to hear it. Not right now. I was still grateful she hadn't been in the room when I'd Googled that one.

"You do realize that discontinuing this pregnancy is an option," the counselor said. Then she droned on about oligohydramnios, hypertension, Potter's sequence and future fertility.

Becca sank into her chair, tilted her head back and muttered at the ceiling. "Twenty weeks. Good God, I can't have an abortion this late. I wouldn't even know where to go."

The counselor told us about a hospital in Detroit where Becca could have her labor induced early, deliver the baby intact, hold her, and say goodbye. She made some phone calls and arranged an appointment for us. It was scheduled for Thanksgiving week.

I'd have to call Ellie and tell her we were coming to visit. She couldn't say I wasn't living until it hurt.

24

Rats

Ellie • Detroit, Mich. • Monday, Nov. 13, 2006

"The bag. Let go, bitch."

My frozen fingers were curled around the nylon strap, refusing to cooperate. He yanked. I hung on. It was exactly what not to do, but it was a reflex, a reaction. God he stunk. I had to get away. I managed to blurt, "I'm pregnant."

"So fuckin' what. Gimme the fuckin' bag." He punched my stomach. Once. Twice. I doubled over and dropped the bag. The little bastard slugged me again, his knuckles burrowing hard under my ribs. He shoved me backward and my butt slammed against the sidewalk. My palms hit the cement too late to cushion my tailbone. I curled around my stomach. My baby. The asshole walked off with my knapsack over his shoulder. Walked, because he knew I wasn't getting up.

My hands were scraped and bloody, shaking. I had to concentrate just to extract the cell phone from my pocket. I called the only person I was sure would answer.

"Shelby? Crap, I just got mugged." Saying it aloud, the enormity of what happened choked me up.

"Welcome to Detroit."

"No, for real. I got hit hard. Robbed. I'm still on the ground."

"What? Where are you?"

I started to cry. "I don't know. Midtown? Kind of past Charlotte Park, around Third Street?" I wiped my eyes on my sleeve. All I wanted was for someone to come and get me out of there.

"Why are you calling me? Call the cops. White girls, I swear."

"Please, Shel. They hit my stomach. I can't walk home. It hurts." I tried to stand, staggered sideways and lowered myself to my knees on the frozen grass. My tailbone burned.

"Ooh. That's bad. They get your purse?" Shelby asked.

"Yeah. $900."

"Right. Like you had that much."

I didn't have the stamina to explain about Saint and his prepaid rent. "Are you going to help me or what?"

"Yes. I'm calling the cops right now, seeing as you don't have the good sense. Lordy." She hung up.

On my knees and elbows in the grass, I texted Reece. *Mugged. Plz call.* No one was coming for me. I had to drag myself to my feet and limp toward home, arms cradling my throbbing belly. Every time a car went by I'd hope it was Reece or a cop coming to help me. My uterus tightened and cramped every few steps. I was sure I was losing the baby. Maybe I shouldn't have been walking, but lying around on the street in Detroit was hardly an option. I forced myself to keep moving.

I'd dragged myself about three blocks when Shelby's bright blue Honda Fit screeched to a stop at the curb. I started crying again, this time with relief.

"What? You thought I'd just leave you out here?"

"Should we wait for the cops?"

"Your call."

"I'm hurt. I'm freezing. I just want to go home."

Shelby helped me into the car. Sitting down was agony. I managed to twist sideways to reduce the pressure on my tailbone. Shelby. She could be a real snot, but at the moment she was my favorite person in the world.

Her ashtray was filled with pink and brown potpourri that smelled like spiced pears. Some talk radio program was on, with callers asking for advice. I was a million miles past anyplace where advice could help me.

"I'm taking you to Emergency."

150

I could just see the hospital bill for that. "No. Don't. I'll call my midwife when I get home."

"You're pregnant. You need to see a real doctor."

"My midwife is great. It'll be fine. She'll probably see me faster than they'd get to me in the emergency room anyway."

"Ha ha. True that."

ଓ

Shelby walked me into the house and made me lie down on the sectional. I became acutely aware of the morning's dirty mugs on the coffee table, Reece's papers stacked on the floor, Saint's grungy bandage draped on the stairs. There was still broken glass on the floor from Stone's toppled shrine. I'll bet Shelby had the kind of floors you could serve tapioca pudding on. She was pretty elegant with her fitted wool coat hiding her Mr. Salty's uniform.

"Call your midwife. I'm not leaving until she gets here, or until your boyfriend, or whoever, comes home. And you should file a police report."

Right. Like the cops were going to find Saint's money. I agreed to file a report anyway.

"I can take you off the schedule for now. Let me know when you can work again. Don't worry if you need a little time, you have more than yourself to consider here. When you can come back, I won't cut your hours or anything."

"Cool. Thanks. Is there any way I can get a bigger uniform? I had to use a shoehorn to get this shirt on today."

"I've checked. They don't have maternity uniforms but they have some XL sizes and men's sizes. We'll figure something out."

Abigail arrived fifteen minutes later, her cheeks flushed, and her silver-tinged hair in a long braid. She helped me into the bedroom and checked me. I wasn't bleeding or leaking amniotic fluid, great news. My blood pressure was higher than usual but Abigail said that wasn't surprising, considering. She said my tailbone was bruised, possibly broken. Pregnancy meant I couldn't get X-rays, but they don't put butts in casts anyway. She said with tailbones, a bruise or a break hurt pretty much the same and took the same amount of time to heal. The real concern was safe pain management.

She gave me some Tylenol-4 left over from when Reece had a wisdom tooth pulled, and said they were OK to take as needed. "I want you on bed rest for the next twenty-four hours," she said. "Call me if you have any spotting, cramping, anything worrisome."

"Don't leave yet," I said.

She took a seam ripper from her midwifery bag and slit the side seams on my uniform shirt, letting me escape it without struggling. Abigail. My hero. She threw the ruined shirt in the trash and helped me into some soft, oversized things of Reece's.

Abigail sat on the bed reading old issues of *Rolling Stone* and munching roasted almonds from our kitchen cupboard. Was this what it was like to have a mother? What kind of mother would I be? I understood maybe for the first time in my life what mothering was. It was being there and caring. Not fixing everything. Not making the bad stuff disappear. But just being there and caring. Shelby had done it for me tonight, and now Abigail. I was pretty sure I could do it too, when the time came.

ॐ

The full meaning of pain in the ass became plain when I tried to sit up. I couldn't. My tailbone was a molten ball of iron. The slightest movement left me gasping. I waved one arm around in the dark until I found my bedside lamp.

"Reece? Hey, Reece? You home?" My stomach felt tender and sore beneath an oversized T-shirt and Reece's drawstring sweatpants. I pulled the clothes out of the way to look at my belly. Even in the shadowy lamplight, devastating purple and red bruises were obvious.

Reece pushed through the door with a tray. "Oh, sweetie, I know. I know. Abigail showed me while you were out of it." He set the tray on the end of the bed and held me. "My poor girl. Our poor baby. How you feeling?"

"Rotten. Everything hurts." I tried to hold still. My tailbone throbbed.

"Are you hungry?" Reece stroked my cheek. His eyes were tired and red. "I made food. I cooked all night because I felt so guilty. I accidently turned my phone off and didn't see your messages." He sat beside me on the edge of the bed. The slight movement of the mattress was agony, but it didn't stop my stomach from answering him with an eager growl. He moved the tray of food to his lap. More pain.

"Can you not sit on the bed right now? I can't take the movement."

He dragged a chair over and settled the tray on his knees. Cheddar-potato chowder, soda bread, rice pudding, double-fudge brownies and a pot of red raspberry leaf tea. The god of carbohydrates must have been pleased. I wanted the food, but there was no way I could sit up to eat. When I attempted it, the pain made my eyes water. I settled back down on my side.

Reece dipped a spoon into the thick soup, got a little on the end and fed it to me. It was buttery and rich, with extra garlic and basil, the way I liked it. He fed me as much as I could eat in tiny, sideways bites and then found a bendable straw for my tea.

After I'd eaten he gave me another Tylenol-4. The relief wasn't instantaneous, but in time the pain became gauzier, and Reece did too. My feelings for him grew all cozy-pink lambswool with the painkiller. He was so sweet. He took such good care of me. And he was cute.

I was drifting off when I panicked about the money. "Saint's rent. The mugger got it." The words were already out when I remembered fibbing about where the money was earlier that day, but if Reece noticed the discrepancy he didn't let on.

"I don't care about that, and neither should you. Don't even worry about it."

That wasn't possible. I owed Saint and I couldn't repay him. We had no rental income, I couldn't work anytime soon, and even if I could, I'd never clear $900 in a month. We were paying Abigail in cash for every house call. She was a bargain compared to seeing an OB without insurance, but it was still well outside of our tight budget. Abigail. I'd fallen asleep without paying her. I asked Reece if he had.

"I tried to, but she wouldn't take the money."

"Why?"

"Sweetheart. Sugar. Look at you. Abigail was relieved you're not in worse shape."

"Aw. That's super nice of her. I hope Saint's as understanding about his rent money."

"Who gives a damn what he thinks? My girl and my baby are all that matter to me."

CR

My mother gave me two treasures. The first was my twin brother. The second was something she'd told me about us in one of her rare moments of lucidity. She'd said, "Your hearts beat in time, you and Clive, always in time." I'd tested her assertion and it usually held true. I'd place one of my thumbs on his carotid artery and the other on my own to feel our heartbeats keeping perfect pace. Not always, but often enough. It was comforting to think about.

That's what came to mind when my brother called. Reece brought me the phone. I was curled on my side in bed, loopy from painkiller.

Clive sounded terrible. And the first thing he said was "Jesus, El, you sound terrible."

I told him about the mugging. He listened and sympathized, then said, "So, looks like the Rafferty doom is in full force right now."

He told me everything they'd found out about their baby. That was worse, much worse, than what had happened to me, but Clive made no comparisons. We both understood too well that while misery loves company, it detests a contest.

"You know that Rafferty family crest you sewed for us?"

"Embroidered."

"Yeah. *We're Fucking Doomed.* Do you ever think it's one of those self-fulfilling prophesies?"

"That's not a prophecy, it's a scientific observation." Man, I'd really missed having these kinds of conversations with him. "I'm like the Isaac Newton of catastrophe."

"So, can you make accurate predictions based on a pattern of past disasters?"

"Catastrophe is a basic condition, no, a law of physics, in the known universe of Honey Jane, from whence we originated."

"Whence. Woohoo. Look at you, Elsworth, *whencing* about all this doom like it doesn't even faze you."

"Oh, believe me, I'm fazed as fuck right now."

"Well, I need to know if we can stay at your place over Thanksgiving. They're sending us to a hospital down there. The procedure is on Wednesday, but we have to come on Monday to do some state law bullshit ultrasound and go through a state-mandated waiting period. You know, in case all that extra time and having to be so far from home makes us change our minds and decide we'd really rather have our kid go through hell before she dies, you know, instead of going out peacefully."

"Geez. Thanks a lot, Michigan. Even with that whole diagnosis laid out, they're making you do all that?"

"No exceptions for fetal or maternal health. Real warm and fuzzy, huh? And our insurance won't cover any of it either."

"Bastards. And yes, you can stay here as long as you need to. Reece kicked Saint out. You guys won't even have to sleep in the loft. Which hospital is it at?"

"That one that's connected to Wayne State."

"That's where we were, after."

After. It was all I needed to say. When you've been through a tragedy with someone, you have these code words. For Clive and I, *after* said it all. After the fire, we were hospitalized there for weeks to recover from smoke inhalation. Before that, we'd been in and out of the system, going home for as long as Honey Jane could keep her poop in a group. After, her custody was permanently revoked. We became wards of the state. She went to jail and later, prison.

"Ah, crap," Clive said. "Not that hell hole."

Later, as I thought about this conversation, I felt like maybe, just maybe, Clive's little girl had spared my baby by taking all that doom onto herself. For once, I didn't care one bit whether my baby was Reece's or Saint's. It was mine. It would get to live.

25

Hard to Imagine

Clive • Detroit, Mich. • Thursday Nov. 23, 2006

We were settled into a dreary room at the maternity ward's dead end. A pinkish plaque above the bathroom door read *God is* ...

In our case, God was apparently constipated. The nurse who'd given Becca the tiny white labor-inducing pills on Wednesday had said that some people were done in a few hours, but it rarely went longer than twelve. We'd been there over twenty-four hours. I was ready to hurl the wall clock out the window.

Becca was clinging to the jagged edge of sanity. I wanted it over too, yet dreaded the end. As it turns out, there is never an opportune time to break it to your wife that your baby has midline craniofacial deformities. I should have let the genetic counselor tell her. But just when I'd screwed up my courage to broach the subject, Becca had dropped off to sleep. After more than a full day of contractions, I sure wasn't going to wake her up to tell her.

A new nurse bustled into the room and took Becca's blood pressure and temperature. Thankfully that didn't wake her. The nurse gave me a polite half-smile, but then her mouth dropped open and she stood there blinking at me.

"Hey, I know you," she said.

I swear I'd never seen this woman before in my life. Wavy brown hair, big boobs, probably in her late twenties. Nope. I didn't know her.

"You lived with me," she said.

She was a complete walnut.

"You are Clive Rafferty, aren't you?"

"Well, yeah. But I don't think I know you."

She started laughing. "Yeah, you don't know me now. But you lived with us, you and your twin sister, uh, Ellie. That's right. Little Ellie. She was like my shadow. I loved her to bits. How's she doing?"

"She's great. But I still don't know who you are."

"Janice Marconi. From foster care?"

I shook my head. The name meant nothing, but that didn't mean she was wrong. I'd probably lived with half the foster care population of Wayne County between 1984 and 1997. "Marconi? What years were you in the system?"

"I wasn't. My mom and dad were licensed. You and your brothers and sister all lived with my family. You were pretty young, but I can't believe you don't remember us. You were with us for the better part of a year."

Becca shivered. I pressed my finger to my lips to quiet Janice, then tugged Becca's blankets up to her neck.

"We can talk in the hall," Janice whispered.

I didn't want to leave Becca there. Even sleeping, she looked tense. Vulnerable. But Janice apparently wasn't going to get lost until I acknowledged this foster family of hers. I kissed Becca's forehead and followed Janice into the hall, nudging the door closed behind me.

"I'm sorry," Janice said. "This room is only used for one thing, and it's so sad to see you, of all people, here. But I can't just walk away. I've wondered what happened to you and Ellie for years. Our family still jokes around about you calling our mom 'Mrs. Macaroni.'"

Holy shit. Just like that, everything tumbled into place. Janice was from the enormous, loving, five-star foster care family all four of us were placed with before the fire. I remember hoping we'd get sent back there and adopted every time we were placed with another family. Instead, we'd never heard from them again. I didn't recognize her specifically, but I remembered them, especially their mother.

158

"The Marconis. Of course. God, how the hell have you been? How's your mom? How are those, what, seven brothers and sisters of yours?"

"Nine. There were nine of us. Two more came along after you guys left."

"And all of your names started with J."

"Not the last two. Mom named them David and Donald."

Those were my brothers' names. This whole conversation was hitting me like a truckload of wet cement.

"When your brothers died and you two were hospitalized, Mom had a nervous breakdown. She never did foster care again."

God damned Rafferty doom. That shit was contagious.

"I'd like to see your mom sometime," I said.

Janice grinned. "That would make her day. Probably her whole year."

I checked on Becca through the narrow window in the door. She'd pushed her covers off and was sweltering, the hospital gown clinging to her skin. She stretched toward a cup of ice chips.

"I've really gotta run," I said.

I went back into the room and fed some ice chips to Becca. Her lips were dry and her eyes were circled in black. I adjusted her pillows and wiped her brow with a damp washcloth.

Janice stood in the doorway, clipboard clutched to her chest.

"Seriously. We'd love to see you and Ellie."

"Yeah. Sure."

"Hey, I know. We'll all be at Mom's tonight. Come by around eight o'clock, have some pecan pie. You should be out of here by then."

"Pie? Tonight?"

"Well, sure. It's Thanksgiving."

The holiday had completely slipped my mind.

"I really can't. Not tonight. Not with all this going on."

"Well, I meant you can bring her too." She scribbled a phone number and an address on a sticky note and handed it to me. "She'll feel better when this is all over. I've seen it many times."

I accepted the phone number, shaking my head. Thanksgiving be damned. Socializing was the last thing I'd ask my wife to do if we ever reached the end of this nightmare.

"Could you give it to Ellie? It would be so great to see her again."

"Sure. Yeah. Good seeing you. We'll be in touch." I folded the note and shoved it into my pocket. "Can you close the door on the way out?"

She did.

Moments later, Becca shuddered. "It's happening."

Ice cold dread crashed over me.

"Oh, God. What do you need? What do I do?"

"Be here," she said.

"I've got to call a nurse."

Her short nails dug into my wrist. "I don't need a nurse, I need you."

I pressed the call button. No one responded.

"I'm getting you a nurse."

"Stay. I don't need anyone but you."

God is … a stoned, greasy-haired carnie, his callused hands on the controls of The Zipper, making unsuspecting townies sick just for giggles.

No one answered the call button. It was still just the two of us when Becca delivered. I was horrified. That was no baby on the bed. It was an angry god flipping me the bird. My tiny, malformed daughter took Rafferty doom to an unfathomable level. I'm not sure how I convinced Becca not to look, probably the expression of sheer panic on my face. I placed a towel over the mess and rang the call button until it jammed.

After several minutes, a different nurse came in carrying a large stainless steel bowl. She inspected what lay beneath the towel. "Oh, good girl, you've delivered the placenta too. Saved yourself a D and C with that. You lucked out."

Sorry Becca. That's what passes for luck when you're a Rafferty.

"I'll get her cleaned up and then bring her back so you can hold her. Not fit for polite company yet are you, wee one?" The nursed

160

snapped on a pair of surgical gloves and lifted the bloody mess into the bowl. She covered it with a cotton cloth and set it against her hip. For all anyone could tell, Grandma's sourdough might have been rising in there.

08

"You don't have to see the baby," I told Becca while helping her get dressed after her shower. "She's ..." *Raw. Deformed. Heartbreaking.* The words that came to mind would only make it worse. "She'll never know if you don't look."

She held my shoulder for balance as she tugged a pair of hospital footies on. "I went through what? Twenty-five, twenty-six hours of labor? I'm going to see Louise. She's mine. I love her. I don't care how she looks."

"Well, obviously we love her."

The nurse returned with a tiny bundle of white flannel, which she laid in Becca's arms. "Take all the time you need. You can press the call button when you're ready for me to pick her up. And, I'm very sorry for your loss."

Becca cradled Louise. "Thank you."

I pressed my fist against my mouth.

"It's alright," Becca said. "Touch her. She's still warm."

I sat on the edge of the bed and accepted the bundle. She was right, it was warm. Louise Clover weighed a thousand pounds and nothing at all.

Becca started to lift the corner of flannel folded over the baby's face.

"Don't," I said.

But she already had. She gasped and turned away.

"I'm sorry," I said.

"Where are her eyes?"

I swept the corner of flannel back over Louise's face and cradled her against my shoulder. "She doesn't want you to see her like this."

Becca sat there, stunned. After a long moment, she reached up and laid her hand on the bundle. "You're right. Of course she

161

doesn't. Louise, I'm so sorry, baby. I'll try to remember you as you were meant to be."

"I wanted to break it to you before the induction, but I didn't know how. I'm sorry."

Her hand fell to her lap. "You mean you actually knew?"

26

Chloe Dancer

Ellie • Detroit, Mich. • Thursday, Nov. 23, 2006

"I f you guys want pecan pie, Janice Marconi says you should go to her mom's place in Royal Oak." Clive dropped this bomb while finishing off a can of Natural Light at my kitchen island, having tucked Becca into bed with some sedatives.

"Wait, what? Janice Marconi? As in *the* Janice Marconi?"

She'd been my foster sister when I was six or seven. We were inseparable until CPS gave us back to Honey Jane. Then all hell broke loose.

"You found Janice? How? When? And why didn't you tell me?"

"It was weird. She works at the hospital. She recognized me, or saw my name on Becca's chart, I don't know. She put it together with me somehow. I didn't actually remember her, but I remember her mom."

"Oh come on, Cliver. She was right in the middle, between Julia and Jay-Jay. We played with her all the time."

He took another beer out of the fridge and popped the top. "If you say so."

"Wow. They really invited us for pie?" I hoped the stretchy gold maternity pants and turtleneck I had on were dressy enough. I was still sore from the mugging, and wasn't up for getting fancy. It wasn't that the Marconis were particular, but I didn't want them thinking I'd grown up to be a complete slob.

"You can go," Clive said, "I'm absolutely fried. And anyway, I'm not leaving Becca."

He looked about as exhausted as I'd ever seen him, but this was important. I pressed him harder. "She's sound asleep. We have to see them. They're the only people who knew us before, and who knew our brothers. What if they remember something?"

"It's not like there's some unsolved crime here. Janice invited us. You're welcome to go over there. So go. They'll be thrilled to see you." He pulled a crumpled pink Post-It note from his pocket and handed it to me. An address in Royal Oak was scribbled on it. "Take Reece. He'll be more fun tonight anyway."

"I already ate at my mom's and I'm stuffed to the gills. Plus, I'm watching the game," Reece said.

"They'll be watching it too." Clive chugged some beer. "You really should take her. I'm going upstairs to crash. I haven't slept since like, I don't even know … Tuesday night or something."

I grabbed Clive's hand across the island. "We need to go. You and me. Those are our people. They took care of us."

"Some other time, then. We have the address. They're not going to flee the country. Becca needs me here. No way am I leaving her."

"She's unconscious. We'll be home in what, a couple of hours? Come on. They knew our brothers. We have to go there."

Even though Clive was tired and worried about Becca, I couldn't believe how stubborn he was being. The Marconis had represented the Holy Grail of families to us throughout our childhood. Finding them meant the world to me. And it had to mean something to him, too. I knew it did. After the mugging and this terrible loss for him and Becca, we needed to do this. Together. Tears of disappointment burned in my eyes.

"I'm sorry, El. But I've had two long, rotten days," Clive said. "I just can't tonight. And I won't leave Becca here after the shit storm she's been through."

"I'll stay with her," Reece said. "She's sound asleep. You and Ellie should go." He stood behind Clive and rubbed his shoulders. "If Ms. Becca wakes up, and that's pretty unlikely, I'll fix her a sandwich and a hot toddy and explain that Ellie gave you no choice."

"She'll kill me. And the Marconis aren't going anywhere. We can visit them some other time."

"But it's Thanksgiving," I said. "They're all there, together, right now. And you hardly ever come to Detroit anymore. If we don't go now we'll never go, and you know it. Reece will watch over Becca for you."

"I've got this, bro. Come on. Trust me." Reece massaged Clive's temples in a circular motion. Clive's jaw relaxed. Sometimes it was easy to see that Reece was the youngest in his family. He knew how to charm people into giving him his way. Or in this case, my way. "I'll take such good, good care of her, just like she was my own sister. And you'll take Ellie to see your long-lost foster peeps. Deal?"

Clive looked me in the eye and half smiled. "You guys. You guys. Ugh. What's with the peer pressure? Didn't anybody ever tell you that no means no?"

"An hour," I said. "Sixty minutes."

"Your wife will sleep the whole time," Reece said.

"No," Clive said. "Anyway, I can't drive. I just drank two Natties."

I put my hand in his. "I'll drive your car."

"You'll get us lost."

"You can navigate. Listen, forty-five minutes. I'm begging. Begging. Forty-five teeny tiny minutes out of your life and I'll never ask you for another thing as long as I live."

"Half an hour. Understand? Thirty minutes," Clive said.

I whooped. I'd have danced around the island, but my tailbone hurt. I fetched his navy blue peacoat from the hook by the basement door.

"That's Becca's now," he said.

"What? This has been your coat for ten years."

"Becca's not going anywhere anyway," Reece said.

Clive shrugged into the coat and pointed at me. "Thirty minutes. Not a second longer."

27

Crown of Thorns

Clive • Royal Oak, Mich. • Thursday, Nov. 23, 2006

Mrs. Marconi lived in a different house than the one we'd stayed in for foster care. It was newer, neater, but still had the familiar scent of garlic and Old English furniture polish. Being there took me back to the safest period of my childhood. Dark-eyed Marconi grandchildren giggled and pouted and climbed the furniture. A toddler whined and a baby strapped in a highchair smeared handfuls of sweet potatoes onto his head. The Marconis, a big pack of Italian Catholics, had grown exponentially over the last two decades. The old boys crowded around the wide-screen and hollered at the football game, waistlines advancing and hairlines in retreat.

Ellie melted into the Marconi family like gravy over mashed potatoes and was about as impossible to extract. She was wedged between two of the Marconi sisters, who were also pregnant, and regaling them with the dramatic tale of her mugging. She lifted her shirt to show off her bruises. They were huge, and every shade of purple. Jesus. I needed to pound the fuck out of whoever had done that to her. And she hadn't even shown those to me, probably out of consideration for everything Becca and I were going through.

Janice kept offering me more pie at the dining room table, nattering on about who knows what. I was too beat to do much more than smile politely and nod. I scooted my chair away from the table and asked her to package a slice of pumpkin for Becca, and some pecan for Reece to thank him for staying with her. She jumped up to do it.

I caught Ellie's eye and tapped my wrist. We'd already been gone about forty minutes, and she always took her time with good-byes. She nodded but returned to her conversation, so I wandered into the kitchen and started helping Mrs. Marconi wash the dishes. Anything to pass the time until Ellie got off her rear and let me get back to Becca. I'd give her another ten minutes, tops.

She'd been right about seeing Mrs. Marconi again. Once we were there, I understood Ellie's insistence. This was soul soothing in a way I couldn't have fathomed, and I think Ellie knew that it would be. My favorite foster mother's hair was now pure white, and she was twice as thick around the middle, but her smile was still a balm and she exuded the same motherly warmth I'd been drawn to as a kid. I washed all of the dessert dishes while she rinsed and dried them. It felt good to fall into this old foster child role, doing what little I could for this woman who had done so much for me

"When Janice said you and your sister might come, I gathered a few old photos from when you lived here. Your second-grade pictures and some snapshots of your brothers. I wish there were more." Mrs. Marconi dried her hands on a dishtowel and pulled a large envelope off the top of the refrigerator.

"We've never had—" the word *any* stuck in my throat.

"Thanks. We really should get going soon. My wife isn't feeling well."

"Oh dear. Sweet little Clive hasn't changed one bit. You had such a big heart and always looked out for everyone but yourself."

Becca sure wouldn't be thinking that way if she woke up before I got back. I thanked Mrs. Marconi again and excused myself. I found Ellie in the family room going through a six-inch-thick photo album with Janice and two of the other girls. I stood in the doorway and waved my arms like I was ground crew guiding a jumbo jet until they all looked at me, and Ellie had to stop pretending I was invisible.

"What? In a minute. It's not even like it's late," she said.

Now, I mouthed.

"You don't have to get all impertinent."

I dangled the keys to my Land Cruiser. "Fine. I guess we're going to see how fast you can get home riding in the passenger's seat of your two-dollar word."

"Impertinent goes for at least twice that much. Anyway, I'm driving."

She stood up and started hugging everyone goodbye, and I joined in. They were one big, huggy bunch, those Marconis. I guess that wasn't exactly a bad thing.

ॐ

Ellie was a decent driver, but her deficit in navigation skills was legendary. I'll admit I spaced out looking through the envelope of precious photos on my lap, and at the suburbs sparkling with early holiday lights. Fat, wet snowflakes hit the pavement and melted. The scent of pumpkin pie came through the plastic wrap over the paper plate on the dashboard. I drew my knees to my chest and tried to hold in the generous dose of warmth and security I'd absorbed from the Marconis. I'd been through so much shit in my life since I'd last seen them, and there they all still were, living their lives and laughing at each other's jokes. It was beautiful.

The residual glow faded when Ellie took one wrong turn and then another. If I'd been paying attention I might have known where we were. But she'd gotten confused after a construction detour and as far as I could tell, we'd wandered onto the set of a *Mad Max* movie.

She slowed. "Did you see a sign?"

"No." I stared out at the gloomy apartment buildings and tatty business awnings. *Payday Loans Today. Bubba's Bail Bonds.* The facades were vaguely familiar but the signage wasn't. We came to the next corner. The street sign had been stolen from the pole. The road ended at a building, so we had to turn.

"Which way?" she asked.

"Left, I guess."

"I'm thinking right." She rounded the corner.

"Why even ask me?"

A slim woman stepped out of a doorway and walked right in front of the headlights. Ellie slammed on the brakes and slid on the wet pavement. The woman kept walking. She didn't even notice us. *Holy shit.* That was LuCretia. I was positive.

"That's LuCretia."

"Nah, no way." Ellie let the car creep down the street. The woman had turned and was walking in the same direction. We passed her. Now I was dead certain it was my ex. I twisted around in my seat.

"That whore was way too old to be Lu-Creep-Show," Ellie said.

"Don't call her that."

"Whore? Or Creep-Show?"

"Go back." I only needed to see that she was alright.

"I'm not following some whore. I thought you were in a red-hot rush to get home to Becca. And in case you haven't noticed, we're in the butt crack of Detroit. This looks a lot worse than where I got mugged."

"It's alright. You're with me. I'd never let anything happen to you."

"Camden. Remember? You lost me after that Pearl Jam show and I got held up by some bitch with a propane torch."

My sister was a guilt-trip ninja. Camden my ass. I'd gotten in line for a T-shirt and she'd kept right on going. Walking on a cloud because she'd scored Matt Cameron's drumstick. But now, conveniently, it was all my fault.

She stopped for a red light. I opened my door. There was never any point in awaiting Ellie's approval when she scowled like that.

"Don't do it, Cliver. No good can come of it. What are you going to do? Give her money? She'll just spend it on dope."

I hopped out. "Lock it up. If you get spooked, you can take off. I'll find a way home."

"That's nuts. Get your dumb ass back in the—"

I closed the door and headed in LuCretia's direction. It had to be her. No one moved with unearned dignity quite the way she did. She never had a care in the universe, even as it crashed around her gem-studded ears.

Ellie pulled to the curb and revved the engine impatiently. The snow fell faster, sticking to my eyelashes.

"'Cretia," I called.

She turned, tilted her head and walked toward me. We met in front of a blinking neon *Michigan Lotto* sign behind cast iron bars. Seeing her stripped my heart raw. LuCretia's beauty was wilting. She'd aged fifteen years in what? Two?

"Rafferty? Is that really you?"

Missing teeth darkened her smile. On her breath was the charred-Drano stench of crack cocaine. Damn. Crack wasn't even her drug of choice. Maybe it was my fault for giving up on her, for moving away. But no. Using was part of LuCretia's package. She was why I'd moved away. Somehow I'd managed to forget that she'd always been too damaged to even realize she was damaged.

"Yeah, it's me," I said.

I didn't even know what the hell I was doing out there. I had to get home to Becca. I was already way late.

"Just saw you and, um, wanted to check on how you're doing," I said.

She brushed snowflakes from her brittle hair. Her dull eyes held the faint glimmer of someone who had known my deepest scars. I'd fallen for her in art school and dropped out trying to save her from herself. With LuCretia I'd been the one with my shit together. A familiar ache, my regret for all she'd never allowed herself to become, filled my lungs like pneumonia.

Her hand grazed my cheek and I recoiled. I remembered something she used to say: *When I get a little money I buy drugs. If there's any left over, I buy more drugs.* I'd been so stupid to ever think I could save this lost cause of a woman.

"You look haunted," she said. "What's gone so wrong in your life? Can I help?"

I was speechless.

"I've got something that will cut your pain," she said.

I laughed. It sounded hollow. Alien. She knew I never did that hardcore garbage she loved. I only smoked weed for the same reason I was drawn to cigarettes, lighters and bonfires: my need to have smoke and flames firmly under my own control, or to burn my lungs with something friendlier.

Ellie gunned the engine.

"I've really got to run," I said.

"At least give me a squeeze." LuCretia wrapped her arms around my waist. She felt flimsy as broom straw and smelled like poison, yet her essence was unchanged from the woman I'd once loved, and who'd needed me. I returned the hug out of I don't even know what. Pity? Habit? Guilt? The things LuCretia made me feel had never made any sense. They still didn't. Maybe everyone has that one inexplicably bad love story. Or maybe I'd won some ass-backward cosmic lotto.

Ellie gunned the engine again and it backfired.

"I've really got to run," I said.

"Goodbye, you." She wouldn't let go of me.

I pried her arms from around me and backed away. "Take care."

"Stay beautiful, Rafferty."

I climbed into the Land Cruiser feeling drained, sick, and soiled. Ellie didn't utter a word. At least I was oriented enough to provide her with meaningful directions toward home. She followed my instructions but continued giving me the silent treatment. I let her sulk for a few miles.

"C'mon. Don't be like this," I said.

"Damn freak bitch."

"She's not, El. Any one of us could tumble down that same rabbit hole any time. You, me, Reece, Becca, Mrs. Marconi ... anybody. No one is immune. It's the one thing you've consistently failed to grasp about addiction. It's not a moral issue. It's a mind sickness."

"Right there. That one. She's the whole reason you moved away."

There was no point in denying that, or in reminding Ellie that it had originally been her idea for me to get out of Detroit and away from LuCretia.

"And now you're, you're all ... all ... ensconced up north and I never see you. It's because of her. I hate her."

"I know. I understand. But moving away really was for the best. Hey, scoot over to the right lane or you'll miss our exit."

She jerked into the exit lane without checking over her shoulder. This elicited a series of furious honks from the car she'd just cut off.

"The only reason I suggested you move away was I hoped you'd get shed of that emotional vampire once and for all. Moving was the only way you could stop reliving Mama's problems through that toxic bitch. We couldn't fix Mama and you couldn't fix Creep-Show."

No point in denying that, either. God, Ellie hadn't referred to Honey Jane as Mama since the fire.

"So you want me to tell Becca you saw your creepy ex?"

"You wouldn't do that to me." I cracked the window and lit a cigarette.

"And you're smoking again?"

I hadn't smoked for almost a year. I'd quit before I'd started seeing Becca. But the pregnancy debacle was too much. All of my strength had gone toward helping Becca through it, and that left me nothing to fight a wicked craving for nicotine. I'd picked up a pack before we'd left Belknap Township for the procedure. Becca had no idea.

"Do I need to remind you that I'm pregnant?"

I took a long drag, cranked the window open further and flicked my cigarette out.

છ

Back at the house, we found Becca and Reece asleep at right angles on the sectional, heads sharing a corner cushion, each of them wearing white earbuds that fed into Reece's iPod through a splitter. Reece's cheek rested against the top of Becca's head. The faint suggestion of pot smoke explained this scene. Normally Becca wouldn't touch it, but this Thanksgiving had taken us all light years from normal. Her right arm stretched over her head and her hand lay in Reece's palm. I read what was playing on his iPod. *Mother Love Bone ... Crown of Thorns.*

Both of them could still surprise me.

Ellie covered Becca with an old yellow quilt that she liked to pretend was our family heirloom, and tossed a throw pillow to me. She knew I'd fall asleep on the floor. As usual, she was right.

28

Swallow My Pride

Clive • Rogers City, Mich. • Saturday, Nov. 25, 2006

Becca and I rolled through Rogers City and were greeted by the sight of the town's Christmas displays. There were a hundred small pines decorated with lights at Lakeside Park, lighted wreaths on all the lamp posts, and the crèche on the lawn of the courthouse in some quaint indifference to separation of church and state.

I'd wanted to go straight home, but she'd wanted to see the lights, and then insisted we stop at Glen's Market for groceries. I offered to take her home and do the shopping myself.

"I'm hardly an invalid. I want to do something that feels normal," she said. "Anyway, we don't have time for you to take me home first. They close in twenty minutes."

At Glen's, she packed a ridiculous array of sweets into the cart. It reminded me of the old days, shopping with that sugar hound, Reece. Pecan Sandies, Swiss Miss, Apple Jacks and Fiddle Faddle. Comfort foods. The best ones always had two names.

Christmas music played throughout the store. I pushed the cart to the beer coolers and grabbed some comfort food of my own, Natural Light. I hoped Becca had enough money because I'd misplaced my wallet in Detroit. I'd noticed it missing that morning. It wasn't anywhere at Ellie's, so it must have slipped out of my pocket at old Mrs. Marconi's. I wasn't concerned. I'd told Ellie about it and she'd said she'd ask Janice to drop it by.

I hadn't mentioned my wallet to Becca. She had enough on her mind. Anyway, she was less than thrilled that I'd taken off to have pie with people she'd never even heard of. I didn't need to add *I left my wallet there* to her resentment.

I slid a case of Natty onto the bottom rack of the grocery cart. When I looked up, Howie was heading toward us with a bag of powdered doughnuts in one hand and a gallon of Sunny D in the other.

"Crowe," Howie said. "How's it going, toots?"

Becca scratched her nose and gave him a wan smile. "Um, good, I guess."

"I understand congratulations are in order."

Becca's eyebrows pulled together. "What? Why?"

Crap. I angled between them. "Hey, how about them Lions?"

"Do you live under a stump? The Dolphins kicked their asses." He moved me aside like a minor chess piece. "Congratulations on motherhood, Crowe. Jeez." He enveloped her in his thick arms with the doughnuts and juice jug still clutched in his big paws. He bent and kissed her cheek. I couldn't object without looking like the insecure little twerp that maybe I was. I pretended to read the ingredients on a container of cottage cheese. How did Becca stand that stuff? Bland, lumpy, cold, yet mildly sour. Probably like Howie in the sack.

She extracted herself and wiped her face with the sleeve of the old wool peacoat of mine she was wearing. "I'm not pregnant. Where did you get that notion?" She gave me a withering look. No one outside of our immediate families was supposed to have known about the pregnancy.

Howie peered down at me and smirked. "Ha. Dude, seriously? 'She can't wait to have my baby.' You made that shit up?"

Blood rushed to my ears. Better to let Howie believe he'd been lied to than crack this rotten egg of private grief all over the beer aisle.

"Pathetic," Howie said.

Becca turned away. She nodded, jaw clenched, arms folded high and tight across her chest. Yep, I was dead meat. I pushed the cart away from Howie and steered toward the checkout lanes.

"I can't believe you actually blabbed that to him," she said.

"Well, only sort of. I did and I didn't. I told him, but I didn't like, *tell him* tell him. Not seriously. I mean, I just said it to get him off my case because he was being a dick about you. I'd probably have said it even if you weren't pregnant."

"I see."

We found an open lane and she slammed a cabbage onto the conveyor belt. We both hated cabbage, but she'd read somewhere that cold cabbage leaves stuffed in her bra would help dry up her milk when it came in.

"Um. I think I left my wallet under the front seat. Did you bring any cash?"

"Uh-uh. I took my cash and cards out of my purse before Detroit so I wouldn't have to worry about them at the hospital. Go grab your wallet. And hurry. This line's not getting any shorter."

My Converse slid on the mix of rain and snow covering the asphalt in the parking lot. Stupid charade. I should have just told her the truth. I paused to light a smoke and headed across the lot to the Land Cruiser. Everything was covered in a silvery layer of slush, but that didn't hide the fact that Howie's Dodge Ram was parked right behind us like a hunk of American cheese with freezer burn. He may not have been a stalker, but he sure had a habit of showing up at the damnedest times. Shivering in my wet sweatshirt, I sucked my cigarette down as fast as my lungs could stand it. There was no way to pay for the food unless I drove home and got Becca's money, and the store was about to close. I tossed my cigarette butt into the slush and headed inside to the checkout lane where Becca was already unloading our groceries.

"I couldn't find it," I said. "Must be at Ellie's. I'm really sorry. I guess I'm a dipshit." The harder I was on myself, the easier she'd go on me. I pulled my six-pack of Natty off the conveyor belt and shoved it under the shopping cart, then started reloading the other groceries into the cart. "Why don't you go sit down? Take it easy. I'll put the stuff back."

"I'm fine," she said through gritted teeth. She tossed her Pecan Sandies into the cart, then her package of super maxi pads, and the bottles of ibuprofen and vitamin B that were supposed to help with her recovery. She grabbed the box of Fiddle Faddle, but before she

177

lobbed that into the cart Howie squeezed past us in line and handed his credit card to the cashier.

"Keep checking out. I got this."

"Howie, no," Becca said. "I can't let you do that."

"Don't be a goof. I know you're good for it."

"But—"

"Honestly Crowe, you look like you been rode wet and put
away hard. I'm trying to help. You know what they say. One good
turn diverts another." He winked at the cashier. "Besides, Cassie
here doesn't want to have to put all of your stuff away. Just take it.
Pay me back whenever."

The shoppers in line behind us burst into applause. One man
said, "C'mon, lady, accept the kindness."

"You can always pay him back, dear," said an old woman in a
knit cap.

"I don't give a crap what she does, long as this damned line
gets moving," said a guy in coveralls with a trio of rug rats in tow.

Howie. What an operator. But if swallowing my pride meant
pain reliever, vitamins and comfort food for Becca, what choice did
I have? I nodded at the cashier, then at Howie. "Thanks, brother."

Howie looked to the ceiling and shook his head.

29

Not for You

Ellie • Detroit, Mich. • Friday, Dec. 1, 2006

Reece had left that morning for an overnight conference. Without even consulting me, he and his mom had decided I should go Christmas shopping with her and have a late lunch someplace nice. I'd have rather stayed home embroidering and watching daytime talk shows. I didn't have any maternity clothes that were suitable for a nice restaurant. Mostly I wore baggy football jerseys and sweats I scavenged from Reece's bottom drawer, or awkward cast-offs from the thrift store. I never scored any vintage-chic maternity clothes. Everything was ten-year-old Kmart humiliation.

I dug around in the spare closet up in the loft and found a royal blue dashiki Reece had bought at the Ann Arbor art fair because he'd gotten baked and forgot that he's an accountant. I cinched it in back with a banana clip and paired it with black maternity leggings, little red ankle boots, and a red ribbon to tame my hair. Marjorie would judge, but I loved my full-on Bohemian earth mama outfit.

Dragging around the malls with Reece's mom was boring, but *someplace nice* ended up being 42° North in the Ren Cen, the restaurant Saint worked at. I'd never been there before, although I'd heard plenty about it from Saint. Thanks to his inside information, I'd be all set if they needed me to bus some tables.

My tailbone still hurt when I sat down, but as long as I scooted to the edge of the chair to keep the pressure off of it, I could stand it for a while. I didn't dare complain in front of Marjorie because

Reece and I had agreed not to tell her about the mugging. She was already hypercritical of the area we lived in and anyway, the baby was fine.

Marjorie had on one of those bedazzled velour tracksuits older women wear when they want to fool people into thinking they're making an effort. Her hair was fresh from the salon. I could tell because it was teased up high enough that I could see right through it. And here's what I saw: Saint Wozniak walking straight for our table. He was looking sharp in a crisp white dress shirt, a black vest, dress pants and wingtips. His hair was smoothed back in a tidy ponytail. Everything I missed about him rushed back at me so fast that I gasped. His expressive face. His alarm blasting *Pilate*. The smell of burnt pumpernickel toast. The way he'd try to tiptoe up the stairs in his clunky Doc Martens when he got home late, but would always wake me anyway.

"Good afternoon ladies. I'm Tim, and I'll be taking care of you. May I start you off with a beverage?"

My face flushed. All I could think was, you may start me off with some Thai stick and finish me off with a slice of orange, Tim.

"Diet Coke. No ice. With a splash of grenadine," Marjorie said.

"I'd like decaf iced tea if you have that," I said.

Saint said, "Sweetened?"

"No thanks."

"With a wedge of lemon?"

"If you insist."

"I'm asking for your preference."

"Yeah, alright, with lemon I guess."

"On the side?"

"Actually, Tim ... could you take that lemon wedge and squeeze every drop of juice into my glass, scoop out any stray seeds and discard the rind wherever it might benefit a passing seagull? That would be my preference."

He jotted a note on his pad. "Very good. Excellent." He set menus in front of us and walked away.

"Goodness. Whatever was that all about?"

I shrugged. "Waiters these days."

"He seemed nervous. I'm sure he's very new at this."

180

I was pretty sure about that too, since at least until the time he'd moved out he'd been a busboy.

For someone who started every other sentence with *I'm sure*, Marjorie had herself one lengthy debate between the almond-crusted salmon and the chicken cordon bleu. I'd long since chosen a salad, set the menu aside, and had to pick it up again because I'd forgotten the name of it.

"I'm going to visit the little girls' room," she said. "If our waiter comes back, order the chicken for me, would you dear?" She toddled off without waiting for me to respond.

"Your tea with tortured lemon, sans rind." Saint wiped the bottom of a stemmed glass with a white cotton towel and placed it in front of me. He leaned over me and whispered, "You should introduce me to your ma."

"Reece's mom," I whispered back.

"Oh. Oh. Now that explains a few things. Your ma would be much cooler."

I looked into his round eyes and waited for him to remember a certain important fact about my mother.

"Shit. Sorry." He rushed off to the kitchen. I had at least seventy-six burning questions for him. Did he hate me? Was he angry about the rent money? Where was he living? How was his arm healing? Where was Tremor Christ?

Marjorie came back to the table and took her seat. "Did you order for us?"

"Not yet."

"But our waiter was just here. I saw you talking. Why would he refuse to take our order?"

I unfolded the linen napkin and spread it over the round ball of my belly. "He was just delivering our drinks. He never refused anything."

"I'm sure he wanted you to hold off on ordering until he's had a chance to read us the specials. That's a good thing, I suppose. I'm having second thoughts about the chicken. That salmon sounds good too, but there might be a third option. What are you having?"

"The spinach salad. It has candied pecans, dried cranberries and some fancy kind of cheese. Maybe gorgonzola?"

I was really looking forward to it. My all-day/all-night morning sickness had stopped abruptly after the mugging. Apparently, my body had decided enough was enough.

"No, no. Soft cheeses are off the menu when you're pregnant. You're risking Listeria. And please tell me you're eating a little red meat these days. My grandbaby needs plenty of protein and iron."

The woman knew I was a vegetarian, and I knew it was perfectly safe to gestate without eating any meat, red or otherwise. I picked up the menu and pretended to reconsider just to avoid arguing. I wanted my spinach salad, damn it.

"Reece tells me you've been toying around with the notion of a homebirth," she said.

Like I hadn't already decided on that. I was in the process of securing a portable tub for a home water birth. All I had left to do was put together my official birth plan. Reece had been going along with me on all of it, so I'd have to assume *toying with the notion* was Marjorie's spin.

"I've done my research. You'd be surprised how safe—"

"Look at you. You're only four months along and you already look like a tick about to burst. I'm sure my grandchild is going to be strapping, just like his daddy. I will tell you this, I thank God every day that I had an epidural with Reece. He was eleven pounds, nine ounces."

"Wow. He was a real whopper."

I pictured newborn Reece catching a bus home from the hospital in a striped polo shirt and a diaper, and frying up some corned beef hash and eggs over easy.

"Well, then you can see why homebirth with a LeFanch boy is the worst idea ever. I wouldn't hesitate to call it child abuse." She subjected me to a sickly sweet smile. "You're risking my grandchild's health and I won't stand for it."

"Boy?" I wasn't finding out the gender, so this was news to me. I'd get to her child abuse accusation in a minute. Or maybe not. You don't throw phrases like that around with someone who's been in the system. But if I tried to mount a defense, things would turn ugly fast. A homebirth didn't mean I was courting disaster for my gigantic, egg-frying baby. It's not like women didn't survive labor before hospitals were invented.

"You're carrying low. I'm sure it's a boy."

Saint came back, read us the specials and took our order. When he was finished jotting it down he said, "Did I hear 'boy'?"

"We're not finding out the sex," I said.

"I'm sure that it's a boy." Marjorie snatched her glass and took a gulp to emphasize her certainty, sloshing Diet Coke down the front of her velour jacket.

Saint raised an eyebrow at me. "More tea?"

"Sure."

I needed to talk to him so bad, but all I could do was sit awkwardly while he filled my glass with tea that he poured sideways from a stainless steel pitcher.

I waited until our lunches were served and Marjorie had just shoved in a big forkful of chicken cordon bleu to announce, "If it is a boy, we're not circumcising him."

Her eyes bulged and she spat her mouthful of food into her napkin. She took a gulp of her drink, miraculously managing not to spill it on herself this time. "Where ever do you get these crazy ideas? A boy needs to match his father."

"Why? So they can put on tuxedo jackets and bow ties, and go out together bare-assed without their penises clashing?"

"I'm shocked at you. At this. Just shocked."

"Think about it. They're not going to match anyway. Reece has got full-on man junk, pubes and all. This baby, if it's even a boy, is going to have bald little baby junk. By the time he's got anything more than that, let's hope they've learned to keep their pants on around each other."

Marjorie's face flushed. "I'd rather not picture Reece's ... good lord. I don't know why he thought this luncheon was a good idea."

"Yeah, me neither." I stuffed some salad in my mouth. That gorgonzola cheese was fabulous.

"I'm relieved you're not planning to breastfeed," she said. "I don't want my grandson developing any inappropriate fixations."

I could not swallow my mouthful of salad fast enough. As a matter of fact, I was totally planning to breastfeed. It was a marvel that Reece had turned out as well as he had, being raised by this old bat. I got my food down and said, "Oh, so you must have nursed Reece until he was three or four then, if his fixation on breasts is any indication."

"You're not being very nice," she said. "I'm just trying to help you, mother-to-mother. I've given birth a few times myself and raised quite a remarkable little brood. I know you don't have a mother figure. I thought perhaps I could fill in some of that gap for you. But it turns out I can lead a know-it-all filly to water but I can't make her drink."

"I'm sorry. I get that you're trying to help. It's just that, well, you had your turn in life to give birth and raise kids the way you saw fit, but this is my turn. I need to do things in my own way."

"We may just have to agree to disagree then," she said.

I didn't think I had ever asked her for anything more than that.

"But you will have that old bus towed out of the yard to make room for my grandchild to have a proper play structure."

My God. This old bag did not know when to quit. Get rid of the Yield bus. She had some kind of nerve to say that to me, like that bus wasn't my only hard asset. My everything. Like it was some broken down hulk when in truth it ran just fine. Now I was getting paranoid that it might have been Reece's idea. He always was a fair-weather Pearl Jam fan. A baby would be just the excuse he'd need to insist I get my bus cleared out of the yard.

"Can you excuse me?"

I hustled off to the bathroom and splashed cold water on my cheeks. I immediately regretted doing so when I realized there were no paper towels in stock and the only way to dry my dripping face was under an air dryer.

That's where I was, bent over with my face under the hand dryer and my hair going all frizapalooza, the red ribbon falling to the floor, the banana clip popping off the back of my dashiki and turning it into a tent, when Saint walked into the ladies room.

30

I Got Id

Clive • Belknap Township, Mich. • Friday, Dec. 1, 2006

The door to the nursery had been shut tight for a week. Becca was taking another of her long grief/depression naps. It killed me seeing her like this. She'd always been, well, not exactly sunny but very bright. Very *on*. Curious. Opinionated. Lively. But leaving Louise behind at the hospital had turned Becca fragile as a drained eggshell.

The only death in the family she'd experienced before Louise was her dad's. I tried to relate to her about losing my brothers. I was eight when they died, and they were only two and four years old. For me, their deaths were akin to a parent losing a child, with all the guilt that entails no matter what the circumstances, and also the loss of who they would have become. My brothers would be 19 and 21 now, young men with their whole lives to look forward to.

Losing Louise Clover was like grieving my brothers all over again, but this time with the heartache of seeing Becca going through it, too. Unfortunately, revealing my experiences with loss just made Becca cry more. I tried to stick to the practical aspects: making sure she ate every day and drank enough water to replace her tears, fielding her business calls, keeping the house neat, and just being around for her.

"What should we do about the nursery?" I'd asked that morning while she was busy staring at the kitchen ceiling with her mug of tea turning cold.

"I don't ... I can't ..." She shook her head. "Figure it out. I've made enough momentous decisions lately. I need a long break from decision making."

ᑫ

During her nap, I decided to pack up the nursery. She appreciated decisiveness, and I figured it might help to put things back to how they were before this pregnancy fiasco. I went into the nursery and quietly closed the door behind me. I folded the bedding and put it on the highest shelf in the cedar closet. I placed Tigger, Piglet and Pooh on top of the bedding, allowing them to grin heavenward. I quietly disassembled the crib, the changing table, and the platform rocker and returned them to their original boxes. Last, I rolled up the densely piled nursery rug and shoved it into the thick plastic sheath it had arrived in. On the way down the basement stairs, it thumped behind me like a dead body. Just in case the basement leaked, I stacked the boxed furniture on top of a pallet. We'd want this stuff to stay nice. We'd need it again someday, I hoped.

I hauled a crate of my art supplies up the stairs, grabbed a can of Natty from the fridge and returned to the empty room. It still felt like a nursery. Christopher Robin and Piglet marched across the 100 Acre Wood wallpaper border. I could have peeled it off, but that would have seemed like doing violence to the room. Everything else I'd just done was only storing things away for some day in the future when we'd bring home a baby we could keep.

I slid down the wall to the floor and drank my beer, picking at the tiny chevrons of oil paint that had been hidden beneath the rug. The pattern matched the soles of my Converse. Tangerine. Red. Cream. Orange. The Smiths, *Louder than Bombs*. That pouting beauty was the first painting I did after moving into this house. I'd listened to the album endlessly while working on it. Those chevrons of oil paint were traces of me, dancing alone, free of LuCretia, free of Detroit, free of so much grief and heavy responsibility. I'd not even met Becca yet. Now *Louder than Bombs* hung over the stone fireplace in her brother's bed & breakfast, and my freedoms were a distant memory.

I'd started my Retro Replicas business a little cynically. My painting skills allowed me to create perfect copies, and I knew Baby Boomers and Gen-Xers were where the money was at. I'd dig up popular older albums at garage sales and thrift shops mostly, as they were a lot cheaper there than at vintage record stores or online. On a whim, I'd tried including the natural wear marks, stains or faded spots on a given record jacket. The funny thing was those "flawed" paintings sold fastest of all, and pretty soon the natural wear of a well-loved album became the signature motif of my work.

Painting album cover replicas had an unintended effect on me: it increased exponentially my appreciation for classic rock— something I'd snubbed growing up during the grunge era. There is nothing quite like listening to the same Steppenwolf, Jefferson Airplane, Hendrix, Stones or Pink Floyd album over and over, deep cuts and all, for several days straight, and having to take the time to flip the LP over, to make you appreciate genre-bending, trippy, psychedelic blues rock from way back when.

Inspired, I carried up my easels, worktable, stool, canvases, turntable, and crate of albums from the makeshift studio in the basement. There had never been enough natural light down there anyway, and lack of it had really sucked away my creative drive. I rolled up the window shades and late afternoon sunlight slanted in. Perfection. I set everything up and started sketching out a mock-up for my next piece, spinning *Quadrophenia* and grooving along to *I Am One*.

"Whoa. What the?" Becca stood in the doorway, a blanket wrinkle on her cheek.

"Like it?"

"You couldn't get rid of the nursery fast enough, huh?"

"You can't be serious. You shut the door to this room the minute we got back from Detroit. I asked you this morning what you wanted to do with it. I got everything packed up and stored really nice. I did it for you."

"Our baby is gone for one week and you've already reclaimed your art studio. For me. I see."

"Well, it was—whether you believe me or not. I'm trying to be supportive, and you're looking for the worst possible motive in everything I do. I just want to get our lives back on track."

"My milk hasn't even dried up yet."

"I'm sorry, Bec. I thought it would help you if I packed that stuff away."

She tapped her finger against the ceramic switch plate shaped like Pooh's hunny pot. "You forgot to get rid of this."

"I didn't get rid of anything. It's all put away. Nice and neat for when … if … when we decide we want to try again. And I left the hunny pot and the border because, I don't know, I really didn't want to erase her." I couldn't articulate the rest. I felt that Louise Clover would always be a presence in this room, and she'd watch over our future children. Until then, she'd be right there with me while I painted.

"You didn't even want her," Becca said.

"That's not fair."

The phone rang, thank God, and she stormed off to answer it.

She was lashing out at me. I understood that. Ellie had done it for a time after our brothers died, but not for long because we'd needed each other too much. Fine then. I'd be the person it was safe for Becca to dump on if that was what she needed right now. Not my favorite role, but one I'd lived through enough times. Grief had an anger stage and Becca was steaming toward it at two-hundred miles per hour. She'd come around eventually.

Becca returned to the studio red-faced and scowling. She clutched the cordless phone against her chest. "So, who's this Lu-Cretia person?"

No way. I'd never given LuCretia my home number. There was no way Ellie would have given them to her. That couldn't be my ex on the line. This had to be Reece or Ellie trying to pull a gag that was falling horribly flat. I held my hand out for the phone.

"Oh, she already hung up on me." Becca gave the phone a dirty look. "She didn't believe you were married, seeing as how she saw you the other night and you didn't bother to mention it."

It was official. I was toast. There was no graceful way to bull-shit my way around this. I'd been kidding myself. I never should have asked Ellie to pull over when I saw LuCretia. Becca deserved the truth. Might as well take my lumps while she was already in a foul temper.

"Look," I said, shoving my hands into my pockets. "She's an old ex-girlfriend. I've told you about her before, but maybe not her name."

"The redheaded heroin addict."

It shamed me to hear her say that aloud. Becca boiled down LuCretia—in all of her fucked up complexity of raw talent, honest joy, soul-crushing sorrow, and fragile beauty—to a pathetic carica-ture: Jessica Rabbit smoking black tar, someone any idiot should have known to avoid. It's too easy to dismiss a relationship based on what ended it. I couldn't blame Becca for that, though. I'd never given her much more to go on.

"It was just one of those weird moments. Ellie got turned around on a construction detour coming back from our old foster family's house. We got lost. LuCretia happened to be walking by, so we stopped for a second to say hi. That's all it was. I never gave her our number and I have no idea how she found it."

"I do. She told me."

"She said who gave it to her?" Whoever it was, I was ready to kick their ass up around their ears.

"It was inside your wallet. Which she has."

Oh, shit. Shit, shit, shit.

"I'm not sure I want to know how someone you say 'hi' to ends up with your stinkin' wallet. But you might want to ask her if she plans on giving it back." She thrust the phone at me. It was hot from her hand.

31

Dissident

Ellie • Detroit, Mich. • Friday, Dec. 1, 2006

Detroit Ellie," Saint said over the drone of the hand dryer. His voice echoed off the tile walls of 42° North's fancy ladies room.

I stood up straight and finished drying my face with the sleeve of my dashiki. "His mother is killing me. She's absolutely positively killing me. I can't take another second. She thinks just because it's her grandchild she can dictate how the rest of my life is going to go, right down to whether or not I can eat gorgonzola cheese."

"If it even *is* her grandchild." He scooped my banana clip off the floor and handed it back to me.

"Saint. God. We really have to talk."

"I know. You totally forgot to ask me which two members of Pearl Jam I'd want backing me up in a fistfight."

"Too easy. Eddie and Jeff."

He shook his head.

"Matt-Cam, 'cause he's tall, and … McCready because he'd swing that ax?"

"Nope."

"I don't know. Boom Gaspar?"

"Uh-uh. Stony. All by himself."

He was going to have to explain that one. And I'd have to look past the fact that he'd broken the rules of his own pop quiz by only picking one band member.

"Why Stone?"

"'Cause I'm a lover, not a fighter. We'd walk away from the fight arm in arm, and grab a beer, and go find some flowers to smell and shit."

I loved it. I could not reach the bottom of how much I'd missed Saint Wozniak.

"Here's one for you," I said. I was about to ask if someone's all-time favorite song is *I Got Shit*, are they actually a Pearl Jam fan or a Neil Young fan. Except right then, the baby decided to kick me for the first time ever. I'd felt sensations that were like a fish swimming against the side of a fishbowl, but never a full-fledged kick. I put my hands on my stomach.

"What? What's your question?" Saint asked.

"It's, um."

The baby thumped at my insides again.

"Hey. Are you OK?"

I nodded. I didn't know if I should tell him. Probably not. What could I say? This baby—who is most assuredly not yours—just reacted to your presence by kicking me for the first time ever.

"Look, if they catch me in here, they'll can me. I just wanted to say..." he reached for my hands and squeezed them, eyes closed. "That's as much detail as I can give you for now."

He left. I leaned against the bathroom wall and covered my face with my hands.

൚

Marjorie pulled her Lincoln Town Car in front of our house to drop me off. She looked at our place and sighed. "He used to live in such a nice area."

I don't know why she had to be all dramatic about that. As Detroit goes, Corktown is pretty chill. It's old, sure, and a little depressing with the abandonment of the old Tiger Stadium, and maybe the houses on our street were packed super close, but it was hardly Mack Avenue and Helen. Anyway, I wasn't the one she should have been complaining to. It was Reece's ex-wife who got the house in Warren.

"I intended to do this over lunch, but we got derailed by a few things." She unclasped her oversized patent leather handbag, took out a gray velvet box and handed it to me.

I cracked it open. Tucked inside was a tarnished ring with some kind of yellowish-green stone, so pale that I wasn't sure if it was supposed to be a citrine or a peridot.

"This was passed down from my Aunt Faye. I'm asking you to wear it because, well, considering your condition it will look a lot more respectable."

I tried to put this as politely as possible. "I'm not super comfortable with that."

"You really would do well to care a bit more about what people think, especially if you're going to be the mother of my grandbaby. Not everything is about your comfort level. You should think of the baby."

I snapped the box closed and set it on the dashboard. "Look Mrs. LeFanch. Marjorie. If and when Reece and I decide to get married, I'll wear whatever engagement ring he either buys for me or we choose together. I'm not ashamed that I love your son, or that we live together, or that I'm pregnant. I'm not the product of a married couple. And the truth is, that's been the absolute least of my problems in this world."

"It's one thing for you and Maurice to choose to live in sin as adults. It's quite another to drag my grandchild into that lifestyle. I didn't raise my son that way."

"Oh, so you raised him to pretend he's engaged?"

I left the ring box on the dashboard and waddled into the house.

32

Trouble

Clive • Rogers City, Mich. • Monday, Dec. 4, 2006

The automatic teller machine refused to cooperate. It spit out Becca's debit card at me. *Insufficient Funds* flashed on the screen. Impossible. Right before we'd gone to Detroit, we'd transferred $2,400, all but $300 of our savings, into checking to cover the bare-minimum hospital fees. And we'd had a cushion of about $500 in there. I shoved the card back into the slot and entered the PIN again. I'd have to settle for getting by without pocket cash. This time instead of trying to withdraw $120, I punched in only the $80 we owed Howie for groceries.

Insufficient Funds.

I was sweating now despite the wind screaming off the city marina and whipping my hair into my eyes. I punched buttons until the machine printed out our account information.

Checking: $0.00

Savings: $0.00.

Available Balance: $0.00

I glared in disbelief at the ugly pile of zeroes on the flimsy paper rattling in the wind. LuCretia had cleaned us out. There was no other explanation.

When my wallet went missing I hadn't bothered to cancel my debit card because I'd thought it was safe with old Mrs. Marconi. Even when I'd found out that LuCretia had lifted my wallet, I figured she didn't have my PIN. But she was clever. She'd known my old PIN, which was my street address backward. This one was my new street address backward, and that number was right there on my driver's license. And yes, I'm every bit as stupid as I look in my license photo.

If the hospital hadn't already cashed the check we'd written them, it would bounce. Then I'd have to tell my grieving wife that thanks to my misbegotten moment of sentimentality, my addict ex had made off like the Grinch with our first Christmas. And there was also the fact that if LuCretia had grabbed the entire $3,200, it was more than enough to fund her into a death spiral. One hello and one hug. Because of me, she might have OD'd already.

When I fuck up, I really fuck up.

I climbed into the Land Cruiser and dug around until I found a piece of paper with the hospital's phone number on it. By the time I got through to the finance department, I was nearly homicidal from listening to Kenny G on hold. I explained that there was a problem with our bank account and I needed to know if our check had cleared.

The clerk put me on hold again. When she came back on the line she said, "It's right here, safe and sound."

"You mean it's not cashed?"

"No. It's right here. It's safe." Her voice was all reassuring smiles.

"You don't understand. It's no good. Someone stole my debit card and cleaned out my account."

"You could put a stop payment on this check and send us another."

That was the dumbest thing I'd ever heard. I re-explained the situation until the clerk pretended to understand. I offered to pay with Becca's MasterCard since I'd already reported mine as lost.

"Are you Rebecca?" The clerk asked after we'd gone through all of the steps of the transaction.

I just rolled with it, feeling ridiculous with my deep voice. "Yeah, yeah, yeah. I'm Rebecca."

That, and the three-digit code on the back of the card, satisfied her identity requirements.

I fumbled to light a cigarette, ended up smoking two back to back, and got my ass on the phone with the bank. Sure enough, our checking and savings were emptied out via cash withdrawals at ATMs across Detroit. There were also a few hundred dollars in expenditures at the Atheneum Hotel and Fishbone's. LuCretia always did have a thing for Greektown.

"We'll cancel your card and send you a new one. That will take a week to ten days. If our investigation proves you didn't make these purchases, we may be able to return the funding to your account. But I should warn you that can take months. Sir, do you have any idea who might have stolen your card?"

I considered ratting LuCretia out, but there was no chance they'd recover a penny from her.

"Nope. No idea."

"You should file a police report."

I thought it over. Plenty of legal trouble had come LuCretia's way as a consequence of her using. The anxiety and shame only fueled her drug abuse. The money was gone, Becca was going to fillet me like a prize trout, and if LuCretia got wind of me filing a police report she'd take it as me paying her special attention. I needed to cut my losses, clean up this mess, and keep moving forward.

୬

When I got home, I found Becca stripped down to her waist and leaning awkwardly over the bathroom sink filled with hot water, soaking her milk-engorged breasts. Cubby was curled around her feet. Not the best time to bring up that, thanks to my idiocy, we were broke. I draped a fresh towel over her back to keep her warm, then rubbed her shoulders.

"I'm so sorry," I said.

"I just keep reminding myself that this part is temporary. Did you pay Howie back?"

"He wasn't home. But I will, I promise."

"I don't want to do Christmas this year. At all. Can we just skip it?"

What a perfectly timed gift. "Sure. Whatever you need."

"I don't want to see Ellie either."

"Really?"

"She's pregnant. I'm not. I can't deal with seeing her like that. Nothing personal. She's been nice to me about everything. But her pregnancy feels like a huge slap in the face to me now. I mean, she takes magic mushrooms, but I'm the one whose baby is all messed up? It's completely unfair."

I didn't think Ellie had really taken mushrooms. I happened to know that she despised them.

"The jury is still out on Ellie's baby," I said. "I don't think she's done much in the way of prenatal testing. I'm pretty concerned, you know, with our luck and everything."

"You guys and your Rafferty doom. That doesn't make me feel any better."

There was no way to tell her that nothing was going to make her feel any better, not for a long time. No way in hell I could bring up that we were broke. And since she'd canceled Christmas, maybe I didn't need to just yet.

"You can go down and see Ellie if you want. I'm not stopping you," she said.

Later, she went to her shop to deal with some paperwork. I got on the computer and turned my Retro Replicas web store into one big classic rock, punk and grunge fire sale. It didn't matter anymore how many endless hours I'd spent painting *Pink Moon, Abraxis, Aqualung, Fragile, Who's Next, Hunky Dory, Never Mind the Bollocks, Raw Power, Siamese Dream, Fly By Night, Toys in the Attic, Blood Sugar Sex Magik, Outlandos de Amour, London Calling, Nothing's Shocking, Highway to Hell,* or *Nevermind.* Everything had to go. I didn't care if all I recouped was the cost of oil paint and canvas. I had to get some money flowing back into our bank accounts before Becca tried to use her debit card again.

CR

A week later, we were watching reruns of *Mystery Science Theatre 3000* in the dark, and drinking Natty. Sometime after midnight, Becca conked out against my chest. I set her beer can on the table, muted the TV, and listened to her breathe. The lights were dim and snow fell gently outside of the picture window. Cubby snoozed at the far end of the couch. There was something extra peaceful about Christmastime minus the usual trappings of decorations and social expectations. Things were settling down with Becca and me. We weren't out of the woods, but there was a clearing, and maybe a path.

The phone rang. I grabbed the receiver before it could wake her. Only Ellie ever called this late, when she couldn't sleep and figured, with eerie accuracy, that I was lying awake too.

"Elsworth," I whispered.

"Uh-uh, Rafferty, it's me. How you doin', old friend?"

Shit. Fuck. Damn. LuCretia. The come-hither croak of her voice pissed me off. With Becca sleeping right under my chin, I muted my anger to a whisper. "Steal my wallet, clean out my bank accounts and now you want to know how I'm doing?"

"Aw, you know me. Nothin' personal."

"Unless you're calling to ask where to send me a check for $3,200, I've got nothing to say to you."

"Rafferty. You know I'm sorry. I'm always like sorry, sorry, sorry—right? I've been trying to get my shit straight, but I'm in a jam. I owe some people. It's not for junk, I swear. Can you help?"

She was that audacious. I'd have been astonished except this was standard operating procedure for her. *Oh, did I fuck you over? How cute of me. Here, let me fuck you over some more.*

"Get into another twelve-step," I said. "Go to NA. Work your program. There. That's all the help you're getting from me."

"Rafferty, come on. Don't be that way. You used to understand me. It was just a little money. I'd do the same for you."

Just a little money. To cover my grieving wife's medical expenses, to pay back her ex for groceries after being completely humiliated at Glen's Market, to keep the roof over our heads. Just a little money. Golly, how greedy of me.

"Woman, you'll be dead before you're thirty."

"Ha. Aren't you some kind of fortune teller. Here I am, thirty-one and living the dream."

Crap. I always forgot she was older than me. I'd felt older than everyone else my whole life.

"I'm not gonna die. I'll get clean sometime. This just isn't a good week for me. Why you gotta harsh on my vibe, Rafferty? Let me get fucked up in peace."

She'd become someone I hated who was trying to kill someone I used to love.

"Hey, you're the one who called me. You can do whatever you want, just don't make my wife and me pay for it."

I hung up. Talking to her was like being vomited on. God, I needed a cigarette. I put my nose in Becca's satiny hair and breathed in the lavender scent of her shampoo until my heart stopped thudding in my ears. She was warm and solid against my chest. The two of us would get by somehow. We were all that mattered. We'd stick together and be just fine here in our no-Christmas Whoville. The rest of the world could fuck right off, especially LuCretia.

33

Let My Love Open the Door

Ellie • Detroit, Mich. • Friday, Dec. 15, 2006

You don't answer the doorbell when you're home alone late at night in Corktown. At least, I don't. My first impulse was to hide in the closet with a baseball bat until morning when Reece was due home, but I chanced it and peered out the bedroom window. On the street below, the roof of Saint's Tracker glittered with ice. He rang the bell again.

I hustled down the stairs, careful not to slip in my mismatched socks. Saint. He would have to show up when I was dressed like last week's laundry: stretched out maternity leggings, a ripped Lions jersey, and my hair all in a kerfuffle.

By the time I'd unfastened the locks, Saint was headed down the front walkway toward his car.

"Hey!"

He turned around, that scarf billowing in the wind, hair tucked behind one ear. "Hey there yourself, Detroit Ellie." He ambled toward the house. "Did I wake you? Got out of band practice kind of late." He checked his wrist, although he never wore a watch.

The damp wind slashed through to my skin. "Just come in."

He leaned against the door jamb. "Is your man gone? I don't see his Buick."

"He's at some conference thingy. Come inside, I'm freezing." I grabbed the ends of his scarf, reeled him into the vestibule and pushed the door closed. "What's up?"

He shoved his hands into his back pockets and leaned against the doorframe. "Seeing you the other day, it just brought up some stuff that needs to get said, you know?"

Oh, did I ever.

"So, get in here and lay it on me."

He followed me into the living room and dove onto his usual side of the sectional like he was part of the paisley pattern. "First off, I'm sorry I left the way I did. I should have talked to you."

"Like Reece gave you a choice."

"That's just it. That's what I wanted to say. All that crap, the bad feelings, it was strictly between me and your man. I was never mad at you, not for a second. We're still cool, yeah?"

I wanted to cradle this moment in the palm of my hand forever. "Yeah, yeah. We're coolio. Always. I mean, you're my friend."

A relieved smile broke over his face. "I was afraid to text or call or whatever because, well, he was so pissed that day. Still, I figured you'd get hold of me—maybe after things blew over. When you never did, I don't know, I thought you took his side. I mean, in your condition that's understandable. You can't just go exploding your relationship. And I figured you might be mad too about what happened to that table with your Stone Gossard stuff getting trashed. I felt bad about that."

"You know, you just might be the only person on this planet who's ever agreed with me that Stony is the sacred heart of Pearl Jam."

"Nah, we can't be the only ones who think that. Anyway, I'm sorry. I should have put Stone's shrine back together before I split. It seemed like bad karma leaving him face down on the floor like that. I mean, it was Stone."

I nodded.

"But then when you showed up at the restaurant. Your face? When you saw me? I wish I had a picture of that," he said.

I sat sort of side-saddle on the sectional. "I didn't get in touch because I didn't know how to tell you what happened to me and what happened to your rent money the night you moved out. Here, just look." I lifted my football jersey and tugged the top of my leggings aside to reveal some of my bruises. Although fading to yellowish green, they were still plenty dramatic. "I got mugged in Midtown walking home from Mr. Salty's. They took your rent money. All of it."

He stood up, his hands balled into fists. "No! I swear I will torture to death whoever did this to you. Was he armed? Are you sure you're OK?"

"I'm fine. No weapons. He slugged me a few times, roughed me up and shoved me down." I readjusted my clothes. "The worst of it now is a bruised tailbone, but that'll heal over time."

"Hit your stomach. Damn, girlfriend. That's evil."

"I'm fine now. Really."

"But your baby."

"My midwife says the baby should be fine."

Hadn't he heard what I said about his money?

"That rent you prepaid me, right before you moved out? I was going to give it back to you, but it was in my bag when I got mugged. It's gone. I'm really sorry. I filed a police report, but you know how that goes. I'll pay you soon as I can, but I'm not even back to work yet."

"Don't worry about that. I'll get by. I can't believe someone would do that to you."

"They don't call it Detroit for nothing."

He wandered over to the turntable and put on Pearl Jam *Live at Benaroya Hall*. I went into the kitchen and rummaged around in Reece's Christmas goody tins. He was hardly ever home, but whenever he was, he'd bake like a fiend. I found the peanut-butter buckeyes, put some on a plate and poured a tall glass of milk over ice for Saint. I brought it all into the living room on a tray.

"I really didn't come here for that money," he said.

"Oh, I see. You're here to ask me … if McCready can play a guitar solo behind his head, shouldn't he try writing a harder one?"

"Nope!" He laughed. "If you can play behind your head, you can play behind your head. Follow? So no, he's not ripping us off with easy solos."

"You would defend him."

"We guitarists stick together."

"Fair enough." I popped a buckeye into my mouth. It was a peanut-butter-sugar-chocolate wonder.

"I've sort of got a small problem," he said. "You remember Nicki?"

I shook my head.

"Yeah, you know her. She's been here a million times. With the tulip tattoo? Kicks my ass at guitar hero, but still gets beat by Lizzie?"

"Oh yeah, Tulip, sure."

"After Reece booted me out, she said I could stay at her place. For me, it was pure practicality, you know? I paid half the rent but I didn't have to be on a lease or anything. Well, she was always a cool chick and we had this understanding. But then after I'm living there, she starts referring to me as her fiancé."

"Oh, wow. That's heavy."

"Tell me about it. So we've been fighting about that. And the neighbors don't like Tremor Christ. He hasn't even done anything wrong. But her apartment complex is technically No Pets, so they reported us to the landlord. She doesn't deserve to get evicted on my account. I needed to get out of there. Last night I grabbed all my stuff and we slept in the Tracker."

"You and Tremor Christ?"

"He kept me warm." He chugged some milk and wiped his mouth with his sleeve. "I was wondering if I could park it in front of your house tonight. I'll be gone by morning."

"How does that work? Where do you shower? Do you leave the dog in the car all day?"

"The gym has showers. My ma has a fenced yard and Tremor Christ can hang out there while I'm working."

"It's getting pretty cold out for that," I said.

"Yeah, I worry about him, but I'm kind of stuck."

"I'm not talking about the dog, I'm talking about you. Sleeping in your car. That's crazy. You have to stay here. It's the least I can do. You've got three months here you've already paid for."

"But Reece."

"Yeah, he's going to have a hissy. I know. But that will be between me and him."

204

"No. It's too much tension for you. I'm not putting you on the spot like that."

"Let me worry about me. And Reece. You're staying here. Now go get your stuff."

When had I ever let Reece stand in the way of me doing the right thing? He'd get over it. He always did.

34

In My Tree

Ellie • Detroit, Mich. • Wednesday, Dec. 20, 2006

Reece never said a word to me about Saint's return. The two had gone out to the Yield bus and talked for a long time right after Saint moved back in. Neither of them seemed very happy about that conversation, and they'd both refused to tell me what was said. After that, Reece treated Saint like ugly wallpaper he was choosing to ignore. His refusal to acknowledge him was awkward as hell. But if it bothered Saint any, he never let it show.

When I tried to talk to Reece about it or explain my reasoning, he'd just say something like, "I wonder what's up with Peter Criss these days."

Whenever I brought it up with Saint, he'd say, "That's between you and your old man."

Every December we went to the pre-cut lot and got a balsam fir, but this year Reece had dragged home a hand-me-down artificial Christmas tree from his parents' house. Originally it had been white, but age had yellowed it to the color of a faded cat pee stain. It had several bare spots where some of the branches had fallen out, and it smelled like mothballs. Putting ornaments on the damned thing would be like putting jewelry on a wildebeest, so it stood at one end of the sectional, naked and pathetic, for a full week. I was much too busy reading the book Abigail had given me, *Spiritual Midwifery*—and writing my birth plan—to bother with Marjorie LeFanch's reject tree.

Reece gave up waiting for me to decorate the tree and did it himself. He covered the thing in green lights and MSU Spartan ornaments, then lashed a grinning plastic Sparty figurine to the top.

"What do you think?" he asked.

"It still smells funky. And I don't think Santa Claus is going to appreciate that up-skirt view of Sparty."

After that, Reece brought home a dozen car deodorizers shaped like pine trees and hung them all over his holly-jolly, helly-smelly, pee-colored Sparty tree. Major improvement: it smelled like mothballs with a hint of fake pine. He was inordinately proud of it.

ᛯ

"You still want a real tree?" Saint asked me.

"I don't know. It's too late. If they're not all sold out they're probably dried out."

He smiled. "Nuh-uh. Bundle up, buttercup."

He drove us far out into the suburbs to a real tree farm. It was after dark and snowing. The farm was well lit, with stacked hay bales for kids to climb on, painted plywood Christmas cutouts where families could pose their little kids for pictures with Frosty or Rudolf, a roaring bonfire, and a concession stand that sold sugar cookies and hot chocolate.

In my whole life, I'd never been anywhere like it. I was going to come here every year. I was going to bring my baby here. I was going to cry. The Christmas tree farm validated my decision to go through with my misbegotten pregnancy. I could give this baby so much, and when I did, that would eclipse all of the things I never had. It didn't matter that I hardly had anything of my own beyond the Yield bus, a GED and a job in a pretzel shop. My baby would have a real childhood, and would always feel safe and loved.

"My parents used to take me and Maddie," Saint said, "until they got divorced." He held a red-handled saw in a few different poses like he was preparing for hand-to-hand combat. "What kind of tree do you like?"

"A tall one."

"I mean like, what species."

208

"We usually get a Balsam. So maybe one of those."

"You sure you don't want to try a Frasier fir? They cost a little more but man, so pretty."

Not as pretty as the snow flurries catching in Saint's dark hair. Not as pretty as his jaw framed in that soft, brown scarf embroidered with bittersweet vines.

"You choose," I said. "Whatever you pick, I'll get behind it a hundred percent."

He selected one that was tall, dark and teaming with little pinecones. He got on his knees in the mud to cut it down, dragged it on a sled to the shaking and baling area, carried it on his shoulder to the parking lot and secured it to the roof of the Tracker with lengths of twine. The entire process fascinated me.

"That's my Merry Christmas for you, girlfriend," he said, tying the twine.

"But I didn't get you anything."

"You put a roof over my head. Don't go pretending that hasn't cost you with your man. I'm staying out of it, but I see."

I couldn't talk about Reece with him. I climbed into the Tracker and changed the subject. "If Eddie had been born two days later, would that make him the second coming of Christ?"

"I like it. Pearl Jam as the Father, Eddie as the son and *Vitalogy* as the Holy Ghost."

"*Yield*. *Yield* would be the Holy Ghost."

"*Vitalogy*."

"*Yield*."

"Actually, I'm not sure Eddie can be the son if Stone is the sacred heart," he said. "It doesn't add up."

"Sure he can. Stuff not adding up is what makes a belief into a religion."

☙

The scent of Frasier fir filled the house. We set the natural tree up at the opposite end of the sectional. This blocked the usual path to the kitchen but there really wasn't any other place it would fit. We had to scramble over the sectional to get there, not an easy feat between my pregnant belly and my bruised tailbone, but worth it for a real tree.

I stacked all of my Ten Club Christmas forty-fives on the record player and let them drop into rotation. Most of them weren't what other people would consider Christmas music, but I have never been other people.

Saint helped me put twice as many lights on my fir, making sure it out-glowed Reece's monstrosity. We trimmed it with dozens of antique glass ornaments I'd collected at rummage sales and thrift stores over the years. I added paper chains, origami stars made from last year's wrapping paper, strings of popcorn and cranberries, and cutwork snowflakes. I found a place of honor for my flat brass Pearl Jam Stickman ornament, then Saint topped off the tree with a pair of fuzzy white baby owls tucked in a nest of silver pinecones. I didn't know where he got them, but they were adorable.

Reece hung out on the sectional, pretending to ignore our tree trimming party. He was eating Rice Krispie treats and reading *Spiritual Midwifery*, which I figured was a great thing.

"We should have a New Year's Eve party," I said. I was talking to both of them, but only Saint responded.

"Quadraphonic Space Trip could play."

"Oh my God. We have to do this. Reece, can we?"

He looked up from the book and shrugged. Normally, he was all about a party.

"C'mon. We need a party to throw 2006 out on its rear. It's been such a gloomy, doomy year with getting mugged, and what happened to Clive and Becca."

"And to my arm," Saint added.

"Did somebody fart?" Reece asked. "I thought I heard a fart."

"Reece," I started, but Saint shook his head at me.

"Do whatever you want," Reece said. "You will anyway."

☙

Reece was snuggled down into bed and still reading that book when I waddled up to our room. I was over the ration of shit he'd given me and Saint about the New Year's Eve party. Sometimes

Reece just needed to be contrary, like that was how he was defining himself. There are worse traits, I guess. He looked cute and serious with his reading glasses on, making notes in the margins. I put on my tent of a flannel nightshirt and climbed into bed beside him. My belly was ridiculous. I didn't know how all of this was supposed to wait until my due date. I was barely into the third trimester and already I looked like Shamu. I started rubbing some cocoa butter on my Martian moon map of stretch marks.

"We need to talk this homebirth deal over some more," he said.

"Why? You told me you were fine with it."

He held the book open to a black and white image of a grimacing, naked woman standing up while her bearded partner supported her from behind. A baby's head was emerging from her body. It was truly beautiful.

"This is too real. Something could go really wrong and then what? There's a reason people give birth in hospitals," he said.

"It'll be fine. Abigail will be there and she knows what's up. She's delivered dozens of babies. Maybe hundreds."

"Well, which is it? Dozens or hundreds?"

I didn't know. I loaded more cocoa butter into my palm and started on the western hemisphere.

He closed the book and set it between us. "I feel like you're jeopardizing our baby with irresponsible, feel-good choices that deny the progress of modern medicine."

I was about to check under the blankets because I was pretty sure Mrs. LeFanch was under there somewhere with her hand shoved way up his ass, making his mouth move and throwing her voice.

"This is my baby too," he said. "My family's baby. We should have a say in how a LeFanch comes into this world."

We. Yup, I sure called that one. Meddling Marjorie was all over this.

"Look what happened with Clive and Becca," he added.

"No. No you don't. You can't throw my brother's tragedy onto the burn pile. What happened to their baby didn't have a thing to do with homebirth."

"I know, but—"

"No. I'm not hearing this. I'm working out a solid birth plan. Abigail already told me if anything at all isn't right, she calls an ambulance straight away and I'm transported to the hospital. Homebirth is a sane choice. Its safety record is well documented, and you can Google that up if you don't believe me."

"What about your friend Janice? She works in a maternity ward. You could deliver at her hospital."

My blood pressure shot upward. Not about Janice, she was cool. And even she had said homebirth was probably fine as long as the baby and I were healthy and we had a very experienced midwife. What pissed me off was that Reece knew I'd spent the absolute worst weeks of my life stuck in that hospital, recovering from smoke inhalation as a little girl. I'd been alone there, knowing that my two little brothers had died, knowing that our mother was in jail, wondering exactly what was meant by *ward of the state*, and not knowing when I'd see Clive again. They kept promising me that he was fine, but I knew they were lying. Something being wrong with Clive was not something that could be kept from me. In my heart, I'd known that he'd suffered smoke inhalation too, and worse than I did. I could feel it. It was terrifying. I was never setting foot in that horrid old hospital again, and certainly not to satisfy Marjorie LeFanch's zeal to micromanage my normal biological functions.

I looked him in the eye. *C'mon Reece. Think.*

"What did I—oh. That's right. That place."

I nodded.

"Fair enough. But you could give birth at a different hospital. Maybe a birthing center, where it's supposed to be homier but there's real doctors and stuff."

"No hospital. No birthing center. It's a natural process. I'm a mammal. I was born to do this and I can do it right here at home. Shoo your mother out of your head, read that book more closely, and you'll see that this isn't astrophysics. It's the same thing every cat and dog does, every squirrel living in the crotch of a tree, every mouse between the floorboards. Humans were doing this for a hundred-thousand years before the first hospital was ever built. It's no big deal."

"Yes it is, actually. We're not having a litter of baby squirrels. Maybe we aren't scared enough. Maybe we *should* be scared. This is our child and we should take every possible precaution to make sure he arrives healthy. There's a baby at the very end of this book, and he was born with anencephaly. It's really sad."

I'd read that story, too. Yes, it was sad. But that baby's problem had nothing to do with homebirth. Reece had missed the point that if anything, that baby's homebirth allowed him and his parents more peace than they'd have had in a hospital setting. I wasn't going to let these LeFanches scare me out of what I wanted. I was having a homebirth, damn it, and my baby would be just fine.

If Reece wanted a hospital birth so bad, he could get pregnant himself and deliver his own dang baby at one.

35

Fuckin' Up

With inspiration from the envelope full of pictures Mrs. Marconi had given me, I spent all day putting the finishing touches on my gift for Becca. Sure, we weren't doing Christmas, but she was going to love this. It wasn't dry enough to wrap so I hid it behind *Quadrophenia*, which was still underway.

She'd worked half days all week and swore she wasn't doing any heavy lifting. But I knew her, and I worried. It had only been a month since she'd given birth to Louise. She was still healing. I wished she wasn't working, but there was no arguing that we didn't need the money. Anyway, if not happier, she seemed a little relieved to have something other than grief to occupy her time.

I was making grilled cheese sandwiches and tomato soup for dinner when she came home. She tossed a pile of mail onto the kitchen table, sat down and started baby talking to Cubby. He came over to get his ears scratched. That beagle worshiped her. Cubby and I had common ground there. Even in work boots and Carhartt's, she was exquisite.

"Glad you're home." I kissed her cheek. It was cool from the outdoors. "Tea? Natty?"

"Has Cubby been out lately?"

I checked the clock. "He could use a break." I pushed the sliding glass door open for him and he shot into the yard.

"Have you been out lately?" she asked.

"I usually pee indoors." I went back to stirring the soup.

"I'm asking if you went out today."

I ran through a quick mental calculation and didn't come up with any errands I was supposed to run and might have missed. I'd worked on her Christmas gift all day under the guise of working on *Quadrophenia*. I'd stopped in plenty of time to clean up and get some dinner together for us. I'd never been a fan of guessing games.

"What'd I forget to do?"

"Pay Howie. For the groceries. From a month ago."

"Oh, shoot. I'm sorry. It completely slipped my mind. I'll get him tomorrow. Or you know, I could swing by the Buckshot right after we eat. He's usually there with his crew on Fridays."

"Don't bother. He came by the shop today. I cut him a check out of my business account. I hate using it for personal crap, but I didn't have that kind of cash or our checkbook."

"I hope he wasn't a dick about it."

"No. He was very polite, actually. He even asked how you were. Remembered your real name and everything."

"That's a shame. I kind of liked being Pete Townshend. He's way cooler than I am. I'll deposit the money from our personal checking to your business account first thing tomorrow." I knew we had the money in our account now that some of the paintings in my fire sale were going. We had yet to bounce any checks.

"I already did." She pulled a piece of paper out of the mail pile and smoothed it out in front of her. "I'm hoping you can explain this. I had them print out our statement when I was at the bank."

I was a dead man.

"We have nothing in savings, checking is way down from where I expected it to be, then I'm going through the mail on the way in and I see this." She pulled another paper out of the pile. "There's a charge on my credit card from the hospital. $2,400. But I know we paid the hospital with a check before they even started my procedure. So how could that end up on my Mastercard?"

The grilled cheese sandwiches started smoking at the same moment the soup boiled over. I rushed to get the food disaster under control, but sopping up the Mastercard disaster was going to take a lot more than a damp rag.

216

"I've been meaning to talk to you about that. Why don't we go get ourselves a pizza at The Lighthouse, and I can explain."

"I think not. You're going to give me some straight answers right here, right now. You want to go to a restaurant so there won't be a scene. Quit trying to manage me and lay this situation out, every penny of it."

I squeezed my rag. Hot soup dripped to the floor like blood.

"Bec, honey ..."

"She took it, didn't she? That ex of yours. Le Crouton. She took it all. And instead of telling me, you protected her. You put her stupid little crouton ass first. The bank said you refused to file a police report. And our check to the hospital should have bounced, but since it didn't you must have paid the hospital off with my credit card. You left me completely in the dark, and you did it for her."

It was breathtaking how she'd sorted all that out between the credit card statement and the bank statement.

"You were grieving hard when all of that happened. I didn't know how to break it to you, so I was trying to smooth it over as best I could."

"Clive. Christ's sake. It's been one lousy month. Four weeks. I am still grieving hard. Right now. Today. Right this minute. I miss her every second of every day. And I did not need this shit. I didn't need Howie coming around when you were supposed to have paid him back ages ago. I didn't need to find out from strangers that Le fucking Crouton ripped us off and you felt it was more important to protect her precious ass from the cops than it was to tell me what happened to our money."

"Look, sweetie, I'm really sor—"

"No." She stood up. "You do not get to apologize and think this just goes away. This is a betrayal of my trust. I thought I knew you." She stabbed her pinky into the air and started counting all the ways I'd fucked up.

"One. You didn't want this baby. It took you damn near getting killed by that dog before you came around.

"Two. You knew there was something wrong with her face and you never told me. I was stunned. If I had known, I'd have been prepared for it, but no. I got blindsided. Do you know how guilty that's made me feel, the way the shock of seeing her face revolted me in those few precious moments I had with her?

"Three. You took off and left me alone at your sister's the night of the termination. Thank God Reece was there. I was devastated—and you were off gallivanting around Detroit, eating pie and running into old exes and passing out wallets like they're leftover Halloween candy.

"Four. You never paid Howie back. I had to do it. You know I hate seeing him, but you stuck me with that chore anyway. And four-point-two, you knew damn well your wallet wasn't in the car that night at Glen's Market, didn't you? I knew you were lying to me, but I didn't get why and I was too destroyed to investigate. Well, I sure get it now.

"Five. You hid all of this huge mess from me, and you can say you did it to protect me but if that's true, it's really condescending. Yes, I have a lot of grief, but we were supposed to be a team. Two adults who tell each other what's up. Not one adult and one frightened little kid keeping Mommy in the dark so he doesn't get spanked.

"Six. You were protecting her from what she has coming: the police, my wrath, everything. You say she's a drug addict. I say you're still enabling her. Right now. Today. Clive, I'm your wife. I'm the one you were supposed to put first. But no. Some crusty old con artist ex comes ahead of me in your book.

"Seven. You put all that money on my credit card without even asking. What, did you think I was just never going to see the statement? That you could keep this kite flying forever?"

"Eight. Did you honestly start smoking again?"

Mercifully, the shredding stopped there. I was guilty on every single count. My ears were scalding. I wanted to disappear into a crack in the floor.

The phone rang. I knew it was Ellie. She felt this. It was her gift, or her curse, to feel my strongest emotions with me. I didn't answer it and neither did Becca. It rang and rang while I rinsed the scorched tomato soup from the rag.

"So now what?" I faced her. "You won't let me apologize. I can't explain it beyond wanting to protect you while you're grieving, but that's condescending of me. And you're right. Everything you said was exactly right. I lied to you. I abandoned you against my better judgment Thanksgiving night. I broke your trust. I enabled my ex. Hell, I even used your grief as an excuse to enable my ex and I'm so blind that I didn't even see that until you said it just now. You should always come first, obviously you should, but I'm so fucked up that I told myself I was putting you first when I wasn't."

I pressed the heels of my hands against my eyes to try to stop the tears that were coming. It didn't work. I was the worst. I didn't deserve her. I was sorry as hell whether she wanted me to apologize or not. I didn't know what she needed from me now, or how we'd ever get past this or through it.

"How do I fix this? Just name it. I'll do whatever you want me to," I said.

She sat down and shook her head.

"What do you mean? Is this it? Are we over?"

"Maybe. Probably. I need some time to sort it all out," she said. "I don't know how I can trust you. You're scared."

"Damn right I'm scared. I'll die if I lose you."

"What I'm saying is, you've always been scared. Even when you weren't losing me. You were scared to have a baby. Scared to talk about your childhood. Scared of that dumb dog. Scared to tell me about Louise's facial deformities. Scared to tell me you'd seen your ex. Scared to tell me she'd robbed us. The more I look at you, the more I see a coward. Why would I want to stay married to a coward?"

"So it's over. No fighting. No counseling. You're ditching our marriage, three days before Christmas."

"Do you really want to drag it out?"

I really did. I wanted to drag this out as long as possible if it kept me connected to the person I loved more than anyone else in the world. *Hell yes. Let's drag this shit out for decades, baby. Drag me behind you like the worthless goddamned appendage I've become.*

"Marshall asked me to spend the holidays with him and Kevin in Montréal," she said. "I'd told him no, but after realizing all of this garbage, I changed my mind. I'm going to start the drive out there in the morning. It will give me some time to think. I'm probably moving into the apartment above the shop when I get back. In the meantime, can you take care of Cubby? I'm not sure if they'll let him cross the border, and I don't need the hassle."

"Thank you."

"For what?"

"Still trusting me enough to leave Cubby with me."

"Howie was too busy to take him."

36

Someday at Christmas

Ellie • Detroit, Mich. • Sunday, Dec. 24, 2006

Janice Marconi laughed at almost everything. Right now she was laughing at the pair of Christmas trees blocking the path through my living room. "It's like Sparty vs. The Nutcracker. Who's winning? I think the Nutcracker peed on Sparty's tree. Is that a technical foul?"

We'd been out all afternoon doing last-second Christmas shopping. I'd embroidered pretty much all of the gifts I was giving, so I mostly just went for the excitement and Christmas spirit, and because I loved hanging out with Janice.

"Well, hiya Ms. Janice." Reece climbed over the sectional on his way to the kitchen and grinned a little too hard at the bounty displayed in the scoop neck of her bright pink sweater beaded with crystal snowflakes. Pregnancy had inflated my breasts to almost the size of hers, but with my beach ball waistline and sports jock maternity wardrobe the effect wasn't nearly as flattering.

Reece had on some Sinatra holiday compilation. He sang every song at the top of his lungs while he whipped up a batch of his extra thick hot chocolate for us in the kitchen.

"You know you're really lucky," Janice said. "He's really darling and he cooks."

"He's a big flirt, and he's making me fat." It was true. Abigail had made me get a glucose test because I was so big that she suspected gestational diabetes. I didn't have it, but Reece sugaring me up was a greater threat to my pregnancy than the homebirth he and his mother were so freaked out about.

"Compared to my ex, he's a regular Barbie Dream Date, hon. I've been divorced eighteen months and have had exactly two dates. It's tough out there on the market. Guys today just want to get their beans dipped. Commitment is dead. Ask them to stay for a cup of coffee and they act like you're dragging them to the altar. I'm never going to find a real man."

"Saint's single," I said, instantly regretting my big, stupid mouth.

She lifted one side of her upper lip, then laughed. "That skinny roommate who never takes off his Dr. Who scarf? Oh my God, girl. You are an absolute scream and a half."

I desperately wanted to defend him, but I wasn't about to pimp him out to her.

"He stuck a little present into that Nutcracker tree while you were in the bathroom."

"Really?"

There weren't any gifts for me under either tree. Reece had stuffed what was obviously a crib box behind the Sparty tree. The tag read *Baby LeFanch*. I knew he'd get me something, eventually. He always waited until the last minute.

I crawled around the Frasier fir looking for whatever Saint had deposited there. Dry needles poked my knees through my maternity leggings.

"No," Janice said. "In the tree, not under it. On the left. By that little high-five guy."

I shook the needles out of my hair and looked at the tree. What did she mean, *little high-five guy?* Then I spotted it. My Stickman ornament. Janice was in serious need of Pearl Jam literacy. I'd have to see to that. Tucked into the branches at the Stickman's feet was a flat box wrapped in plain green tissue, no ribbon, bow or gift tag. I turned it over. On the bottom, in neat lettering around a foil sticker of a snowman, he'd printed *Li'l Wozniak*.

The balls on that boy.

I balanced the gift on the branch where I'd found it. "It's not for me."

"Who, then?"

"Um, his dog, I guess."

Janice rearranged her bangs and inspected her long fingernails. "So … what about that brother of yours?"

"He's married."

"But you said she left him."

"Yeah, they're sort of having a trial separation, but he's still very married and wants to stay that way. He's definitely way, way off limits." It couldn't be overstated. Clive was so vulnerable and brittle right now. His pain was a cinderblock on my chest. I felt guilty for having blurted his situation to Janice while we were out shopping.

"Do you get along with her? His wife, I mean."

"She's alright. We don't especially relate, but she's a pretty sharp lady."

"When she's not walking out on him," Janice said. "At Christmastime."

She was right. How dare Becca leave Clive? He'd told me what LuCretia did, and how he'd tried to cover for it, and about the humiliation of Becca's ex-boyfriend buying their groceries and all that, but still. My brother had the most humongous heart of anybody I'd ever known. He was the kind of person the phrase *benefit of the doubt* was invented for. Becca, of all people, should have realized that.

"He's hella cute," Janice said. "Those dimples. That deep voice. All those crazy curls."

"He's a hair farmer, alright." That was the Raffertys for you: shitty luck, outstanding hair.

"I felt awful for him when they were at the hospital. I mean, he looked so lost. I wanted to hug him and make him all better. And then, you should have seen the way his face changed when he realized who I was. He's just precious."

"Married," I said. "Married. Married. Married."

❧

While Reece was outside scraping frost off the windows of the Roadbastard, Saint gave me the gift he'd tucked in the branches beneath the Stickman ornament.

"Before you open it, who do you consider your immediate family?"

I didn't have to answer. I just smiled.

I tore through the wrapping paper, pretending not to notice the name written on the underside. It was a black Pearl Jam onesie and a Ten Club membership made out to *Li'l Wozniak*.

"You can email them to change the name when he, or she, is born, I checked," he said.

I stood on my tiptoes and kissed his stubbly cheek.

"Again," he said.

I tugged his scarf. "Don't get crazy."

◌

Reece and I went to Hazel Park for Christmas Eve with the LeFanches. His parents played the same Frank Sinatra music Reece had been subjecting me to all season. Marjorie LeFanch's brand new artificial tree was glimmering white with turquoise lights and turquoise ornaments that twirled slowly on motorized spinners.

I sat in the fluted chair and opened my gifts among the doilies. This was by far the biggest pile they'd ever given me. His mom usually gave me a Yankee candle, or some bath splash, or a basket of little soaps or some other generic, obligatory gift stuffed into a festive bag. This year the gifts for me gleamed with Mylar wrapping paper and iridescent bows. The tags bore my name, but as I unwrapped them I discovered that each was intended for the baby. That wouldn't have bugged me. The LeFanches, excited that their only son was finally giving them a grandchild, wanted to make sure the newest member of their big brood arrived in style. But none of the things they'd chosen were things I intended to use. Baby bottles, an electric bottle warmer, pacifiers, a case of formula, newborn-size Pampers, a Diaper Genie, and a robotic teddy bear with a heartbeat to fool the baby into thinking its mother was nearby.

Obviously, Reece and his mom had been commiserating about my decisions: breastfeeding, cloth diapers, co-sleeping. He laughed and thanked his parents for every gift as I opened them. With each one, I felt more betrayed. Still, I forced polite smiles and said thanks like the perfect little grandchild gestation device they expected me to be. Then I hid in their cranberry Renuzit-scented guest bathroom and cried into a hand towel decorated with snowmen wearing cowboy hats and waving American flags. No wonder all of Reece's sisters lived as far from Michigan as possible. If Marjorie LeFanch was my mother, I'd flee the planet.

There was only one thing that could make me feel better. I closed the toilet lid, sat down and called Clive. I knew he was doing even worse than he'd let on when I heard Elliot Smith singing *Clementine* in the background. This was heartbreaking. I begged him to come down and spend Christmas with us tomorrow. He made some lame excuse about icy roads and having to take care of Becca's dog. I told him to bring Cubby along, but no, he wanted to stay up there in Presque Isle County and be a sad bastard all by himself. I refused to let him off the phone until he'd at least agreed to come to our New Year's Eve party.

I slipped Janice's name into the conversation.

He said, "Who?"

After we finished talking, I pulled myself together the rest of the way and returned to the LeFanches family room. I gave Marjorie her present, a handmade apron I'd embroidered with an equation consisting of an apple, a plus sign, a heart, an equal sign and a picture of a steaming apple pie. It was my own design. Maybe it was corny but I knew she'd love it, and I wasn't wrong.

She put it on and modeled it for us. "It's the cutest thing ever. Did you find it at one of those craft bizarres?"

"No, Ma. She embroidered it herself," Reece said.

"Oh my goodness. Really? That's so thoughtful of you," she said.

That made me feel a little better. I started thinking about alternative ways I could use the baby gifts. The bottles could make cute vases. I wondered if I could compost vegetables in the Diaper Genie. I'd have to check the Internet for ideas.

As we were about to leave, Marjorie said she had something else for me. I hoped it wasn't that godforsaken hand-me-down pretend engagement ring.

She reached into the front hall closet and produced a nubby swing coat the exact color of Grey Poupon mustard. I marveled at its hideousness while thanking her profusely for being so thoughtful.

37

Interstellar Overdrive

Clive • Detroit, Mich. • Sunday, Dec. 31, 2006

C ars were lined up and down Ellie's street for three solid blocks. I parked the Land Cruiser two streets south and walked Cubby on his leash to the house. It was already packed full of people, which was exactly what I'd hoped for. I'd arrived late so Ellie would be too busy to grill me about Becca again. She wanted an angle that would make it all Becca's fault, and I didn't have one. She wanted to know what would happen next, and I didn't know. She wanted me to be happy, and I wasn't. Talking about it changed nothing. I'd made the trip down here only because it seemed important to her.

The furniture was shoved against the walls and that weirdo Saint was on a makeshift stage in front of his band, playing *Interstellar Overdrive* on a guitar painted flat black. He wore knee-high boots, a Mookie Blaylock basketball jersey, and a long, fluttering scarf. His hair fell past his shoulders and over his eyes. An angry scar zigzagged down his fretting arm. I wondered how he could even play.

Inexplicably, Ellie had put up two Christmas trees and they blocked the normal traffic pattern in the house. I had to climb over the back of the sectional to get into the kitchen to hang my peacoat on the hook by the basement door. I wondered if she subconsciously knew I didn't have a tree this year and had made up for it by setting up two. If that was the case, I had dibs on the live one, not that Sparty monstrosity dripping with Reece's college pride.

Cubby cowered by the front door, his big brown eyes pleading for me to get him the hell out of there. By the time I'd climbed over the sectional again, a collection of skinny girls with mono-chrome black hair, kitty-cat eyeliner, tattoos and Chuck Taylors were fussing over him like he was Leo DiCaprio.

Shit, I was wearing Chuck Taylors myself. Time to seriously reevaluate my choice in footwear.

I scooped my trembling dog into my arms amid their protests and carried him through the crowd of strangers and up the stairs. He rested his chin on my shoulder like the giant baby that he was, and I whispered into his silken ear that he was going to be fine. The door to my old room was locked, so I took Cubby up the ladder to the loft and left him on the bed while I got him some food and water. He settled right down on the only pillow.

My whole life could probably be measured in events that Ellie had insisted I attend. Concerts, tailgates, Tiger games, bonfires, beach picnics, canoe outings, camping trips, ice skating parties. I'd never been in less of a social mood, but here I was, the dutiful brother about to join in her New Year's blowout wearing a reindeer sweater covered with beagle fur.

Reece stuck his head through the loft opening. He had on a pair of glittering *2007* sunglasses. A brass one-hitter was clenched between his teeth. "Heyyyy, my man. What's the haps?"

"Spark that bad boy up," I said.

He pushed the sunglasses to the top of his head. "C'mon down."

"Uh uh. Up here."

"Alright, you damned hermit." He hoisted himself through the opening and sat on the edge with his legs dangling through. "Hey, I just want to say I'm sorry about your old lady."

"Can we not?" I sat down cross-legged on the painted pine floor. "I'm here with a prime directive to forget that my life is a whirling, swirling sucking vortex of shit, interrupted by brief eddies of false hope."

"Bitchin'. Got a lighter?"

I handed him my red Zippo. He flicked it and held the flame to his one-hitter. We shared it, refilling it for each other from a baggie

228

of weed he'd set on the floor between us, and passing the one-hitter and the lighter back and forth like some kind of ritual. I lost track of how many hits I'd had. Too many. I was blitzed.

"It's cool, Reece said. "But if you want to talk about Becca later, hit me up."

"That Saint guy," I said, by way of changing the subject completely, "Is he living here again? I mean, my door was locked. And I could swear I spotted a codpiece hanging on the bathroom door-knob."

"Yeah, uh. Speaking of *can we not.*"

"Oh, really?" I started laughing. It was hard to stop.

He took a long drag and rolled his eyes up while he held it in. "For real," he said with a puff of sweet smoke.

"Well, hit me up if you want to talk about it later."

He grinned and released smoke from his nostrils. "Asshole."

"We cannot talk about my asshole. How many times do I have to tell you? That subject is strictly off limits."

ೞ

There were now roughly twice as many people downstairs, and the music was three times as loud. *The Pusher.* Steppenwolf. No shit. The mood of it was dead-on true to the original, yet the sound itself felt entirely rejuvenated. No one had ever told me that Saint's band was actually terrific, or that Saint could play and sing, or do such incredible things with ancient psychedelic rock. And I didn't even want to like that weirdo, let alone respect him.

When the song ended, I worked my way toward the kitchen, climbing over the sectional again. I plunged my arm into a galvanized tub full of ice and beer bottles, closed my eyes and made a random choice. Michelob. People still drank Michelob?

Under the music was an eerie howling. I recognized the voice of Saint's dog. Tremor Christ. The name gave me chills. I swear to God he was trying to back Saint's vocals on *We Love You.* Or maybe the flowers I'd just smoked with Reece were a little too spectacular. I took a swig of beer, leaned against the refrigerator and closed my eyes. I just wanted to stay there, but a woman kept yelling my name.

Not Ellie.

Not Becca.

I gave up ignoring her and opened my eyes. Janice Marconi was squeezing through the kitchen door between the people crowded around it.

"Clive!" She was sporting a *Happy New Year* tiara and waving with a can of Mike's Hard Lemonade in her hand. I wiped my dripping palm on my jeans and extended it toward her. She skipped the handshake and went right in for the bear hug like we were long-lost amigos.

We shouted "What?" in each other's ears a few times. She pointed at the back door, and I followed her, snatching my peacoat off the hook on the way out. I took my smokes and a lighter from the pocket and slung the coat around my shoulders. The little piece of paper with Marshall's number in Montréal fluttered away and caught in the gap between the decking boards. I grabbed it and tucked it inside the cellophane wrapper of my cigarette pack for safekeeping.

Janice was all dolled up for the New Year in a black velvet mini skirt and stiletto boots. Her candy apple red sateen blouse was open one button below awkward, revealing generously freckled cleavage.

"2007. I can't even believe it," she said.

I could.

She beamed at me. "I was sure hoping you'd be here."

I wasn't.

I decided to be polite, just for the hell of it. "Hey, I can actually hear you now. Cigarette?"

"Please. I tried to quit, but then my life started to suck too much."

"Same here, sista, same here." I lit one for her from the tip of my own. Our fingers touched as she accepted it from me. Her raspberry lipstick stained the filter tip.

"So. Ellie told me your wife split."

"That's Ellie for you. Sees all, knows all, tells all."

230

"Want to talk about it?"

I had no urge to discuss what had happened with anyone, let alone any overly demonstrative childhood acquaintances I barely remembered. I leaned against the pressure-treated lumber railing and blew smoke at the starless sky, wondering if the stars were out in Montréal tonight. I didn't owe Janice any juicy tidbits of my personal disasters.

"What's with the crazy bus?" she asked.

I told her about it, not believing for a second that Ellie hadn't already given it to her chapter and verse. She was trying to make conversation and it was a safe subject, at least. I could be nice as long as she wasn't asking me to talk about Becca.

"I like Pearl Jam alright," she said. "My favorite song of theirs is *Arms Wide Open*."

Priceless. If Ellie ever heard Janice blaming her beloved Pearl Jam for something by the loathsome Creed, she'd summon the gods of grunge to split the earth open and swallow Janice whole.

"I've seen two concerts. Ricky Martin and Celine Dion," she said. "How many times have you seen Pearl Jam?"

"Ellie has our tickets on a corkboard in the vestibule if you ever want to count them. I lost track sometime after twenty-five."

"That's insane."

"Not especially. Lots of people follow them on tour. Most of them know the Yield bus and come to us for a good time. We're a rolling party. It's how she met that Saint guy who lives with them now."

"I think he's kind of strange," she said. "The other day Ellie was like, 'Well, you know, Saint's single and ready to mingle' and I'm like, 'Oh hell to the big fat no.'" She laughed. "Did you see he's wearing eyeliner?"

I hadn't noticed. I scraped at the damp label on my beer bottle, making an accordion-fold tear.

"That supposed to mean you're sexually frustrated," she said.

Now there was some cheap barstool psychology for you. Metallic flakes clung to my fingers as I hastily smoothed the label back into place.

"Can you get me a peek inside the bus?" she asked.

"You should let Ellie do the honors. That's her sacred temple of Pearl Jam worship. I don't want to commit sacrilege." That was true, but it was still a lie. I had my own key to the bus and was every bit as welcome onboard as Jeff Ament and his fur hat. I loved the band as much as Ellie did, but I never needed to be Pearl Jam's Biggest Fan™. I just didn't want to be alone on the bus with Janice because she obviously wanted to be alone on the bus with me. I mean, I may be a complete idiot but I'm not stupid.

Janice texted someone, waited for a reply then showed it to me. *Tell him I said show it to you. He's just being stubborn.* "Looks like she's totally cool with it."

I whipped out my phone and texted Ellie. *Remembering this next time you want me to hold your spot on the rail while you take a whiz.* I pulled my keychain out of my pocket. The bus key was longer than all of the others. I led the way across the muddy lawn and around Tremor Christ's stinking deposits. Janice teetered in her boots and clung to my arm for balance. Her perfume made my nose itch. Becca never wore perfume. Her scents were limited to Aveeno lotion, shampoo and cutting oil.

We climbed aboard and I turned on the overhead lights. The fact that they came on meant the battery in this bus was some kind of Pearl Jam Chanukah miracle. Even in the winter, it smelled like diesel fuel and incense. I loved Ellie for hanging onto this old thing.

Janice's nipples protruded against her shiny blouse. "I'm freezing," she said, rubbing her arms.

It really wasn't a cold night, maybe only in the mid-forties. I slipped my peacoat off of my shoulders and helped her put it on, to cover her cleavage more than anything.

"Thanks. You're still a sweetheart." She removed her foil tiara and stuck it in my hair. "I had the biggest crush on you when you lived with us."

A crush? How was that possible? I was only seven when I lived there.

"Do you remember?" She plucked a tuft of Cubby's fur from my sweater.

I didn't. In my memory, the Marconi kids were a homogenous group. Dark haired, dark eyes, all of their names beginning with the letter J. When I'd met Janice at the hospital, if she'd have told me her name was Jennifer or Jamiroquai I'd have reacted exactly the same.

"Don't even tell me we played doctor," I said.

She guffawed, sloshing her hard lemonade on the sleeve of my sweater. "Nah. But we played house together. You were the husband and I was the wife and Donald was the baby. Remember?"

It came back to me, but not with the warm, nostalgic effect she'd probably intended. Donald's name fell from her mouth and brained me. Ellie and I rarely spoke directly about our brothers. It was just too hard to verbalize, even all these years later. At Thanksgiving, the Marconi clan had considerately maneuvered around the subject of our dark past. Alone, Janice lacked the simple grace to let my baby brothers be.

I sank onto a futon and put my face in my hands, allowing myself to see Donald as my son in a game of house. Pilled and faded footy pajamas, laughing eyes, Chiclet milk teeth, and a deep dimple in his chin exactly like mine and Ellie's. He'd belonged to me. I could almost smell his peanut-butter breath, feel his sticky fingers, and hear the way he used to chortle when I talked to him in a Donald Duck voice. For a victim of extreme parental neglect, he'd been one sunny little guy.

Janice sat next to me and draped her arm around my shoulder. Becca had worn my peacoat right through the end of her pregnancy and it still felt like her somehow. I leaned into it, indulging myself in the memory of Becca so close to me, still pregnant, still happy, still mine. I didn't fight it when Janice moved in for a full embrace. I needed this. It was as close as I could come to holding Becca.

"I'm sorry. Did I say something wrong?" Janice asked.

Her talking ruined the effect. It made me aware again of her cloying perfume and her strangeness. I pulled away.

"I believe everything happens for a reason," she said.

That was stupid. There wasn't any reason that could justify my fractured childhood, or Trisomy 13, or the woman I loved with all my heart leaving me. Alright, so there actually were some good reasons for that last one, but still.

"What reasons," I said. It wasn't a question. It was a challenge.

"I got divorced, and now you're getting divorced. And then we run into each other and nothing's changed between us. Who'd a thunk it?"

Nothing's changed between us. For fuck's sake, I barely remembered her. I stood up and she looked at me expectantly. She was Ellie's friend, she had some wrong ideas about me, and I could straighten this out without being a dick. There was no harm in letting her down gently. She reached for my hands, and I pulled her up off the futon.

"Listen, Janice. It's been neat to catch up with you after so many years. And it was cool of you to invite us to your mom's on Thanksgiving. But I think you're confused."

"Don't you believe there's a reason we lived together?"

I shrugged and headed for the exit. She tagged behind me, hooking a finger into my belt loop. "It's not just a coincidence that we lived together as kids and then we run into each other out of the blue. There's a reason. There has to be."

I stopped near the exit steps and faced her. "Yeah, there is a reason. It was because your mother is a saint and mine was a drug addict. Anyway, I'm not getting divorced."

Her face fell. "Ellie said you were."

I rubbed my neck and looked down at her pointy-toed patent leather boots with silver buckles. If those were Becca's work boots, I'd have been on my knees kissing them.

"Ellie said there's no way you two can work it out. That she's bitter, and she doesn't even get you."

The sting of my own sister's doubts was still registering with me when Janice grabbed my head and mashed her mouth against mine. I froze. This kiss felt completely wrong. Lipstick. Cigarettes. Hard lemonade. She was everything Becca was not. I let it happen because it underscored how completely I belonged to Becca. She'd owned me from our first soul-splitting kiss on the frozen sand at Forty Mile Point.

Reece opened the door to the bus. Janice and I leapt apart.

234

"Oops. Sorry brother, Reece said. "Just looking for my beer bong."

"Haven't seen it," I said.

Janice sashayed down the bus steps and picked her way across the dog poop minefield back to the house. I turned to leave, but Reece kicked the door closed. "She called here for you."

"Who? Janice?"

"Ha, that chick calls every day. But no, I mean Ms. Becca. Remember her?"

I hated the judgment in his eyes, mainly because I agreed with it.

"When?"

"A couple of minutes ago. She wanted to wish you a happy New Year, hear your voice or something. It was hard to understand her over the party."

"Well, shit."

"I'll say." He jerked his thumb toward the door. "What the hell was that?"

I shook my head. "Nothing."

"I don't know bro-ski, it sure looks like something to me."

"It was beyond nothing. It was so nothing it left a vacuum."

"A Hoover?"

☙

Little Wing was perfection in Saint's hands. I didn't know a thing about Quadraphonic Space Trip, but I wanted them providing accompaniment for every event I had to attend for the rest of my life. Right now though, I needed to get my coat back from Janice. She'd walked off with it. My phone, car keys, cigarettes, lighter, and the number for Marshall's bed & breakfast were in the pockets. Becca had instructed me not to call her cell while she was in Canada because she didn't have international coverage.

I spotted Ellie, roughly the size of a modest beach cottage, gabbing with a lean, stylish black girl in the front vestibule. I climbed over the sectional once again and worked my way through the dancers, the drinkers, and the screamers. Everyone I knew was giving me a thumbs up or yelling "Go Clive" or "Dude" at me. I didn't realize people had missed me that much. I kept moving until I was inside the vestibule.

The girl was saying, "This party has got to be the whitest thing that ever happened in Detroit."

"Sorry to interrupt, ladies. El, have you seen Janice Marconi? Did she leave?" I asked.

Ellie snickered. "Oh my hell, Cliver, that's something. Don't move." She whipped her little Polaroid camera out of her pocket and pointed it at me.

"I'm serious. Put that thing away. I have to find Janice, like, right now."

"I'll bet you do, action pants. By the way, this is my boss, Shelby Williams. Shelby, my brother Clive."

"Uh huh," Shelby said with a smirk. "Nice 'do, brother Clive."

I had no idea what she was talking about.

Ellie snapped my picture and waited for the camera to spit out the print. She was being completely useless. I turned to walk away and she grabbed my elbow. "Get your buns back here, princess."

"What? I have to find Janice."

She flapped the picture to dry it. "You're like Robert Smith with that lipstick all over your mug. I'm embarrassed for you."

I put my hand across my mouth. *Ugh.* I was coated with lipstick.

"Destroy that picture or I'm disowning you," I said.

I went upstairs and got into the line for the bathroom, hanging my head so my hair curtained the mess on my face. Something tugged at my scalp. I reached up and found Janice's insipid 2007 tiara stuck in my hair. I yanked it out and threw it to the floor. Every time I wiped my mouth, I got raspberry red lipstick on my hand. She must have bought her makeup at Insta-Lube. I started hoping she'd ditched my coat somewhere so I wouldn't have to deal with her again.

A pair of girls in ponytails, fishnets and high-tops tumbled out of the bathroom and fell to the floor laughing. I stepped over them and went in to face the mirror. Damn. Robert Smith was an understatement. More like Crusty the Clown. I found a clean wash cloth and got to work scrubbing the crap off my face.

Someone knocked on the door. "Hurry up in there. I gotta take a wicked piss."

Screw it. She'd have to wait. I continued washing my face.

"Hurry up." She pounded some more.

I checked the mirror. Maybe a little raw from scrubbing but definitely passable. The pounding continued. *Christ. Calm down.*

I flung the door open. "All yours."

It was Janice. And she took the *all yours* completely differently than I'd meant it. She threw her arms around me. She still had my peacoat on. "Ellie said you were looking for me. Well, here I am, cutie."

She was flat out loaded. I mean swaying, staggering drunk. Only ten or fifteen minutes earlier she'd been fine and now she was in some kind of condition.

"What happened to you?" I asked.

"Ha. Watermelon Jell-O shots. You missed out." She shoved me back into the bathroom and pushed the door shut with her hip.

I asked her for my coat.

She took it off and dangled it in front of me like a bullfighter on a bender. "Trade you for your pa-ants."

"You've had a lot to drink, Janice. You're a nice girl from a nice family and you don't mean that. Now, give me the coat."

"Ooh, my mother was a saint, but I'm not. Come here, little cutie."

I snatched the coat from her. Something small and dark flew into the air then skittered across the floor.

"My fingernail! You broke my fingernail." She showed me her hand, one nail an inch shorter than the others. It was a real tragedy.

"Sorry. I need my cigarettes." I reached for the doorknob. "You said you had to go. I'll get out of your way."

She hiked her skirt above her hips and backed toward the toilet. "I'm not shy. I got brothers."

I slammed the door behind me. She yelled something about meeting her in the kitchen for Jell-o shots as I pounded down the stairs.

38

Last Exit

Clive • Detroit, Mich. • Sunday, Dec. 31, 2006

Instead of meeting Janice for Jell-O shots, I met myself on the front porch for a cigarette. Outside, Saint's incredible psychedelic cover band was muffled to window-rattling bottom end. *White Rabbit.* How did they make it sound like it was written just yesterday? Like they'd invented ring modulation? It was crazy good. I lit a cigarette and took a deep drag. Relief. Sometimes I wondered why I ever even bothered trying to quit. I fished around in the cellophane for the scrap I'd written Marshall's number on. It was gone. There was a fortune cookie slip in its place. I squinted at the faded orange text under the porch light. *Everything is not yet lost.* On the back, Janice had scribbled her name and phone number.

I lit the fortune on fire with the end of my cigarette, dropped it onto the concrete stoop and watched it burn to a cinder. I ground it under my heel for good measure.

I walked down the street and around the corner toward my Land Cruiser. I'd lived in one part of Detroit or another most of my life, but had never considered the implications of bringing up kids here. Even when LuCretia was pregnant, I hadn't thought that far ahead. With her, it had been about seeing her through each day sober right up until she miscarried anyway. Ellie's baby wasn't even born yet and already had been the victim of a mugging. I'd moved up to Presque Isle County—with all its pristine beaches, woods, and farmland—to get untangled from LuCretia and get my own head on straight. But for the first time I understood what a cool place that would be to raise children.

If only.

My car was pinned in between a minivan and a red Grand Prix with heavily steamed windows. It didn't matter. I wasn't going anywhere after the beer and pot I'd had. I got behind the wheel and turned on the radio, flipping through the stations until I found one that wasn't hawking car insurance or playing a cheesy top one-hundred countdown.

A familiar and poignant chord progression washed over me. *Ziggy Stardust.* I turned it up and slouched in the seat, absorbing the sweet reminder of Becca. I lit another cigarette and wallowed in feeling completely bereft and adrift. *Suffragette City* and *Rock 'N' Roll Suicide* followed. She'd referred to this as *The Stardust Trilogy.* The way she made up things like that—as if anyone but her had ever called those three songs together *The Stardust Trilogy*—was one of a zillion things I loved about her.

Dear Becca, I spent my New Year's Eve smoking alone in my car and crying over how much you loved David Bowie. How did you spend yours?

How long was the drive to Montréal from here? Eight hours? Ten? Did I have enough money to cover the gas? Could I smuggle Cubby across the border? Would it be pulling a Howie to show up uninvited? I could handle anything but Becca thinking I was as pathetic as Howie.

Wait. I'd passed that point—and then some—with her the second she'd realized I was lying about my wallet at Glen's Market. She didn't want to see me. I still wasn't going anywhere.

The Grand Prix's door opened and a disheveled chick climbed out, laughing. I was pretty sure I'd seen her at the party earlier. She stood on the sidewalk, tucking in her blouse and smoothing her short, pink-tipped hair. A guy got out of the car next and squeezed her waist. It was Reece. No shit.

They kissed, long and slow. He walked her around to the driver's side and opened the door for her. She got in, started the car and rolled the window down. He leaned in and they continued talking and kissing for another five minutes. Everybody knew he was a flirt, but I'd never seen him stoop this low.

She pulled the car away. Reece waved as her tail lights disappeared around the corner.

I got out of my car. "Let's talk, Maurice."

He spun to face me. "Clive. Hey! Where'd you come from?"

"You're fucking around on my sister? My pregnant sister? Who fucking adores you?"

"Hell no. I mean, I know what that probably looked like but—"

I stepped up and stuck my face close to his. "But what?"

"She had something in her eye!"

"Oh yeah? Something in her eye? Like your prick?"

"Chill." He shoved me. "Wasn't that your tongue down Janice Marconi's throat half an hour ago?"

"Bite me, LeFanch. Nothing happened."

"Yeah, 'cause I walked in on you. Sneaking her off to a bus full of futons."

"My wife left. I can bone whoever I please. What's your excuse?"

He shoved me again. I snatched him by the lapels of his leather jacket. "Maurice LeFanch, you Hazeltucky punk." I pushed forward, forcing him to scamper backward over the curb. I rammed him into a chain link fence. It jangled and every dog in the neighborhood went insane. He smelled like peach schnapps and pussy. I could've killed him right there.

"Calm the fuck down," he said.

I pressed him against the fence.

"Cool it. C'mon, I can't breathe."

"Bullshit." He was talking, so I knew he was breathing.

"Then get the hell out of my business. You don't know how it is around here."

I slammed him against the fence again. "Regale me, fucker."

"I love her. You know I do. But she's been tighter than the Virgin Mary and twice as boring ever since she got pregnant. I mean, we never. I'm going apeshit. And she's hanging out with that freak all the damned time. She moved him back in without even asking me. I'm like a third wheel in my own house."

I dropped his lapels and stepped back. "Yeah, so? It's your house. Kick him out. Don't make it an excuse to fuck around on her."

"It's not that simple."

"Are you saying they're fucking? Is she actually fucking that guy? She moves him in against your will and she's fucking him—right under your goddamned nose? 'Cause if that's the case, I'm going to drop this and go have it out with her right this minute."

"Don't. Don't. I never said that. It's hard to explain. It's like … she's better friends with him now than me. They've got all these inside jokes. She listens to him. Trusts him."

"No shit, LeFanch. You're out here getting it on in the backseat of a sedan with some random chick and Ellie's back at the house holding that whole party down by herself. And you think it's some big mystery that she doesn't trust you like she used to. Wow."

"You don't get it. Their friendship is …"

"So now she's not allowed to have friends? That's fucked up. It's not how you used to be, or she never would have dated you in the first place."

I wanted to punch his stupid face. I turned to walk away.

He snagged my arm. "For Christ's sake, brother. Promise me you won't tell her."

"She's my sister." I yanked my arm out of his grip "I'm not covering for you, asshole."

"Yeah, you are. 'Cause here's the deal: keep this quiet, and I don't mention to Becca about you and Janice."

"There is no me and Janice. And Becca's not your goddamned sister."

I walked away from him backward down the sidewalk, lighting another cigarette. "Tell Becca whatever you want. She's lost to me. Nothing you can say will make it worse."

CR

Nothing mattered anymore. Life was a Mongolian cluster fuck with shrimp-fried rice. I walked alone in the dark, knowing exactly where I was headed, but not why. I half hoped I'd get jumped so I could beat the ever living shit out of someone.

There was no other option but to tell Ellie about Reece. I couldn't let that twerp blindside her the way I'd let Louise's face blindside Becca. If I covered for Reece, Ellie would never trust me again. I was done with Reece. Becca was done with me. My life was hemorrhaging people.

I absolutely had to handle this right. I'd introduced those two. It was my fault. I'd been the one to put Ellie in this situation. And now she was hugely pregnant and hugely vulnerable.

I walked fast with my hands shoved in the pockets of my peacoat. Revelers in knit caps and down parkas dotted the streets, guzzling from paper sacks, using their cars like cocktail furniture. They yelled "Happy New Years" at me and I nodded and said it back. Fireworks exploded in the sky. The neighborhoods grew rattier, the window bars thicker, the cyclone fences higher, the barking more savage. I just kept going.

Near midnight, I hit Brush Park. I hunched my shoulders as I turned down our old street. The boarded Victorians with caving roofs were menacing in the dark. I reached the deserted lot, our lot. The hollow mansions that flanked it were our brothers' brick tombstones. The Queen Anne was baby David's, the Second Empire, Donald's.

No one had ever told us where, or even if, our brothers were buried. If there'd been a funeral, it was while we were hospitalized. For all I knew they'd been cremated like Louise. Who was I supposed to ask? And did it even matter? Finding out what happened to their remains wouldn't bring them back.

We had this place to remember them. The empty lot verified their existence. Here, I knew they'd been mine and not some figments of the recurring nightmare that passed for my childhood.

Louise didn't even have this much for a memorial. We should have done something permanent to acknowledge her short life. She was never going to live, but she'd been alive. She'd been ours, together. Without her, we'd fallen apart.

I walked across the muddy weeds to a concrete slab jutting from the earth. I crouched and made myself as small as I could, hugging my knees to my chest in the darkness. In the final two months of this year, I'd lost my baby, my dignity, my fantastic wife and now my best friend. If I mishandled this with Ellie, I could lose her. Then who would I have? It would be just me and Cubby until Becca took him away, too.

It hit me that Becca hadn't called Ellie's. Reece was just laying a head trip on me when he saw the opportunity. I probably owed Janice one for replacing Marshall's phone number with her own. She'd saved me from making an even bigger ass of myself in Becca's eyes.

A car alarm bleated unchecked. Some nearby cats were either fighting or fucking, maybe both by the horrible yowling they made. I wanted to implode and disappear from this earth like ashes in a stiff breeze.

Fireworks boomed. I looked up at the purple and green stars exploding in the sky and falling to earth. Maybe 2007 would be better for me.

No.

I would be a better man for 2007.

39

Grievance

Ellie • Detroit, Mich. • Monday, Jan. 1, 2007

New Year's Day arrived too soon and too sunny. I'd had my heart set on sleeping in, but the baby had decided that dawn was the optimum time to practice the Humpty Dance on my bladder. Boy, by the time this kid was born, it'd better have those moves down cold.

The house had a severe case of post-party halitosis. I waded through the aftermath with a big, black trash bag collecting Solo cups, streamers, paper plates and discarded tiaras.

Saint was sprawled across the sectional sound asleep, bathed in the early light. He wasn't wearing a shirt but he still had on his boots, jeans, and scarf. His black eyeliner, which he'd had me apply for him in the bathroom right before he performed, was smudged. His arms were draped around a pair of girls in mini-skirts and tank tops. They were so alike they might have been sisters. One's clavicle was tattooed with a shooting star, the other with a bouquet of tiny pink roses interspersed with black skulls. Shooting Star's thumb plugged her mouth, and Skull/Rose was drooling. It was a Polaroid moment for sure. I set down my trash bag and found my camera, my heart swelling with motherly affection as I snapped their picture.

I covered the trio with our old yellow Rafferty family quilt. Pregnancy hormones were some crazy stuff.

I was rinsing beer bottles and returning them to their soggy cases when Reece padded into the kitchen wearing the same jeans and sweater he'd had on last night. His eyes were puffy and his hair stuck up on both sides like it wanted to play Batman.

"Rough night, Reece's Pieces?"

He rinsed the empty coffee pot and pulled a tub of Folgers out of the cupboard. "Did Clive talk to you?"

"Uh uh. I barely saw him last night, and he's not up yet."

"He split."

"No!"

I couldn't believe it. He'd come all the way down for the party and I'd only seen him for a grand total of fifteen seconds, maybe twenty. I didn't know whether to cry or call him up and chew him a new asshole. How could he sneak off without talking to me? My feelings were seriously hurt.

"Well, next time you hear from him, ignore whatever he says about me. He's completely full of shit," Reece said.

I dried my hands on a dishtowel and stared at Reece. My brother was far from perfect, but if there was one thing he wasn't, it was full of shit. I waited for him to explain. Whatever it was, it had to be why Clive had left without saying anything.

Reece filled the pot with water and dumped it into the coffee-maker, splashing the countertop.

"Come on. Out with it. What happened between you two?" I asked.

"He totally misconstrued a completely innocent conversation I was having, made all kinds of assumptions, jumped to a bunch of stupid conclusions then started shoving me around." He crammed the pot into place in the coffeemaker. "He had the nerve to accuse me of cheating on you."

"But he knows you better than that. A lot better."

"Exactly. I think it's his own guilty conscience. I didn't say anything to anybody, but I busted him making out with Janice Marconi on your bus. It's like, projection, you know?" He scooped coffee grounds into the filter basket, scattering them onto the countertop and floor. "I catch him with her, and then like half an hour later he sees me talking to some girl I hardly know—I mean literally, Sugar. I don't even know this girl's name and she was basically just asking me for directions—and he goes, 'You're cheating

246

on my pregnant sister, and I'm going to tell her right this minute. And I'm like, 'Bro, what the actual fuck?"

"You detonated a guilt bomb."

"Yeah, that's about the size of it. And now it's like he wants to trash my credibility in case I tell Becca. As if I'd ever do that. I mean, they're separated. She left. Why would I stick my nose into that?"

I shook my head. This wasn't like Clive at all. If he was accusing Reece of cheating, it was because he really believed Reece was cheating, even though I knew he wasn't. Hell, *I* was the cheater ... that one time, at least.

Reece poured us each a glass of orange juice, sloshing it all over the island. "He's in such a rage right now. Honestly, I'm pretty worried about him. It must be the stress, you know, Becca taking off, losing the baby and everything. I still can't believe he'd dare accuse me of something so vile. I never even cheated on the girls I went with in middle school."

"I'll try calling him. He's always straight with me. I can get to the bottom of it."

He yawned. "Don't. Don't. Let him cool off. He owes me an apology, big time. Honestly, my feelings are hurt that he'd even say shit like that. And he shoved me around, too. Pushed me right into a fence. He knows how I am about you. This was so far out of line."

I wrung out a dishrag and wiped the water, juice and coffee grounds from the countertop. "I know baby, I know."

"I say we let him alone until he comes to his senses."

The phone rang.

"Speak of the devil," Reece said.

I snatched the cordless before he could get to it.

"Sorry to call so early," Clive said. "I couldn't sleep so I figured—"

"Janice! Hey! No, it's fine. Really. I'm wide awake, just having some OJ and cleaning up the party mess." I stuck my tongue out at Reece.

"He's standing right there, I'll bet," Clive said.

"Sure! Yeah! Absolutely!" I covered the mouthpiece and asked Reece, "Should I get rid of her?"

"No, it's cool. Talk to your girlfriend. I'll come back when the coffee is done." He headed for the stairs, taking his empty mug with him.

"You can call me later if it's not a good time, but we really have to talk," Clive said.

"It's fine. I'm right here." I peered around the kitchen doorway to make sure Reece wasn't hanging out in the living room. "He's gone."

Clive told me the very things Reece said he would, but with more detail. He claimed he witnessed Reece making out with a girl with pink hair in a car. I remembered seeing a pink-haired girl at the party, but I didn't know who she was.

"Hate to be the one to tell you this El, but I saw it. Saw it."

"No … he told me what you believed you saw. He was giving her directions. He doesn't even know her."

"Oh, fanfuckingtastic. That means he's getting it on with complete strangers. What if he gives you a disease or something? How is that going to affect your baby?"

Ha. I was the one who'd been guilty of picking up an STD.

"I know you mean well, but you don't know what you're talking about."

"You're in denial, El. He basically admitted it to me. The truth is scary, but you have to know that as long as there's a roof over my head there will always be a roof over yours."

The coffeemaker beeped and I heard Reece heading down the stairs.

"I can't talk right now."

"Then go someplace where you can talk. This is too important to leave for later."

"Hang on." I headed down the basement stairs, closing the door behind me. My approach made Tremor Christ grumble, but he was locked in his crate. I sat down at the bottom of the steps. "What do you mean, 'admitted'?"

248

On the other end of the line, there was the metallic click of his lighter followed by the silence of him taking a drag on a cigarette. I hated that he was smoking again.

"He started giving me all these lame justifications. Like, he's sexually frustrated because you're pregnant, and he's bored, and your friendship with Saint makes him feel like a third wheel. If he was just giving somebody directions, why would he say all that to me?"

"I don't know. Maybe he needed to talk about it. But that doesn't mean he's cheating. You're filling in a lot of blanks. Maybe you're projecting your own marital problems onto my relationship."

"I'm telling you exactly what I saw, sis."

If Clive understood that I was the cheat in this relationship, he'd hate me forever.

"Reece told me he caught you kissing Janice, and you felt guilty and that you'd try to say this stuff about him in case he told Becca."

"You're not making any sense. Are you blind? He's acting like a total dirt bag and he's lying to you and he's saying this shit about me so you won't believe me when I'm telling you the truth."

"He's been your best friend for years. You're hurting because Becca wants a divorce. And now you're trying to tear up my relationship. Why? So I'll move up to the sticks with you and you won't have to be lonely? You can't replace Becca and her baby with me and mine."

"That's straight up ridiculous. I'm telling you this stuff because I don't want to see you get hurt."

"Look, I know you probably feel guilty about the thing with Janice, but you need to take back all these baseless accusations and apologize to Reece. And me."

"El."

"I'm hanging up now."

"Ellie."

"I'm hanging up."

"Elsworth, would you listen to me?"

I hung up.

40

The Needle & the Damage Done

Janice came into Mr. Salty's on a Tuesday in mid-February and ordered a cinnamon pretzel and a coffee for inside. I hadn't seen her since the New Year's Eve party. I told Shelby I was taking my break and sat down in a booth with Janice. I had to turn sideways to fit. Since coming back to work, I'd gone from a men's large to a men's extra large uniform shirt, and now even that was getting snug.

"Look, I hate to stick my nose in, but I've been thinking about you a lot lately, and we need to talk some more about that home-birth thingy," she said. "At the party, I thought you looked a little LGA. And seeing you now, it'd be irresponsible of me to not say anything. Unassisted birth might be kind of risky for you."

"I have a midwife. That's hardly unassisted. And I don't even know what LGA means."

"Large for gestational age." She tore off a piece of pretzel, dipped it in vanilla icing and took a bite.

"I just have a small waist so I'm carrying way out front."

She shook her head and finished chewing. "I've seen this. A smaller woman carrying a larger baby can get in a lot of trouble with natural childbirth. Not always, but if it goes bad, you're going to want to be at a hospital."

"But Reece is under six foot. And I'm not that tiny."

"You could have gestational diabetes. That would make the baby bigger."

"Nope. I got the gnarly sugar-drink test for that. Don't have it."

"Twins, then."

I looked up at the ceiling. I'd been hearing *twins* and even *triplets* from every clueless wannabe midwife on the planet in response to my size and due date. Sure, I was pretty big, but there was only one heartbeat. I'd listened to it myself many times.

"My midwife says my fundal height is within normal ranges, just at the high end." I was proud of knowing a proper midwifery term like *fundal height*.

"I wouldn't be so sure, Ellie."

"Uh uh. You're not talking me out of a homebirth. Reece has tried to, his mother is still trying to, and if they can't talk me out of a natural delivery at home, well, you should learn to spot a lost cause."

"They're not nurses in a maternity ward."

Shelby was on the other side of the counter, giving me her pulled-down-nostrils face which meant she thought my break was already over. She needed to learn how to tell time. I waved at her, nodded, and kept talking to Janice. "Think about it. The last thing any midwife wants is a high-risk delivery. If you're that worried, come hang out with me when I go into labor."

"I could lose my job attending a homebirth, even on my free time, even if everything went great."

"And it will." I squeezed out of the booth and stood up. "I'm sorry, I really gotta get back to work."

"Hey, have you talked to Clive?"

We hadn't spoken in six weeks, a world record if you didn't count that time they locked me up in a girls' correctional facility and we'd had no choice. It was killing me, but Reece kept saying I should wait for my brother to call and apologize. I was afraid that next time we talked wouldn't be until I called him to let him know the baby was born. Tears sprang from my eyes.

"Ellie?"

"Damn these pregnancy hormones all to hell. He got in an argument with Reece on New Year's Eve. We haven't talked since."

"Oh, no." Janice stood up and hugged me. "You guys were always super-duper close."

"I don't know what to do."

"Maybe I could take you up there to him sometime. It might even be fun."

Reece would never go for it, but Janice was the best—even if she was yet another person trying to talk me into a hospital birth.

ॐ

Abigail came over for my regular exam after work that day. She let me listen to the heartbeat again. One heartbeat, fast and strong. I was sitting on the edge of my bed with her portable Doppler to my belly. Reece was making apple empanadas downstairs, filling the house with the scent of apples and cinnamon.

"Did you see that story in the newspaper about the lady they found?" Abigail asked.

Newspaper. Now, there was a quaint notion. Every once in a while, Reece would bring home a copy of the Freep because I wanted the grocery coupons and he liked the comics. But having a paper subscription was right up there with having milk and eggs delivered. How newspapers even stayed in business anymore had to be some kind of sorcery.

"No. What lady?" I asked.

She took a folded section of the Freep out of her bag and showed me an article. I read the headline. A woman's body had been found in a guest room at the Leland Hotel. No surprise there. The place was a notorious fleabag that should have been condemned.

"Did you know her or something?" I asked.

"No. I don't know her. But it's really awful."

"Was she murdered?" Even that wouldn't have been surprising at the Leland.

"No. Much worse. She checks into a room on the eleventh of December. That was two months ago. She pays for only one night. Never checks out. The room is never cleaned. This week, somebody else checks into that same room. The woman is in the bathtub, no clothes, no water. They say she had turned black, like a mummy."

That was pretty bad. Even for the Leland.

"My cousin used to work at that place. She quit because it was so terrible. Read it, read it." Abigail said.

I read the grim story. The coroner was calling it a drug overdose. Heroin. I got to the part where they identified the body and just about fell off the bed. It was LuCretia.

☞

I sat at the kitchen island, staring at my plate full of untouched empanadas. Reece wasn't eating his either. We'd never liked LuCretia, but that didn't mean we were glad she was dead.

"I have to be the one to break this to him, face-to-face," I said. "Can you drive me up there?"

"I'm the last person he wants to see. You should just call him."

There was no way. I knew my brother. I knew when he'd need me. He was already wallowing in Elliot Smith/Jeff Buckley-level despair over his marital problems. A telephone call wasn't going to cut it with this rotten news.

"Please. I know you guys aren't getting along, but he's going to try to blame himself for her death. That's just how Clive is. He's already so down in the dumps with Becca gone and everything. I have to be there for him. It's the only thing I can do."

"I agree, you should tell him this in person. But I'm working tomorrow and the rest of this week. It's tax season, so I can't just split like that. Could someone else take you? And by that I mean literally any human being on Earth other than Saint."

I refrained from pointing out that calling Saint a human being was a huge upgrade from how Reece usually referred to him, and said, "Janice, maybe."

Reece smiled. "Janice. Perfect. You know what, give your brother this for me." He reached into the black backpack that he used instead of a briefcase and dug up a small baggie of Acapulco Gold. "Maybe it will take the edge off for him."

I didn't think it would make a dent in how Clive would feel when he found out LuCretia was dead. I also didn't think it would make him forgive Reece. But it was worth a shot.

41

Red Mosquito

Clive • Belknap Township, Mich. • Tuesday, Feb. 13, 2007

For six weeks straight I'd been painting Seventies album covers day and night on my mission to get Becca's credit card paid off. I'd let my work spill out of the studio/nursery and into the living room. My stomach rumbled and I promised myself I'd break for a sandwich and a smoke after I got this white carnation— pinned to the lapel of Alice Cooper's tuxedo—painted just right. *Welcome to My Nightmare.* I was pretty sure the cover artist had swapped in a young Warren Beatty because Cooper hadn't looked this good on his best day. Tonight it was just me and this fellow Detroiter rocking in my snow-encrusted purgatory while birch logs crackled in the fireplace.

A pair of headlights fishtailed up my long, snow-packed driveway.

I don't know how, but I was sure it was Ellie even before she emerged from the passenger's side of a VW Beetle, wearing a huge triangular coat the color of Dijon mustard. We hugged in the doorway, icy air rushing in and her tummy a friendly foreign nation between us. She'd embellished the coat's ridiculousness by embroidering a laughing pickle in a trucker cap on its wide shawl collar.

She pressed a tiny baggie of ganja into my hand and said, "Reece sent you his strongest flowers."

Janice stood behind her, grinning awkwardly.

I stuffed the baggie into the pocket of my jeans. There'd be no smoking anything with Ellie, and no way was I toking up with

Janice. God only knew what kind of nymphomaniac she'd turn into on weed.

Janice asked where my bathroom was and I pointed her down the hall. I knew it was a mess, but I wasn't looking to impress her anyway. Ellie's expression immediately turned grave and she dragged me off to the kitchen and spoke in a hushed tone.

"Look, I'm really sorry. I hate being the one to break this, but who else, you know?" She took a newspaper clipping from her coat pocket and handed it to me.

The headline read *Corpse Discovered in Hotel Tub*. I dropped the clipping to the floor and pressed my fist to my mouth. *Not this. Not her. Not yet.* I couldn't breathe.

Ellie nodded, her lips pressed together in a grim line, confirming what I already understood. I didn't need to read a word of the article to know it was about LuCretia, that she was dead and it was entirely my fault. Ellie put her arms around my neck and stroked the back of my head. I hated that I was crying but I couldn't stop.

I broke away from her and picked the article up off the floor.

"Please don't read it," Ellie said.

I had to. I owed LuCretia at least that much.

"I shouldn't have brought it. I should have just told you." She tried to take it from me. "Don't. Clive. I mean it. Just don't."

I crumpled the paper against my chest. "That's my call."

She backed off and hung her head as I read the hideous words blurred through my tears.

LuCretia had checked into that hellhole, the Leland, on December eleventh. That had to have been the same night she'd called me. Over two months, and no one had filed a missing persons report. The article focused more on the condition of the hotel and failings of its management than it did on the woman who'd died there.

It had been me who'd insisted we stop on Thanksgiving, me who'd failed to cancel my debit card in time, me who'd refused to file a police report against her which might have landed her someplace safer, like jail or rehab. Worse, I'd been thoroughly unkind that night when she'd called. What if I'd been slightly less than a complete asshole to her? What if I'd shown her a fraction of compassion or forgiveness? I'd enabled her and then I'd turned my back on her. My God, this could not have been more my fault if I'd cooked that shit down and injected her myself.

Ellie blotted her tears with a dishtowel. "I hate her so much for making you feel like this."

We heard Janice flush the toilet. Ellie handed me the dishtowel and I dried my eyes.

"Don't you dare feel guilty," she said. "Those were her choices. And don't forget she's cost you your wife."

I shook my head. I'd cost me my wife. I wasn't putting that on LuCretia. She may have been royally fucked up but my marriage had never been her responsibility. Ellie wasn't making things any better by trying to dictate how I should feel.

Janice popped into the kitchen. She saw my face and said, "Oh. Poor baby. I know. I know. Do you need a hug?"

"That's ... no. What I need right now is a stiff drink. Seriously."

"Well, I sure need a hug," Ellie said.

Janice embraced my sister. She looked over Ellie's shoulder at me and said, "Let's get you that drink."

ᴂ

We were at the Buckshot, which was thankfully Howie-free at the moment. I'd grabbed the last stool at the end of the bar and helped Ellie into the next one to create buffer between Janice and me. Janice had spread her Michigan Lotto tickets in front of her and was staring open-mouthed at the winning numbers on the wall-mounted flat screen.

I nudged Ellie. "You two are hanging tight these days, huh?"

"She's cool." Ellie leaned close. "Try to be sociable. You're turning into one of those hermit crabs."

I supposed it was pretty generous of Janice to bring Ellie all the way up here to deliver the distressing news about LuCretia in person. The bartender brought over our drinks: alcohol-free O'Doul's for Ellie, a Long Island iced tea for Janice and a double shot of scotch for me. My usual Natty was not going to cut it tonight. The kitchen was taking forever with our cheeseburgers and onion rings, but the scotch went down smooth and easy, and was especially

effective on an empty stomach. Ellie and Janice were chattering endlessly about water birth stories. By the time I'd down my third or fourth double I was ready to hop in a pool of warm water and dilate myself.

Janice toddled off to the bathroom and Ellie spun on her barstool and chugged from the O'Doul's bottle. "This is as close as I get to drinking anymore. Alcohol-free beer and spinning 'til I'm dizzy." She stopped mid-spin and pressed my hand to her daisy printed maternity top. "Feel this."

A rolling pressure moved against my palm. Wow. That was my nephew. Or niece.

Ellie giggled. "Did you feel it?"

"I really did." I kept my hand in place, waiting to feel the baby's movement again.

"See, it's not all gloom and doom. We need to kick back and focus on the things we do have. Each other. Friends who come through for us like Janice. A baby on the way. Our good health." She clinked her O'Doul's bottle with my glass. "You think they've got *Red Mosquito* on that jukebox?"

"Not a chance, unless Kenny Chesney covers it."

She slid from her stool and strolled past the foosball tables to the jukebox. She was adorable pregnant. Round and wholesome in the bluish glow of the beer light, her wild, wavy golden hair smoothed away from her face with a silk headband. She turned to me and made a gagging motion to indicate there wasn't one thing on the jukebox that met with her approval—no surprise there— and veered toward the ladies room. It hit me how much I'd missed her these last several weeks. I reached into my pocket and fingered the baggie Reece had sent. I knew it was some kind of bribe. I was still angry with him for cheating on Ellie and making me out to be the liar, but he was trying to set things right in his own half-assed way.

I knocked back the rest of my drink and told the barmaid, "Another scotch, and one of your buck-fifty carnations."

She brought me a white one. I poked the bloom into Ellie's empty O'Doul's bottle and analyzed the play of light and shadow on the crinkled petals, thinking about how to bring the carnation on Alice Cooper's lapel to life.

Along with my fourth (or was it my fifth?) scotch, our food was delivered. I scorched my fingertips on an onion ring, flung it to the floor and dunked my fingers into my drink. I was sucking scotch off my fingers and realizing that damn, I was drunk, when I spotted Howie's reflection in the giant Budweiser mirror. The guy was a Peterbilt truck in a Toronto Maple Leafs jersey. Not even the Red Wings. Now that was just low.

He headed straight for me, a bottle of Bud clutched in his big fist. Fucking stellar. Towering above me, he stuffed a couple of my onion rings into his mouth and didn't even react to the heat.

"Help yourself, muffin," I said.

He washed the onion rings down with beer and banged his bottle on the bar. "What the flying fuck did you do to Rebecca?"

"Huh?"

"I ought to throttle you over the head. Girl looks like a rabbit strung up by its toes and bled dry."

I didn't know what he was talking about. The last time I'd seen her she'd been in fine form in our kitchen, jabbing her fingers in the air and giving me a painfully accurate accounting of my cowardice.

"What in God's name happened to her?" Howie pushed a finger into my chest. "It's like you broke her."

An icicle of hatred slid through me. How could this asshole accuse me of breaking her? On her worst day she was stronger than the both of us put together.

"You're talking out of your ass," I said.

"Yeah? I just ran into her at Grulke Hardware. Ain't never seen her that sick. And here you are hanging out at the bar, boozin' it up."

"She's sick? Did she say what's wrong?"

Howie smacked the bar. "What'd you do to her, you long-haired hippy weasel? Tell me. Right now."

"What do you mean, 'sick'?"

"Fuck does she see in you, man? You're a midget fuck, Rafferty."

I gritted my teeth. "Thanks for noticing."

"Diamonds before swine."

"Pearls, moron."

"Nuh-uh. Rebecca is diamonds."

There was no remedy for his idiocy, so I stared into my scotch glass hoping he'd get bored with me and leave. But he stayed there, waiting for an explanation I couldn't possibly provide.

Ellie returned from the restroom and I helped her climb onto her barstool.

"Oh my hell, girlfriend's in there completely redoing her makeup." She sniffed the carnation. "Aw, Cliver, did you get this for me? That's super sweet. I guess we're all made up now and coolio and everything." She kissed my cheek. "So, who's your big friend?"

Howie looked from my face to Ellie's burgeoning midsection and back again. Color rose in his thick neck.

"Get in the car, El," I said.

"What? Why?"

"Grab Janice and just go."

Howie glowered, jaw jutting, Budweiser bottle clenched in his fist.

"Look, it's not what you think. That's my sister."

"Bullshit." Howie cracked me upside the head with his beer bottle.

Ellie shrieked. Ice cold beer soaked my shirt and groin. I fell off the stool and onto the carpet. I was flat on my back, head throbbing. White dots swirled against the water-stained ceiling tiles. Ellie was still screaming. I touched my head and found broken glass tangled in my hair, which was now slick with beer and blood.

Howie straddled me with the jagged bottleneck held high.

That's gonna hurt.

Ellie screamed "No!" She grabbed at Howie's arm and he swatted her away. She lunged at him again. He shoved her. She stumbled and landed flat on her ass. She gasped and her face contorted. "My tailbone!"

Seeing Ellie hurt unleashed a volcanic fury from deep inside me. I pulled my knees to my chest and rocked backward until I was out from under him. I slammed my feet into his brick wall torso. Howie went over backward. I pounced on him.

He struggled to throw me off. I spread my knees wide and dug them into the dense muscles of his shoulders. I hadn't been in a real fight in years. Not since foster care. That my body was still a master at this surprised my drunken brain. I pummeled my fists into Howie's stupid movie star face like his head was an obstacle to pulverizing a hole through the floor.

The face changed from Howie to Reece to the betting doctors to LuCretia's dealers to Honey Jane's pimps to every punk who'd ever attacked me.

Then I didn't see faces at all. I saw flames. I had to put them out with my fists.

"Clive stop! You'll kill him!" Ellie cried.

I wanted to stop. I didn't know how.

Two farmers grabbed me by the collar and the seat of my jeans. They hauled me to the door and threw me face down into a snow bank. One twisted my arms behind me.

"Got him?"

"Yeah."

"Sit on him. I'm calling the sheriff."

He sat on my back. Jesus, he was a heavy old boy.

"Get an ambulance while you're at it."

42

Of the Girl

Clive • Rogers City, Mich. • Wednesday, Feb. 14, 2007

The deputy frog-marched me through the police station and into the jail attached to the rear of the Presque Isle County Building. Last time I was here, Becca had taken my hand in marriage. This time, they took my coat, belt, wallet, keys, cigarettes, lighter, and shoelaces. They'd missed the baggie stuffed in my pocket.

"Pissed yourself," the deputy said.

It was Howie's beer on my jeans, but if it was keeping the deputy's hands off Reece's weed, good.

"Uh, yeah," I said, feigning deep shame. "Sorry 'bout that."

The deputy curled his lip. "Turn your pockets out for me."

"Yes sir." I pulled out as much fabric as possible without revealing the baggie.

"Alright, son."

I'd never have gotten away with that in Wayne County. Even so, I was missing the ever lovin' fuck out of Detroit at the moment.

He locked me in a bright, chilly cell. I waited for the hallway to clear, then approached the rust-stained commode attached to the wall. I unzipped my wet jeans, dumped Reece's finest flowers into the water and pissed on the golden flecks. I flushed and watched my last few grams of slightly decent luck swirl down the vortex.

The place stank of old urine on concrete blended with over-zealous pine disinfectant. My hands were burning, aching, raw. I slumped on a concrete slab that sucked what little warmth was left from my body. Becca would have called that a heat sink. Becca. All of this was because of her, because she was sick and I hadn't known it, and that dumbass Howie had decided he needed to "throttle me over the head" for it. When I got out of jail, the first thing I was going to do was send that dipshit ex-boyfriend of hers a dictionary of his very own.

ୡ

I lay with one arm behind my head and the other shielding my eyes from the harsh light of the caged bulb. The only sounds were the dry tick of the wall clock, the intermittent crackle of a police scanner, and a distant, tinny radio faintly playing *Beast of Burden*. So much for my New Year's resolution. It was only mid-February and the sole thing I'd gotten better at was fucking up. LuCretia was dead. I was behind bars. If and when I got out of jail, I was going to ditch my land contract and move back to Detroit. Or start over someplace else entirely, like Oregon. Or maybe China. I'd never been so desperate for a cigarette.

I passed the long, cold night losing a truly valiant battle to not think about how completely the fight had blown whatever scant chance I had of getting back together with Becca. Each time I started drifting off to sleep, I saw LuCretia's rotting remains grimacing in a hotel bathtub. Sometimes she was holding Louise, the corner of white flannel peeled back from her tiny, eyeless face.

ୡ

In the morning I was arraigned and advised of the charges filed against me.

Resisting Arrest. Not exactly, but not all that surprising either. Never disagree with the fuzz. But if you must, best avoid the term *douche nozzle*. North of Oscoda, even *Officer Douche Nozzle sir* is unacceptable.

Public Drunkenness. That didn't seem quite right. In Wayne County, they'd have charged me with drunk and disorderly.

Assault with intent to do great bodily harm less than murder. What was that even about? In my head I tried to replay the fight with Howie, but only remembered Ellie's contorted face, my scorching anger, and trying to beat out flames.

Because I had no priors, the magistrate set my personal recognizance bond at $500. I just had to sign a few papers and I was free until my pre-trial hearing. That was the good news.

I had a swollen cut on my cheek, a roaring headache, and severe cottonmouth. My unlaced shoes flopped under my feet as I followed the deputy to his desk. A plastic bag filled with my stuff sat among the stacks of files and forms. My red lighter was in it but my pack of smokes was conspicuously absent. My peacoat was also missing, but I figured it got left behind at the Buckshot. I had to sign a pile of forms before the deputy would let me use the phone to call Ellie for a ride. While it rang unanswered, I touched the tender lump on the side of my head through hair stiff with dried blood and beer.

I couldn't reach Ellie. The snow blew horizontally in the harsh wind and stuck to the windows. It would be a miserable trek home on foot in punishing cold, but I didn't relish hanging out around the Presque Isle County Jail.

"If you fail to show for your preliminary hearing you'll owe us $500 and you'll be taking up residence here in jail until your court date," the deputy said. "Meantime, find yourself a good lawyer. And you might want to trim those lovely locks before your date with the judge, Rapunzel."

I didn't stop to put the laces in my shoes. I pushed through the glass exit door and into the dry heat of the vestibule. What awaited me there was so beautiful that I dropped my plastic bag.

◌

Becca leaned against the wall-unit heat grate with my peacoat folded over her arm. The hot current made her hair flutter like my stomach. With crystal clarity, I understood Howie's outrage. Her brown coveralls were unzipped to the waist, and a blue thermal shirt clung to her ribs. The dark circles beneath her eyes contrasted with the spectral shade of her skin. Her cheeks were a fevered pink. *A rabbit strung up by its toes and bled dry.*

"How are you here?" I asked.

"Your sister called me. She couldn't get that hunk of junk Toyota of yours started."

I didn't understand why Ellie would need my car—unless Janice had ditched her. That would have been an awfully shitty thing to do.

Becca's voice was low and hoarse. "I tried to jump start it for her, but, well, let's just say that after thirty years on the road, it doesn't owe anyone anything." She dissolved into a violent fit of coughing.

"Oh, Bec. You should be home in bed, not out in this Arctic cold messing with jumper cables. Especially not for my sake."

"I couldn't just let you walk home. It's six below. You wouldn't last ten minutes in this wind chill."

"Exactly. And you're sick. You shouldn't even be out in this. You're going to end up with pneumonia if you don't have it already."

"That's the least of my worries. They took Howie away in an ambulance last night. You're in some seriously deep doo-doo."

"Holy shit. Is he alright?"

She handed me my coat. "He'll live, but he's in the hospital in Alpena with a broken jaw. Why'd you have to hurt him? I mean, fighting over me? How'd you think that was going to go? Neither of you had me. Everybody loses. You're like a couple of cavemen. This whole town is talking about your scrap last night like it's my fault. For cripe's sake, I'm home nursing the worst case of bronchitis I've ever had in my life, and you two are getting drunk and brawling at the Buckshot. Howie ends up with his jaw wired shut, and it's all on me according to the Rogers City gossip mill. I did not need this today. Valentine's Day. What a joke."

I could have explained that I'd drank too much to dull the guilt of LuCretia's death. And that Howie had bashed my head with a bottle and shoved Ellie to the floor. But I knew when Becca was in no mood for excuses, which was basically always.

She zipped up her coveralls. "I'll drop you home on my way to the hospital. I have to see him for myself. And I want to hear his side of the story."

"Bec, I'm sorry. Really sorry. About all of this. And tell him, tell Howie I didn't mean it. I was drunk. I don't know what got into me."

"Save your apologies for Ellie. You scared the crap out of that poor girl. And how is she so pregnant? She's huge. I don't even think she should be alone right now."

I could tell by her tone that it had been difficult for her to see my sister still pregnant. The contrast between the two of them was hard enough on me. It had to be hell for Becca.

She shoved through the door. I trailed her into the blinding sunlight and blowing snow. I grabbed her hand. She laced her fingers with mine. My raw knuckles stung, but her warmth was heavenly—right up until I realized that it was a fever making her hand hot.

"Come home with me," I said. "Let me take care of you."

She laughed, then stopped, doubled over and seal-barked against her sleeve, then laughed some more. "I don't need your brand of help. Look at yourself. You're a mess. Go home and take care of yourself and your sister. Let me worry about me."

Sparkling puffs of snow blasted my face. The packed snow on the sidewalk squeaked under my feet like tortured Styrofoam. I pulled up the collar of my peacoat.

"Where's your van?"

"Parked around front. I had to file some paperwork at the county clerk's."

Scalding panic made me forget the cold. She'd been filing divorce papers; I knew this like I knew my own middle name. She was done with me. She held my hand and stalked ahead of me like the mother of an errant five-year-old who's just been expelled from kindergarten. She let go when we reached the van. I followed her over the snow bank and into the street to open the driver's side door. Her dark hair blew across her face. I brushed it away, skimming her burning cheek.

"Why'd you come for me, really?" I asked.

269

She shrugged. "I guess I've never been the kind of person who leaves her dog at the pound."

43

No Way

Ellie • Belknap Township, Mich. • Monday, Feb. 19, 2007

Before we hit the road, I need to lay down a few ground rules," Becca said. Shapeless and intimidating in her brown winter coveralls and fingerless work gloves, she clutched the enormous steering wheel of her company van. She turned away from me and coughed violently into her shoulder. "I swear it's not as bad as it sounds. I'm on antibiotics."

Right. I could have smacked Reece for sweet-talking her into giving me a ride home. The night of the fight, Janice had completely freaked out and high-tailed it back to Detroit in a tizzy. I'd refused to go with her because my brother needed me. Clive couldn't take me home while his 1978 Land Cruiser was in the shop awaiting parts that had to be ordered from overseas. It had been no surprise that Reece—with tax season looming—couldn't get the time off. While I'd enjoyed my little impromptu vacation hanging out in the boonies with Clive, I needed to get home for a prenatal appointment and my job at Mr. Salty's.

Saint had readily agreed to pick me up even though it was a minimum ten-hour round trip for him. But Reece couldn't deal with me spending a few lousy hours in a car with Saint, despite these facts: the guy already lived in our house, he had a harem of hotties trailing him wherever he went, and I was roughly the size of Jupiter and in no mood for sexy times in a rusty Geo Tracker in the dead of winter. Reece was being flat out ridiculous. He'd called Becca, promised to make her a pan of his famous cream cheese marbled brownies and who knows what else, then informed Saint that I no longer needed a ride. By the time I'd found out and tried to put the original plan back in place, Saint had already agreed to take someone's shift at work.

Not to mention, Becca had some kind of death-rattle bronchitis which I really did not need exposure to in my delicate state.

I was mad, but Clive was livid. The last thing he wanted was Becca having to chauffer a pregnant lady around while she was still grieving the loss of Louise Clover. Or while she was fighting the aforementioned bronchitis. Or having her realize he hadn't kept his shit together enough to have a running vehicle on hand. Or, especially, having anyone pester her for a huge favor on his behalf.

Clive had already lectured me about what I couldn't discuss with Becca: My pregnancy. Her abortion. Their marriage. The fight. Howie Peterson. Janice Marconi. LuCretia. The fire. Our mother. Politics. Religion. "And for God's sake, don't bore her going on and on about Pearl Jam."

Honestly. What was left? Recipes?

Becca's first ground rule was, "I don't want to hear about pregnancy. Yours or anyone else's." She had stopped the van at the bottom of Clive's long driveway and put it in park. Clive was waving at us from the picture window. I waved back, but she either didn't see him or she was pretending not to.

"Alright," I said.

"And no questions about if or when I plan to have kids. Really, just no baby or kid talk, period."

"Sure."

"Nothing about me and Clive. Nothing. Not past, present, or future. I don't want to discuss what happened, what's going on now or what's going to happen."

"He already told me not to bring up any of that stuff."

"Good. For the purposes of this drive, let's agree to pretend that he doesn't exist."

"Why would you even be giving me a ride, then?"

"Let's just say my friend Reece asked me to do him a favor, and luckily I didn't have any jobs scheduled and I needed to pick up a certain furnace motor in the greater Detroit area anyway."

"Got it."

Becca backed onto Rabbits-Honey Road and I pushed the visor down to block the glare of the wintry sunrise. Well, everyone called it Rabbits-Honey but it was really just a rural route with a number. Down the street from Clive someone who sold rabbits and honey had stuck a hand-painted sign near the ditch at the corner, inadvertently christening this end of the rural route with a weird name.

She turned up the stereo volume for T. Rex, *Planet Queen*. I was just grateful it wasn't Creed. Janice had insisted we listen to them during the entire drive north—she was sure I'd like them if I just gave them a chance—and I still hadn't quite recovered from that assault on my musical soul. I'd spent that entire journey counting mile markers, dreading telling Clive about LuCretia, and thinking about a Frank Zappa song Reece liked to sing called *The Torture Never Stops*. This trip was shaping up to be about as much fun, even if T. Rex was a lot more tolerable.

"So, what's a safe topic?" I asked.

"Don't worry about it. You don't have to entertain me with sparkling conversation. I really am just doing this for Reece."

"Oh. Well, did he inform you that Saint was totally coming to get me until Reece called you up and begged you to do it instead, and then he turned around and told Saint I already had a ride arranged?"

"No way. Reece wouldn't do that."

Lord. This was how it always was with Reece and every other woman alive. They were all so sure he was just the sweetest thing, and oh-so-cute, and not a devious bone in his supplement-fueled, sugar-addicted body. *And by the way gals, he can bake. Order your very own Reece LeFanch today and we'll throw in free-weights, a pill sorter, and damp towels we guarantee he'll leave on the floor just for you.*

"He's French, right?" she asked.

I dropped my head against the headrest and looked at the corrugated metal of the van's roof. Reece was about as French as I was Labrador retriever. I pressed the soles of my wool clogs against the dashboard. Her van was old and cluttered with papers and tools, so I didn't figure a couple of footprints would make it any worse. "He's a mix. Mostly Polish. His mom's maiden name was

273

like Mazcieweski or Matazewski, one of those M-ski names. So yeah, he's pretty much a Polack despite the fancy French last name. I think his dad was adopted anyway. Who knows? And you, I'm guessing, are at least part Native American."

She touched her nose. "You can tell?"

"Crowe. Your dark hair. Yeah, it's not such a stretch."

She pulled onto the highway ramp. "Crowe is actually a very old English surname. But I'm one-sixteenth Ottawa, if Crowe family lore is to be believed. And obviously, you're Irish."

"I am?"

"Well, yeah. Rafferty is Irish."

"Rafferty may or may not have been one of our mother's aliases." Whoops. I'd just broken one of Clive's cardinal *Do Not Discuss* rules. Oh well. "No idea about the paternal side of things. Our dad could have been black, for all we know."

She laughed. "Right. With your strawberry blond hair, freckles and sky-blue eyes."

"But Clive's hair is brown. And have you ever seen how fast it dreads if he doesn't wash it?"

"Fortunately, no. He's been pretty hygienic since I've known him. And we're not talking about him, remember?"

Sheesh. She was the one who'd brought him up. I decided to quit trying to make conversation.

The baby hiccupped inside me, kicking and turning, trying to get comfortable. This whole pregnancy, I'd never felt comfortable and I knew why. One day my deception would come to light. My child would demand the truth about his or her father. What credibility would I have with my own kid if I lied about that?

Curled in the stiff passenger's seat, with great puffs of snow blowing across I-75, I made an important decision. If the baby was obviously a LeFanch, I'd take my indiscretion to the grave. If the baby was a Wozniak, I'd come clean about that with everyone and not ask a single thing of Saint. I'd accept whatever hardships this caused me, because I was the one who'd made the mistakes. Who'd cheated. Who was still pretending this baby was a LeFanch when I knew damned well it might not be.

If it wasn't obvious right off who the father was, I'd pay for paternity tests. This decision made, I could go forward into motherhood with a clear conscience.

The single indulgence I allowed myself was the continued hope it was Reece's baby. He drove me nuts half the time, sure. But the truth was I needed Reece. I loved him. He'd always been good to me.

"What made you decide to come all the way up here to our vast, frozen snowscapes in the dead of winter, anyway?" Becca asked.

I had to think fast to put it in terms that didn't violate any of the taboo topic zones she and Clive had laid out for me. "Someone we used to know died. I felt I should deliver that news in person."

"A family member?"

"No."

"A friend?"

"Not really, no."

"Your old foster mother?"

I shook my head.

She pulled off her gray knit cap and stuffed it into a cup holder. Strands of her satiny hair floated with static. "Alright. I give up. Who is it that died, that was so important that you had to get someone to give you a ride all the way up here to break the news in person, and yet this very important, recently deceased person is neither family nor friend?"

"I'm not at liberty to say."

"Oh, my God."

"I'm sorry. I'd tell you, but I promised my brother that I wouldn't discuss certain subjects with you. His list was pretty much the same as yours, but more specific. As it happens, the deceased is near the top of the *Do Not Mention* list."

"No. I meant, *oh, my God* as in, *oh, my God—I know who it was.* I know exactly who it was. Holy cow. She died? She's actually dead? She OD'd, didn't she? She took all of our money, spent it on drugs and did herself in. Oh, my God. That's just horrible."

"Yeah. I hated her guts, but I never wished her dead. Not like, for real anyway."

"Same," Becca said. "Now I feel bad for calling her Le Crouton."

"Nice. I usually referred to her as Lu-Creep-Show."

"So I guess this means we've both earned our Girl Scout asshole merit badges. What happened to her? I mean, she did actually OD, right? What was she on? Where did it happen?"

"I don't really know the details," I said. "I'm sure it was just typical drug-addict whatever. You know, they overdo it, and nobody's around to help, and that's the end of that." I figured I'd already violated Clive's rules badly enough without bringing up the gruesome scene at the Leland Hotel.

"He's got to be feeling like absolute garbage about this. You know how he is. He's probably been kicking himself up and down the street for days now," she said.

"Yeah, pretty much. We're not discussing him, however."

Becca started coughing, covering her mouth with her arm and turning away from me. She grabbed her water bottle and took a long swig.

"No. We're really not," she said. "And we absolutely will not talk about how this news must have affected his emotional state, possibly leading him to drink too much of something a lot stronger than Natural Light, and then brawling with my idiot ex-boyfriend at the Buckshot Tavern."

"Yeah, please don't mention any of that." I twisted in my seat so I was facing in her direction. "And I won't bring up how your ex knocked me flat on my ass right before a certain someone lost his mind and started beating the crap out of him."

"No! No fucking way. I can't believe it. Howie actually hit you? Neither of them told me about that."

"He didn't hit me, he shoved me. And I fell down on my already-bruised tailbone."

Her mouth dropped open. "Oh, that's right. That's right. From when you got mugged last November. God, Ellie. That's just terrible. And that weenie bastard had me convinced the fight was all Clive's fault."

"But we haven't discussed any of it."

"Right. And now I know how a fight we didn't talk about, between two people we're absolutely not mentioning, went down. Wow. I'm so glad we didn't talk about this at all," she said.

"Yeah, it's a good thing we stuck to talking about recipes."

She nodded enthusiastically. "Especially since I don't cook."

I was really beginning to appreciate what it was that Clive saw in Becca. What a shame that it was over between them before we had a chance to become friends.

ॐ

I'd been holding my pee, figuring we were getting close and I'd rather use my home toilet. Then Becca veered off to pick up that furnace motor, adding another half-hour to my agony. She probably would have stopped for a bathroom again if I'd asked, but my bladder-dancing fetus had already caused us to visit nearly every rest area from Alpena to Clarkston. It had to be trying Becca's patience even if she didn't show it.

Finally, we got home and I made a mad dash for the bathroom. When I came downstairs she was in the kitchen with Reece, who was wearing a lavender gingham apron over his work shirt and melon tie. He played the role of perfect boyfriend expertly, serving her fresh brownies with homemade whipped cream, raspberries, and peppermint tea. She was talking about how great she thought Tremor Christ was, and Reece was saying, "Take him with you, please. Consider him a parting gift."

"Don't be giving Saint's dog away," I said.

"I'm planning to kidnap him one of these days," Becca said. "Saint doesn't know how to handle him anyway."

"Actually, he's been teaching him a bunch of new stuff," I said.

Reece put his hands on his hips and repeated my words exactly, wagging his head around. He was straight up jealous of Saint. I couldn't say a word about him lately without Reece mocking me.

"I want to see Tremor Christ before I go. I brought a little goodie for him," Becca said.

"Ooh. And did you bring a goodie for me, too?" Reece asked.

"As a matter of fact, I did. Her name's Ellie."

Abigail showed up for my prenatal appointment right then, so I crammed a brownie in my mouth and let her inside. By the time we came back downstairs from my exam, Becca had left and Reece had gone back to work. I tiptoed down to the basement. Tremor Christ was asleep in his crate, dreaming about something, his big paws flippering. I hadn't really thought she'd kidnap him, but I had to check.

Reece had left his brownie baking mess all over the kitchen, and for some inexplicable reason had dragged out a shoebox full of photos that I'd been meaning to organize. Right on top was the picture I'd taken New Year's Day morning of Saint sleeping shirtless on the sectional with two chicks. I pawed through the box and everything seemed in order, so I stuffed it back under the sectional where it belonged.

44

I Wanna be Your Dog

Clive • Rogers City, Mich. • Friday, Mar. 9, 2007

Cubby followed me up the slush-covered outside stairway to Becca's apartment. Against my chest I hugged the envelope of divorce paperwork she'd asked me to sign, and the small painting wrapped in brown paper. A flock of nervous moths fluttered inside my chest. I didn't want this. She did.

I knocked.

"It's open."

I turned the knob and stepped into the brilliant warmth of her kitchen. Her boombox was blasting *I Wanna Be Your Dog* while she knelt to pry open a can of latex paint. Cubby ran in first, greeting her with muddy paws and a wet shake of his fur.

"Out, boy," she said, and then, "Clive. What's up?"

What was up was that I'd smoked five cigarettes end-to-end while pacing up and down Rabbits-Honey Road in the dark, trying to work up the nerve to deliver these things to her. Scribbling my signature on the divorce papers was signing away the love of my life. I'd never have done it if she hadn't asked me that fourth time. I'd brought the painting I'd always intended to give her. This wasn't a good time, but now there never was going to be a good time, so I had to settle for tonight.

"Uh … looks like you're in the middle of something. This stuff can wait." I needed to put the envelope and painting somewhere safe, but at this point I didn't feel welcome to walk through her kitchen and into the living room. I tucked everything into her

Reagan-era microwave, large enough to ruin a Thanksgiving turkey. "Looks like a big job. Need a hand?"

"Yeah, that'd be great actually. You're a painter. Grab yourself a roller." She bent forward at the waist and fastened her hair into a haphazard bun.

I hadn't thought she'd take me up on it. It made me smile even if I wasn't that kind of a painter.

"Sure, sure. Absolutely." I took off my damp sweat jacket and turned my T-shirt inside out. It was black with a strip of highway beneath a cirrus-clouded Montana sky and a yield sign. Ellie had given it to me years ago. She thought it was a lucky shirt but I'd worn it only because I was behind on laundry and it was the last thing in the drawer.

"You know what? Could you take the rest of the hardware off the cabinets first?" Becca handed me a screwdriver.

"Of course, sure."

"Please don't do that."

Now I didn't know what she wanted of me. "So, you want the hardware left on?"

"No. I meant don't say 'Sure! Sure!' You're like a desperate puppy. Grab yourself a beer and pretend you're my equal."

Called right out for being inadvertently pathetic, I yanked open her fridge and was greeted by the sight of familiar blue cans. But she hated Natural Light. I pulled a can out of the six-pack collar and held it up. "What's the story here?"

"I stuck it in my cart out of habit. I didn't even realize what I bought until I got home. While you're in there, grab me a real beer."

By that, she meant a Bell's Two Hearted Ale. I handed her the bottle but refused to let go until she looked at me. Our eyes met and a grin broke across her face. I let go and cracked open my Natty. It tasted like she might still love me.

I sat on the floor and started unscrewing a cupboard knob, watching her from the corner of my eye. The buttercream latex she poured into the roller pan looked like cake batter.

"Don't get too much in there," I said. "It'll slosh."

"So, we'll wipe it up. I'm not trucking down the ladder every four minutes for a refill. This isn't art. It's maintenance."

"I can do your refills."

"You're doing the hardware, and at sloth-neck speed, too, I see."

She carried the roller pan up the ladder, hooked it in place and tossed her flannel over-shirt onto the counter. I watched her reflection in the bare window, her pale blue Superman tank top with no bra, her firm arms, that brash, unapologetic confidence she exuded. I'd missed everything about her. I'd missed *us*. But this wasn't us, it was a faint, distorted shadow of who we'd been together. The proximity to Becca hurt me down to my soul. I caught myself staring up at her reflection, distracted by her muscular grace as she cut in the corners with a paint brush in one hand and a damp rag in the other. Secretly gazing at her felt wrong. She wouldn't want me doing that even if she was, for the moment, still technically my wife.

She stretched to brush the crown molding, one leg stretched behind her for balance, toe pointed in her canvas slip-ons. She clamped the paintbrush handle between her teeth and reached to daub a paint drip with a rag. It was beyond her. She leaned out further and the ladder tilted with her. Two of its legs lifted off the floor. I scrambled to my feet as she pinwheeled her free arm and shrieked. The paintbrush flew through the air. She clung to the tilting ladder like a cat on a rollercoaster.

I reached her as the ladder rocked back and the legs slammed into place. The roller pan flipped off and dumped a torrent of cold paint over my head. I squeezed my eyes shut and clenched my fists. Thick humiliation coursed down my face and neck.

She jumped to the floor. "Oh my God. Clive. I'm so sorry." She squeezed my shoulder and started wiping at my face with a rag. "Keep them closed. Keep them closed. You alright?"

I nodded.

The faucet ran. She led me to the sink and wiped my eyes again, her cloth hot and wet, her hand steady on my cheek. "Don't open your eyes." She continued rinsing the rag and smoothing the cold paint from my face. "My God, I'm so sorry. Keep them closed. You don't want paint in there."

Her voice, her gentle touch, her lavender scented shampoo, the ale faintly on her breath. I absorbed her essences for what I knew would be the last time.

"I think you're safe to open them," she said.

I blinked.

"Is it in your eyes?"

"No. My mouth. And it's not buttercream flavored, either."

"You should see yourself." The concern in her voice melted to giggles.

I rinsed my mouth with water and spat into the sink a few times. I downed the rest of my beer to wash away the residual tang of latex. She grabbed another Natty out of the fridge and opened it for me.

"Your hair." Becca snickered. "You look like a loaded paintbrush."

I tried to push my hair back, but my fingers got stuck in the mess. This delivery of divorce papers could not get any worse.

"I could paint the walls with your head." Becca laughed harder. Hugging her sides, she collapsed to the floor and fell backward in a fit of hilarity.

"Hang on a minute while I wring my hair out in the paint can," I said.

That made her screech with laughter. I dropped to my knees and made my hair glide across her bare arms, smearing her with cold semi-gloss. She snorted and wiped at the tears spurting from her eyes.

"Ha! What are you doing? It's cold!"

I rubbed my nose with hers. "Just pretend I'm your equal."

She grasped my paint-soaked T-shirt in both hands and pulled me down on top of herself. She kissed me. Oh, that soul-splitting kiss of hers. It was endless, yet over much too soon.

She giggled. "Your hair's so gross."

"Mmm hmm." I kissed her, melting for her like a pat of butter in the middle of a stack of hot pancakes.

"You taste like latex," she said.

282

"Yet you can't resist me."

"I'm twisted like that." She kissed me again. "And cheap beer."

"Admit it. You secretly love Natty. You're not fooling anyone with that 'accidently bought it' story."

"And something else. Let me taste that again." She kissed me long and slow.

My heart was either going to burst or break. I pulled back from her and looked deeply into her onyx eyes. She slid her hands down, squeezed my ass and rolled her hips against me, looking into my face the whole time. We peeled away our clothes and got down to business, our skin sticky with paint. The newspapers crinkled beneath us on the hard floor. I savored every inch of her, not allowing myself to think about what this could mean or if it was our last time ever.

Afterward, we showered together. She shampooed paint out of my hair until the hot water ran cold. We toweled each other dry and collapsed on her brass bed. We'd have one hell of a mess to deal with tomorrow, but tonight—Oh God, *tonight*.

ରୁ

I tiptoed into the disaster zone of Becca's kitchen at dawn and let Cubby out into the drizzling gray morning. Thick splatters of paint had dried on the cupboards, the countertop, and the appliances. Her discarded tank top clung to my T-shirt forming a textile sculpture of unadulterated lust.

While the teapot was heating, I tugged my paint-stiffened jeans on and borrowed the flannel shirt that was draped across the counter. Had she been scratching an itch last night? Was our delicious mishap actually a goodbye screw? Reconciliation couldn't possibly be this easy.

I gathered ruined newspapers from the floor and crammed them into the trash can, soaked the paint brushes in hot water in the sink, and started scraping the dried latex off of her countertops and faucet.

Becca wandered in, raked her fingers through her hair and blinked at me with puffy eyes.

"Mornin', beautiful," I said.

Her smile was equal parts glad-you're-still-here and pure embarrassment.

"I haven't been this hungry in months," she said.

I filled a mug with hot water and dropped a teabag into it for her. "Did we ... last night ... was that for real?"

"It happened. I've missed you." She frowned into her cup. "But I'm not sure if it changes things. I mean you're still ... and I'm still. And for all of our issues, sex was never the problem."

Damn. She was right, as usual.

"Hey, I brought you something," I said. The painting seemed smaller, less significant, as I pulled it from the microwave, leaving the envelope of signed divorce documents inside.

She tore away the brown paper, revealing my painting—a newborn baby girl combining Becca's beauty and the snapshots of my brothers that Mrs. Marconi had given to me. Little Louise's mouth was as sweet as a candy kiss, her eyes wide and clear, her wispy hair black like Becca's. The dimples on her cheeks and chin were pure Rafferty, and she was swaddled in a blanket covered in clover in reference to her middle name.

Becca touched my hand. "You've put her together. You've made her alright."

I wanted to say I wished I could do the same for our marriage, but this wasn't about that. I knew enough to quit while I was, if not exactly ahead, maybe breaking even for the first time in months.

Cubby scratched at the door. Becca let him in, along with the cold, damp air. He shook off, spraying us both with the smell of wet beagle.

"I should probably get going," I said. "You were lovely to me last night. Stunning. I'm so grateful. Even if we can never work this out, I want us to try to stay friends." I put my sweat jacket on.

"Wait. Listen. There's something that's been eating at me, something I need to understand." She pulled open a drawer and slapped a Polaroid photo on the counter. "Was this the girl with the pie on Thanksgiving?"

It wasn't a picture of a girl. It was me with a stupid New Year's tiara stuck in my hair, my mouth smeared with horrid raspberry lipstick, my eyes reflecting every ounce of the cowardice that Becca had called me out on. I wanted to barf.

"Who gave you that? Reece? That Saint guy?" There was no way Ellie would have.

"I stole it, I'll admit that. Right out of your sister's shoebox of photos that day I gave her a ride home. New Year's Eve, Clive. Right here is why Reece couldn't find you, isn't it? It's why you never called me back."

"When he said you called, I totally thought he was pulling my leg."

"Now who's pulling whose leg? I heard this same chick was in town the night you beat up Howie. What's her name? Janet?"

I looked at the floor. There was no point in engaging in an argument about Janice Marconi. She wasn't worth the oxygen it would take.

"So, want to know how I feel about this picture?" she asked.

I braced myself against the countertop, my ears hot with shame.

"I let my damned dog loose. I don't get to complain if he eats dinner somewhere else."

"Baby, please. I never ate at Janice's. How can I make you believe that?"

"It doesn't matter. That's my whole point. I stared at this picture for hours trying to kill my love for you, trying to hate you, and I couldn't do it." She pressed her palms to her temples. "I can't hate you. It's not in me. Last night, I couldn't even resist you." She started to cry. "You're my Kryptonite. You have to leave me alone. I'm begging you."

"What? No. Please, Bec. Listen. We belong together. Both of us want this, deep down. After what happened with us last night, I feel sure we can work it out. I can be so much better, I swear. There is nothing I wouldn't do to make you happy."

She shook her head.

Cubby carried over one of my paint-ruined shoes and dropped it on my toe. That dog always knew what was up.

45

Suggestion

Ellie • Detroit, Mich. • Sunday, Mar. 11, 2007

I ndigestion and the baby's incessant hiccups made sleep impossible. At 2:30 a.m. I'd given up trying to teach myself to play *Release* on the ukulele and was separating strands of gold embroidery floss. My due date was still five weeks away. At my appointment that afternoon, Abigail had said I was dilated to one and partially effaced. The rented birthing tub, set up behind the sectional, was sanitized, covered in Saran wrap and ready to be filled at a moment's notice.

The front door crashed open and in tumbled Saint with Double Roses and my least favorite entrant in the skank parade, Cross. The stink of her cigarettes, cheap body splash and hairspray assaulted my nostrils from across the room. She didn't bother wiping the mud from her vinyl ankle boots.

To be polite, I said, "Evenin' kids."

"Oh, it's awake," Cross said.

Saint gave her a playful shove. "Be nice, Chelsea. That's my landlady you're talking to." He was wearing the bittersweet scarf, like always.

"Member of your immediate Jamily, too," I said.

"El, you're looking well, uh, well-rounded this evening," he said.

I laughed.

"Holy shit. Saint, you never told me you got a Jacuzzi," Double Roses said.

I hopped off the sectional. "It's not a hot tub. That's my birthing tub. Don't touch it. It has to stay sanitary."

"Yeah," Saint said. "She could blow any minute. Don't mess with her tub."

"Why do you care, huh Saint?" Cross sat on the edge of the tub and poked her fingernail through the plastic wrap.

"Chelsea, I'm totally serious. Don't even mess with her tub. It's no joke," Saint said.

"Let's fill 'er up and go for a skinny dip." Cross tore away a strip of Saran and swung her muddy boots into the tub. She stood up right in the middle of it.

I couldn't believe it. The whole tub would have to be sanitized again. I was ready to fill it and drown Cross's skank ass. I glared at Saint.

He grabbed Cross under the arms and dragged her out. "The kitchen. Both of you. Now." He pushed them toward the door and looked over his shoulder at me. "Sorry. I'll clean it. I'll clean it, I swear."

The bottom of the tub was soiled with Cross's muddy boot prints. I hated her, and the other one. I hated every last one of them except for little Harajuku Goth Rosebud/Lizzie, who had apparently moved along to some other psychedelic band called The Black something or other. If the baby came right now, I'd have an audience of gothic morons.

I brushed past all of them, went down to the laundry room and gathered bleach, a bucket and cleaning rags. Tremor Christ's crate was empty. He was in the backyard.

"Aw, is that her practice baby?" I heard Cross ask as I headed back up the steps.

"It's Tremor's gummipuppe. For training," Saint said.

There were peals of girl laughter. "Say that again. Tremor's whoodi whaddi?"

"Gummipuppe. Give it to me."

"Yeah Chelsea, give Saint his dolly back," Double Roses said.

When I reached the kitchen the doll was flying back and forth between the two girls. But Saint wasn't dumb enough to engage in their game of keep away. I ducked through the kitchen and he followed me into the living room.

"They're drunk. I said I'd clean it for you. Let me do it. I'm really sorry. Please. Just sit down and relax," he said.

"Can't you send them home? They'll wake Reece. He has to work tomorrow."

"Yeah, OK."

There was another shriek of laughter, followed by hysterical giggling and the slam of the back door.

Saint hurtled into the kitchen. "What'd you do?"

Both girls cackled.

"Die gummipuppe?"

"Die goopy poopy!" More hysterical giggling and snorting.

"Never, ever screw with my dog. Now get out of my house, both of you."

"Get out, or Saint's going to let his badass mutt eat us."

"Your Alpo's not good enough for my dog," Saint said.

The girls clambered out the front door, clinging to each other and cackling. Cross yelled, "Buh-bye!"

Reece was standing at the top of the stairs in his boxers, shaking his head.

"Aw, I'm sorry they woke you, sweetie. They're gone now. Saint made 'em leave," I said.

"Sugar, come to bed. I miss you."

I patted my belly. "She's practicing the Cha-Cha Slide. No sleep for me. G'night, Reece's Pieces."

Saint filled the bucket with hot water and pushed his sleeves to his elbows. While he cleaned the tub, I sat on the edge and asked him why he even hung out with girls like that.

He shrugged. "They gravitate to me, maybe 'cause I don't judge them."

"Except when you're calling them Alpo."

"Yeah, Chelsea gets her mean on when she drinks brown liquor. Plus, she's been jealous of you ever since I moved in here. That's the last time I buy that little wench any Captain Morgan's."

Chelsea. I still thought of her as Cross. And I never would have dreamed that any of Saint's groupies envied plain old me.

289

"What's her issue with me?" I asked.

He wrung his rag into the bucket of bleach water and wiped away the muddy boot prints. "You're really good at being yourself. No pretenses. You don't even care what's cool or not. You're chill. You're the real deal, Detroit Ellie."

It might have been the nicest thing anyone had ever said to me.

When he had the tub sparkling again, he put on his training gear and went out back. He was out there a long time. I checked on him through the back door window. He was slumped on the deck, his face buried in Tremor Christ's shoulder. The dog looked every bit as dejected as Saint.

CR

I drifted off to sleep sitting up on the sectional. Saint walked in and laid the headless torso of the gummipuppe on the coffee table. And one leg. And half of its perpetually grinning face.

"I really tried," he said.

I knew. I knew how hard he'd tried to train Tremor Christ to be gentle.

"He was provoked," I said.

"If he hurts your baby, it won't matter whether or not he was provoked. His whole problem is that he's provocable."

"Hey, sit down." I tipped my head toward the seat next to mine.

He plopped onto the cushions and picked up the maimed doll torso. "He behaves for me, but that's it. He needs to behave for everybody. I love him so much, but I can't seem to turn him into a good citizen. Everybody is afraid of him but me."

"A rescue organization?"

"What if they give him to someone who puts him in dogfights? Or doesn't follow through and train him regularly? Or if he ends up with some rescue hoarder with a yard full of starving animals in crates, no money and even less sense? He trusts me. I can't do him like that. He needs some kind of, I don't know, major intervention."

"A dog whisperer."

290

"No. He needs the opposite. He needs to learn to respect people who aren't dog whisperers. People like your brother."

Saint was a genius. That was exactly what the dog needed, and although Saint didn't know it, it was exactly what Clive needed, too.

"I'm calling him. If he says yes, you'll take the dog up north, stay at Clive's and train them together. They'll both benefit."

"Nope. No way. I have to work. I have my band. He's self-employed. He doesn't have a boss to answer to. And it's going to take weeks. He comes here or no deal."

I grabbed the phone.

"What are you doing? It's four in the morning," Saint said.

I punched in Clive's number. It took him forever to answer.

"Elsworth?"

"Cliver. Wake up."

"What time is it? Oh my God. Did you have it?"

"Shh, no. The baby's still simmering. But I have a plan for you. It's too good to wait."

Saint sat at the other end of the sectional making futile attempts to reattach the gummipuppe's leg to its torso.

"I know how you can get Becca back," I said.

"Too late. She asked me to stay out of her life. I don't like it, but I'm respecting her wishes. At this point, it's pretty much the only thing left that I can do."

"It was your fears that drove her away," I said.

"Yeah, I'm pretty sure I'm the one who told you that."

"If you can overcome your fears, though, she'll come back to you."

"I doubt it."

"So anyway, here's the plan. You come down here and stay at my house for a while. Saint shows you how to work with Tremor Christ. You master the dog. You maybe even take the dog up north to live with you."

Saint poked me with his toe and shook his head. He pointed at himself and mouthed *my dog*.

I ignored him. "Becca sees that you're overcoming your fears. Becca comes home."

Clive laughed for a long, long time.

"Good morning, sis. Still eating that big ol' bowl of crazy flakes for breakfast every day, I see. Is this your idea of an early April Fools'?"

"Did I mention Becca has a total dog crush on Tremor Christ? She was threatening to kidnap him after she brought me home. You should see them together. They're practically soul mates."

"Look, El. I love you, but this might be your most harebrained scheme yet. I'd ask what you were smoking, but I know this is Eleanor Rafferty, unenhanced."

"Great. Whatever. It's a limited time offer."

"Act now and we'll throw in this set of thirteen Ginsu knives. A $100 value!"

I waved the phone at Saint, hoping he might take a crack at talking some sense into my stubborn twin brother, but he only shrugged. I took one last swipe at convincing Clive. "Get your butt down here. Saint says he'll work with you on this. You could learn a lot from him. If you won't, well, fine. I'll be way, way disappointed in you until the end of time. And Becca will never come back. But ultimately, it's up to you."

"It's a dumb idea and it's dangerous. I'm not doing it. Anyway, she's not coming back, regardless. This isn't some stupid sitcom. It's real life."

"Forget it. Don't come."

"Call me when you have that baby," he said.

After I got off the phone, I put fresh bedding in the loft and added Natty to my grocery list.

46

Aye Davanita

Clive • Detroit, Mich. • Wednesday, Mar. 14–28, 2007

I was Becca's Kryptonite. It was an insult, a compliment, and an obligation all rolled into one. She didn't want me, but she couldn't resist me. If I could just become worthy of her, her weakness for me wouldn't be a risk to her anymore.

But how was that even possible? My preliminary hearing was in a few weeks and my case wasn't looking so hot. Howie was out of the hospital and back to work, but his injuries were well documented. My lawyer, Bob Mulberry, was talking plea deals. That would mean a conviction. If I was lucky I'd get probation. If not, I'd be taking up residence in the Presque Isle County Jail. Given the Rafferty propensity for doom, I had a pretty good idea how that would go.

Ellie's notion of having me work with Tremor Christ was a half-baked yam, but I'd rather spend my last few weeks of freedom courting disaster in the D than hanging around Presque Isle County alone. I packed up my art supplies and took the highway south.

છ

I trailed Saint through the mud in Ellie's narrow backyard and pulled up the hood of my sweatshirt. I'd studied his list of German dog commands with pronunciations, and read a book he'd recommended on adult dog rehabilitation.

I forgot everything when Tremor Christ crawled out from under the bus. The long steel chain snaking behind him was attached to an eyebolt set in concrete. That chain could only be as secure as its weakest link. I mentioned this to Saint.

He unwound his embroidered scarf and draped it over the bus's side-view mirror. "Weak link. Right. Say that three times fast."

I did. It sounded like *weakling*.

"Fear is the weak link in this game. Your wife unhooked him. How do you think she got away unharmed?"

"She didn't show fear?"

"Close, but no. There's a difference between not showing fear, and not having fear. No one can master an animal they fear. Your wife didn't fear him, she respected him."

He squelched across the mud in his tall leather boots and stood in front of me, then pushed up his sleeve to reveal a mess of fresh, bright pink scars all over that dog's tattooed name. I'd seen it before, but never up close. If Saint didn't want me scared of that dog, he had a funny way of trying to change my mind.

"After he tore up my arm, he sensed my fear. I lost control of his discipline. He forgot who was boss. That was the period when he attacked you. My fault."

The weirdo was a lot smarter than I'd given him credit for. And Saint had been right about Reece back then, too. Realizing this had actually been a big factor in my decision to go through with Ellie's goofy dog mastery plan. I'd dismissed Saint's concerns about Reece way back in August when I should have listened. The guy genuinely cared about Ellie's wellbeing, and now he was offering to help me. It was high time I gave him a chance.

"Go ahead and unhook him," Saint said.

"He'll kill me."

Saint smirked.

"I'm going in." I started walking toward the house.

"You can't overcome a fear with baby steps. You have to do something bold. Prove something to yourself. Walk right up to him and unhook him. Show him who's in charge."

I came back and stood next to Saint.

294

"Go ahead," he said.

I took one step toward the dog. Tremor Christ growled and bared his teeth. I froze.

"You're not ready and neither is he." Saint stepped between me and the dog. "Go wait outside the fence for a minute."

When I'd closed the gate, Saint unlatched the dog and threw a tattered stuffed animal for him to fetch. Graceful. Comfortable. In charge. He led the dog into the house and returned alone a few minutes later, a wide leather dog collar around his own neck. He attached himself to the tie out.

I couldn't stop laughing. "Are you going to attack?" I pushed through the gate and approached Saint. The guy was a riot.

"Fear I will, and I will."

"So I just—I just pretend you're the dog and unhook you?"

Saint charged at me. "I'm going to kill you!"

I dashed out of reach. Wrong reaction. "So, uh, I showed fear there, right?"

"Weak link. Weak link."

"I'm supposed to dominate you," I said.

"Nope. It's not about dominance. It's about the relationship. Show him respect. Confidence."

I reconsidered my intimidation. Saint was taller, sure, and sinewy. But I'd landed Howie Peterson in the hospital without even meaning to. That guy outweighed Saint by around a hundred pounds, all of it dense muscle and bone. Hair flopped around Saint's eyes. That codpiece? Pointless. I could take this kid down, no sweat. But I didn't want to hurt my sister's friend. She was inexplicably fond of him. And in his own weird way, he was trying to help me.

I walked over and unfastened Saint from the chain.

"Good," he said. "Now praise me."

"You're a gentleman and a scholar."

"Ha. Love it. Let's go again."

"Wait." I ran out front to my Land Cruiser and grabbed a box of Lemonheads Becca had left in the glove box. It rattled as I headed across the lawn.

Saint was on the chain again, positioned to run at me. "Out of my yard, intruder. I'll rip your nuts off."

I faltered.

"I said get the hell out!" Saint yelled.

I got my shit together. "Hey, you're kind of cute when you're mad." I sauntered up to him. "Calm down, boy. Sitz."

He squatted.

"Braver hund." I shook the box of candy.

"Lemonheads? Oh wow. They still make 'em? Man, I love those things."

I popped one of the sour candies into his mouth.

∞

Saint and I worked together on training for a couple of one-hour sessions each day. Our role playing probably looked down-right bizarre to the neighbors, but it all made some kind of sense. I trusted in Saint and the process. I threw sticks for him. I scratched behind his ears while he pressed his cheek to my thigh, panting. I walked him around the neighborhood on a leash. Once I even waited, eyes averted, as he pissed on a telephone pole. Fortunately, he drew the line at mating in public. While he worked with Tremor Christ, I'd sit on the deck rail and observe.

I began to understand why Ellie was tight with Saint. He was every bit as crazy, smart, and unconventional as she was.

Unconsciously, Saint and I started carrying our training roles into the house. We were settling in for the playoffs on TV. He grabbed me a beer and I said, "Braver hund" without even thinking about it. He sat on the floor and rested his chin on my knee.

I was absently massaging his scalp when Reece walked in and burst out laughing at us. "Give that bitch a bath, and don't forget to squeeze out his anal glands."

"Don't be disrespecting my dog," I said.

"When did you get so weird?"

"Probably around the time you completely lost your sense of humor."

He went into the kitchen and started banging pots around. I felt a little sorry for him. He was already jealous of Ellie's friendship with Saint, and now Saint was hanging out with me. But the damage between Reece and me dated back to New Year's Eve. Reece was the problem.

ଔ

By the end of the first week, Saint was observing from the deck rail while I took Tremor Christ off the chain.

"Pretend he's me," Saint had told me.

It worked. I let him off the lead, tossed a tennis ball around the yard for him, and ran through all of the basic commands in German. I wasn't afraid in the least. This dog was intelligent, loyal and eager to please. He hardly felt any more threatening to me than Cubby did.

But after several days of working like this with Tremor Christ, I knew we were still missing something. I was trained in how to deal with the dog, but he was still a danger to anyone who couldn't handle him. I'd changed, but now it was the dog that needed to change.

"He's a smart one," I told Saint during one of our walks with the dog. "We should teach him his commands in English. I mean, it seems like he should understand our native language. And he needs to spend more time in the house, hanging out with us."

"Better socialization. I like it. But Reece is going to have conniptions."

I didn't think so. I'd been keeping an eye on Reece and he didn't seem all that afraid of the dog. The way I saw it, he was using Ellie's fear of the dog to try to turn her against Saint. That wasn't working so hot for Reece anyway. Since Ellie also had a healthy trust in both Saint and me, I didn't think it would be hard to convince her to see Tremor Christ for who he was now instead of the bogey-dog he'd been made out to be.

"It'll be a start," I said. "He needs a bigger yard, and more exposure to other animals so he can settle down and be part of a community, not some loner who spends all of his time in isolation."

I realized I could have been describing myself.

We walked from Corktown to Brush Park. This was the third time we'd ended up there in the last week. It wasn't even intentional on my part. Sometimes I thought there must be Clive magnets under the earth there. I stood in front of the empty lot, with Tremor Christ's leather leash wrapped around my palm.

"What is the deal with you guys and this empty lot?" Saint asked.

"It's our ground zero."

"I don't get it. There's nothing here."

"Nothing, except everything that ever mattered to us."

"You're going to have to explain that."

I told Saint our whole story. It was the first time I'd ever laid it out for anyone from beginning to end. I watched his face change from mild interest, to fascination, to anger, to fear, to sorrow, to outrage.

When I was finished, he hugged me and said, "Oh, man. Ellie never told me."

"We just keep moving forward, you know?"

"All I knew was that your mom died pretty young. That's it. I had no clue you guys had been through so much shit."

I shrugged. "We're not big on talking about it. Once people know, they have a hard time seeing past it. It becomes the totality of who we are. But it's not who we are at all, it's just something— well, a bunch of things—that happened to us."

Tremor Christ jumped up and pulled the leash taut, barking and growling. An orange kitten was tiptoeing across the back of the empty lot.

"We should get going," Saint said.

I had a better idea. "Hold him." I gave Saint the leash and walked toward the kitten. She froze and eyed me warily. I squatted down and pointed my index finger at her. Like every cat I've ever met, she couldn't resist coming over to have herself a sniff. I scooped her up and tucked her inside my sweat jacket. She felt bony, underfed. She immediately began to purr.

"What are you going to do with that?"

"Tremor Christ needs to learn how to make friends."

ℭ

I kept dog treats in my pockets to reward Tremor Christ every time he was calm around my kitten. It didn't take long for them to bond. Pretty soon, she was napping in his crate.

Ellie started calling the kitten Davanita, and it kind of stuck.

47

Push Me, Pull Me

Ellie • Detroit, Mich. • Thursday, Mar. 29, 2007

Two hours into my late afternoon shift at Mr. Salty's, I sprung a leak. I couldn't reach or Reece or Abigail, so I called Clive.

He answered on the fourth ring. "You've reached the offices of LeFanch, Rafferty, Wozniak and Christ." That was the fantasy law firm he wished was defending him. His pre-trial hearing was a few weeks away. He needed to get back to Rogers City soon to strategize with his bargain-bin attorney, some guy who specialized in defending poachers and was known to take venison as payment.

"I need a ride home," I said.

"What a coincidence. I'm at home, watching the *Pimp My Ride* marathon."

"Cliver—" A contraction grabbed me hard. I waited for it to pass. "Can you help me get home? My water broke. I'm having contractions."

"Whoa. Why didn't you say so?"

"And before you head out, start filling that birthing tub for me."

To assess my contractions, I talked through them. Abigail had told me that when they're mild, you can talk but when they're strong, it's impossible. All the way home I recited *Push Me, Pull Me* along with the stereo in Clive's Land Cruiser. He joined in with his baritone, tapping the rhythm on the steering wheel while the windshield wipers swished against the steady rain. Every time a strong

301

contraction seized me and I couldn't talk, he'd clutch my hand, never missing a lyric. I'd pick right up again as soon as it passed.

CR

The house smelled like popcorn and the air was steamy from the hot water running from the kitchen tap to the birthing tub. Neat stacks of laundry lined the sectional—Clive had done everyone's, even Saint's. On TV, Xzibit feigned shock over the sorry condition of a Ford Escort.

I got into a robe and dipped my toes in the warm water. I'd have to wait for Abigail to clear me for splashdown. I left her another message. And another for Reece. Where the hell was everybody?

Clive helped me time my contractions. They were two minutes apart and I couldn't talk through them. If I'd been planning a hospital birth, this would have been the time to head to the hospital. I was starting to get nervous. Maybe Janice had been right.

Tying his thick hair back, Clive said, "You sure you're ready to do this thing? Sure you don't want me to take you to a hospital?"

"No way." Another contraction seized me, and I waited for it to pass. "Abigail will come."

"Your call. I'll be here with you no matter what. Just let me know what you need."

"Could you turn off the TV? Put the lights lower? Play some music?"

Within minutes we were bathed in the soft glow of string lights. Clive put Pearl Jam's *Mansfield Pre-Set* on the turntable and recited the intro where Eddie advises the crowd to pace themselves. Great advice.

He cleaned up his popcorn mess, put all of the laundry away, left Reece another message, then rubbed my feet.

Abigail arrived in a long denim skirt, her braids dripping on her cotton blouse. She checked me in the privacy of my room, said I was dilated to five and fully effaced, and helped me downstairs to the tub. The warm water, the buoyancy, made the intense contractions far more bearable. She talked me through each one. Soothing. Encouraging. Motherly.

I wore my bathrobe right into the tub. My contractions hit faster and harder. I couldn't keep up. I let out a high-pitched whine.

"Keep your sounds low. Guttural. Like a big bad bear," Abigail said. "Now, I want you to pick one thing and focus on it."

I focused on Clive. He was on the sectional with Davanita on his shoulder, scratching behind her ears. A contraction overtook me and I growled. He laughed and growled back. Davanita jumped off of his shoulder and tore up the stairs. Tremor Christ started to follow her. Clive calmly told the dog "Leave it," and the dog turned around and settled at Clive's feet.

Clive and I took turns trading growls for the longest time. More than anything in the world, I loved the way he was here with me. I wished I could return the favor for his hearing, but Rogers City would be a long way to travel with a newborn.

The front door burst open and Reece walked in, wet and grinning. I was relieved to see him but the moment he hugged me, my contractions stopped. I knew why. If the baby was obviously Saint's, Reece would throw me out on my ear. I'd never really allowed myself to believe it was Saint's, and, on the off chance it was, I didn't expect that to be evident at first glance. But it might be. If the baby was Saint's, I was committed to telling Reece the truth. The looming possibility that I'd need to make that hard confession stopped my labor cold.

I'd never told Abigail about the small chance that Reece wasn't the father, but one look at me and she knew something wasn't right. She'd picked up that it was Reece's arrival.

She massaged my shoulders. "Are you comfortable with everyone here?"

I nodded. Reece had no idea how intense my labor had been before he'd walked into the room. I had to find a way to set this right. There was no asking him to leave. My only choice was to do something counterintuitive.

"Reece should get in the tub," I said.

He looked at Abigail. "Is that even allowed?"

"Sure, hon. Couples do that all the time. In fact, if you hold or caress Ellie, that'll release oxytocin to speed her labor."

"What about germs?" he asked. "Won't she get an infection?"

"Everything's flowing away from her amniotic sac. Picture a leaking saltwater balloon held under fresh water. No fresh water will get inside the balloon because saltwater is forcing its way out."

I adored Abigail.

Reece stripped down to his boxers and climbed in. I reminded myself this was my Reece, who I'd been with for years. I loved him. He was this baby's father. He had to be.

He sat behind me, his knees on either side, chin resting on my shoulder. "This better?"

"I need you to tell me something," I said. "Tell me that no matter what happens today, you'll love me."

He squeezed his arms around me. "Sugar, you know I will."

"Say it." Maybe it wasn't fair extracting a ridiculous promise like that. If things went wrong, I didn't expect him to keep it. But I needed to hear it anyway.

"We should get married," he said.

That was not the statement I was looking for. "Say you'll love me no matter what happens."

"After you say you'll marry me."

Clive and Abigail stared at each other, frozen by the awkwardness of a conversation that should have been private.

I needed Reece's assurance he'd love me no matter what, so I said, "Fine. I'll marry you."

"Then no matter what happens today, I will love you."

Tears welled in Abigail's eyes, but not mine. Clive shook his head. At last, I had a contraction. My labor resumed quickly, harder and faster than before. When it comes down to it, labor is really just a big old head game.

Everything started to happen in a blur. Blood bloomed in the water and Abigail thrust her arms between my legs.

"When you feel the urge, bear down. And keep breathing, for you and the baby. Reece, remind her to breathe," Abigail said.

I knelt in the water, Reece behind me, balancing me, telling me "Breathe. Breathe." A burning sensation intense as a blowtorch left me gasping.

Clive stood nearby with an armload of fluffy towels, his gaze steady on my eyes. No matter how bad this got, Clive would be there like always, making everything alright. Focusing on my brother's face, I bore down hard. I didn't care what happened as long as the burning, the steamroller pressure, ended.

"She's crowning," Abigail said. "Now give us one good, hard push. Push for your life. Good. Good. There's the head. Now take a deep breath and push for me. Push like you're pushing a bowling ball uphill with your anus."

Clive threw his head back and laughed. Everyone laughed. I laughed. The pressure of my laughter forced the baby out. Abigail lifted him from the water and put him in my arms while everyone was still laughing.

That's right. *Him.*

Abigail aspirated my little boy. He gagged and began to cry. She said he looked great and gave him a nine/ten Apgar score, followed by ten/ten. Reece held him while I delivered the placenta, then I held him while Reece cut the cord, squinting like it might squirt him in the eye. Abigail weighed the baby with her portable hanging scale. Seven pounds, seven ounces. A big, healthy boy.

My baby looked like himself. Like me. Like Clive. Like our brothers. Like a real Rafferty.

"Wow. He looks exactly like me," Reece said.

"He does," Clive said.

I guess I could see that, too. With his white-gold hair and round cheeks, he did resemble the LeFanches. I burst into sobs.

Abigail helped me out of the tub and held up a blanket to give me privacy while I dried off and changed into a fresh robe. I couldn't stop crying. Everyone assumed I was crying for joy, but it was pure relief. The heavy cloud of uncertainty I'd lived under for nine months had dissipated with one look at my baby's face.

Reece got dressed and Clive fixed me some tea while Abigail looked me over to make sure I was in good shape.

On the sectional, Reece snuggled next to me and gave me the baby. In the history of history, there'd never been a baby as beautiful as mine, even if his head was a little pointed from the trip down the birth canal, even though cheesy vernix clung in the creases of his fat rolls. He extended his arms, his eyes wide and calm.

"Did you know your mommy said she'd marry me?" Reece said to the baby. Already he was a great dad. Our little family was perfect.

Abigail showed me how to hold the baby to nurse him. Ear, shoulder, hip in horizontal alignment. She put pillows under my arms and explained about proper latch-on, and where the baby's tongue ought to be. The baby got right down to business like he'd been nursing his whole life.

"Look at Van go," Reece said.

Labor had made me forget that we were supposed to name him. But Van? I'd been sure Reece was joking when he'd told me he liked the name Van LeFanch because it was like Van Halen or Van Morrison. In my book, naming him Van was no different than naming him Bus or Cab or Utility Trailer.

"Vedder," I said. "I thought we'd decided on Vedder Ament."

He made a sour-pickle face.

"Alright then, maybe Vedder Maurice," I said. "Your mom would probably love that."

"Ugh. I've always hated Maurice. At least Vedder Van," Reece said, "if the middle name is up for grabs."

"No Vedder Van. That's dumb. It sounds like a van full of Eddie Vedder clones. If you don't want Maurice, maybe Vedder Cliver." I threw it out there thinking if Reece agreed to it, it might heal the rift that was still simmering between those two. But saying it aloud, I liked Cliver for a middle name a lot better than I liked Maurice.

Clive brought my tea in during the middle of this exchange. "No Cliver," he said. "This is Reece's son. He should pick the middle name."

"Van," Reece said. "Van, Van, Van. I want Van. You know what, I want Vedder Van Cliver LeFanch. I can't think of anything better than getting Van and my best bud's name in there." He jumped up and hugged Clive.

That's how my firstborn son ended up with a name three times larger than he was. Vedder Van Cliver LeFanch. Like there was a surplus crop down at the V farm and we got them three for the price of one.

The uterine cramps were agonizing when the baby nursed. I ask Abigail if this was normal. She explained that my cervix was in the process of closing, like labor in reverse. This reassured me only a little. I just didn't feel right.

Vedder fell asleep. I dressed him in an infant gown and let Reece hold him. I needed to nap but the discomfort and after-pains kept me awake. Nothing I'd heard or read had prepared me for the intensity of after pains. I thought that they were supposed to be like bad period cramps, not like *Contractions, the Sequel.*

Mr. and Mrs. LeFanch showed up with a green bean casserole. I hated green bean casserole, but Mrs. LeFanch was trying. She handed it to Clive and instructed him to put it in the oven, then oohed and ahhed over her newest grandchild. Little Vedder was passed around the sectional, with everyone confirming that he was every inch a LeFanch baby.

Like there was ever any question.

∽

Exhausted, I drifted into a twilight sleep while everyone else continued a merry conversation about babies and weddings. I dreamed I was swimming underwater with baby Vedder's vernix-coated arms around my neck. He was burbling "find him," into my ear, but I didn't know who we were looking for.

Reece stroked my cheek until I awoke, and Abigail had me latch the baby on by myself this time. I tried to orient myself to the purple paisley sectional, the happy faces. Nursing made the after-pains excruciating. I needed to use the bathroom, but the baby nursed endlessly. I allowed him to until I couldn't hold on for another second. I told Abigail I had to use the toilet. She showed me how to slip my pinky into the corner of Vedder's mouth to break his latch without hurting my nipple. Reece and Clive politely looked away. Mr. LeFanch didn't.

I decided not to give a rip. I needed the bathroom. Now. I handed Vedder to Clive and stood up. Blood gushed out of me and made a mess of the floor.

"That's normal," Abigail said. She took my arm and helped me get up the stairs. I told her I'd handle it from there.

"Don't let the blood scare you. You may even pass some clots. It's all part of the program." She smiled. "You did great today. I'm so proud of you. And your baby, he is just beautiful."

"I love that you've stayed. Please don't go yet."

"I'll wait," she said.

I shut the bathroom door and fell to my knees.

ଔ

Desperate urgency opposed excruciating pain and either way, I was the loser. I leaned forward on the toilet and groaned.

Abigail knocked on the door. "Ellie? Ellie? Everything alright in there?"

Pain and confusion made answering her impossible. I grunted. Panted. Chills covered my face. I shuddered. Hot fluid gushed out of me. This was all wrong.

"Ellie?"

She came in and closed the door. "What's the matter, hon?"

I was in too much agony to reply. She yanked towels out of the cupboard and spread the biggest one, my Pearl Jam beach towel, over the floor. She scoured herself up to the elbows at the sink. "Let's check you. Can you get on your hands and knees for me?

The movement was torture. She helped me to the floor and palpated my stomach.

"Do you feel the urge to push?"

"Yeah."

"Resist it. Don't do anything until I say."

Did she seriously expect me to crap on a towel? If this was a regular part of childbirth aftercare, no wonder it was kept secret. Her hand went high inside me. My whole body shook.

"Don't be scared. You might be passing a large clot. It happens."

What if Abigail didn't really know what she was doing? What if she wasn't actually a registered midwife at all? Maybe my uterus had come loose and she was trying to pack it back inside me. I panted and whimpered. I was out of my mind with the need to bear down.

"Don't push," she said. "Fight the urge, Ellie. Fight it. Breathe."

"Am I gonna die?"

Her other hand pressed on my stomach. I retched. Herbal tea came out through my mouth and nose. Sweat poured down my face. I *had* to push.

Her hands were inside me, pulling on something. The pain was unbearable.

"Alright hon, bear down now, strong and steady."

I didn't care what happened. I didn't care if I died, as long as this horror ended. Panting and sweating, I bore down as hard as I could. Abigail pulled and I pushed. Something overwhelming was happening to my entire body. I swear I was turning inside out from the crotch. I retched again. Bile. God-awful.

"I'm dying."

"You will not die today, I promise. Push once more for me. Come on. Be strong."

Ashen roses whirled before my eyes, but I refused to faint in the puddle of vomit. I bore down as hard as I could. The pain stopped abruptly. I believed I had died. What a relief.

I blinked and there was the vomit and the towel. I was still alive.

"Oh dear Jesus," Abigail said. "Jesus! Jesus, Mary and Joseph. Call nine-one-one!"

I turned around. What was that bloody thing in Abigail's hands? Where did it come from? Had that actually come out of *me?*

She was holding a motionless, gray-blue baby with thick, black hair. It was maybe half the size of Vedder. How in the hell? My head swam. I may have actually fainted, then. I'm not sure.

"Is that mine?" I asked.

She pulled a bulb aspirator out of her apron pocket and cleaned out its throat and nostrils. She flipped it over and vigorously rubbed its back. Nothing happened. The gray baby hung over her forearm, limp and lifeless as the gummipuppe.

"Call 911!" she yelled. I yelled it too. We screamed it in unison until we heard feet stampeding up the stairs.

A placenta plopped out of me. I hadn't even pushed. It was smaller than Vedder's. Blood dripped from the bathroom cabinets, from Abigail's arms. My orange towel was soaked in crimson.

Reece flung the door open. "Ellie? Holy fuck. What's happening in here?"

Everyone was crowding behind him, forcing him into the room. He looked from me, to the baby, to the floor. His mouth fell open and the color drained from his cheeks.

Clive was clutching a phone. "I called them. On their way. What happened? What can we do?"

"Another boy. Pray," Abigail said. "And shut the door."

Clive did. Then it was Reece, Abigail, the gray baby and me in the bathroom.

I tried to convince myself I was still napping on the sectional, having some lurid nightmare, and that everything was fine and we'd be choking down Marjorie's green bean casserole soon. I smelled it burning.

"Breathe," Abigail said. "Breathe, damn it. Breathe." She held my lifeless gummipuppe by the ankles and smacked his narrow behind. Once. Twice.

Reece held me and stroked my hair. "I'm sorry. You're alright though, aren't you? And Vedder's fine. We'll get through this, sugar. I'm sorry."

He might get through it. Vedder would. But not me. I thought of Becca's daughter Louise and Patricia Wozniak's son Brody. Now my very own baby was dead before he was even named. My chest ached for our collective losses. Stillbirth was a timeless heartbreak that no woman, no matter how rich or poor, careful or careless, was immune to. I'd thought I understood that before, but I didn't. Couldn't. Even with the consolation of a healthy baby downstairs, I was destroyed.

310

Abigail smacked the gummipuppe again. Its slender arms flailed. Tiny fingers spread then made fists. Blue lips parted. Gasped. Released a mewling cry. Screaming his tiny, weak squalls he turned from gray to lavender to pink.

"Oh, thank God," Reece said.

"Thank Abigail. Abigail, thank you!" It was completely inadequate for the miracle she'd just performed, but it was all I could manage through my tears.

"Congratulations," Abigail said. "You have another son."

She swathed him in a fresh hand towel and placed him in my arms. He was tiny and screaming and beautiful. I held him to my chest and pressed my lips to his wet hair. My son. I breathed him in.

He smelled like roasted cashews.

48

Truth Be Known

Ellie • Detroit, Mich. • Thursday, Mar. 29, 2007

My unbearably small baby stopped breathing twice in the ambulance. Their equipment dwarfed him. He needed me, but the ambulance crew rejected my tearful pleas to hold him. Vedder was strapped down too, and wailing. Minutes into motherhood and already I'd failed them.

No. I'd failed these two souls at conception.

In the ER, they said my unnamed baby was four pounds, one ounce. They considered that premature even though my pregnancy went to thirty-seven weeks. He was unstable. They whisked him off to the NICU. In a strange way, I was relieved. Professionals who knew what they were doing would keep him breathing and make sure he survived, hopefully.

Vedder, on the other hand, easily passed his ER examination, protesting the entire time. They returned him to me like an uninteresting, if somewhat noisy, token brought to a show-and-tell. They checked me out and decided I was alright, too. I had to fill out a long questionnaire about my health and social history. *Was I in an abusive relationship? Did I take drugs? Had I ever had an STD? Did I finish high school? Did I take money in exchange for sex? Did I know who my baby's father was?* When I finished filling it out, they looked it over and finally let Reece into the room.

Reece closed the striped curtain around my ER examining cot and I got down to nursing Vedder.

"Twins. How did we not know this?" Reece asked.

"Everybody said I was too big."

"We should sue for malpractice. I mean, shouldn't your midwife have heard two heartbeats?"

Abigail had just saved my baby's life, and probably mine as well. There was no way I'd even consider suing her. I traced the folds of Vedder's velvety ear. I'd listened the heartbeat through the fetal Doppler at every appointment with Abigail. One heartbeat. Once or twice I'd even asked about the possibility of twins. After all, it did run in my family. And maybe Saint's. We'd listened all over my belly. There had only ever been one heartbeat. One.

I felt Vedder's temple, his quick pulse. That was when I understood. Vedder and his surprise brother were like Clive and me. Their hearts beat in time.

Later, they brought us double paperwork for the birth certificates. Vedder's full name seemed grandiose, while the name line on his twin's paperwork remained stubbornly blank.

"If he was a girl, we'd have his name," Reece said. "Maybe we should give him some of Vedder's name. I don't think he'd mind sharing." He balanced Vedder face down on his forearm. "Let's call the other one Van, take it out of Vedder's name. It is a little longish."

Van. I still one-hundred percent hated it. I made random doodles on the name line. Berries bursting out of angular casings. Bittersweet.

"If you're giving him a symbol name, no flowers," Reece said. "I know, draw a mushroom. He can be the baby formerly known as—"

"Can the jokes at least wait until they tell us if he's going to live?"

He gave me a sheepish look. I knew he'd only been trying to cut the tension, but geez. Anyway, there was no hurry to name this baby. It's not like there was a statute of limitations and if you didn't pick a name in time, the powers-that-be named your kid Jacob.

Right then, the only name possible for this baby came to me all at once: Brody Saint Wozniak.

Before I lost my nerve, I scribbled the truth on the line.

314

49

Rearviewmirror

Clive • Detroit, Mich. • Thursday, Mar. 29, 2007

Didn't I tell her homebirth was a terrible idea?" Mrs. LeFanch said into her cell phone for the fourth time, despite signs everywhere forbidding their use in the ER waiting room. She'd been calling all of her daughters, reliving the juicy details of the good news/bad news about the latest additions to the LeFanch family. "But my opinion doesn't count for dog doo-doo. If that baby doesn't make it, I'll never forgive Little Miss Crunchy Granola Pants. And I can't fathom what's keeping your brother from getting his buns out here and telling us what's going on."

Mr. LeFanch started complaining about his blood sugar, dinner time having long since passed in a haze of cremated green bean casserole, and ambulance sirens. With Mrs. LeFanch still griping about Ellie to her daughter, the two of them headed for the cafeteria. I stayed back. I didn't envy Ellie her impending in-laws.

I couldn't erase the gory bathroom scene from my mind. Poor Elsworth. I was sick with worry. They wouldn't tell me a thing at the desk.

Half an hour later, Reece burst out of the treatment area and booked past me, red faced, with dried bloodstains on the knees of his chinos. He hit the exit door and broke into a run.

I chased him, sprinting down one long hallway after another.

"Reece! Wait up!"

I didn't catch him until he reached the elevators to the parking garage. He jabbed the button and folded his arms.

I ran up to him, doubling over to catch my breath. "What's going on? What's happening in there?"

The elevator doors squealed open and Reece got on. I stepped inside with him. He punched a button and the elevator rattled upward. He was fuming.

"Whatever's happening, I'm sorry," I said.

"Sorry? You're sorry? It's your sister who should be sorry."

"You two need to stick together. Blaming Ellie isn't going to help."

"Fuck that noise."

The elevator stuttered to a halt and the doors slid open. Reece shot out of there.

"Trust me, I know something about this." I hurried after him, my voice echoing off the cold concrete. "I wish I'd been more sensitive to Becca when we lost our baby."

Reece broke into mirthless laughter.

Whatever it was, it was bad. Ellie was all alone now and dealing with God only knew what. I grabbed the sleeve of Reece's starter jacket. "Come on. Let's go back to the ER. Ellie needs us. Your parents are going crazy not knowing what's going on."

The more I said, the harder Reece laughed.

I put my arms around him. "Brother, I know. I know. I've lost a baby, I understand." As a matter of fact, I'd lost three. My brothers and Louise. Four if I included LuCretia's miscarriage. "It's scary. It hurts. Believe me, I know."

"Dead? You think it's dead? Shit, I wish it was dead."

I stepped back. "What the hell happened in there?"

Reece headed for his big Buick and unlocked it with a remote.

"That baby isn't even mine."

"That's insane. Obviously, he's yours. That kid's a carbon copy of you."

"No, not Vedder. Vedder's mine. Probably. That's what she's claiming, anyway. The other one. Fuckin' Wozniak's scrawny fuckin' wartling."

Whoa.

"Saint's? She thinks it's … For fuck's sake. What is she smoking? That's flat-out impossible."

"Yeah? Go ask her yourself. Hetero-specialo-fukwondernation or some shit." He yanked the car door open and threw himself behind the wheel. "Gotta go congratulate the father."

Reece's tires squealed as he fled the parking garage. Shit. He was going after Saint. This was crazy. I texted a warning to Saint. I'd have raced out to defend him, but Ellie needed me even more. This unexpected sickly twin, this tragedy, was making my sister lose her mind.

50

Brother

Ellie • Detroit, Mich. • Friday, Mar. 30, 2007

For someone whose family size had just doubled, I'd never been lonelier. I didn't know how I was going to care for two babies alone. I didn't know how I was even going to survive if Brody didn't. That was an unfathomably scary prospect that kept seeping into my brain no matter how forcefully I tried to push it away.

Sometime after Reece stormed off, the hospital staff decided they were finished observing me and Vedder. We were relocated to a carpeted waiting room near the NICU. A candy striper brought Vedder diapers, a little blue cap and a flannel blanket in a donated infant car seat. For me, she had cold bottled water. As much as I'd been anti-hospital, they were pretty kind to me. In my head, I composed thank-you notes and after that, long, futile letters of apology to Reece, Saint, and my baby boys.

I don't know how Clive found me there.

"You alright?" he asked.

"I've been better."

He sat next to me and pressed his palm to my forehead. "What are you thinking, Elsworth? You're losing it. C'mon. They can't have different fathers."

"They do."

"That's impossible. I don't think it's ever happened in the history of the universe."

He was wrong. I told him about heteropaternal superfecundation. I'd learned about it on one of my daytime talk shows. I couldn't remember if it was on Montel, Springer or Maury, but supposedly it's pretty rare. They said something like one or two percent of all fraternal twins are half-siblings, and if you suspected your fraternal twins had different fathers, to contact the show about paternity testing.

Once again I was cutting edge Jerry Springer material. I wondered if Clive and I had different fathers, too. Not that it mattered to us, but that would make one hell of a Springer show.

"So, you and Wozniak?"

Even as Clive shook his head, I saw his disbelief lifting. Now that he knew Saint better, maybe it wasn't so hard to imagine.

"Only once. It just kind of happened. You know … *Yellow Ledbetter*, Thai stick." As if that would excuse anything with my brother, who'd been livid New Year's Eve thinking Reece was the one screwing around on me. "Do you hate me?"

"Nah. We all make mistakes."

"This was a doozy."

He lifted Vedder from my tired arms. "I'd call it spectacular. You know what you've done, don't you?"

Sure I did. I'd lied to everybody I cared about for months on end. I'd brought two innocents into a tangled paternity mess. I'd guaranteed homelessness for myself, my babies, and Saint. Oh my God, Saint. How was I supposed to explain this to him?

"You've brought us back our babies," Clive said. "You and me, we have two little guys to take care of again. This time, we're old enough to manage."

"We?"

"Well, yeah. I'll help you any way I can."

My throat tightened and I fought back tears. I didn't deserve this mercy. I didn't deserve this brother of mine.

He put on his serious face. "And the first thing I'm doing is straightening you out about Reece. Whether your other baby is Saint's or not, don't you dare feel bad about what you did. He's not faithful to you, either."

"Clive, don't."

"You look right past it. The guy's a player. When I caught him in the act on New Year's Eve, he knew I'd tell you. And I did, didn't I?"

Reece was a flirt. I was the cheat. Yet, come to think of it, Reece had been bent on discrediting Clive on New Year's Day. I still didn't want to believe it. Accepting that would change everything I thought I understood about the years I'd spent with Reece. But it hardly mattered now. Brody was all that mattered.

A nurse stuck her head in the doorway. "Eleanor Rafferty? Mom of the homebirth preemie? Doctor will see you in a moment."

Still cradling Vedder, Clive clutched my hand. We waited in silence for another twenty minutes, staring at the E! channel news ticker on the muted television. Everything going on out there in the great world seemed trivial. A Spice Girl had given birth to her second baby. Usher got engaged. Marie Osmond was getting a divorce. Britney Spears had separated from Kevin Federline. I couldn't care about any of it. All I could think was *my God, who cares?* The only news I wanted was to know if my tiny boy Brody would survive.

An East Indian pediatrician came in and explained the situation. I struggled to understand her thick accent. The gist of it was, Brody was stable. They'd ruled out twin-to-twin transfusion syndrome, whatever that was. Brody was just smaller because he was smaller. He was breathing on his own now, but because of his apnea in the ambulance, they wanted to monitor him closely. The hospital was lending me an electric breast pump to start collecting colostrum for him immediately. They encouraged kangaroo care. As long as Brody remained stable, they wanted me to hold him skin-to-skin as much as possible. They had a room for me to do that in, and I was to report to it straight away.

My little cashew-scented baby was going to live.

"Can his Uncle Cliver come along?"

"Uncools, they are vedy important too, yes," the doctor said.

The room she showed us to was little more than a warm, dim closet with a couple of vinyl recliners and a window facing the NICU. Clive held Vedder and a nurse brought Brody to me. He squalled. He seemed even tinier now than he had at home in the bathroom. Monitor leads were taped to his delicate skin. I was proud of my boy, breathing all on his own and expressing his miniature fury. He had every right to be mad at me.

She showed me how to recline and snuggle him against my chest, carefully rearranging his wires. I tried to think of good and calming things, but it wasn't easy with everything I was still worrying about. Eventually, he settled down.

Clive knelt beside me and took a good look at him. "I can sort of see why you think he's Wozniak's."

"No question."

"This is so wild. Different fathers. Something like this would only happen to the Raffertys." He smiled. "We really are doomed."

We'd concocted our family motto when we were fifteen, sitting on the porch of a foster care home we were locked out of because the parents refused to give us a house key. We'd smoke a couple of sorry little roaches, and snickered, and played with some chalk the younger kids there had left out on the sidewalk. Clive drew the crest, and I came up with *The Raffertys, We're Fucking Doomed.* It was perfect at the time. It meant we'd learned to expect the worst, and together we'd handle it. It had served its purpose, but our next generation deserved so much better. Already our doom had taken Louise. Now we had Vedder and Brody to consider.

51

Better Man

Ellie • Detroit, Mich. • Friday, Mar. 30, 2007

Clive was a natural with my tiny boys. But then he'd always been great with babies, even when we were kids. He sang Vedder and Brody to sleep and stayed with us through the night in our NICU closet. At dawn, he took Vedder along to look for some breakfast for us. Vedder's chubby hands were tangled in Clive's hair.

I wanted a shower. Clean clothes. A chance to brush my teeth. But that would mean giving Brody back. I couldn't yet. We needed each other. I never knew it was possible to love anyone as much as I loved that skinny little monkey and his chunky brother. I adjusted the recliner and closed my eyes.

"Detroit Ellie."

I startled at the sound of Saint's voice, and gasped when I saw his black eye. It was swollen shut. His lower lip was distorted, fat, and split down the middle. It hurt me to the core to see him like that. I knew instantly that Reece had attacked him. Because of me. Because of what I'd done to Reece.

"Aw, Saint, I'm so—"

"Don't even say it, girlfriend. I had this one coming."

"No, it's my fault."

"OK. Both our faults. Can I see him?"

I shifted to allow him a good look at Brody.

Saint got down on his knees and rested his chin on the arm of my recliner. He gazed at Brody for a long time, like he couldn't believe it and he couldn't disbelieve it. I brushed his hair away from his face and he looked into my eyes.

"I'm really worried about you," he said.

"Why?"

"Your old man. He's on a vicious tear."

Reece had never laid a hand on me, but then again, I'd never given birth to someone else's child before. Still, I couldn't see him doing to me what he'd obviously done to Saint.

"Just keep far away from him until he settles down," Saint said. "When he told me, I was like—brother, you're high. But I guess I can believe it now that I see the baby. What am I supposed to do?"

"Just love Brody, if you can. That's all."

"Brody? My mom's going to flip her lid."

"Everybody's flipping. Who'd have guessed a four-pound baby could kick up such a fuss? He's a force of nature."

"Reece needs to come off it. He's hardly innocent. I knew all along what he was up to. He was afraid to kick me out after the first time, 'cause when I came back I warned him that if he made me leave again, I was gonna tell you everything."

Here I'd believed I was the one who'd let Saint live with us. But I saw it clearly now. Reece never did follow through on his threats of eviction. He'd hardly made a peep when I let Saint move back in. I'd taken that as Reece being tolerant of me. I'd mistaken his manipulation for indulgence. I wondered if I would have even believed Saint. I hadn't wanted to believe Clive when he'd tried to tell me.

"Remember that day you got all mad about those panties under your bed? I never set foot in your room," he said. "He had some-one up there the day before, while you were at work."

"You were covering for him?"

"Guilty as the devil. If I told, he'd kick me out. I just kept my mouth shut. And I never had Chlamydia, either—that was from him."

My heart sank. I'd trusted Reece and Saint, and they'd both been lying to me. "But we were friends. How could you keep all that from me?"

He pushed his hair out of his face, wincing when his finger grazed his swollen eye. "You gotta understand, I really needed a place to live. I always liked hanging out with you. And that one night? In the kitchen? I don't know, I felt like I was making things right. Like, he couldn't treat you that way. You deserved some joy of your own. I was settling a score, I guess."

I kissed the top of Brody's head. "Dang. When you settle a score, you really settle a score. He even smells like you."

Saint sniffed Brody's hair. "Mmm. Eau de Wozniak. Can I hold him?"

I showed him how. He pulled off his T-shirt and settled into the recliner next to mine. I put Brody to his father's chest.

"God," Saint said. "Regardless of whether he's mine, I think I just fell in love with him."

©©

I stayed at the hospital around the clock until Brody was released. Five days. Janice bragged to her coworkers that it was her friend who had the unexpected twins, and they brought us all kinds of baby gifts. They also let me take showers in an empty room at the far end of the maternity ward. A plaque above the bathroom door read *God is …* I didn't know what God was, but if he existed, he'd given me more than I ever deserved. I had two healthy baby boys, a brother who loved me, and Saint's promise to stick around and help us any way that he could.

Reece's anger was understandable, and the one thing I probably did deserve. He'd kicked everybody out, so Clive and Saint had packed up my stuff for me and loaded everything onto my Yield bus. They were living out of it in the patient parking lot. Tremor Christ, Davanita and all.

The hospital let me keep Vedder with me. He nursed like a champ and brought my milk in for his brother, who took it through a nasogastric tube. Clive brought me fresh clothes off the bus and take-out food. While I ate, he'd talk like Donald Duck for the babies.

For good measure, I had those paternity tests performed. They came out exactly the way I figured they would: Reece had fathered Vedder and Saint had fathered Brody. Jerry Springer would have been so proud of me. I wasn't proud, but this was our situation. Somehow I'd make the best of it for my babies.

52

Cinnamon Girl

Clive • Belknap Township, Mich. • Tuesday, Apr. 24, 2007

Brody's fussing didn't leave me much mental space to stew about tomorrow's hearing. I took a small tin of bag balm from my pocket and swiped the golden goop onto his crusted nostrils, then coated his narrow butt and fastened his woolen diaper wrap. The poor little guy's cold was wearing everyone out. At three in the afternoon, Ellie was finally getting a shower after a long day of nursing him in fits and starts.

Veddie sucked his thumb in the baby swing. Unlike his brother, he had the good manners to nap on something approaching a schedule. I tucked fusspot Brody into the fabric sling on my chest and scrubbed my hands at the kitchen sink.

Out back, Tremor Christ and Cubby were playing tug-o-war with an old sock. Cubby was hilarious when he climbed the chain link fence into my yard to play with his new best friend. I'd taken Tremor Christ on, which allowed Saint to move into an apartment building above a restaurant in Greektown. He took custody of Davanita, who didn't need nearly as much attention as the dog. I'd promised Saint he could visit Tremor Christ anytime he liked, and have him back if he ever moved somewhere dog friendly. I'd been right that the dog just needed to belong. He had a lot more room to run and play in my yard than he'd had at Reece's house.

The Alpena radio station played *Cinnamon Girl* then *Look Out for My Love*, and I boogied around the kitchen until Brody quieted. When he stopped crying, I heard Becca's whistle. It was the one she used for calling Cubby. We hadn't spoken since our butter-cream paint debacle. Understanding that she considered me her Kryptonite, I'd stayed well out of her way. Now she was right there in my backyard, leash in hand, trying to collect her dog. I watched from behind the sliding glass door. I still loved her—I can't even say how much—but I was going to be fine. I had so much here with Ellie and her babies and that big old loveable lug, Tremor Christ.

Intent on winning the battle for a filthy sock, both dogs ignored Becca. She headed toward them, then stopped, looked at the sole of her boot and grimaced. Dog crap. She wiped her foot in the grass.

I shoved the sliding door open and put my arms around the sling to shield Brody from the damp breeze. "Bummer."

"I know. Gross. Got a paper towel?" She smiled, as much out of embarrassment as anything.

I'd missed her smile most of all. It had left me long before she did. I invited her to kick off her boots and come in.

Becca. In my kitchen. Stocking feet. Still smiling. She checked out the fabric sling that rested against my chest. "Nice purse you got there."

"I should warn you, a purse like this can get pretty loud. And sometimes it leaks." I pulled aside the bit of fabric obscuring Brody. He was awake, but quiet—a real rarity. He blinked his round, dark eyes at Becca.

She gasped. "Look at Mr. Teeny Tiny. Is that Ellie's baby? A boy? How sweet. Oh my gosh, can I hold him?"

"Sorry. Just got him settled. His name's Brody, but we're think-ing of changing it to The Tumor because he's only happy when he's attached to someone. Usually me. Our big guy is a whole six pounds now."

"I don't believe it," she said. "There's that dog living here. And you're taking care of a baby. I never, ever imagined I'd see this."

"Two babies, actually. Twins. Vedder and Brody."

"What? No way. Twins? Honestly? I can't even believe it. Did she know?"

"Nope. This little stinker right here took us all by surprise."

I headed for the living room to check on Veddie. The swing had stopped and Veddie was gearing up to complain, making all the furious faces he'd make before letting out an actual yell.

"Can you grab him for me? Quick, before he blows," I said.

She lifted him out of the swing. Veddie wailed in Becca's arms and she looked at me helplessly. I put him on my shoulder and patted his back. He let loose a major burp.

"Look at you. Just look at you," she said. "Talk about having your hands full. This is amazing, Clive. Looks like you're doing great."

It was true. I'd never been happier, not even when we were newlyweds. But her approval didn't fill me with the pride or hope that it once would have. She was only stating the obvious. Ellie, her babies, the dog, were simply my life now, my responsibilities, and my loves. They weren't window dressings to lure her back, and how she felt about all of it wasn't what really mattered.

"I enjoy them," I said. "Well, not when they're waking me up at three a.m., but you know what I mean."

"Did Ellie and Reece split up or something?"

"Yeah. It's a long story. She's staying with me for now."

I didn't feel like laying out the details of their custody issues. Reece was trying to fight for full custody of Vedder, but since he'd kicked Ellie out—essentially leaving her homeless—the Friend of the Court had been cool with Ellie taking the babies and moving to Belknap Township with me. He was ordered to pay child support. Saint had arranged to pay his share too, voluntarily.

"Are you still mad that I left?" she asked.

I sat on the couch, laid Veddie across my knees, and rubbed his back. That always helped when he was gassy. "Was I ever? Mad? Sorry you left, absolutely. Beyond sorry. But I was never mad at you. Hell, Bec. You were right. I was a total coward. I look back on how I was when you left, and I feel like I don't even know that guy."

"You're still wearing your wedding ring."

She wasn't. She sat on the arm of the couch and put her hand on my shoulder. "Us. Again. Do you ever think about it?"

Always. But this was phenomenally bad timing for us to reconcile.

"You know, tomorrow's my preliminary hearing. My case is most likely going to get bound over for trial. I'm dealing with a lot of uncertainty, legal expenses, and if things go how they usually do for me, I could end up in jail. As much as I'd love to just say yes— I've never wanted this marriage to end—I'm thinking about how the charges I'm facing could affect you. Anyway, I thought you filed already. I left those divorce papers in your microwave."

"I came close. I took them to the courthouse and sat out front in my van with that envelope on my lap. I wasn't at a hundred per-cent, you know, and I was trying to figure out what percent I was. So I took a drive to Forty Mile Point to walk around and think eve-rything over some more. I remembered that kid who was throwing snowballs at us on our first date, and the way you'd looked at me when I was talking to him. And I just, I ... "

"Yeah?"

She smiled. "Well, it was really cold at the beach that day. I ended up building myself a little bonfire."

"You've got to be kidding me."

"No. Twisted up, those documents helped get the kindling going."

Incredible. I would have loved to have roasted marshmallows over that fire.

"I've left you out in the cold for a long time. I hope I'm not too late," she said.

"In the interest of full disclosure, you should know that I'm still smoking."

She grinned at me. "You're smokin' alright."

"Seriously, Bec. Your Kryptonite is addicted to nicotine."

"Yeah, I spotted the coffee can of butts by the back door. It's not what you'd call a deal breaker for me."

I pulled off my wedding ring, pressed it into her palm and fold-ed her hand over it. "Take some time to think it through. Depend-ing on what happens tomorrow, you can get rid of this or return it to me whenever you're really sure."

"I've already decided."

"No. Wait on this. Sleep on it. I'll call you when the hearing is over. We can talk about it some more."

"But I'm sure, Clive. I've never been so sure of anything in my life."

"I can't accept it yet. I won't. You deserve better than some loser doing time in county jail." I kissed her hand and held it to my cheek.

53

Given to Fly

Clive • Rogers City, Mich. • Wednesday, Apr. 25, 2007

My attorney, Bob Mulberry, jiggled a bony knee and drummed his pen on the oak defense table. He wasn't more than forty. His shoe-polish black toupee swooped across his pockmarked forehead. His breath stank of coffee and cheap cigars, but he was the only lawyer in three counties who'd agree to take an oil painting for payment. He'd asked me for a cover replica of *Thriller*. If he didn't do a decent job of representing me, I planned to update Michael Jackson's nose.

Saint had taken time off of work and come up north to look after the babies so that Ellie could attend my hearing. She was somewhere behind me. Becca was there too, with my wedding ring on a chain around her neck.

The bailiff hiked his gun belt under his potbelly and cleared his throat. "All rise. The Eighty-Ninth District Court is now in session, the Honorable Marcus Wisnewski presiding."

Wisnewski. This judge had made me uncomfortable when he'd officiated our wedding, saying he was sure he knew my name from somewhere. Earlier in his career he'd been a prosecutor in Wayne County, so it was possible. But I had no memory of him. He wasn't the judge who'd overturned my teenage joyriding charges.

The judge entered in a swish of dark robes. He sat down and blew his nose. "Please be seated. The prosecuting attorney is requesting this court enter charges of public drunkenness, resisting arrest, and assault with attempt to do great bodily harm less than murder. Mr. Rafferty, do you understand the charges?"

"Yes, Your Honor."

"When you were arraigned, you pled 'not guilty' to each charge. Is this still how you plead?"

"Yes, Your Honor."

"Thank you, sir. Ms. Graves, you may proceed."

The prosecutor strode to the front of her table and addressed the judge. "As to the charge of public drunkenness, Mr. Rafferty was arrested outside of the Buckshot Tavern. Breath analysis showed he had a blood-alcohol level of point-one-nine."

"Mr. Mulberry, how do you intend to refute that?" the judge asked. "Clearly, your client was drunk at the time."

"Your Honor, he admits he imbibed too much scotch on an empty stomach and as you can see, he is not a large man. However, the bar is privately owned, therefore his drunkenness was not in public."

"He was arrested outside the bar," Graves said.

"My client was removed from the Buckshot Tavern against his will. Therefore, it isn't his fault he was drunk in public. We can't go tossing people out of bars and calling it public drunkenness."

The judge said, "Nice try, Mr. Mulberry. Undoubtedly, the defendant was removed from the premises to stop the fight."

"Then the prosecutor should have charged him with drunk and disorderly conduct, not public drunkenness."

"Ms. Graves, why did you not charge the defendant with drunk and disorderly?"

"Well ..." She adjusted the crisp, white collar of her blouse. "Because he was in fact outside at the time of the arrest. May I amend the charge, Your Honor?"

The judge looked at the ceiling and then pointed at her with his pen. "Ms. Graves, can you see the silk tie I'm wearing under my robe?"

She nodded.

"It's a good two decades older than you are. So, I'm thinking no, I shouldn't allow you to amend this charge. Let this serve as an object lesson. Get your charges right the first time. I'm dismissing it."

I scraped my fingers across my scalp. One down, two to go.

"Your evidence as to the charge of resisting arrest, Ms. Graves?" the judge asked.

"I have the sheriff's report. At the time of arrest, the defendant verbally abused the sheriff. His exact words were, 'Go arrest that fuckwit who attacked my sister, officer douche nozzle sir.'"

The judge pressed his lips together in a good imitation of seriousness. "Ms. Graves, you do realize that by definition, resisting arrest refers to physical resistance?"

"But he called the sheriff a douche nozzle. Now, maybe flouting authority is acceptable in the slums of Detroit where Mr. Rafferty hails from. However, I'd like to send a firm message that disrespecting authority doesn't fly in the county of Presque Isle."

"Slums of Detroit? I see. Do you have evidence demonstrating how Mr. Rafferty's insult physically deterred the sheriff from making the arrest?"

"I suppose not, Your Honor."

"Then it's dismissed."

The judge made another note on a yellow tablet. "Last, we have a charge of assault with intent to do great bodily harm less than murder. Is the victim, Mr. Howard Bartholomew Peterson, Jr., in the courtroom today, Ms. Graves?"

"Yes, Your Honor."

"Would Mr. Peterson please rise?"

Howie stood tall. The judge appraised him, then peered at me. "Mr. Rafferty, please approach the bench."

Heart thrumming in my ears, I obeyed.

"Mr. Peterson, please come up here and stand next to Mr. Rafferty. I trust you'll both behave like gentlemen in my courtroom."

"Yes, Your Honor," I said.

Howie slouched next to me.

"Mr. Peterson, take a page from Mr. Rafferty's book and stand like a tin soldier. I want your feet together and your shoulders back. Chin up. That's right." The judge placed his palms parallel to the bench, then raised one hand and lowered the other until he'd approximated the height difference between the two of us—about nine inches. He made a similar comparison with the breadth of our shoulders, measuring me about a half-foot narrower. Shame prickled from my scalp to my knees. It was one thing to be a runt, another to be publicly sized against Becca's former lover.

"Comparing these two, I'm wondering why the defendant isn't pleading insanity." The judge leaned forward and locked eyes with me. "Tell me young man, what started the altercation between you and Mr. Peterson?"

"He confronted me. He'd run into my wife, who's separated from me. She'd been sick and looked pretty bad. I guess he was angry about that. Upset."

"Was Mr. Peterson a factor in your marital separation?"

"Oh, no, it wasn't like that at all, Your Honor. It had nothing to do with him. She left me because we'd lost a baby and I—"

"That's more than enough information, Mr. Rafferty."

My face went hot. I shouldn't have blurted out our personal problems. From now on I was sticking to answering the specific questions.

The judge leaned back, lacing his fingers across his chest. "Mr. Peterson, if you weren't involved with his wife, why did you confront Mr. Rafferty?"

"He wasn't taking good care of her."

"Why should that interest you?"

"Rebecca was my girl. I loved her first and he stole her from me."

"I see." He looked at me. "How did you respond to him, Mr. Rafferty?"

"Your Honor, I don't remember if I said anything. He was the last person I wanted to discuss my marriage problems with."

"I still want to hear how this fight got started."

"Sure. Well, while Howie was confronting me about my wife, my sister came up to us. She was very pregnant."

"How was that relevant?"

"He didn't know I had a sister. He assumed she was my girl-friend and he smashed a beer bottle over my head."

"Is that true, Mr. Peterson? You believed Mr. Rafferty had a pregnant lover, and you attacked him?"

"He bought her a flower. She kissed his cheek."

"Are you admitting to assaulting him?"

I raised my hand and the judge nodded.

"Your Honor, Mr. Peterson made an honest mistake. I get how things looked to him. And my wife's condition at the time was, well, worrisome."

"Yet according to Mr. Peterson's medical records, you broke his jaw. Why?"

I looked at Howie. He was scowling at the floor.

"I'm not sure, Your Honor."

The judge spread some papers across his bench. "By all witness accounts, including that of your sister Eleanor Rafferty, you pounded Mr. Peterson relentlessly."

"Yes, Your Honor, I admit to that." I clasped my sweaty palms behind my back and hung my head.

"Mr. Peterson, the police statement provided by Ms. Eleanor Rafferty says that you shoved her to the floor before the defendant began to fight back. Is this true?"

"Well, yeah. But she was trying to pull me off of him."

"I see. Prior to that, had Mr. Rafferty struck you?"

"I don't know. I guess not."

The judge scribbled another note on his pad. "Mr. Mulberry, you've read the prosecutor's complaint?"

"I have, Your Honor."

"Are you not objecting to her intent to bring up the defendant's juvenile record?"

"What?"

"That's 'What? Your Honor.'"

"My apologies to The Court. No, I was not made aware that my client had a prior record. I preemptively object on the grounds that it's inadmissible as evidence. To even suggest including it is highly irregular."

"It's relevant to the case, Your Honor," Ms. Graves said. "It establishes the defendant's proclivity for criminal behavior."

The courtroom was hotter than Satan's balls. My brain felt like it would float away. I bent my knees and pumped my thigh muscles to keep my blood flowing. My dress shoes pinched. I'd been standing in front of Judge Wisniewski's bench for an eternity and a half. The only juvenile record I knew of was the joyriding thing, which had been overturned. It didn't make any sense to me that the prosecutor would try to use it, or that the judge would allow it.

"I'm allowing it," the judge said.

While Mulberry objected, I concentrated on breathing. Panic clouded my mind. I struggled to follow what my lawyer was saying. Something about juvenile records, inadmissibility, no priors, mistrial, appeals. The words swooped around my head and a rushing sound filled my ears.

Mulberry tugged my sleeve. "Come on. Hizzoner told everyone to sit down. You look like shit. Don't pass out."

Plunking into the wooden chair was a huge relief. I'd have given my canine teeth for a cigarette. Or water. I grabbed a paper cup from the stack at the center of the table and lifted the thermal carafe. It was empty. There was nothing for me but thirst. And doom.

"Mr. Rafferty, you've admitted to beating up Mr. Peterson. Please explain to this court why you did so," Judge Wisnewski said.

Mind blank, I stared at a knot in the oak table.

"A reason, Mr. Rafferty." He clicked the top of his pen several times. "Presumably, you don't normally jump a man twice your size."

Words stuck in my parched throat. I forced them out. "He hit me with a bottle. At first, I was confused. Then he shoved my sister. She was hurt. Crying. I had to protect her. Then something snapped and I couldn't stop. After that, it wasn't about Howie or anything he did."

I leaned back in my chair and looked over at Howie. "I'm sorry. Seriously, man. I'm really sorry."

"Please refrain from addressing the alleged victim."

"Sorry, Your Honor."

"So, you're admitting to me you used Mr. Peterson like a punching bag, took your frustrations out on him?"

"He didn't deserve it, Your Honor. But in a way, he volunteered."

"Are you saying you took the pain of your wife's estrangement out on him?"

"That, and much more, I've realized. Things that go back twenty years, even longer."

The judge nodded as if this was what he'd been waiting to hear. Mulberry looked at me and shrugged.

"Sir, according to your juvenile record, you were convicted of joyriding at the age of fourteen, and that conviction was later overturned," the judge said. "This will, in fact, be inadmissible as evidence. Frankly, Ms. Graves should have known better than to even attempt to bring it up. But I digress.

"Along with your juvenile record, she submitted to the court your foster care record. Also inadmissible." He removed his glasses and rubbed the bridge of his nose. "However, reading through it jogged something in my brain about an infamous tenement fire. At the time it happened, I was an attorney in the Wayne County Assistant Prosecutor's office."

My heart lurched into my throat. He knew about me. He knew the fire was my fault.

"You're one of only two survivors of the Brush Park inferno. Eleven people died, including two infants. Those were your younger brothers, correct?"

I nodded.

"Please answer aloud for the court recorder."

"Yes, Your Honor." A bead of sweat trickled down the side of my face.

"You show a great deal of remorse for your actions."

"Of course. That fire was my fault. I have to live with that … with that … fact." I covered my face. Had I just admitted guilt in open court? Did that mean I'd be convicted for the fire? It was an accident. I'd been a juvenile. Did that matter? Eleven dead. Was there a statute of limitations on manslaughter?

"Mr. Rafferty, you were what? Seven years old at the time of the fire?"

I twisted my hands in my lap and tried to understand what the judge was getting at. "Eight, I think. Your Honor."

"Mr. Rafferty, have you never read the fire inspector's report on that incident?"

"No, Your Honor. I was there. I saw everything."

"Working in the assistant prosecutor's office at the time, I was privy to the facts in the case of that tragedy. This morning I reread the record to refresh my memory. It was ruled an arson, started on a mattress in the basement. The landlord was convicted, but that was appealed and overturned."

My mind clawed for traction in a free-fall of morphing realities. I gasped for air and tried to understand, but nothing made sense to me now. I knew better than to argue with the judge, but I had to ask for clarification.

"Pardon me, Your Honor, but I don't get this. I don't get it at all. My mother went to prison because the fire was my fault. It started in our third-floor apartment. They held her responsible because I left some candles burning. She told me that herself."

I looked behind me, searching for Ellie. Her face was hidden in Becca's shoulder, and Becca was stroking her hair and looking straight at me. Whatever the hearing's outcome—no matter what the judge decided—they were mine and I was theirs. I could get through this, through anything. I turned and faced the bench.

"As I recall," the judge said, "your mother, Honey Jane Rafferty, was incarcerated for multiple counts of reckless endangerment, gross child neglect, flagrant parole violations and possession of narcotics with intent to deliver."

My relief that the fire and our mother's imprisonment weren't actually my fault whirled with the shame of hearing her stripped bare in public. And if it wasn't my fault, why had she forgiven me? It had been her forgiveness that made me willing to shoulder the blame.

"I'm allowing your juvenile record as a mitigating factor. It is this court's opinion that you struck Mr. Peterson in self-defense, and in defense of your pregnant sister. I understand that your sister, the only other survivor of that fire, is your sole living family member. This court stands behind your right to protect her.

"Having considered the relevant factors in the complaint, I find insufficient evidence to bind this over to Circuit Court. I hereby dismiss all charges against Mr. Clive Ellis Rafferty." He raised his gavel and struck the bench.

54

I Believe in Miracles

Ellie • 40 Mile Point, Mich. • July 4, 2009

The scent of pink primroses basking in the sunshine filled the air at Forty Mile Point Lighthouse beach. Saint hauled the cooler out of my twenty-year-old Volvo wagon, a decent trade for the Yield bus. I doubted I'd ever get a chance to see Pearl Jam live again anyway, at least not until my boys were older.

We trudged across the sandy lawn toward the beach. Saint's frayed and faded scarf fluttered behind him. Veddie was heavy in my arms and clutching my ukulele, which I'd gotten pretty good at playing. He offered his usual babbling brook of consciousness. "Gwass. Seagoos. Twees. Bwody."

Brody marched ahead of us, pausing to investigate a bug on a wild daisy. His silky black hair grazed his narrow shoulders. The baby we'd called The Tumor had grown too independent to hold my hand. People said he was Saint in miniature. He was, but Brody was his own little person, too.

"Uncoo Cwive!" Veddie stretched for his hero, though we were still several yards away. Clive waved at him then helped Becca spread our Rafferty family quilt over the sand.

Right after Clive's hearing, in the vestibule of the Presque Isle County courthouse, Becca had put his wedding ring on his finger and handed her ring to him so he could put it on hers. They'd helped move the boys and me into the furnished apartment above Crowe & Father Home Heating. The kitchen floor was spattered with dried buttercream yellow paint, but the place was rent free and all ours. Becca even loaned me a bunch of brand new baby gear they had stored in their basement, but gave me a heads up that she might need it back if they had any luck with trying again.

Sundays after his brunch shift, Saint made the long drive up to Rogers City and stayed until Tuesday mornings to help with the boys. He slept with his legs dangling off the end of my couch, and I'd wake to the scent of burnt pumpernickel toast. He played his music too loud, but took excellent care of Veddie and Brody, who both called him Papa. This arrangement gave me the time I needed to apprentice with Becca. I was grateful for the chance to be something more than a salt sprinkler in a pretzel shop. The awning at the shop would soon read *Crowe & Rafferty Home Heating*. In exchange for teaching me her trade, I was showing her how to embroider. She still pulled her stitches too tight, but she was learning.

I helped her set up our Independence Day picnic while Clive and Saint played Frisbee with the dogs. Our birthdays were coming up so we were celebrating those, too. We'd gone all out with guacamole, fresh salsa, queso dip, enchiladas, Spanish rice, and empanadas.

After we'd stuffed ourselves to the verge of regret, Saint gave me a birthday card. Inside was a printed email confirmation from Ten Club for tickets to see Pearl Jam two nights in a row in Chicago in late August. I could have fainted right there in the sand.

"Me and you, in the pit again," he said.

"I love it, but what about the boys?"

"We'll watch them," Clive said.

"Thanks, man, but I've got this all worked out with Reece. He's taking them both that weekend."

I couldn't believe it. I met Reece halfway for his visitation with Vedder one four-day weekend each month. Reece always returned him clean and happy, with a tin of homemade treats to share with Brody. But as far as I knew, Saint and Reece weren't even on speaking terms.

"How'd you get him to agree to that?" I asked.

"I guess during his visits, Veddie's been crying for Brody. Reece called me up to talk about keeping our boys together more, and I threw this out there. He's not completely unreasonable."

"No, not completely."

Our paternity situation could have turned hideous, yet it hadn't. I understood now that Saint, Reece and I didn't belong on any daytime tabloid talk shows after all. People had to be full of anger and hate for that, and that wasn't who we were.

"But you need to understand something about me taking you to this concert." He leaned forward and whispered in my ear. "It's a date, girlfriend."

We were already great parents together, and good friends, and immediate Jamily. Why not?

I smiled. "Wozniak, it's on."

Clive gave me a painted portrait of my babies. He'd captured Vedder on the verge of saying something, and Brody about to dash away with a fat red Magic Marker in his hand. He sure understood his nephews.

"Beautiful, Uncool Cliver. I'll let Becca give you your present. It's from both of us, but, well, you'll see."

Becca ran out to her van and came back with her ponytail askew. She was breathless as she handed Clive a silver gift bag. Inside was a reworked version of the Rafferty family crest. We'd changed the motto from *We're Fuckin' Doomed* to *Multum in Parvo*.

"What's it mean?" Clive asked.

"Much, in little," Becca said.

In place of the torn clover leaves that had represented our lost brothers, there were whole leaves of pure white. The once blackened stem was green and sturdy. Becca showed Clive the fresh new clovers unfurling beneath the original. "Your nephews. And this butterfly is for Louise."

I'd encouraged her to add that pale yellow butterfly, and resisted the urge to fix her puckered stitches. It had meant a lot to her. Almost as much as the slender shoot that the butterfly was fluttering over.

"Here's the best part," she said.

Clive looked from the crest, to Becca, to me and back to Becca. "Is that—is that what I think it is?"

"You bet," Becca said.

"Really?"

"I'm due February twentieth."

He slipped his arms around her. "Bec, oh my God. That's so perfect. But are you alright? Are you scared?"

"A little. Maybe more than a little."

"Me too," he said. "But this time we're going to be alright, no matter what happens."

The End

Acknowledgments

Many thanks to Michael Ombry for always believing in me, and to my children, Charlotte and Seth, for being their wonderful selves.

I'm also deeply indebted to many friends from Absolute Write, the Saginaw Bay Wombats Nanowrimo group, and every last one of my beta readers, proofreaders, and cheerleaders.

Special thanks to Ray York II for designing the cover of this book, and to Mary Jo Hoffman of stillblog.net for the image of bittersweet that graces the cover.

And of course I am forever grateful to Pearl Jam for their bottomless musical inspiration, as well as to their wonderful fans—many of whom I'm lucky to count among my friends.

Also by Grace Ombry

Smokin' & Cryin'

The Rise & Fall of Smoky Topaz

August 27, 1972. Robin Chelsea, teenage lead singer of Smoky Topaz, disappears into the Atlantic Ocean mere weeks before the group's double album, *Smokin' & Cryin'*, is released. Recorded over one blistering Savannah summer in the dungeon of an antebellum mansion, it's threaded with candid snippets of the band members' dirty secrets, bitter arguments, and deepest fears.

In the wake of Robin's disappearance, *Smokin' & Cryin'* flies off store shelves and dominates radio airwaves to become the obsession of a generation of music lovers. But what really happened to Robin Chelsea?

More than four decades later, the discovery of Robin's candid writings—juxtaposed with news clippings, legal documents, reviews, letters, personal notes, and interviews—make it possible to finally piece together the tangled truth behind this mysterious rock and roll legend.

About the Author

Grace Ombry writes pop culture fiction. Some of her favorite writers are Barbara Kingsolver, Lauren Groff, Maria Semple, Kurt Vonnegut, Nick Hornby, Nick Sheff, and John Krakauer. She has a degree in journalism from Central Michigan University. Weekdays, she's the Marketing Director for the greatest glue factory on earth and editor of Epoxyworks magazine. She lives in Bay City, Michigan.

Read more graceombry.com

About the Publisher

Founded in 2016 and based in Michigan, The Ledbetter Press is a tiny but mighty independent publisher of entertaining, character-driven fiction.

theledbetterpress.com

www.ingramcontent.com/pod-product-compliance
Lightning Source LLC
Chambersburg PA
CBHW051327250626
47155CB00007B/2484